CENTURION

Quintus Roman Thrillers
Book Four

Neil Denby

SAPERE
BOOKS

CENTURION

Published by Sapere Books.

24 Trafalgar Road, Ilkley, LS29 8HH

saperebooks.com

ISBN: 978-0-85495-523-7

To Tilda and Max and Ivy, who continue to bring me hours of joy and delight.

ACKNOWLEDGEMENTS

Thank you as always to my family and friends, whose input has been vital, and also those readers who provide constructive criticism in their online reviews. A good review puts a spring in my step for a week.

There are wonderful historians out there to whom I owe a huge debt of gratitude. To explore this time period more thoroughly I can recommend Mary Beard, Guy de la Bédoyère, Adrian Goldsworthy, Tom Holland and Lindsay Powell, to name but a few.

I: CASTRA HIBERNA

Julius Quintus Quirinius had never been so cold. His head ached from it; his fingers were stiff, his toes numb. Though he blew on his hands and stamped his feet, he could not get warm. He envied the men below who were at least partially sheltered. They could walk the length of the wall on their guard duty whilst he was confined to the small square of the tower. The raised edge of the wooden palisade protected them from the sharp bite of the wind. He was exposed.

He had a brazier, spitting and fretful and unwilling to release its heat. The men below had fires. He sighed. When Quintus had been forced to join up, even as his younger brother found his father's favour, he had never imagined such a posting — devoid of warmth, riches, fame and civilisation.

'May Jupiter damn this snow to Hades,' he cursed.

'It is just weather, friend. It will pass.' So shrugged his primus amicus, Crassus, who fought beside him in battle. He was heavyset, with the neck of a bull, his dusky skin and curly hair giving away his ancestry somewhere in the south. By trade, he was a blacksmith, his muscular physique attesting to this. He looked up at Quintus from where he huddled over the brazier. 'Perhaps it is worse up there, Mac?'

Quintus was used to sarcastic references to his height. He was probably the tallest man in the legion, certainly the tallest in the cohort. His nickname, used with affection, was Macilentus, 'lanky'.

'The time will pass more quickly if you do not invoke the gods,' said Marcus in a tone of mild rebuke.

Tullius, his comrade, face as long as ever, just nodded.

9

Marcus, an evocatus — called again to the colours — and ex-centurion, had fought under Marcus Antonius in Armenia and, like many, switched his allegiance to Octavius at Actium. Now he served Octavius reborn as Augustus Caesar. He was soft-voiced but solidly built, a natural wrestler. Tullius had served as long. He had fought in the Sicilian wars and bore two long, jagged scars down his right cheek, one more recent than the other. He revered the gods, believing his eye had been twice saved by them. His beard was sparse and the hair on his head almost non-existent. Only when he removed his helmet could his wolf-bitten ear and its silver earring be seen.

Quintus stopped complaining, and instead turned to look out over the white expanse by the river and the snow-laden trees beyond. He knew he would be relieved, and that Jovan and Maxim, the Macedonian slaves attached to his contubernium, would have hot broth and a roaring fire. He could wait.

The winter had been harsh, beginning with a great storm blowing in from the north and west. Snow came flying in on a vicious wind, bringing with it a depth of piercing cold the likes of which the Romans had never before experienced. It piled up in drifts against the sides of the fortress and narrowed what could be seen of the river to a mere stream. It then froze solid, so that unprotected shins were cut when the surface broke beneath a man's weight. The shimmer of the sweeping white mantle of snow in the winter sun hurt the men's eyes. The passing of the hours was marked by the long black shadow of the fortress crossing the ground below the treeline.

Quintus made sure that he spent as much time up this cursed tower as the rest of his men, though as optio — second to the centurion, Galba — he could have sent others. He was also the elected leader, the decanus, of his tent-party, and he believed in leading by example.

His gaze turned to the fort below. One tower, the north-east, could no longer be used. Burned by the enemy, it emerged from the snow like a blackened tooth, impossible to repair without rebuilding — and that would have to wait for spring. Other weather damage was also apparent. The canvas roof of the junior officers' tent had caved in, along with the protection erected over the blacksmith's forge. The auxiliary horsemen of Cantabria had been forced to move their lodgings next to the porta decumanus, closer to the Anatolians than they wished, but sheltered.

The timber-built roof of the prefect's own house had collapsed, whether from the weight of the snow, or from the slaves sent up to clear it, no-one knew. Of course, the slaves were blamed and whipped — but no more than whipped, since manpower was in short supply. It was not replaced; instead the commander moved to his campaign tent, leaving much behind to soak and rot.

Looking outwards, Quintus watched the river Rhenus, which never froze. It continued sluggishly, carving a path through banks of snow, lumps of ice tumbling down it. In the shortest days of winter it looked possible to cross the river on foot, though none dared. Across the water he could see the icicle-laden figures of crucified tribesmen.

Before the worst of the weather had arrived, a tribe of Germani had attacked the fortress. They captured legionaries and humiliated and killed them within sight of their comrades. They burnt the north-east tower and attempted to batter down the gate. It was only a returning patrol led by Quintus that allowed the garrison to emerge and rout the tribesmen. The patrol was bringing back a great prize — the stolen eagle of the Fifth. The threat of attack remained, even though executions were carried out as warnings. The Romans could not drop their guard.

The frozen corpses of five of the executed enemy stared back at Quintus from the far bank. They had been captured in the fight and crucified on bankside trees. The white frost exaggerated their agony and made their twisted limbs glisten and shine horrifically. Crows and weather would usually have rendered them faceless quickly, but these men kept their icy gazes fixed on the fort. They invaded the sleep and inhabited the nightmares of the soldiers. The men made the warding sign against them whenever guard duty put them in sight.

Only when it began to thaw could the Romans hope these cursed beings would rot and be eaten. But the rictus grins of the executed men instead grew wider, seeming to mock the legionaries. At last the commander ordered that they be taken down. The duty fell to those men stationed at the gate. They fought their way through the slush and dug out the little raft from the snow, poling it across the water. With relief they dragged the dead down and tumbled them into the river.

'Now perhaps the spring will come,' said Quintus.

He was right. It seemed that as soon as the corpses were removed, the sun rose higher, the days grew longer and the snow began to melt. Shoots of grass could be seen poking through the snow. The buds on the trees opened.

On yet another guard duty, not as cold, Quintus' contubernium watched as a small group of riders approached from the south. Foraging and hunting parties had been sent out; the Anatolian archers serving as auxiliaries had proved to be invaluable in bringing down game. But this was not them returning. This was something else.

'Enemy?' Crassus asked, as he shaded his eyes to look.

'I don't think so,' said Quintus.

II: CURSUS PUBLICUS

A group of five riders approached, definitely not tribesmen of the Germani. A hail from the gate tower greeted them.

'*Quo vadis?*'

Their reply floated up to Quintus. 'A courier of Rome, a rider of the *cursus publicus*.' The words made Quintus look over at them in wonder. These men must have come from the centre of the empire, from the warmth of the seven hills. He was amazed to think that the network of public roads used by these riders extended this far. *Of course it doesn't*, he chastised himself. *These men are extending it now.*

The group was small but impressive. At its head was an imperial courier, wearing a full breastplate like a noble officer, with his paludamentum draped over his shoulder and fixed with an ornate brooch. His tunic beneath the thick red cloak was white, and his shins were protected with black leather greaves. He rode a sturdy roan mare, chestnut and white. His four companions were fully armed and armoured. Two, either side of him, wore high-crested centurion's helms and carried javelins from which flew long banners of red and gold. Two heavily armed soldiers rode behind, leading extra horses.

The castra had seen visitors before. A small group of engineers and surveyors, tracking the course of the river, had stumbled across it. Reports must have found their way back to Rome. This courier knew what he was looking for.

'I seek an overwintering cohort of the Ninth Hispania,' he called up in a clear voice. 'Have I found it?'

'The same,' came the reply.

'Who commands here?'

'The prefect, Titus Flavius Pusio of the noble order of equités,' the voice responded.

'Then it is he to whom my messages are addressed. Open the gate.'

The gate was swung wide and the horsemen entered, clattering along the via principalis and dismounting in the forum from which the melting snow had been cleared. The prefect took a while to appear. When he did it was in armour, with his own red cloak over his shoulder. He greeted the visitors from the tribunal in front of the cohort standards. Only the eagle of the Fifth was not there. Its place was in the alae, the sacred space of sacrifices, where the gods of the legionaries lived.

The courier greeted the prefect stiffly then dropped to one knee, and, arm straight, held out a tightly rolled cylinder of soft leather.

'From Augustus Caesar, imperator, divi filius, tribunicia potestas, consul for the eleventh time, greetings.'

Quintus could see and hear what was happening from his vantage point in the south-east tower. He was glad that the courier had decided to use but a few of Caesar's long list of titles.

'Of "imperator" he should be rightly proud,' said Marcus. 'Only victorious troops can hail him as such.'

'"Son of a god" would be my favourite,' said Crassus. 'As heir of the divine Julius.'

'"Tribune of the people" shows his links to the common man,' an impressed Tullius added. 'He is one of us.'

'And "consul" demonstrates the loyalty of the Senate and the populace of Rome,' Quintus finished with just a hint of weariness in his tone. 'These four titles are sufficient.'

Beneath them Flavius took the roll and felt its quality. Goatskin vellum, a writing surface he could never hope to afford unless his career was somehow jolted back on track. The wax seal, the head of Augustus Caesar framed by laurel wreaths, was unbroken. He bowed his head in thanks, saying, 'I will break the seal and read it in private.'

But the courier was not finished. He beckoned forward one of the centurions. The man reached into a pouch and handed over a round image of Augustus Caesar, a sort of raised sculpture made of bronze, within a cowl of silver.

'This is for the cohort to display, a new idea. The face of Augustus should be carried before all of his troops. The man who carries it takes the rank of signifer,' the centurion said.

'Vanity,' muttered Quintus, though he was careful that none heard him.

Titus Flavius ordered the visitors to be fed and housed, then took the message inside. A few moments later, his scribe, the thin and busy figure of freedman Cornus, came looking for the senior officers. In the tent, Flavius sat, while the officers stood, Quintus beside them.

'We have been given a job to do,' he told them. 'Rome is clearing a road through the Alps and along the Rhenus to the sea. It will link Italia with the new province of Gaul, Tres Gallia. We are tasked with clearing out any nests of Germani between here and the advancing legions. We work our way along the river until we meet with imperial forces. We march in three days.'

'Where are the legions now?' Centurion Galba asked.

'I have no idea,' admitted the prefect, 'but it seems that they are not close. They are fighting tribes in the high mountains, according to the courier, a confederation called the Raeti. He spoke of six changes of horse stationed up the river. He was unsure whether the enemy were Germani, Celt or Gaul, but was convinced that the young general opposing them, adopted son of great Caesar, would defeat them all.'

'Of course.' Quintus nodded dutifully. The others followed suit, agreeing with the prefect's assessment.

'Do we keep the fort as a base?' Felix was centurion of the Fourth. His men were the least experienced, but keen to fight. If the fort stayed, it would be his century that would — reluctantly — garrison it.

'Our camp is too far north,' said the commander. 'We need to follow the river upstream, past where the Fifth were attacked. I am told that at the threat of the emperor's wrath, Maelo and his men have returned across the river. They have even given up hostages.'

Maelo was the tribal chieftain who, with other tribes — long sworn enemies — had led a deadly raid across the Rhenus. The strength of this confederacy was unknown to ex-consul Marcus Lollius, leading Legio Five. The legion had been caught and routed by the cavalry of the Germani. It had taken others, including Quintus, to rescue the eagle that was stolen. The news of the loss had reached Rome — the courier knew of it. But no-one outside of the fort knew that the eagle had been recovered.

'Clearly this is no raid or punitive expedition,' said Galba. 'It is an attempt to complete the work of Divus Julius, to rid Tres Gallia of malign influences and push the borders of the empire at least to the Rhenus.'

'How far do we go?' Quintus asked.

'Until it is no longer safe, and we encounter hostile tribes. That is as much as the courier would tell me.'

'At least some of these tribes are friends to Rome already,' Quintus added, not sure why Rome was fighting them. 'My father traded cheese and honey and wax from the Raeti.'

'And we use Norican iron in the forge,' said Galba, 'but that does not mean we can trust any of them.'

The others agreed. They had all fought with barbarian tribes in the past, and many had been betrayed by them.

'Start dismantling the fort today,' Flavius ordered. 'Leave nothing but the contents of the latrines for the enemy.' He smiled at his own humour as the officers filed out.

Quintus hung back. 'The eagle...' he began.

'Stays with the cohort,' interrupted the commander quickly. 'It is far too great a risk to send such a trophy unprotected. In any case, as soon as the courier knows of the eagle, so will the general and, soon enough, Caesar. Augustus would begin to ask why it had not been brought back earlier, rather than reward those who returned it.'

'The information on Britannia...' Again the commander was brusque, although this time anger coloured his tone. 'This is not the time, soldier. Don't worry, I will make sure the emperor knows of the Druids.'

Quintus made to speak again but the commander raised a flat palm to stop him. The matter of the eagle and the Druids was, for now, dismissed. As Quintus turned to leave, the courier came back into the tent to speak with the prefect. Behind him, Quintus heard the prefect saying, 'I have a favour to ask of you...'

He hovered by the door flap, keen to hear if the Flavian was trying to take advantage of the information and the eagle that he, Quintus, had rescued. But it was more mundane than that. There were women in the camp. The Flavian did not want to take them further into unknown territory.

'Take my wife back with you,' he said. 'She can ride, and so can her companion. Their body slaves will accompany them, and I can spare a legionary guard.'

'I must respectfully decline, my friend,' the courier replied. 'My purpose is speed. I do not have litters, nor spare horses for ladies. Do they wish to go?'

'They do and they don't. They long for baths and society and decent food, but they also wish to be where the men are. They cannot do both. I would point them towards Rome. I would have them safe.'

'Then you should not have brought them on campaign with you,' muttered the courier under his breath, but loudly enough for Quintus to hear. The idea that campaigning in hostile territory was akin to some sort of holiday seemed to irk him. 'With great respect, sir, they will be safer here than with a single messenger and his escort.'

'When do you leave?' Flavius asked curtly.

'With your permission, at once.'

There was an exchange of salutes along with other formal niceties that Quintus did not stay to hear. He slipped out and waited for the courier, grasping his arm and speaking urgently with him. 'I have valedictions. Can you return them to Rome?'

'Men you have lost?'

'Yes. One of them of the equités, a knight, though he enlisted under an assumed name. His friends would recognise him.'

'Very well,' agreed the courier. This was a duty, a noble duty, that he could perform.

Quintus handed over a frame of thin wood with a lid that could be closed. Within, on two wax tablets, were the valedictions that detailed the heroic and honourable deaths of Nox and Lux, the comrades lost between Britannia and

Germania. He had dictated them to Cornus, who had carefully inscribed the wax. The whole package was sealed and tied.

The courier added it to his satchel. 'I will try,' he said, 'but I give you no guarantees.'

Quintus stepped back and saluted. 'I know you will do your best.'

By the time the evening muster was called, the men knew that something was happening. They had been ordered to start dismantling the fortress. All spare posts and lines, where slaves had hung clothes to dry, were taken down. Areas set for recreation — gaming or wrestling — were cleared. Extra fires were doused, and every structure the bored men had built for entertainment and convenience was removed.

The contents of the message were revealed by Titus Flavius. The commander stood in front of the newly minted image of the emperor, which was mounted on a pole. Quintus did not recognise the man holding it, now with the new rank of imaginifer. Aquila still stood proudly bearing the eagle of the Fifth. The men cheered to see it was still with them, fearing the courier might have claimed it.

Flavius spoke quietly, learning from Galba that this was better than shouting. The men would strain to hear, but they would listen. 'General Decimus Claudius Drusus, the emperor's son, is in the high passes to the south with many legions,' he said. 'He intends to subdue the peoples of the mountains and then to work his way down the river. The Germani tribes, including those that plague us, will be given the choice of alliance or conquest. The noble senate also promises reinforcements.' His arm swept across until it pointed south. 'We offer them friendship or death. We march in two days. By then, this fortress will have vanished.'

III: EXTA

In the grey light of the pre-dawn, the tuneless note of the cornu woke the legionaries, its call echoing away mournfully down the valley. The men emerged from their tents bleary-eyed, warming themselves by the fires the slaves already had burning. The same slaves were briskly ordered to tie the legionary armour.

'Help me,' ordered Sextus as he sat by a fire, chewing a piece of meat skewered from the pot that boiled. As usual he seemed to be somehow neater and tidier than the others, as if he had a personal body slave. He hadn't — this was just Sextus: good-looking, cheeky, fortunate. A lucky charm. Jovan hurried to tie the overlapping chest armour at the back.

'Help yourself to more meat,' encouraged red-bearded, red-haired Rufus, sitting beside him and waiting his turn for the slave. 'There is plenty this morning.'

Unusually, this was true. The animals unfit for travel had been slaughtered and a feast eaten the night before. What remained was still being consumed or dried.

'Where are we going?' Rufus asked.

'That way,' said Sextus. Where he pointed the smoke from the various cook fires was mixed with a low mist. 'It looks like the road to Hades.'

Germania was plagued with fogs, and this morning was no exception. The river Rhenus, once more wide, carried a ghostly pall. Stubborn patches of snow still clung to the ground. The tall evergreen trees on the far bank were seemingly rooted in a milky haze, the oaks and elms yet to come into leaf.

'Are you not glad to leave this place?' Quintus asked the two comrades. 'To be on the way to Rome?'

'It is a fair step before we see the Temple of Jupiter on the Capitoline,' said Sextus, shaking his head. 'This year, do you think?'

Quintus shrugged. He would not care to guess.

This morning the hearts of the soldiers were just a little lighter. They were finally going to leave this cold, wet castra hiberna, the winter camp on the banks of the sluggish river. At least, they were if the gods willed it.

Quintus, as optio, had been one of those directing the destruction of the camp. With practised efficiency the legionaries tore down most of the palisade. They were still in enemy territory, so the destruction went on in full armour, with guards looking on. Towers, walls and gates all went, along with the bridges over each ditch, except the one in front of the river. The ditches were then filled with earth and debris. For something that had stood for so long, and resisted so many enemy attacks, it was demolished in a remarkably short time.

In the place where friendly Germani tribesmen had been allowed to congregate and do business, a huge bonfire was constructed and lit, fed with the timbers ripped from demolished walls and buildings.

Marcus, sweating from his exertions, called a man across to where he stood. 'Pollio,' he shouted. When Pollio came, Marcus pointed at a particular stake, still fixed. 'I think you should do the honours,' he laughed.

'I thank you.' The man gave an exaggerated bow, then with his trenching tool uprooted the stake and flung it on the blaze with a curse. Marcus knew that Pollio had good reason to burn the whipping post.

The reservoir dug within the walls, which the men had expended so much energy in building and waterproofing, was hard to destroy. The legionaries had made an excellent job of it, and needed trenching tools, axes and levers to pull it apart. The remnants of the commander's abandoned house, however, which was supported on green timber, fell down almost of its own accord.

The horreum where the grain was stored, the quaestorium where equipment and uniform was issued, the alae that housed the gods and altars of the cohort, the blacksmith's forge — all had to be dismantled. First to go was the horreum, its contents packaged and labelled. There were only a few sacks; the reserves they had built up before the winter were heavily depleted, and the cohort had become used to living off the land. Felix, centurion of the Fourth, was directing operations here. The stores and equipment from both the horreum and quaestorium were loaded into saddlebags to be carried by mules. The animal pens by the north wall were emptied, horses were led out and checked, and birds were caged.

Quintus was at Galba's side by the river when the commander came across.

'Centurion, what shall we do with the barges?' Titus Flavius asked. 'We cannot burn them or sink them.' The two barges had been on the river all winter and now sat low, waterlogged.

'We can do both,' said Galba, nodding. 'Quintus, light fires on them, then set them adrift. They will be of no use to the enemy.'

The Romans would not leave behind a single paling, a single stone set upon another. They would not even leave the remnants of a sack, or a length of twine.

All that was left were the tents, a basic perimeter defence and the tribunal platform. The commander's documents and maps were stored in travelling chests. The remains of his house, along with the furniture he had forced carpenters to waste time on, were already cinders. He would have liked to keep the couches but, unable to justify taking up a cart with them, he satisfied himself with his curule chair and a desk. The alae, housing the sacred objects of the cohort, was pulled apart attentively, with the tripods carried out with reverence and carefully stored. One was kept out for the sacrifices. If the haruspices were unfavourable, the cohort could not move.

As dawn broke, light fell on the backs of the officers standing on the tribunal platform, the centuries assembled before them. The commander had lost weight and seemed tougher now. His hair, which had been light and thinning, was gone. The barber had been instructed to shave his head, and this did much to make him look sterner. His old boxing injuries also helped — though Quintus still thought him small for a soldier. Quintus had to bend his knees to speak to him.

His solid breastplate gleaming, Galba shook his head at the lack of numbers. There were just about four complete centuries, so two short of a cohort. There was less than a troop of cavalry plus the auxiliary horsemen — Cantabrians and Astures of Hispania. Along with Anatolian archers and his own staff, they numbered fewer than five hundred men.

To his left smoke rose from a tripod as a white chicken was ritually sacrificed and opened. A soldier with his cloak pulled over his head — a priest for the moment — approached the commander, his head also now covered, carrying the exta of the offering. Titus Flavius inspected the innards of the bird, then raised his arm and shouted, 'Jupiter be praised, Mars be praised, the omens are good.'

A great cheer arose from the assembly. Quintus watched as the exta were burned on the tripods — food for the gods —

and smiled as he wondered what they would do if the fates did not augur well. It would have taken a pitch-black goose liver or a three-headed calf to stop them now.

The two noble ladies, Antonia Flavia and her companion Aurelia, peeked out from behind the less than adequate curtains fixed to their makeshift litter then drew them tight. They had no part in this ceremony. For the next few weeks, their world would be bounded by canvas and wood. Titus Flavius had instructed his carpenters to construct the litter for them, carried on the shoulders of four slaves. It was furnished with blankets, pillows, waterskins and wineskins, as if they were in Rome.

The fires now burning could be seen for many miles, but this did not matter. The legionaries were not attempting to depart secretly. To blasts of brass, jingling harnesses, multiple shouted orders and, soon enough, soldiers' marching songs, the four centuries of the depleted cohort departed, signiferi with standards leading them.

Rufus, as a signifer, bore the standard of Century One and marched behind Aquila, who carried the shining eagle on a long pole. The new image of the emperor was hoisted behind them. The cavalry brought up the rear, its splendid gear glinting in the sun as it rose above the thick trees on the opposite bank of the river. It chased away the mist, which swirled in protest before vanishing. Finally came the auxiliaries, slaves and carts.

The risen sun vied with the bonfire to provide the morning light, even as the tribunal platform, ripped down by a rearguard of slaves and legionaries, fed the flames. The cohort travelled down the beaten earth that would once have been the via principalis, crossed the wooden bridge and turned sharply right, following the path of the river. Quintus, as optio, marched at the rear of his century, tall hastile in hand.

Crassus, by his side, asked, 'Are you not glad to be going once more into battle?'

'I am, friend. This sitting around watching snow melt was getting to me.'

'We are all glad,' echoed another.

So they marched, seeking an enemy they could not see, on orders from an emperor they would never meet, to join up with a general about whom they knew nothing. But at least they were no longer confined, and they looked forward to fighting.

IV: DEORUM VOLUNTATEM

The two arrows that thudded into the newly made imaginifer arrived so close together that they must have been fired from different bows. They were sharp and accurate. Just like the Parthians who had outranged the legionaries at Carrhae, these bowmen were well out of sight. But they were near enough to aim at the man carrying the imago of the emperor. One of the shafts quivered from the imaginifer's neck, his focale being no protection, whilst the other punched through his lorica laminata, the new segmented armour favoured by the emperor.

He fell, the imago falling with him.

'Grab that,' shouted the commander as his hand shot up to stop the march. Centurion Galba barked swift orders to present shields. The imago was rescued, the man holding it less than happy about his sudden unwelcome promotion. The wolfskin and the standard made obvious targets for enemy arrows.

The legionaries crouched behind their tall curved scuta, ready to fling spears at the enemy, but no more arrows came. It was the third time that day they had been forced to stop, and they had yet to see an enemy. The imaginifer was yet another victim with crest or standard.

When he was certain no further attack was imminent, Titus Flavius called his officers to him. 'I have had enough of being stung,' he announced. 'It is time we swatted these insects.'

The centurions readily agreed, although Quintus did not understand how they could swat an insect they could not see.

'I think, sir,' he said, 'we need to tempt them to come to us. We need to provide a pot of honey.'

'If we find them, we have no need of such tricks.' The Flavian was dismissive. 'We will just find them and wipe them out.'

Titus Flavius committed three centuries to finding and defeating the tribesmen, but whilst they sought the enemy, a much larger band attacked the baggage train. It was almost unprotected, although slaves fought hard and shouted for assistance. Felix led his century, supposedly in reserve, and wheeled them round to repel the natives. But there were losses. Many slaves were killed, others injured beyond surviving, and many food beasts were driven off.

In the camp that night, there were whispers about the ability of the Flavian to command. He had little battle experience and was no tactician. He needed common sense and experience at his side. At a meeting of the officers, Centurion Felix dared to suggest that Galba could provide it. To their surprise, the commander agreed.

Galba thus became praefectus castrorum, responsible for logistics and battle tactics, and Quintus, by general acclamation of the men, moved into his place at the head of Century One. The other centurions, called upon to endorse him, did so immediately. Here was a tall man, skilled in battle, who listened to advice but who, above all, kept a cool head.

His own 'chosen man', his optio, was of course his friend and long-time companion, Crassus. Though they had new jobs and new responsibilities, they knew that they would not receive any more pay. At present, they were being paid nothing, although Cornus diligently recorded their new titles and the amounts that they should have received. Until they defeated a wealthy enemy, or found a town that they could sack, there was nothing with which to pay them. To their frustration, the Germani did not seem to build towns.

Galba persuaded the prefect to adopt a more defensive posture. These tribesmen did not like open battle. Drawing up troops on a chosen piece of flat ground did not tempt them to face their enemy. Instead, like gnats in a marsh, they bit and stung and flew away. They might attack from the side. They might put up a few men to draw the legionaries forward, then attack at the rear. They might fling a few spears and then vanish into the forest.

The cohort had to become warier, to march in close order, to protect its slaves and baggage. It slowed them down. Each night the men built a marching camp, basic but better than nothing. Galba had ordered a pause in their march, so that they could take stock and plan. Therefore, this camp had been their home for more than one night.

They were frustrated. This enemy needed to be drawn out. Sitting around the fire in the evening, officers recalled tactics and campaigns — from Macedonia, Tres Gallia, Hispania; from the clearing out of the pirates by Pompeius Magnus and the great victory of Alesia by Divus Julius; from the social wars, the servile wars, the civil wars.

'In many cases,' Quintus was saying, 'the enemy was one that refused a straight fight, that used subterfuge and guerrilla tactics.'

'I know,' said Marius, centurion of the Third. 'So what do you suggest?'

'We have to provoke them,' Quintus replied. 'We have to make them so angry that they come to us. Like hitting a wasps' nest with a spade.'

Felix shivered. 'There would be many stings,' he said, shaking his head.

'We have no spade that would work.' Black-bearded Furius Lentulus, centurion of the Third, was thoughtful. 'And I do not think insults will lure them, nor jibes about their mothers.'

'*Deorum voluntatem.* The will of the gods,' Quintus interrupted excitedly, suddenly struck with inspiration. 'That is how we will make them fight. If we insult their gods, that should provoke them.'

'Their chief gods are the one-eyed Wotan and the one-armed Týr. They appear to be revered and respected by many of the tribes, if not all. The Suebi, I know, venerate Wotan; the Tencteri, Týr. There are other tribes, but we do not hear much of any other gods. These are their main ones. They are gods of war, rage, justice, vengeance.'

'They sound like Jove and Mars, I would say,' Felix said.

'And what would you do if an enemy insulted Jove and Mars?' Quintus asked, smiling grimly. 'We will shame their gods. It will make them angry enough to meet us in open battle. The next time we can, we'll take prisoners. We'll use these to provoke them.'

'How?' Galba asked.

'Watch,' said Quintus conspiratorially.

The following day they captured six Germani — not in battle; these were coming to steal, so as far as Quintus was concerned, they were already devoid of honour. They were tied back to back to stakes and beaten just enough to silence them.

'What do we want with captives?' Crassus asked.

'You will see,' Quintus replied.

He sought out Jovan, the Macedonian slave, as a messenger. 'Find me Caius of Legio Five,' he commanded. 'He speaks some of their language.'

The slave ran through the camp shouting the name. 'Caius of the Larks, the Centurion calls you.' He found his quarry playing knucklebones at a makeshift low table with three others from the Fifth. 'Centurion Quintus seeks you, sir.' The slave bowed from the neck. Though he belonged to the army — a fact inked on his forehead, hidden by a tied cloth — he did not consider this man to be his master. Nevertheless, he showed him respect.

'Lead on,' Caius said. The ruddiness of his cheeks had faded as the cohort's wine supplies diminished, although he still looked gruff, with a short beard. He was an evocatus, too. He had returned to the legions when the land allocated for his service proved less interesting than fighting. He rose and followed.

Quintus then spoke quietly to Maxim, cousin to Jovan, who carried his request to the Anatolian archers. It was a strange entreaty, but one they felt they could fulfil with relative ease. They would be ready.

Quintus came with Caius to inspect the captives. He decided to question two, who were smaller and dark-haired. 'Find out about their gods, Caius. Tell them ours are greater — make them brag.'

One of the men was sullen and uncommunicative. His nose was spread across his face and one eye was closed and swollen. The other, more productively, was boastful. Within a couple of hours both were handed over for execution.

He eyed up the four remaining captives, a ruthless smile crossing his face. He chose the two biggest ones, with the fairest and longest hair. These he would use.

As the morning light grew, two strange silhouettes could be seen on the flat field chosen by Quintus. A field that would benefit the Romans, providing they could tempt the Germani to attack them. Two stakes were driven into the ground, about ten paces apart. A naked man was tied to each, their feet barely touching the floor.

On one side, the man's fair hair had been pulled from his face and tied. It tumbled down his back in a ragged ponytail. His moustaches had also been roughly trimmed to highlight the angry red socket where his right eye had once been. At the prisoner's feet two dogs, taken from the semi-feral pack that followed the baggage train, were tied on short lengths of rope, so tightly that they could barely breathe. Even so, they kept pulling and whining. Round the man's neck hung two dead birds, a jackdaw and a blackbird. This man's tongue had also been removed. His hands were firmly tied behind his back so that he could not reach the spear plunged deep into the ground in front of him.

Quintus explained the menagerie. 'Wotan has a spear, two ravens and two wolves. The dogs can be the wolves, the two birds at his neck the ravens.' He nodded in approval towards the archers. 'The Anatolians shot them down specially.'

The Romans did not bother with the hair of the other, which hung untidily about his shoulders. They left one arm untied — the arm that ended in a blackened stump, covered in tar and bound with a rag. The victim's chest was shaved and a wide arrow pointing upwards painted on the flesh. Alba had suggested burning it on, but Quintus wanted the man alive.

'What is it?' Tullius asked, fearful of any disrespect to the gods, even someone else's. He had already sacrificed to his own patron to expiate any possible sin.

'Just a rune,' Quintus said. 'Apparently Týr has his own letter in their writing.'

The two effigies were gradually revealed by the rising sun.

Though the Romans pointed and laughed, the tribesmen watching were not amused, recognising the travesty in front of them.

Wotan, the Allfather, had given up his eye to Mimir to drink from the well of knowledge. He was known by his eye-patch, his spear, his two wolves and his two ravens. This was clearly meant to be him. The rune that indicated Týr, along with the hand the god had sacrificed to help bind the wolf Fenrir, identified the other.

The trap was baited. Now Quintus ordered the next part of his ruse.

V: TENCTERI, SUEBI ET AL

The centuries were drawn up behind a low rise, partly hidden by scrubby bushes. Quintus commanded that no more than one group at a time should insult each god and that they should stroll back and forth nonchalantly, but keep their shields raised. He did not want to risk more than a few men.

Only when the light strengthened did the Germani see, with horror, that small groups of men were taking turns, in threes and fours, to urinate on the prisoners. They laughed loudly. Many also spat. Some went further, petting the dogs, slapping the backsides of the men, even weighing their balls in their hands and sniggering.

The Germani, Quintus reasoned, were not stupid. Of course they would know it was a trap. But the way in which their revered gods were being humiliated would cause their ire to rise, and commonsense to depart. Eventually, they would be so incensed that they would try to rescue the men. At least this is what he hoped.

It began with arrows peppering the legionaries' shields. Then the Germani began to gather in greater and greater numbers. It looked like the provocation had worked. Galba smiled and ordered the cohort into battle formation.

The group of tribesmen grew. They seemed to fight as much with sound as with weapons. They shouted and cursed. They let forth strange ululations that rose and fell, sounding like paid mourners at a funeral. The noise rebounded from the forest and echoed from the bare earth. They leapt and waved their spears, axes and long blades.

He observed his foe, taking in the different hairstyles, the fantastic moustaches, the plaited beards. The men wore colourful tunics and cloaks with cross-tied trews. Each style identified a different tribe; they were all tribes that had been defeated — many more than once — by Rome.

These were Tencteri or Usipetes or Suebi or Raeti — or perhaps something unfamiliar to Quintus and his comrades, now that they had travelled this far up towards the mountains, following the twists and turns of the meandering river ever higher. In the thick forest lands above the right bank of the Rhenus, there seemed to be innumerable varieties of Germani, branches of the Celtic nations. They all spoke similar languages and even shared their gods.

Individuals dared to dart forward, trying to tempt the Romans to fight. But none did; instead, a line of legionaries quietly rose up from the opposite side of the field, making a wall of shields. Standards also now flew openly. The crowd of tribesmen thickened.

The note of the cornu rang out, and the echo from the opposite flank was immediate. It signalled a slow march. The legionaries set their jaws and turned their eyes to the standards. With deadly purpose, they began to move.

The standards rose in anticipation. On each flank were the sigils of each century. To one side of the centre flapped the cohort's own image. To the other shone the silver cowl housing the emperor's face. A tesserarius of the Third had taken it, despite the fate of its previous carrier. He now wore the wolfskin cloak. In front of both and proudly above them all, flew one of their own gods, a bronze-beaked eagle rescued from the enemy. Its shining head was turned to the right — the side for victory. Though it was not an eagle of their own legion, it was still an eagle, still divine.

The sweat beaded on Quintus' forehead under the weight of his helmet. Its horsehair crest was magnificent, but made it heavy. He understood why Centurion Galba preferred his tucked beneath his arm.

All the men were tall but he stood a head taller than most of them, the difference made even more obvious by the crested helm of the centurion. Armour protected his chest, back and abdomen, and the tough leather straps of his cingulum covered his groin and the upper parts of his legs. His cloak was thrown over his shoulder and fastened with a pin bearing a wolf's head — one of the few spoils of this endless war of attrition with the numerous tribes of the Germani. It looked like gold, but was probably base metal, an ingenious counterfeit.

On his left he held his scutum, a shield two thirds his height, his forearm thrust through the two vertical straps. It needed to be held in this way to stop it being turned.

Rectangular and slightly curved, it was painted leather-clad wood for the most part, but with a metal boss — a fearsome weapon in itself. At his side, hung on a baldric, was his sheathed gladius, the short, two-edged sword that had turned the Republic into an empire. Unlike the men behind him, his weapon hung on his left. It was the privilege of a centurion to stand alone, and therefore have the room to draw his blade across his body.

Now, at the sound of the cornu, he pushed back his cloak, drew his sword and pointed it at the heavens. Quintus' men were on the right flank, he on their left side, nearer the centre. In the centre itself, Centurion Furius Lentulus and Centurion Marius led the Second and Third centuries. Behind them was a group of Anatolian archers. On the left, leading the Fourth, Centurion Felix was at the head of the latest recruits, whom the veterans called the rabbits. An unfair nickname now, as they had been with the army for more than a year, and none were new to battle.

Behind each century, an optio stood sternly with his long hastile, metal-tipped at one end and rounded at the other. It was up to him to choose which end he used to push back any men who fell out of line.

To either side was the cavalry — not many, but enough to protect the wings, along with a few mounted auxiliaries from Cantabria. Between them these formed a thin reserve. To Quintus' right, Galba sat on horseback above the battle plain, his mount shoulder to shoulder with that of Titus Flavius. The dip and sway of the standards indicated their orders. To the disappointment of Galba, he would not fight this day unless the reserves were needed.

Some of the men prayed to the gods of the state and the legion, as well as their household deities — the ones that guarded their families, their homes, their trades and guilds. There was lame Vulcan for the blacksmith, Ceres for the farmer, Diana for the hunter, Apollo for the musician, Mercury for the thief. They also prayed to Fortuna for luck, and blood-red Mars, of course, for war. Century One revered Juno, her noble beast, the cow, counterpart to the black bull of Legio Nine shown charging on the red field of the cohort standard.

The tang of sweat, dung and urine filled the air, not fear. It was the smell of battle.

VI: VALHALLA

At a signal from Galba, a raised standard dipped and twisted, meaningless to the enemy. The movement was repeated at the other edge of the field. A cornicen sounded a different note and the pace quickened to a standard march. A wall of shields advanced. In contrast to the tribesmen, the legionaries moved silently but for orders and the steady tramp of their caligae.

Quintus' raised sword urged the men forward as the instrument sounded. This time the centre maintained pace, whilst the two wings increased theirs. Still the army did not run. Instead, there was another order, and the wings adopted a jog-trot, double time but more so. An undisciplined run would open gaps in the ranks. The strength of the formation was in its shape, its closeness, its overlapping shields. It took a lot of training to hold the line straight and not break.

These men had endured a lot of training. The army was a team, a collective, or as Galba had once described it to Quintus, 'an animal with many legs, many arms, one that does not need all of them. It needs just one head.'

For most men, he knew, survival was the goal. Survival for themselves and their amicus and their standards. Survival without dishonour until night fell or the trumpet called one of two notes. *We are victorious, pursue*; or *forward, protect the eagle*. Never defeated, there was no trumpet call for a rout.

The gap was closing fast between the opposing forces. The Germani were already careering towards them, running flat out. Arrows, then spears, plunged deep into the two prisoners tied to the stakes. Death came quickly. There would be no more shame here.

37

There was no discipline in their attack. It seemed that honour went to the one who reached the Romans first, who was the first to die. The lines closed. The Germani overtook the stakes and the dead men vanished, torn out in fury. The dogs and birds were freed and discarded in rage. The thunder of the enemy's feet on the ground made it shake.

Quintus narrowed his eyes in concentration. His ears stopped themselves to all but the sound of the cornu. His tread beneath him became soft and silent. His heart slowed to a fist-struck bass drum rhythm, regular and deep and irresistible. His head cleared, all but the spark of battle banished. His thoughts — strike, fight, win — ran clear and true as a deep-rooted mountain spring.

For the tiniest moment he paused on the brink. Between paralysis and action. A second. Less. Then sound and air and heat and light, sweat and smell and brotherhood, all tumbled in, like a great river throwing itself down a cataract, like the beating rain of a summer storm.

Another note. Two short, one long. A swarm of spears flew over his head and towards the enemy. They were accompanied by a shower of arrows, halting the Germani charge.

Arrows flew in both directions. There were only about twenty Anatolian archers, but they would keep shooting for as long as their quivers allowed. Their shafts flew high and then plummeted into the enemy, carving gaps in their rear. The Romans relied on their scuta to keep them safe; the small, round bucklers of the Germani were not enough to protect them.

Quintus gave the next command as the cornicen sounded again. '*Gladium stringe* — draw swords!'

The note of the cornu reached the men even if Quintus' shout did not. Every man with a gladius reached down and drew it with his right hand, the soft swish of each as it left the scabbard joining together in a sound like a wave breaking on a shore. Every wrist turned, every point thrust upwards at the same time and, like a many-clawed animal, the men raked the Germani. The right wing engaged first, their shields held up to eye level so that their bodies were protected. They rammed into the tribesmen as their sharp blades sought flesh.

They were no cowards, these Germani, but nor were they organised. They tripped and blocked each other, needing room to swing and slash. They tried to strike over the shields or between them, or to thrust at the eyes. But the scuta were close together and curved, and there was no room to stab with a long sword, and no way through for an axe. The legionaries, in contrast, stabbed upwards with minimum backswing, efficiently making use of the confined space. They held their ground. If a comrade fell, they moved swiftly to close the space. The reek of sweat and dung was soon overpowered by that of blood and opened guts.

Quintus could barely breathe, the air between him and the enemy was thick, the space confined; his world collapsed into a prison of darkness, no sun, no sky, no river, no grass. The noise and stench assaulted his senses. He was as much trying to fight his way out as to defeat the enemy. Every few minutes, there was a pause, and hope rose in the men's breasts. Then the two sides laid on again as they caught their breath.

It was only as he stepped over a fallen tribesman that Quintus realised the legionaries were gaining ground. He dared to look left and right and was relieved to see that his line held, though the centre had outpaced the wings so that now the line took the shape of a bent bow.

Slowly, the right wing first turned, then outflanked the tribesmen, pushing them back onto their own men. The centre held its ground. The left, as planned, gradually gave way. Before they realised it, the tribesmen were all but surrounded.

Suddenly, beside the river there was room for the Germani to breathe, room for them to swing their swords and axes. But here there was no enemy, just water and earth. They could return to the mêlée and take some more Romans with them before they were themselves cut down. But for this they needed to be fired up. Most were not, not any more.

The alternative was to follow the river, to save themselves to fight another day. A few decided to join their gods and heroes in Valhalla — to go back into the fight and die. Most took the opportunity to escape.

The legionaries hurried the tribesmen along by flinging spears after them. The Anatolians nocked arrows and let fly, bringing down some more. They would be entitled to the spoils from any that they killed. The cavalry did not pursue. The decurion waved a languid arm and turned his mount away from the fight. This particular confederation of tribes appeared to have no mounted warriors.

The tribesmen who had chosen to die fighting rushed at the legionaries, some even throwing down arms. Galba signalled and the cornicen sounded the general engagement, allowing the men to break ranks and choose a foe to engage one-on-one.

Quintus sighed with relief. The battle was over.

VII: PONTEM AUREUM

'Do you think we destroyed the nest?' Quintus asked Rufus as he squatted by the river, wringing out his focale. He had used it to wipe the sweat and splattered blood from his skin. Though he rinsed it thoroughly, it was still not clean. He squinted at it with distaste before tying it back around his neck. Either the slaves would boil it, or he would obtain another from a fallen comrade.

'This one, perhaps. There will be others, I think,' Rufus replied, raising his bushy eyebrows. He squatted beside Quintus, washing his face, his wolfskin cloak carefully laid out beside him. His drooping moustache made him look like one of the Germani, and his red hair stood on end.

Further down the bank, tribesmen's bodies were being tipped into the river by slaves. All their weapons, jewellery, furs, leather ties and belts had been removed. A small group of prisoners huddled nearby, destined for flogging and crucifixion. Their bodies would be displayed as a warning to any enemy who might dare to attack. The prisoners had not surrendered; they had fought hard not to be captured, but had been overpowered. Now their hands and feet were tightly bound. If they could have reached a blade, they would have willingly killed each other, and themselves.

'Why did they not run with the rest?' Sextus asked as he joined them.

'They did, but were caught,' Rufus said, shrugging. 'Their bad fortune that they were captured. Now they will die a slow death.'

'They could have chosen to die honourably,' said Quintus as he adjusted his damp focale. He took Sextus' helmet from him in order to scoop water. The crest on his own helmet prevented its use as a vessel. 'They could have fought, but they ran. They took the only road left open to them.'

'The golden bridge,' said Sextus, taking the helmet back.

'Exactly.' Quintus nodded. 'That's what Scipio Africanus called it — the *pontem aureum*. It makes sense. If you are surrounded, you only have two options: die, taking as many of the enemy with you as possible, or flee.' He pushed a hand through his wet hair. 'The clever commander creates a way out, an escape route. The defeated man now sees a way to salvation. Instead of fighting a desperate rearguard action, he remains defeated and runs. With luck, he throws away his weapons as he goes.'

'But these did not escape,' Rufus pointed out.

'Not all of them, no,' Quintus said. 'For the running man is now vulnerable, has made himself weak. He can be slaughtered or captured.' He nodded towards the prisoners. 'These were just not fast enough.'

Rufus returned to Quintus' question. 'You must think there are more tribes?'

He grinned. 'Enough to keep even a workshy wastrel like Sextus busy.'

Sextus rose and pretended to shove his centurion into the water. He was known as a ladies' man, too fond of his own appearance. 'I think there are many more beyond this god-cursed river,' he said. 'They do not know when they are beaten.'

'I know,' said Quintus seriously. 'Whenever we defeat a tribe, even taking the heads of chieftains and leaving behind prisoners hammered up on tree branches, another springs up in its place. It is like Cadmus sowing dragon's teeth.'

Rufus pointed at the thickly growing trees that came right down to the water on the opposite bank. 'I think the forest goes on further than we can imagine. And in it there must be tribe after tribe of these Germani.' He lowered his voice. 'Perhaps we should leave them be.'

Quintus pretended not to hear. Rufus's comment would count as defeatist talk, and if reported he would lose his position as a signifer and possibly receive a whipping. Sextus had no title. He refused all promotions, not wanting the extra responsibility and not believing he would ever receive the extra pay. 'Double nothing is still nothing,' he was fond of saying.

The three of them set off together to investigate the field hospital. Quintus knew that Crassus was safe; he had seen him. Marcus, the evocatus and optio, had been seen with Galba and Titus Flavius, no doubt discussing the tactics of the battle. Dour Tullius, his amicus, was squatting near where the slaves went about their grisly work, one eye on them whilst he sharpened his already razor-edged pugio. There were others who they had yet to find.

The field hospital — more a dressing tent than anything — was almost empty, but they did find Alba the capsarius carrying a severed leg under his arm.

Quintus nodded towards the limb, taken off above the knee. 'Will he survive?'

'Unlikely,' said Alba, then, in a lower tone, 'better if he doesn't.'

The patient would be sent — along with any others who lived — back to the marching camp. A cart pulled by a mule and guided by a couple of slaves would take them. The camp was currently garrisoned by the ill and the injured. It also housed the noble personages of the wife of Titus Flavius and her companion, who were looked after by their body slaves. Although this camp had lasted longer than a single night, it was still very basic, with a ditch and bank, a simple palisade, and a felled tree for a principal gate. It was certainly not safe.

Quintus spotted something else going on down by the river. One man, a legionary, was on the bank with his arms pinioned by two others. Another two men were taking it in turns to pummel him. The group of men watching closed ranks when they saw the centurion approaching.

'Not for officers, sir,' said one, politely but firmly.

Quintus nodded. He and his companions continued walking. This, they knew, was someone being punished by his own. They would break no bones, except perhaps the man's nose; cut no flesh, except perhaps his lip; and use no weapons except their fists. The man would know that his action, or inaction — Quintus had no idea how the man had sinned — was being punished. Better this than a flogging in front of the whole cohort or an execution — even more of a morale-destroyer.

They stepped out of the way of Century Four, mustered ready to return downstream. It would escort the wounded and take first watch. Felix was proud of his rabbits, and made sure they pulled their weight. The two centurions exchanged a salute. For now Quintus was letting his own century gather what poor spoils there were. Galba walked towards the group, vine staff in hand. His helmet, as ever, was tucked under his arm. 'Uninjured?' he asked briskly.

'Uninjured, sir,' Quintus and Rufus responded, fist to heart in salute, whilst Sextus began to tell of the cuts to his shield arm. Quintus playfully punched him in the other arm.

'Uninjured, sir,' Sextus echoed glumly. There were bruises, of course, and minor lacerations, but no breaks, and nothing that would put them out of action.

'The rest?' Galba knew how close-knit this particular contubernium was.

'Not all found yet, but we think all survived.'

'Good.' Galba tried to be gruff, but his voice was soft. He liked these men. Addressing Quintus, he went on, 'Your ruse succeeded, centurion. We may at last be able to strike camp and move upriver. The commander is happy, though I see your tricks do not gain universal approval.' He looked at two legionaries close by, subtly making the warding sign of the cornua at Quintus, afraid that this man had offended the gods.

Quintus shrugged. If getting the job done made him unpopular, so be it.

'Another tribe comes — they will be here in two days,' Galba continued. The men sighed; they thought they had earned some respite. Galba was quick to reassure them. 'We can take a breath. Apparently they wish to become our allies, so maybe we won't have to fight them.'

VIII: SENATOR CORNUS

The Germani tribe that sought an alliance were not to be allowed anywhere near the camp, lest there be spies amongst them, so a meeting place was arranged, a rock in the shape of a horse's head a mile to the south. It was also away from the battleground, the place where their chief gods had been so insulted.

In the camp, the commander's tent was busy. Titus Flavius was contemplating how many men to take and how many standards, symbols and vexilla to carry. He did not want to reveal their true strength. If the tribe knew that they were dealing with an undermanned cohort, they might think twice about an alliance.

'The eagle and the cohort standard come with us,' he said, 'and you, the tall centurion who tricked them with their own gods, bring ten men, an honour guard.'

Quintus nodded and saluted. As he turned to leave, he heard the prefect start to explain how diplomacy worked. He paused to listen.

'When Rome meets with its enemies and erstwhile allies, it matches pomp and ceremony with simplicity.' Flavius stroked his newly shaven head. 'I have seen the Parthians, Armenians and Egyptians arriving draped in gold and silk, surrounded by slaves, acolytes and noble beasts and accompanied by the sound of trumpets and flutes.' He lowered his voice, as if imparting a secret. 'The Egyptian queen, Cleopatra Philopator, lover of both Divus Julius and the defeated Marcus Antonius, was most famous for this. She sailed into Ostia with many ships, then unloaded many carts and wheeled platforms for her procession into Rome. It took two days to bring it all within the gates.'

'Or not.'

Quintus was surprised to hear a woman's voice. Antonia Flavia, higher born than her husband, seemed less convinced by such stories.

'Much of this is conjecture, husband,' she offered helpfully, 'written by her enemies. My father was present in the city — the two days is a myth.'

Flavius did not respond. Quintus could only imagine his withering look. He had never seen the court of an eastern monarch, but had heard tell of fabulous displays of wealth and power. He had also heard tales of Cleopatra's entry into Rome, bringing a son she claimed was fathered by Divus Julius.

'In contrast,' the Flavian continued, 'Roman ambassadors often comprise a single red-shoed senator, with a couple of legionaries in attendance. The power of the toga should not be underestimated.'

Quintus pursed his lips at this but said nothing, slipping out of the tent. Outside, he called Rufus and Aquila to him. 'The standards — including the eagle — come with us. We need to look like we represent a legion.' He dropped his voice. 'Apparently the commander believes in the power of the toga. I would rather we had ten good soldiers with us.'

'You are right,' agreed Aquila. 'It is not the power of the toga, nor displays of hauteur and disdain that convinces our enemies.' He smiled knowingly. 'It is the fully armed legions camped on their doorsteps.'

'Wealth here is different,' said Rufus. 'Here they do not seem to sport gold or silver — at least not if the meagre takings from this action are anything to go by. They do not build palaces or even cities. They are a poor people, and may be bought with cattle or grain.'

'Neither of which we have in abundance,' Quintus said.

'That does not stop us from promising them,' Rufus grinned. 'They don't know we don't have them.'

'And with luck they don't know the history of Roman alliances either, and how many times a friend has become an enemy,' said Aquila. 'Rome often bargains with what it does not have. You know my father served with Caesar in Britannia. He was also at Alesia. Vercingetorix himself was made many offers that were not in the gift of the general. Not least, citizenship.'

'And the barbarian pretended in return,' said Rufus. 'He kept spreading rumours that the rest of the Celtic nation was close, just over the horizon. He even received messengers — men that Caesar suspected he had despatched himself. Apparently this is called diplomacy.'

'Did you not see Vercingetorix die?' Quintus asked.

'I did,' Rufus replied. 'That's when I heard these stories. Vercingetorix may have fronted a great nation, but he did not wear gold and silver. When he was dragged to his knees in front of Divus Julius, he was clad in furs and linen, not silk. And when he was strangled, he wore no ornamentation.'

'It is strength they respect, not wealth,' agreed Quintus. He repeated the order. 'Ten good men. Fully armed and armoured.'

He went back into the tent to see what more was needed. The commander turned to him. 'Centurion, do they know our strength?'

'I think not, sir. Though of course they may have spies.'

'Then we do what we can to conceal our numbers. Move centuries, change guards, make noise. We must make sure they think that we are strong, a *full* legion with cavalry and auxiliaries. Galba, tell the decurion we need mounts.' He looked at his freedman through narrowed eyes. 'I think we will even take staff. Cornus will ride with us.'

The scribe would have objected, but he knew it would be useless and would put him in a bad light. Instead he smiled thinly and dipped his head.

'Red shoes be damned,' Flavius continued. 'I am going to flaunt our strength, not hide it. We will ride to this meeting, and, centurion, I want archers and auxiliaries as well. I will also hint at reinforcements on the way. It's no lie — General Drusus is somewhere to the south.'

Cavalry horses, as richly draped as possible, were brought for all of them, even the archers. The legionaries all wore full lorica laminata and helmets, the crests of the centurions making them look impossibly tall. Titus Flavius wore his shining metal breastplate, beaten out to make it look as if he had the torso and ribs of a Hercules or a Hector. Aquila and Rufus and the cohort's signifer and imaginifer all wore their animal skin cloaks, the wolf heads snarling above their helms. Ten legionaries rode as escort.

After a brief discussion between Flavius and Galba, a cornicen was also mounted. The curved length of his great horn was intended to impress the tribesmen, but it would also be ready to call reinforcements should a trap be sprung. Quintus was happy with the deputation; it smacked of Roman might. Most impressive was the shining eagle, held aloft by Aquila.

They picked their way over the rough land at the side of the forest, avoiding the battleground entirely. Scouts were sent ahead to ensure the route was clear up to the large, oddly shaped rock that marked the meeting point. The scouts were also instructed to report on when the Germani arrived. It would not do for Rome to be kept waiting. Flavius would make sure that the tribesmen were in place before entering the glade.

When the Germani were gathered, the Romans moved forward slowly, harnesses jingling and horses blowing.

Quintus saw that these supplicants looked no different to the other tribes they had encountered. They were dressed in short tunics and woollen trews, cross-tied with leather. Their heads were mostly bare, aside from the occasional headband. They wore multi-coloured cloaks held in place with bright metal, which looked more like bronze or iron than gold or silver. There were intricate designs to the brooches, but no sign of precious stones. They carried long, curved swords — of little use to infantry in close combat — sharp knives and tall spears. There were approximately ten of them, all fair-haired and with full beards and moustaches.

'We have seen similar in Britannia,' Quintus whispered to Rufus. 'Surely these Germani are cousins to the Britons.'

'Maybe to the Gauls, too, from their dress.'

The leaders of the party dismounted. Cornus sat awkwardly on his horse. He was not used to riding and had no intention of trying to dismount. At a soft order from Galba, one of the legionaries lifted the scribe from his saddle and gently placed him on the ground. As he brushed the dust from his pale tunic, he threw the man a look of thanks.

The Germani watched this little mime, talked amongst themselves quietly and urgently, then seemed to reach an agreement. One man, seemingly their leader, stepped forward and addressed the simply dressed Cornus in heavily accented Latin.

'Welcome, Senator. We come to you as friends and trust you will be friends to us.'

Cornus looked confused and was about to say something in protest when Quintus intervened. 'A formal answer will suffice, *Senator* Cornus, and then this man can get down to business with our general.' He indicated Flavius, who also realised what was happening. Luckily, the scribe recognised the game, looked to Flavius for confirmation, and on receiving a slight nod, continued the conversation.

The tribesman had clearly sought out enough history to expect to be met by a senator, and he knew that the man would be the most plainly dressed of the visitors. Quintus could see that it would be useful to have an imitation politician here — someone who might be able to confirm treaties, or who might need to send to Rome for advice. An excuse to delay was always a good negotiating tactic.

Caius, who spoke some of the Germani's language, was with them. He looked relieved that this chieftain spoke Latin, although the men swiftly realised that his knowledge of the language was poor. Perhaps the chieftain had learnt this opening speech by heart, as he looked confused when Cornus replied with a formal phrase — one that was not really appropriate, unless you were inviting a guest into your home. 'Rome bids you welcome to share fire and water at our hearth.'

The chieftain turned to one of his own men and spoke briefly. This appeared to be the Germani's translator, a small man, fairly young and simply dressed. He wore both his hair and beard short. Unlike the others, he was dark. He replied to Cornus in passable Latin. 'Thank you, your honour. I trust that you and your people will share this fire and water that you bring with the earth and air that is already here.'

'A rebuke, do you think?' Quintus whispered.

'A mild one, if it was,' Rufus replied. 'Is he a slave? He is not of their race.'

'I think he may be a Celt. Although he reminds me of the Britons.'

The chieftain spoke again to the Celt and he addressed Cornus. 'My master wants to know if you have men with you with ancestry along the great river.' He waved a hand towards Rufus, with his large moustache and bright red beard.

'I am a freeborn Roman citizen,' spluttered Rufus proudly, slapping his fist to his chest to emphasise the point.

'He is not of your race,' Caius confirmed.

The Romans unloaded folding camping stools, on which the commander, Galba and Cornus arranged themselves. Aquila stood at their back so that the eagle was above them. The Germani chieftain and his advisers and translator squatted on the ground.

They spoke informally of countries and families, fortunes and gods. Luckily, the chieftain did not seem worried about the insults offered to Wotan and Týr, nor was he bothered about the tribes already defeated. They were clearly not kin. However, Galba — who led the negotiations — could not extract any military information. Titus Flavius intervened now and again, whilst Cornus nodded sagely but said nothing.

It was agreed that each side should withdraw and speak with their own groups privately. Cornus was relieved at this, and said so as soon as he was out of earshot of the Germani.

'Masters, I am not sure how much longer I can keep up this charade. I am no senator.'

'You make an excellent senator,' Quintus assured him.

'Excellent,' agreed Galba. 'Just act slightly deaf and stupid and you will be fine.'

Titus Flavius threw a black look at his senior officer, but that was all. Senators were not to be mocked.

IX: SAGUM

The discussion between the men was brief.

'Do they really want so little?' Titus Flavius asked in wonder.

'They do not wish to be an enemy to Rome,' said Quintus. 'I do not think that this tribe is allied with any other.'

'Nor do I,' said Galba. 'They seem to be less than warlike. All they want is enough land to farm, enough forest to hunt in, and enough river to fish.'

'We can provide this,' said the commander confidently, as if the land was Rome's to give. 'Most of these tribes seem to be enemies with each other. Only when they come together do they pose any threat.'

'So, if we ally with this tribe, it wins us the enmity of others, but safe passage for the next few miles?' Galba asked.

'I think so,' said Quintus. 'I think that is the best we can hope for.'

'We can offer them land, any of that behind us on the left bank, all the way to the sea,' the commander said, with not a trace of doubt in his tone.

'And the senator here can offer them grain, sir,' Quintus added, nodding at Cornus. 'It is just that it will have to be transported from Rome, so may take some time to arrive…'

Galba nodded. 'So we make them our ally. We need something with which to seal the pact — a hostage, really.' He looked at the legionaries, the signifer and the centurion. None of these could be spared — or risked, for that matter.

Quintus had a suggestion. 'We should ask them what they want. They may not wish to take another mouth to feed.'

'Nor, I think,' said Galba, 'do we wish to take one of their warriors into our camp and confidences. Such a man could easily escape and take our secrets with him, if not to this tribe then to others. You are right; we will ask them.'

Returning to the negotiations, the two sides had clearly both made decisions. The tribesmen asked for land and for grain with which to feed their people until their farming was settled and productive. Unexpectedly, they also asked for Roman protection from certain of their fellow tribesmen.

Flavius granted the land over which they had just marched, leaving the Germani to choose which tract suited them best. He did not mention that they would probably have to fight for it.

Divus Julius had pushed tribes from one side of the river to the other, and all along its length, trying to fit them into pockets of land like a neat patchwork. Flavius had no intention of attempting this, knowing that it gave rise to conflicts and shifting alliances as each tribe was displaced.

The true part of the negotiation was the demand that this tribe — who identified themselves as the Vangiones — lead them safely over the land that they currently occupied, as close to the mountains as possible. At the last moment Flavius also matched the plea for protection with the idea of a formal alliance — which meant that this tribe would be expected to provide auxiliaries to fight for Rome when called on. This made them once more seek private counsel.

'I do not think that was necessary, sir,' said Galba tetchily.

'I do,' snapped Flavius. 'I would have this as genuine an agreement as possible. A general would not ask for anything less, and a senator certainly wouldn't.'

It took a while, and seemed to involve a great deal of discussion and arm-waving, but eventually the chieftain and his translator came back to where they had been speaking with the Romans. They did not squat as before. This was going to be brief.

'This could signal a refusal,' muttered Galba into Quintus' ear. 'I knew he should not have gone so far.' He fell into step with Flavius and Cornus. They too, did not sit, though the camp stools remained.

The chieftain signalled back towards his men, and a black colt was trotted forward. It had four white socks and a white blaze that served to accent the sheen of its coat. It was a spirited beast, clearly not yet broken, and it whinnied as it was brought forward. The chieftain spoke, and the translator told Flavius what he wanted to hear. 'My master agrees to your offer, and to your terms. This pony is a token of his commitment. The exchange of this beast with a gift from yourselves will seal the bargain, and the alliance.' He paused. 'My master asks what you would give in exchange.'

Quintus sensed that this man was not about to accept something that he could not display to his fellow tribesmen. Therefore, the promise of citizenship or a trip to Rome would not suffice.

'What would he have?' Flavius asked.

The tribesman pointed at Aquila and Rufus and said something. For a moment Quintus thought that he meant to take them as hostages, or at the very least to take the standard — perhaps even the eagle. He tensed. None of these could be allowed.

'The cloak, my master would have the wolfskin cloak,' the Celt explained.

Quintus was quicker than any of them, clutching his cloak tightly. 'Tell him that the sagum, the red cloak of war, is the most precious thing to a soldier. It is more important than his sword or shield. We could not possibly pass the red cloak of a centurion to a foreign power, even if they are allies.' He put on a stern face and clutched his cloak to his breast like a new mother with a baby.

The German holding the colt began to walk it away and it looked like all negotiations and agreements had broken down. Galba, realising the ploy, pleaded theatrically with Quintus and he, in turn, feigned great reluctance before unclasping his cloak and handing it across. They tried to hide smiles as the exchange was completed.

'I will even authorise a new one from the stores,' promised Cornus in a whisper, 'without the need to produce the old one first.'

'Very noble,' said Quintus sarcastically as he took possession of the colt, but he accompanied the comment with a warm smile that only Cornus could see.

'An agreement, then?' Galba asked.

'Let it be so,' said the Germani chieftain through his translator. 'Our scouts will make sure the path is clear for your people.'

The two groups parted, one admiring their hard-won 'red cloak of war', the other the high stepping gait of the colt.

Quintus walked the animal back to the camp, which was finally struck.

The Germani not only kept the road clear, but were also adroit at avoiding natural obstacles. They took the cohort around marshland, rivers and streams, past dense woodland and around deep clefts in the land. The legionaries followed at around two stades' distance, with sometimes just the tails of the ponies at the rear of the tribesmen in sight. The arrangement suited Galba, who did not wish to reveal their true numbers, although by now their guides must have gleaned that this was no full strength legion.

As a 'senator', Cornus rode, just in case the Germani should spot him on foot and conclude that he was nowhere near as important as was claimed. It was a rare luxury for the freedman and he quietly relished it. The colt was walked beside him.

The legionaries marched four abreast where the forest paths allowed, with mounted auxiliaries keeping watch over the wagons, mules and the rest of the baggage train. Cavalry protected the closed litter, relays of slaves carrying it on their shoulders at a brisk pace.

They were followed by a motley band of local tribespeople offering various services. There were hucksters, hair-pluckers, bloodletters, fortune tellers, and prostitutes — female and male. They were not permitted within a spear's throw of the wagons, nor within the temporary fort at night, on pain of a whipping, but that did not stop many of them from breaking this rule.

Sometimes, the cohort swung so far west that the men could no longer see or hear the river. Then Galba was concerned, and Quintus insisted that a runner was sent to make sure they were still on course. That runner was the legionary Agnus.

Agnus had acted as a runner and messenger when the winter camp was being besieged. Now he ran ahead of the vanguard in order to check the position of their guides. Sometimes he rode, but most of the time he was happy to run wearing just a tunic and caligae, no armour, though he kept his belt and sword. On every occasion he returned with news that the Germani were not leading them astray, that soon they would see the river again. Being on foot meant sacrificing speed for greater freedom beneath the trees and on broken ground.

He reported movements back to the column. 'They are going around a steep hill, rather than going over it. It looks like we will be outside this stretch of forest soon, then turn east back into it in a short while.'

Agnus also carried messages between his commanders and the tribesmen. From the Germani to the Romans came warnings of difficult terrain, wild animals and even possible enemies, though this was their own territory. From Roman to Germani came one daily message only, in mid-afternoon: 'Time to stop and make camp.'

This caused great amusement amongst the tribesmen, who could see hours of daylight left. The camps were made in places with water and wood — defendable spots with sightlines up and down the river and across the plain, if they could see it. Pioneers went ahead to mark out the perimeter and to fell the necessary timber to clear a space. Some of the great trees defeated them, but many smaller ones, plus brush and shrub, fell easily.

Once the ground was cleared, they constructed a camp laid out in the familiar cruciform shape, with two roads bisecting each other and four gates, each closed with a single tree. If they were not close enough to the river, they dug latrines and fetched water for the animals. They lit fires and erected tents for the men, larger ones for the officers, and an even more elaborate pavilion for the commander, with separate quarters for the women. Simple stables were constructed for the horses. An altar and brazier was set up near the commander's tent so that thanks could be given, pleas made and haruspices could be taken. The injured were unloaded. Some of them expired, including the one-legged man. Others recovered enough to walk.

The Germani stayed in temporary shelters made from branches and leaves, and they posted guards rather than constructing palisades. They crept close enough to the Romans to watch them build their camp, and in the morning, they knew from the smoke that it was time to move, even though it was before dawn.

X: CONGREGA

The Romans and their guides traversed a series of low hills under a dull and metallic sky. As they crossed a small and muddy stream, Galba looked for a place to halt.

'It is almost time to stop for the day. The sun passed its zenith some time since,' Galba told Flavius. 'It will be dark early; this cloud is thick.'

'There is a storm coming,' said Quintus, walking beside Galba.

Agnus came jogging down the hill. 'At the top of the next rise, it is flat,' he said. 'The Germani are moving beneath the trees.'

The ground around them was grassland and low scrub. The forest was thick and forbidding to their left, with stony, broken land to their right.

'Camp or shelter?' Galba called.

A long roll of thunder and a flash of lightning in the distance answered him.

'Shelter,' said Quintus. He called across to the runner. 'Agnus, go and tell our friends we are halting.'

The men still crossing the stream were irritable, the heaviness of the day and the approaching storm affecting their mood. There was murmured chatter, but no singing or jocularity. The sky seemed low above their heads and was stone-grey. Quintus was a farmer and countryman. He knew the signs. He felt the change in the air as it became closer and denser; the storm had gathered strength somewhere near.

A wagon became stuck crossing the stream, and Quintus ordered his men to break ranks and help the slaves who were trying to move it. They struggled.

'Put your shoulders to it!' Quintus yelled. 'You are better fed than the slaves, and better trained. Shift the cursed thing. Do you want to be ambushed? This is as good a place as any.' The four slaves carrying the women crossed the stream a little further up, their cavalry escort with them. Quintus was minded to have them put the litter down so they could help with the cart, but he did not dare.

Finally the recalcitrant wheels turned and the wagon lurched out of the mud. Helped by slaves pushing and the mule pulling, it came out of the water and began trundling towards the top of the rise. The rest of the cohort, knocked out of rhythm, were milling around in disarray, a broken formation that would have shamed an optio or brought laughter down on a junior officer's head on the Campus Martius, the sacred field outside Rome where legionaries trained.

Quintus was furious. 'Form up,' he shouted, waving his vine rod angrily. 'You look like the mob turning out from the games rather than soldiers.'

With obvious reluctance, the men began to reassemble in proper order, looking with apprehension at the black clouds that approached.

The first sign that the storm was upon them was the grasses beginning to whisper and shiver. The dried detritus at the feet of the legionaries lifted from the ground in small waves and eddies. The sky went eerily quiet as the birdsong ceased. The wildlife that had leapt out of the way of the march grew still. Even the insects were silent.

For most men, such storms came with little warning. For the herdsman, the farmer and the sailor, these early signs were clear. The sky rapidly darkened to a shade of night, then fat drops of rain began to fall heavily.

Many of the men moved behind a horse, mule or cart for shelter. The prefect dismounted and sought protection behind his horse, his cloak whipping around in the wind. The women were still in the litter. They must have parted the curtains to give instructions as their bearers lifted it and hurried them under the trees. Quintus sniffed the air and looked at the bruised sky. Then he shouted to Flavius across the rising gale. 'If we stop now, we will be caught in the eye of the storm. We must find shelter quickly.'

A camp constructed would withstand a storm. A camp being built would not. Quintus knew there would be no time to finish it. The wind had arrived stealthily, at first brisk, then strong, now hard and irresistible.

'Your advice, centurion?' Flavius replied.

'I doubt we can outrun it. Our protection is in the trees.'

The wind was now roaring and it would be impossible to unload the carts. One tent, a badly packed edge caught by the wind, was ripped from the hands of men trying to rescue it and shredded as it was borne aloft. Horses were shying and whinnying, trying to turn their backs to the tempest. The colt struggled, tossing its head in an attempt to part from its handler. Men knelt down, lest they be blown over, cloaks pulled over their heads as if they prayed. The slaves cowered where they could behind the carts. The rearguard of native service providers had disappeared.

'Galba,' shouted Flavius. 'The forest?'

'The forest,' called Galba in response. 'Make it so.'

Quintus ran across to the cornicen and grabbed his arms so that he could yell into his ear. 'Cornicen, blow the congrega, the reveille,' he shouted.

The cornicen hesitated. Quintus raised his vine rod threateningly, until the man lifted his curved horn to his lips and blew. Four short notes, one long, three times, much of it lost on the tempest. The men, crouched double against the wind, looked up, astonished to be told to rise as if it were morning.

'Again!' Quintus shouted. 'Blow it again.' He caught sight of the cohort standard stiff in the wind. 'Signifer, make the sign.'

The man struggled to lift the tattered standard but managed, dipping it despite the heavy cloth trying to leave its pole. As the cornicen made the second call and the standard signalled the same order, the men began to form up. The mules were still in the traces, the carts still packed.

'The trees,' Quintus shouted, pointing. 'The trees will protect us.'

The men now saw the sense of it, and the four centuries coalesced into a single column, dragging carts, horses and slaves with them.

'Sound the quick march,' commanded Quintus, and the cornicen once more blew. The men more than ten feet away heard nothing, but the word was swiftly passed. The legionaries broke into a trot with the mules and carts encouraged to keep up. The cavalry pulled their mounts into the trees, talking the beasts away from their panic. Their horses might be trained to war, but that did not mean that they would not react unpredictably to thunder and lightning.

As the cohort moved, the next blast of heavy rain swept across, needle-sharp with the weight of the wind behind it. Ahead of them it formed a blanket, blurring the shape of the treeline. The sky darkened further, and a great peal of thunder was followed almost immediately by lightning. Quintus knew then that the storm sat directly overhead.

He remembered Wotan and Týr and the power they might have over this land. The Romans were a long way from the home of their own gods, and Tullius and Sextus had warned him about respecting foreign deities. Back in Rome, no business could be conducted in the Senate if Jupiter was heard to be angry, nor in the law courts or the Curia. If Rome itself trembled beneath the fury of its gods, should not Germania?

Perhaps the storm would pass as quickly as it had arrived. Quintus prayed that it would, invoking Ceres and Mars, but most of all, mighty Jupiter.

The forest soon swallowed the cohort. The men left the raging storm behind, the violently pelting rain with all its tumult and commotion. They left the blackness of the tempest and entered the deep gloom beneath the trees. It was like changing worlds. Like leaving the busy shouting of the hawkers and the lawyers in the Forum Boarium, the old cattle market in Rome, and entering the riverside gardens of some senator or ex-consul. Like shutting fast an oaken street door. The sound of the storm continued, but it was subdued, muffled, heard as if the head was underwater.

It seemed impossible to rally everyone; legionaries, horses, auxiliaries, slaves, mules and carts were all out of place, scattered through the forest. Many of the horses neighed and fretted, their riders on foot holding them tight. They comforted them even as the rain beyond the forest's edge continued to fall in relentless sheets, curtains of spume blown around on the stiff and capricious wind. There was another peal of thunder, and lightning followed a few seconds after, meaning the storm was now further away.

Quintus found his optio. Crassus was shooing in the last of the cohort, the cart that had proved so reluctant to cross the river. He had the black colt with him and was stroking it and whispering to it.

Crassus turned to his amicus. 'We need order.'

'I know,' Quintus replied tersely. 'Find me a cornicen — that will be a start.'

Crassus ducked away into the trees, the horse trotting beside him. Quintus followed. Both men shouted for the cornicen, bumping into men and carts and horses in the Stygian gloom. One man recognised Quintus. 'A clearing, sir,' he said. 'There is a clearing here where we can muster.'

The men were glad to be out of the worst of the storm but still feared attack. An army that was scattered and undisciplined could be annihilated in an instant. Its strength was in its formations and brotherhood. They needed a place to gather.

'Show me,' Quintus commanded.

XI: AQUILAM DEFENDE

Quintus followed the soldier to where a tree had long since fallen. It had lain long enough for its twisted shape to be covered in slippery moss, colourless in this night-in-day; long enough for spindly growths to struggle skywards from the black and broken tooth of its stump. Around it was a clearing, where trees and bushes had failed to sprout when the fallen giant had been in its prime.

'This will have to do,' he said. 'Point any you find in this direction. I still seek the cornicen.'

The legionary set off, calling to men to go where he pointed, to bring beasts and carts with them. Slowly the clearing began to fill. Centurion Felix arrived, with at least twenty of his rabbits who had been disciplined enough to stay with him. Their signifer was with them, standard intact. Quintus hurried them in and spoke to Felix, putting his fears into words. 'Galba? The commander?'

Felix shook his head.

'Aquila? The eagle?'

Another shake. Then Centurion Furius Lentulus came crashing through the trees with some of his century, forty or more men. They hadn't seen Titus Flavius or his first officer either.

Cornus arrived, unmounted and dripping. He, too, shook his head when asked about the senior men. 'What about the ladies? Are they safe?' he asked. But no-one had seen them either.

Men of Quintus' own century also appeared. 'The eagle?' Quintus demanded of them.

'In here somewhere,' Vetruvius replied confidently. 'Aquila would not lose it.'

'You should be with him,' Quintus scolded. Vetruvius was amicus to the aquilifer.

Around half the men by now had gathered, sitting on the moss-covered branches or squatting on the ground. Amongst them carts and mules and slaves were scattered. Though there was a good hour of daylight left, the storm and the trees made it as dark as night, and there were no torches. At least the thunder seemed to be moving further away.

Then, at the same moment, Aquila and Crassus both burst into the space in front of Quintus, Aquila triumphant with the eagle, Crassus dragging another with him.

'The aquilifer,' he said, panting, 'and the cornicen. I have found them.'

Quintus looked at them, trying to decide what order to give. 'Aquila, stand by the stump. Hold the eagle high — the men will see it when lightning flashes. Cornicen, stand by his side and blow the rally. *Aquilam defende.* Don't just blow it once — blow it again and again, until you have no breath left.'

This was a battle call, not a marching order or a disposition. It told fighting men that all else had failed, that they should seek the eagle and not go forward of it. It demanded that they find their brothers and form a line behind the standard. It said that the enemy were pressing in overwhelming force. It was a desperate call, one that indicated that the soldiers should soon expect to die.

The aquilifer and the cornicen ran to the tree stump, where Aquila raised the standard and the cornicen sounded the call. Some of the men had heard it before — but only a few. It was not a call used on the Campus Martius.

Marcus Antonius and the Egyptian queen had fled Actium with its notes ringing in their ears, but that was because the eagles of the general's legion had switched their allegiance to Octavius Caesar. Some veterans remembered this as the last time they had responded to it.

The men knew what the call meant, drew their blades and hoisted shields on to their forearms before setting off at a run towards the sound. The call was reserved for the midst of battle, often blown only once, seldom more than twice, but this time it was repeated again and again. They ran as best they could in the dark, tripping and sliding, suddenly full of energy, hoping to find a foe to warm their wet bones.

They were ready to strike at an enemy. They shouted support for each other, cries of 'to me' and 'on me' coming from the senior men. They closed up, shoulder to shoulder, with other men, as much as they could, parting to go over or around obstacles, clambering and leaping. The call was meant to fire up soldiers for a final push. Defend the standard at all costs. Victory or death. The thunder rolled and crashed high above them, reverberating round the trees. A bright flash of lightning followed, a great forked bolt with many fingers spread to the ground. It showed the bright outline of the eagle.

More men soon arrived in the clearing with their weapons drawn, looking around for an enemy. One of the men climbed onto the tree stump beside Aquila and the cornicen.

'Stand down,' he yelled, the silhouette of his tall crest revealing his rank. He grabbed the cornu from the man blowing it and the call was cut short. The cornicen seemed to be in some sort of trance, and the officer had to tussle with him to take away his instrument. As soon as the notes ceased, the noise from the men grew.

'There is no enemy,' the officer on the stump was shouting. It was Centurion Galba. 'Stand down. Sheathe your weapons. The call was used to gather you, not as a call to arms.'

Many of the men needed to be told twice. The call was designed to put fire into their hearts, to prepare them to die. For many, the flames took a lot of quenching.

Once they had settled down, Quintus and the other centurions, along with their signiferi, tesserarii and optiones, gradually organised the men. Though it was still dark, they could at least see the dim shapes of each other.

The orders were repeated by each centurion. 'Each man first find your century, then make sure your amicus is with us and unhurt. Finally, look to your equipment and slaves.'

There was no room to form columns in what had become an overcrowded space. Quintus' order may have brought all the men together, but they had come too quickly and were now in each other's way. If they had been left to arrive more slowly, or a different command had been blown, there would have been less chaos than there was now.

Galba chided Quintus with this. 'You gathered them, yes, but a call to muster would have brought them more slowly, and with swords sheathed.'

Quintus bowed his head briefly, accepting the rebuke, though he still believed his call was right. Having scattered, the men had needed to be mustered quickly, and now they required a place to settle for the night. Both Titus Flavius and his wife were still missing.

'We are here now,' Galba said. 'We will make camp.'

To one side was a trod, a highway for the animals of the forest, heading towards the fields where they grazed. Galba handed the cornu back to the cornicen, ordering him to call the pioneers.

The note of the cornu was now a long and effortless one, and the pioneers recognised it. The various engineers and surveyors gathered in front of Galba. There were a score of men, enough to mark out the lines and begin digging post holes and ditches.

'Down there,' said Galba, pointing, 'until you are out of the trees. Then find us a campsite.' He turned to Quintus. 'Centurion, send men in search of the prefect and the litter — perhaps he is with it, defending it. Order them to find lost comrades, loose horses and slaves.'

Quintus complied, though there seemed to be few if any missing.

'Felix, can your rabbits make fire? They are going to need light, and so are we,' Galba went on.

Felix gathered his men, who managed to strike a light even though the air was sodden. Enough material and oil was found for a few torches for the pioneers, the lights bobbing and vanishing into the dark.

That the prefect had failed to appear meant that he had not heard the call of the cornu. The absence of the litter meant the bearers had probably run in the wrong direction, or hidden from the storm. Both the prefect and his women needed to be found.

XII: NEMO

The storm abated as quickly as it had grown; the thunder was intermittent now, the lightning barely visible. The almost-white sky of early summer returned, the wind stilled and raindrops fell sporadically down through the branches. But the men needed more room than this clearing afforded, and they hoped the pioneers would return soon with news of a campsite.

Quintus and his contubernium gathered by the tree stump. Aquila fixed the eagle of the Fifth into the soft earth. Vetruvius was now by his side, as was Sextus and signifer Rufus, bearing the standard of Century One.

Marcus was on the edge of the group. Promoted as optio to Furius Lentulus, his allegiance now lay with Century Two, but he was drawn to his old comrades. He could be heard speaking softly to a long-faced Tullius — he of the double scar, the earring and the wolf-bitten ear. Crassus tethered the colt before checking on the other animals.

The storm finally blew away on the wind. True dark came, and the men settled down for an uncomfortable night. Galba ordered a rotation of pickets posted and fretted that the pioneers were not back, and the commander and women had not yet been found. He came and sat by Quintus.

'Where do you think they are, centurion?' he asked.

Quintus knew who Galba was referring to. 'Hopefully not captured. I would not trust these Germani to keep their word; they have proved false before. Maelo was sworn a friend; he had even been offered citizenship, yet he betrayed Rome, defeated Legio Five and mutilated his captives with beheadings and crucifixions. I fear for the ladies if they have been taken.'

'I agree, but it is the way of war,' shrugged Galba. 'It is what men do.'

He would not be the only one that had seen Rome do worse things. Cities of the east had been burned and their populations slaughtered and enslaved, down to the killing of the last dog and cat and caged bird. The dictator Sulla, they said, would have killed the very insects in the air if he could have but caught them.

A silence fell between them as they looked around at how the men had organised themselves. They were impressed. They were also disappointed as the search parties returned empty-handed.

Nemo. No-one had been seen — no commander, no ladies, no pioneers.

The cornicen reported that he had blown the recall many times in the forest. The two officers came to the same conclusion about the pioneers. 'They are not coming back, are they?' said Galba. Quintus nodded in agreement.

Later in the night the rain returned, but without the thunder and lightning. This was different, no summer storm. It settled into an incessant drizzle, no longer a torrent, forming a veil wherever the forest and the darkness beyond met. The wind remained stiff, smacking staccato sheets of water into the trees. The fires provided little heat or comfort, spitting tetchily. Torches struggled to stay alight.

Galba turned to Quintus and spoke softly. 'Your use of "protect the eagle" was naive. Men could have died. But in the end it did us no harm.' He pursed his lips ruefully and shook his head. 'My use of the pioneers to find us a camp was worse than naive. It was foolish — a rushed decision, made without thinking of the risks. I have been accused of haste before, and stupidity.'

Quintus began to protest, but Galba raised a hand to stop him. 'No, no. I know the stories. I am neither deaf nor simple, whatever men have said. In this case, however, you would be right to report me, centurion.' He paused, lowered his eyes. 'Do you wish to report me?'

'No, sir,' said Quintus. 'Anyway, there is no-one to report you to.'

After a pause, Galba asked, 'Do you think they have fled?'

'No, sir. I think they have died.' Quintus took off his helmet and brushed the hair from his forehead. 'And reporting you will not bring them back to life.'

'I should have sent horse with them. If not horse, then at least an armed unit.'

'They were armed, sir.' Again, he emphasised rank. He needed Galba to lead, not to wallow.

'Pioneers, Quintus. You know as well as I do that they were lightly armed, unencumbered by a pack or pilum. Also, they were not expecting an attack, and about as wary of an enemy as an aqueduct builder in a city.'

'Agreed,' said Quintus brusquely, before moving on. 'Now, what do we do?'

Galba appeared to rouse himself. 'Are all the search parties back?'

'Yes,' said Quintus.

'Send no more for now — it is too dark, too uncertain. We spend the night here. In the morning, we can continue searching, but as soon as there is light to see by, the rest of us march out in good order. Tell the men.'

Quintus called his optio. 'Crassus, pass the word. We march at dawn. Build up the fires, break out marching rations. Double pickets all around. No foraging, not even for water. Unhitch mules and unsaddle horses, but keep them all tethered and feed them. The prefect and his wife are still out there, as are the pioneers. Watch for them. Stay in pairs to sleep and watch in turn. No-one goes into the trees on his own, not even to piss. This is enemy country, and we must treat it as such.'

Crassus saluted and immediately began to pass on the orders. Quintus could feel the men's tension lessening as they worked. The animals were fed with fodder from the carts, Crassus personally taking charge of the black colt that had been gifted to them. It was full of nervous energy and needed gentling. Crassus had the skills. When he left it, it was calm.

'Maxim, take over,' Crassus called to the Macedonian slave of his contubernium. Once a farmer, he was also skilled with animals.

'Keep him quiet, and keep him warm but away from the fires. I think the flames spook him.'

'Yes, master.' Maxim stroked the colt's neck. 'A fine beast.'

Crassus nodded then made his way round the now settled camp. Quintus watched him make sure that every century had the message. The other centurions would, he supposed, join them later when they had settled their own men. He recognised the silhouette of the man that approached him, the biggest of the fires at his back. Then his long, dark hair and neatly trimmed black beard came into view. It was the other slave of the contubernium, Jovan. He wore a headband to hide his slave mark, a plain tunic tied with rope and thin shoes of animal hide. He had brought a bowl and spoon. 'It is not much, master,' he said, 'but it is hot.'

'And for Centurion Galba?'

'I have two, master.' The Macedonian produced another bowl out of the dark as if by magic. Quintus took it and handed it to Galba.

'Will there be anything else, master?'

'No, Jovan. Just look after the men.'

The slave bowed and left.

'You are well served, Quintus.'

'Jovan has travelled a lot with us, in Hispania and Britannia, as well as here. He does not let us go hungry.' Quintus waved an arm in the direction of the camp. 'Maxim, his cousin, is good with animals. He is helping Crassus.'

The pottage was thin but welcome. For a while, neither officer spoke.

'Where do we march to, sir?' Quintus asked eventually.

'Three choices,' Galba said. 'One, we go back the way we have come, along the river until we reach the sea. Two, we go back as far as the plain from which we fled the storm, then navigate south, without our guides. Three, we take ourselves along that track to find the pioneers.' He pointed towards the now guarded opening. 'They might be sheltering, or they might have been killed or taken prisoner. What do you think?'

'I think we can dismiss the first choice. Our mission is to clear the enemy from this bank of the river, to meet with General Drusus. If we go back, we are in retreat, defeat even. We are also disobeying orders.'

'Seems certain enough,' said Crassus, who now joined them. 'The sea is a long way away and may be no safer than here. There is no guarantee that we could reach Tres Gallia.' He lowered his voice. 'Nor is there any guarantee that these men would march that way. I believe they would be happier going forward, to possible victory and plunder, rather than backward to possible defeat and certain shame.' He looked at Quintus. 'And you, my friend, promised to bring these men back to Rome. I still dream of handing the eagle and the information about the Druids directly to Caesar Augustus.'

'And the rewards that would bring,' Quintus finished for him. 'Remember I also have my appointed task, and a holy vow to go with it. I must take Ursus' armband and his wishes to his family.'

'Ursus?' Galba said, with curiosity.

'A man killed unjustly — a friend,' Quintus said simply. 'I carry his will and a promise to his child.'

Galba nodded in understanding. Such missions were not uncommon. 'Not back then,' he said. 'That leaves us two choices. Field or forest. If we return to open country, we may yet find our allies and they may still lead us. They will have also fled from the storm. Do we have no intelligence on them? I thought we had a spy, a runner?'

'Agnus,' Quintus replied. 'He is also missing. He was heading towards our guides when the storm struck. Of course, he may still be there and safe. He, too, is lightly armed by his own choice, for speed. If free, he should have been back hours ago, though we are not where he supposes us to be.'

'He could have met up with the pioneers,' said Crassus hopefully.

Galba and Quintus both shook their heads, doubting that this was the case. A quiet settled on them.

In the camp an argument broke out, voices were raised, a throaty laugh barked into the night. A sharp admonition from centurion Felix cut the laugh short. The crack of a vine rod on someone's exposed flesh — an arm or the unprotected back of the leg — stilled the noise.

'The third option ...' Crassus began.

This was the course that they had not wanted to think about. It was both the most perilous and the most likely.

XIII: STRATEGOS

Quintus outlined the nature of the choice. 'This course is the most dangerous. The pioneers have not returned, and even the call of the cornu did not reach them. Of course, they could be safe but it is unlikely. If they were, someone would have reported back.' He looked at the opening to the trod, judging its width. 'There is room for four abreast at the most, and no room to protect flanks with cavalry or bowmen.'

Galba expressed doubt. 'A narrow track through tall trees is ripe for ambush. I would not like to be the one who loses the eagle of the Larks a second time.'

Quintus nodded. He could see that Galba, whom the men respected, would be more honourable than ex-consul Lollius. The general had abandoned the eagle to the enemy whilst he himself fled with his native bodyguard. Galba would fall on his sword.

It was only through the actions of Quintus and his companions that the standard had been retrieved from a tribal temple. But it had not been returned either to the emperor in Rome or even to the defeated legion, the Fifth, the Alaudae. Some of the men with the lark's wing helmets who had escaped the massacre were serving with them now. To lose the eagle again would be unconscionable.

'Then the eagle stays protected,' Quintus said. 'All the standards stay protected. We must make use of what we have — archers, cavalry, auxiliary horsemen, wily veterans.'

Crassus smiled. Though still a young man, he guessed he counted as one of these 'wily veterans'. Quintus understood, matched his smile.

Galba leaned forward eagerly, the flickering light of the fire reflected in his eyes. 'It seems like we have made a decision, *strategos*.' He honoured Quintus with the title the Greeks used for a master planner. 'We take the most dangerous path, probably into the teeth of the enemy, to face the same destruction we believe has been visited on the pioneers.'

There was no sarcasm in Galba's tone, just a question. He was sure that Quintus would have an answer. He had seen him do the impossible before. He had seen him plot the defeat of the Catalonian tribes in Hispania, and the rescue of the garrison at the winter camp. And just a short while ago, Quintus had drawn the Germani into open battle.

'All we need is a way to track the path ahead whilst casting our eyes behind and seeing through the trees,' Galba went on. 'Oh, and a way to convince the men that they are not marching to their certain death.'

Quintus and Crassus nodded in agreement.

'A vanguard,' said Quintus thoughtfully. 'A proper vanguard — a long way in front of the main column.'

'But not so far that a warning of attack could not be sent back,' Galba added.

Quintus nodded. Having a vanguard meant that a few legionaries would be bait. He would not keep this back from the men. He decided that the vanguard must be volunteers, and be aware of the possible outcomes. 'The vital thing will be to keep the route back to the column open, so that warning can be given. For that we need the auxiliaries, the Anatolian archers and the Cantabrians. Their small ponies are better suited to such work than our cavalry horses.'

He paused. He was working out the possible formation in his head. What was most efficient? What presented the least risk to the men?

'At the front, there should be four or five Cantabrians, mounted. The Germani will not recognise them as Roman and should not see them as a threat. They should be able to see things that a legionary would not. They will travel slowly, as if they are an undisciplined foraging party. Then there will be soldiers — a small group, ten at most. Enough to provide resistance if attacked, not so many that their loss will be noticed.' Galba began to protest. 'They will know what to expect,' said Quintus sharply.

'Behind the legionaries, there will be two or three Anatolians,' he went on. 'Their job is to fire arrows back down the track as a signal. A white fletching to halt the column, a black one to bring it on at speed. They must keep shooting as long as they can. If the column sees a black fletched arrow in the ground, the vanguard is under attack.'

Though they debated other formations and possibilities, this remained the bare bones of the strategy. In essence, it was simple. Risk the Cantabrians in the hope that they would fool the Germani. Provide a small force ready to fight and hold off an attack. Devise a way to signal to the column that they were under attack — a black-fletched arrow would travel faster and further than either man or horse.

'Crassus, call the other centurions across so that we can finalise the details.'

The tall, bearded figure of Furius Lentulus — centurion of the Second — was first to appear, his eyes glittering in his tanned face. Once he had been nicknamed 'little Caesar', owing to his height and his hairiness. The emperor would have not found such a jest funny, so it was no more. Then Felix and Marius arrived, as did, uninvited, some of the evocati. First came Tullius and Marcus, comrades to Quintus; then Piso, the wrestler; then Caius of the Larks.

Between them they put more detail into the initial plan, debating whether the Cantabrians and Anatolians would be reliable, and if it would be better to have Anatolians at the front to fire on any attackers, and Cantabrians at the rear to warn the column. But the arrows were key.

The decurion of cavalry suggested his squadron of horse should have a role, to which all the officers readily agreed, but none could see a way in which they could fight. They would be unable to manoeuvre. The track was too narrow for them to ride the flank, and their presence at the front would reveal the Cantabrians as a ruse. They would be best utilised guarding the rear and the baggage train. Quintus made sure the decurion understood that this was a place of great danger, and great honour.

Felix suggested that the vanguard could be made up of the rabbits of Century Four armed with javelins. No-one took him seriously, although nor did anyone scoff. It was just Felix's way of promoting the progress and maturity of his century.

In the end the initial plan remained largely intact. Mounted Cantabrians would ride at the front of the vanguard, and Anatolian archers would run at the rear. They decided on thirteen legionaries in the centre, four rows of three with the centurion at their head. Three from each century seemed fair, if volunteers could be found. They would proceed at a pace that allowed the Cantabrians to look like they were relaxed, keeping a gap between themselves and the advance party.

'They must be willing,' Quintus insisted. 'They must be warned of the dangers, that if they have to fight, their chances of survival are minimal.'

As the fire sparked behind them, his companions muttered agreement.

'They will be bait,' Quintus admitted.

Marcus immediately volunteered to lead the party, Tullius at his side. Tullius had received permission to move to Century Two as amicus to Marcus, but would not accept promotion. 'I have been there before,' he said sadly, 'and have yet to be paid. Also, I am not deserving.' He would not tell anyone why.

'Quintus will lead,' Galba told Marcus. 'But, of course, you will take point position on the first rank.'

'And I, too, will march in the first rank,' said Crassus.

He was also destined for disappointment. 'Apologies, optio,' Galba said. 'But as your centurion leads, you will remain and command the First.' He turned to Quintus. 'Much as I would like to join you, I must stay here to command if the cohort is ambushed from behind, and to keep searching for Titus Flavius and his ladies.' He smiled mirthlessly. 'Who else do you need?'

Quintus looked at Centurion Marius. 'I need your optio, Caius, for his language skills, so sadly I think you must stay with your century here.'

Marius nodded in disappointment and Quintus turned to Furius Lentulus. 'I seem to have gained your optio too, friend.' He nodded at Marcus, whose determination to go would not be turned. 'So you must also remain. Tullius is also of the Second. Can you find another?' Both centurions saluted and left, ready to fill their quota.

Only Felix was left. 'Felix, you represent Century Four, if you will. I would like the capsarius, Alba, to volunteer. We may have use for him.'

'I agree — and I will persuade him.' Felix rose to his feet. 'Any more?'

'One other, friend. One you can rely on.'

'It will be difficult, Quintus. I can rely on them all.' Felix chuckled as he, too, saluted and left.

Sextus quickly offered to go. He revelled in such challenges, daring the gods to strike him down with a smile on his face. He also persuaded Vetruvius to make up the numbers for Century One. Quintus knew him as a gambler, rake and womaniser, but a good man to have at your side in a fight. Rufus and Aquila wanted to volunteer, but it was already decided that all the standards would remain with the majority of the cohort. They could not be risked.

'What about the auxiliaries — the Cantabrians and the Anatolians? I could order them,' Galba said.

'That would not be just,' Quintus said — and at least some of the men agreed. Marcus was most vocal that they should be apprised of the risk in the same way as the Romans. He appointed himself to speak to them.

'How many, sir?'

'Five or six of each. We could still manage with just a couple of archers.' He clapped Marcus on the shoulder. 'Do your best.'

Quintus need not have worried. Marcus returned with five archers and six Cantabrians. 'I could have brought more,' he said. 'They are keen to fight.'

Galba found men who could translate for the auxiliaries. Although they had basic Latin, the centurions wanted to make sure that they understood the risks, despite Marcus' protestations that he had explained already.

Quintus was curious. 'What did you tell them?'

'I explained that this was a secret strategy, a ruse, involving a one-sided fight and almost certain death if the bait was taken.' He smiled broadly, white teeth showing. 'And that they were the bait.'

The translation did nothing to dissuade them. The Cantabrians were a hardy people, small, dark and tough, much like the ponies they rode. They occupied the narrow strip of land between the northern coast of what was now the province of Hispania Tarraconensis and the high crags of the Picos mountains.

'Can you trust them?' Galba asked. 'Are they not of the same race as the Germani?'

'They all seem to be related,' replied Quintus. 'They are a Celtic people, somehow brothers to all other Celts and Gauls, but for a long time they have been wedded to a life of freedom and brigandage. I know that some fought in the civil wars for the dictator Sulla, and some even rode with the boy-general Pompeius. Others fought against him.' He looked at them. 'They are loyal to their current masters.'

'They are mercenaries, really, rather than auxiliaries,' Marcus added. 'They seem uninterested in political comings and goings. Many threw in their lot with the Gauls against the generals of Divus Julius and were defeated.' He shrugged. 'Then they changed sides.'

One of the Cantabrians grinned at Quintus, showing gaps in his teeth — a result of a battle blow or of some of the strange plants they chewed. 'My grandfather fought against Hannibal,' he boasted gruffly.

His companion clapped him on the back. 'And mine fought for him,' he laughed, turning the man away. 'Do not listen, master. We are fighting for you now.'

XIV: MÁKHAIRA

The Cantabrians were armed with knives and short javelins, but their favoured weapon was a long, single-edged curved sword, like a sickle, which they called a mákhaira. Many of them were given female names out of affection. Most of the hilts were shaped into horse heads, a detail that Crassus found fascinating. The blacksmith was also impressed by the quality of the iron — laminated, forged and hammered like any good blacksmith would.

'Not as strong as Norican iron,' he said as he admired a blade. 'But a good second best.'

The Anatolians were lighter-skinned than the Celts, but still dark. They were taller and tended to be more serious, and were a coastal people — mostly from the northern shores of Mare Nostrum, what was now the province of Asia.

'I tried to draw one of their bows,' Quintus admitted. 'I failed, yet the man whose bow it was drew it effortlessly. Look.' He tapped the right arm of the nearest archer, who held it up proudly. 'This arm is bigger, more muscled, than the other. Years of training does that.'

'These men can be trusted,' said Galba, with a nod. 'I have fought alongside them. They would call themselves Lydians or Phrygians, but all their tribes were defeated when Sulla destroyed King Mithridates in their grandfathers' day. Since then, they have been loyal to Rome.'

'We understand,' their leader said seriously. 'We know our duty.'

Quintus and his men had no idea how long it was until dawn. Centurion Galba waited with them, ready to rouse the camp the minute they left, so that the cohort could follow at a distance. The gap was determined by how far an arrow could fly. The chief of the Anatolians claimed he could cover two stades, though the others clearly thought that in the conditions this was over-ambitious. Galba decided to follow around three stades behind, far enough back to be out of sight, but near enough to arrive swiftly if the alarm was raised.

The sky was still a forbidding deep grey, and though the rain had finally paused, the air was saturated. Quintus decided that they would go as soon as he could pick out the branches of the tree above from the sky behind. That would be a sign that dawn was breaking. He wished for the clever water-clock that he knew the commander had once possessed, but did not know if the clepsydra had even made it to Germania. He suspected that, along with many other treasures — and many men — it had found its way to the bottom of the sea when the cohort's ships were wrecked.

The centurion collected his troop of auxiliaries and legionaries and stationed them at the end of the track. The Cantabrians led their ponies and continuously talked to them in soft voices. When they rode, they rode bareback, gripping the beasts with their knees, feet almost touching the ground. They carried many different spears and blades, including the curved sword so admired by Crassus. They had some protection — round leather shields, leather jerkins, and even leather caps. Enough, thought Quintus, to give them confidence. Not enough to turn a blade or stop a spear.

The Anatolians carried unstrung bows and baskets of arrows attached to their backs by plaited hide straps. They would string the bows before they marched. They wore leather that appeared soft, more decorative than useful. They would have preferred the role of the Cantabrians, putting themselves at risk, rather than their own part, which was to give warning. As soon as the column was warned, they were determined to join the fight.

The low murmur of conversation amongst the waiting men was cut short by an urgent message, hissed by Furius Lentulus, appearing out of the dark.

'Bad news, sirs,' he reported to Quintus and Galba. 'We have deserters. Some of the men have vanished into the woods. Not for calls of nature, either. They are gone, and some of the supplies with them.'

Furius Lentulus paused to let the message sink in. 'Do we go after them?'

'How many have gone?' Galba demanded.

'Eight or nine, we think.' Furius Lentulus waved an arm back at the camp. 'Some of the slower ones we caught before they made good their escape. Including that rat Hirtis.' He spat in disgust.

Hirtis had once been his project. He had been determined to turn the insolent, overweight oaf into a soldier. He had even made him, temporarily, his optio. But the man spent forever quoting the minutiae of the law in defence of why he should not do anything that benefited anyone but himself. He was lazy and venal, with no concept of honour, bravery or brotherhood. Furius Lentulus was baffled as to how the man had ended up in the legions. He had eventually tired of him and demoted him.

'I thought I was making progress there,' said Marcus, who had included Hirtis in his basic training of the men.

'I have had to silence him,' said the black-bearded centurion. 'He was still quoting the lex something-or-other, so I gave him the lex punch-in-the-mouth.'

Quintus thought quickly. He was angry; he did not like his careful plan being complicated by deserters. If caught, they would be sentenced to fustuarium — being beaten to death by the comrades they had betrayed. Their names would be expunged from the legion's roll. Any hope of entering the fields of Elysium would be taken from them; there would be no ferry, no coin, no Charon. They would be stranded on the wrong bank of the Styx, condemned to wander in agony as ghosts, like the dead boy called up by Erictho the witch for General Sextus Pompeius. A boy whose descriptions of his torments almost drove the general mad.

'We cannot afford the time to chase them now,' said Galba bitterly. 'They have chosen their time well.' He took a deep breath. 'Quintus, do not delay. You must go as soon as it is light. The cohort will follow.'

'We cannot let the deserters go,' interrupted Marcus urgently. 'It is tantamount to condoning the crime.'

Quintus responded swiftly. 'Let the wolves have them, my friend. Or the Germani. I doubt they will last long if they are all of the same stamp as Hirtis.' He addressed his fellow centurion. 'Any veterans, Furius?'

'No veterans, Quintus. No evocati.'

Felix raised his head in question.

'You need not worry,' Furius went on. 'No rabbits, either. None of your boys.' He hawked again. 'Curse Hirtis!'

'How many did you catch?' Quintus asked.

'Three, including the fat bastard. One fought to escape capture and has a broken arm.'

'What should we do with him?' Quintus looked to Galba.

'Execute him.' Galba turned to Furius Lentulus. 'Strip him, cut his hams and leave him behind — no food, no water. Make sure he is tied in a place that the column can see him as they leave. Nail him to a tree if you have time, but leave him alive. Cut out his tongue. I do not want the men distracted by his pleadings.' He looked across. 'At least that shows we do not condone the action, Marcus.'

Marcus nodded reluctant agreement. 'And the others?'

'Disarmed, of course, belt and apron confiscated. No deserter deserves the protection of baltea and cingulum. They will advertise their shame by being forced to wear their tunics like women. Tie their hands and put them in the care of their comrades. Let the men know the nature of their crime and that they will be punished as soon as we have a proper camp.'

'Punishment?'

'They will be placed beneath the yoke and scourged,' said Galba.

'Then handed over to the men for further chastisement,' Quintus added. 'They may not survive it.'

None questioned what was, effectively, a death sentence on all three captured men. The maintenance of discipline was necessary — and such men could never be returned to the ranks. Their ideas would spread like poison.

'Aquila's own father was many things,' Vetruvius muttered to himself. 'One of them a mutineer.'

Marcus heard him. 'I thought he was the hero of Caesar's fleet,' he said.

'He was, later,' said Vetruvius, leaning forward conspiratorially. 'Before, he was of Legio Ten Equestris, unpaid, unhappy — and mutinous. They were not the only ones; the Old Ninth also rebelled, a mutiny that started with desertions. A result of indiscipline and foolish ideas spreading. Luckily for them, the general treated them leniently.'

'We do not have that luxury,' Quintus interrupted. 'We are in hostile territory with depleted forces.'

Furius Lentulus saluted. He, too, knew why the punishment must be harsh. 'I will stake the man to the ground next to the entrance to the track. A placard with his crime inscribed will be hung from his miserable neck.' He shook his head, then raised his eyes to the sky. 'Morning comes. We must move.'

Furius Lentulus set off quickly, intent on carrying out the sentence on the deserter with the broken arm. Galba followed him, having wished '*bon Fortuna*' to Quintus.

Quintus hissed orders at his waiting squad. The Cantabrians mounted their ponies, weapons hung at their sides, shields slung on their backs — trying hard not to look like a war party. The legionaries began to form up, but not with the alacrity expected by the centurion.

'What is the delay?' Quintus demanded. The men parted to let him see. Tullius stood in the centre of the track between the two men guarding it, his head covered and his arm raised.

'Janus, sir,' said one of the men. 'He found a little oil somewhere. We will invoke Jove with our sword-tips when he is done.'

'As long as you do it quietly,' said Quintus, 'and quickly.' The god of beginnings and endings should, of course, be venerated, as should Jupiter Optimus Maximus.

'It is only right,' said Sextus. 'It may at least bring us good fortune.'

Tullius had already finished and turned to the men, raising his sword. 'Jupiter,' he said quietly but forcefully, his sword tip pointing skywards. The men followed suit, then sheathed their swords and formed up — four rows of three, as ordered, with

Quintus at their head. He sent the Cantabrians ahead, counted aloud to estimate the gap that he wanted, then set off with the legionaries. The Anatolians strung their bows, then followed, keeping the rear of the squad in sight. Each carried both black and white fletched arrows.

A watery sun filtered through the forest canopy and cast long shadows across the path like the bars of a cage. The bars might be just tricks of light and shade, but of such things were omens and auguries made. Some of the men shivered, and many made the warding sign of the horns. Some grasped charms or talismans, Sextus gripping the leather pouch containing the unbroken bulla at his neck — the amulet retained by him as none had ever sponsored him for a manly gown.

As the sun rose higher, the bars vanished. The track opened out, and Quintus allowed each man to join his amicus where possible, or choose a new partner in a formation of four by three, a more normal width for a marching column. They seemed to be climbing, each hill higher than the last, the forest following the contours.

Three hours passed, and as they crested yet another hill, Quintus was considering a proper pause for rest when the tails of the Cantabrian ponies came into view, then the men themselves, on foot. Wondering why they had dismounted, Quintus quickened the pace, slowing only when he saw the reason they had stopped. One man, a legionary without armour, lay face-down in the dirt, a javelin sticking out of his back, his hands splayed forward as if in supplication. A messenger, Quintus surmised, stripped down for speed, carrying news back to the cohort.

He feared it was Agnus. The hair was right. He tried to turn the man over to look at his face, but could not. He tugged at his arm but he could not shift him. The spear had been thrown with such force it had gone straight through the body and fixed it firmly to the earth. There was no time to investigate further.

'Free him and identify him,' Quintus ordered the nearest men, then quickly approached the Cantabrians. He needed to see what lay beyond the horsemen before telling the archers to fire.

XV: TABULA RASA

Quintus hurried forward and crested the lip of a shallow bowl. There his eyes were met with a grisly scene of death and destruction. On the other side of the hill the pioneer group was no more. This was not just the slaughter of a patrol, casually carried out before the perpetrators had ridden off. Unlike the pinioned messenger, these deaths had taken time. They were designed to send a message.

There was no sign of an enemy.

He made a swift decision. 'Halt the column,' he ordered the Anatolians. 'White fletchings.'

The Anatolians each nocked a white feathered arrow and bent their bows. Five arrows soared into the clear air above the path, vanishing even before they began to fall to the ground.

Ahead lay a scene from the deepest realms of Tartarus. In the centre of the clearing, a group of four bodies, legionaries, were arranged lying on their backs in a circle. Their arms and legs were fixed to the ground with short stakes and leather hide. The stakes should have been used to mark out the castra.

They were, of course, headless — heads were prized as trophies by the tribesmen. They had been stripped of their armour and their caligae, pointing outwards, had a gruesome symmetry to them, each marking a different direction. Their tunics were ripped apart to expose their chests whilst what remained of their garments was torn, with material pushed deep into their flesh.

The soft, rain-sodden ground revealed the progress of the torture and execution. Their deaths, as far as anyone could tell, had been caused by horses riding over them. There were hoof prints around the macabre arrangement, and deep indentations in the pink flesh of the bellies and thighs. Ribs and limbs were broken, white bone showing. Some arms and legs were severed completely, parts crushed into the earth. The enemy had left the men with baltea and cingulum. This was all that truly held the mangled corpses together.

The light that spilled into the glade was filtered by the tops of the trees, adding a ghoulish green and yellow tinge to the horror as Alba the capsarius knelt by the bodies, touching some of the wounds gingerly.

He indicated a long length of twisted grey tube, still attached to one of the victim's stomach. 'This is where the hoof of a horse caught the insides of the gut, and dragged it across the ground.' He was detached and professional as he moved on to the next victim.

'Speak,' demanded Quintus. 'What have you found?'

Alba spoke quietly, so that only the centurion would hear. 'This wound was inflicted while the victim lived, his blood flowing still. The others did not bleed. Their injuries were inflicted after death.' He indicated the grey length of gut. 'This disembowelling was of a man already dead.' He looked away from the carnage and directly at Quintus. 'I would have said they were killed in a frenzy if it had not been for the careful staging.' He examined one of the dead men's necks, touching it gently with his finger. 'The heads were severed after death. A small mercy, but it is certain.'

'And what of these?' Quintus demanded, pointing to the marks that the capsarius had not mentioned but which they had both noted. There was a design carved on each man's chest, the rain having washed the blood away — two patterns or letters, one above each nipple. The broad, flat chest of a fit legionary provided a perfect tabula rasa, like a freshly scraped wax tablet.

The first sign, on the left side, Quintus thought he recognised as the rune sign for Týr, the god he had so insulted in order to bring the tribes to battle. It was an arrow, pointing up towards the throat of the dead. This could be revenge for his hubris.

Sextus and Tullius would think their concerns about the misuse of the gods of the Germani were justified. Sextus would not be slow to point this out to his centurion. Tullius would demand the appropriate sacrifice — to Nemesis for vengeance, or Clementia for forgiveness. Probably a white heifer or a brace of virgins, Quintus thought, something either improbable or impossible.

The second symbol was a cross between two vertical bars. It could have meant a crucifixion, except the arms of the cross were sloped.

'This one is Týr's own letter, I think.' Quintus pointed to the vertical 'T', then switched his attention to the other. He did not want to touch it. 'This one may be the symbol for Wotan.'

The capsarius did not know what the other symbol meant, only when it had been carved. 'Done whilst the man lived and breathed, sir, though he may have known nothing about it, if his other injuries were severe enough.'

'Sir!' Caius called across from the other side of the clearing. He pointed to a man's body. This one had its head. The man was naked but for his caligae. He had been nailed between two saplings, hands and legs both outstretched. His hair was tied to a branch above to keep his face pointing towards the slaughter. His eyelids had been sliced off. He was dead, but Alba could not see an immediate cause.

'He does not seem to have taken a heavy blow. He is not stabbed or cut — except for this.' He indicated the T-shaped carving on the man's chest.

Marcus approached quietly. 'There are more, Quintus. Arranged in this shape.'

'Where?' Quintus asked.

'Over here,' said Marcus, leading the centurion away from the butchery still being inspected by Alba.

It seemed the pioneers had chosen the site and started to clear it. A few small shrubs were cut down, and stakes hammered into the ground. Beyond this point, raised on a small hill, three headless, naked corpses hung. Each had their ankles and wrists tied to posts so that, seen against the pale blue sky, they made the same shape as that which was carved in blood on their chests. The other symbol was also there. The men still wore their caligae, that much was true, but the heavy sandals hung from a string around the stumps of their necks, their feet still in them. Alongside them hung their hands.

'Alba!' Quintus called and the capsarius came running. There were no obvious wounds on the men, apart from the missing hands and feet and the symbols carved. Their stomachs were whole. Even their manhood was intact. 'How did they die?'

'Slowly, sir. These bled out. The hands and feet were cut off and then they were tied here, and here, not tightly enough to stop the bleeding.' He looked across. 'I can see that their heads were taken after they had died.'

'The symbols?'

'Whilst they lived.'

'The other,' said Sextus, approaching up the rise, 'I think died from shock. He was meant to be a witness, to tell what he had seen, but his will gave out.'

'Maybe,' Quintus agreed as he turned on his heel, nearly crashing into a dazed Cantabrian.

'Caius,' he called. 'Tell these men to stand guard on the track. To look out for enemy.' He took Caius by the shoulders and spoke with urgency. 'Borrow one of their ponies. Go back down the track swiftly and meet the cohort. Speak to Galba. Tell him of this murder in private. He should prepare himself. Delay the advance to give us time to clear the worst of it.'

'The Anatolians?'

'They stay,' he decided. 'They can help the Cantabrians. Go. Hurry.'

He turned his attention to the disorientated men who now wandered the charnel pit. 'Search,' he ordered. 'Find the rest. Sextus, Tullius, find some dry kindling. I know it is god-cursed wet,' he shouted to quell their protests. Tullius heard the curse and, out of habit, made the warding sign of the horns. Quintus was about to shout some more, but, with an effort, he restrained himself. 'I want a pyre,' he went on. 'I want these bodies burning before the column gets here. Make it on that rise. We can bear witness to it, but they do not need to see it. If they do not see it, perhaps any curse only applies to us.'

'I suppose so,' said Tullius dourly, stroking the double scar on his cheek.

'Make sure they are all here,' said Quintus. 'There should be nineteen bodies, plus the man we found on the spear. We have found eight. Go — Alba will help.' He hurried the men away.

They soon found the others. The causes of death were many. Some men had been torn apart, probably by horses, frayed leather braids still attached to their wrists, though their arms were no longer attached to their bodies. Some had been smashed against the bole of a tree. Yet others had been staked out and ridden over like the first corpses they had found. All were headless, so denied passage across the river Styx unless they had managed to secrete an obol beneath their tongue before death.

They seemed to be either arranged to form a shape, or had the letters for Týr and — Quintus was sure — Wotan, carved into their chests.

'What I do not know is why such bizarre ends have been inflicted on these men,' Quintus said to Sextus, hoping he might have an inkling. 'Was it a ritual? Part of a sacrifice? A warning? A curse?'

Sextus shook his head. 'I cannot say, Quintus. It is beyond my experience.'

A single Cantabrian, deprived of his horse by Caius, sat at the foot of a tree. Suddenly, he jumped up and shouted excitedly at a movement in its branches. A thin figure began to climb out, shinning down the rough trunk with difficulty. The Cantabrian drew his mákhaira, at sight of which the man almost fell, holding on with one arm whilst waving with the other and desperately shouting. '*Amicus, amicus, amicus sum!*'

He was ragged and half naked, but his caligae and weaponry identified him as a legionary. He still had a tunic and a baldric, with his gladius and a pugio sheathed at his belt. The Cantabrian stood back and allowed him to descend. He shouted to Quintus, who ran across.

'Sir.' The Cantabrian made a sort of obeisance to the centurion — not quite a salute, not quite a bow, but enough to show respect. 'I seem to have caught a spy, a naked man in a tree,' he said with a grin. 'Will you come and look?'

Quintus was glad to come away from the gruesome work of identifying how victims had suffered. He whispered to Sextus as he saw the Cantabrian's expression. 'How can men could find humour in such carnage?'

'Because the gods enjoy their games,' Sextus said. 'And who are we to not join in? It is only death, after all. Father Dis will have his due.'

Quintus immediately recognised the thin man who had emerged from the tree. 'Well met, friend.' He embraced the bony figure of Agnus, the runner. 'I thought you were lost.'

Agnus could not stop himself from shaking.

'Water,' Quintus shouted. 'Bring him some water. And a cloak.'

Sextus offered his own cloak and Crassus brought water. They helped the messenger to sit, and he took a few sips from the waterskin. He then inhaled deeply, clearly stifling a sob.

'Capsarius!' Crassus called across to Alba.

'Not necessary,' Agnus said, holding up his hand. 'I will be fine in a minute.'

Quintus waved Alba back to his grim task. The pile on the makeshift pyre looked like a scene from a plague pit or the twisting of the damned in Hades. The remains sat atop a wooden structure, a platform a scant few inches off the ground. The space beneath ensured it would burn.

Quintus cupped Agnus' face in his hands. 'Tell me,' he said gently, moving the messenger's gaze away from the mangled mess.

'I saw it happen,' Agnus said slowly. 'I saw it all, but could do nothing to stop them.'

XVI: QUAM MOX OBLIVIONI SUNT HORRORES

Quintus sat back on his heels. 'Leave nothing out.'

Agnus bowed his head. 'I arrived as the man on the track — carrying messages to the cohort — was speared. I sought cover. I climbed a tree. Should I be punished, centurion? Should I fall on my sword? Am I a coward? Should I have tried to save them?'

'You would have died,' Quintus said flatly. 'Now you are a witness. Tell us what happened. That will help us to avenge these dead.' He put a hand on Agnus' shoulder to reassure him, feeling him tremble beneath the cloak.

Agnus spoke rapidly, a flood of words tumbling one after the other. He barely drew breath.

'I have seen death, sir. I have been in battle and seen faces shorn off, seen arms and legs severed, seen guts hanging out. I have seen piles of bodies tipped into ditches, or burned, or left where they fell for the animals and birds. I have been to the funeral games and seen gladiators fight to the death. But there was always a purpose to it — battles, arena fights, disposal of the dead...' He took a sharp breath and looked at Quintus. 'Here, I saw no purpose. These men were not allowed to defend themselves. They were stripped, gutted and beheaded without being able to resist. I do not think they were even sacrifices.' He was not just shocked, but outraged. 'It seemed to be done for — gods above and below forgive me — amusement.' He spat the last word as if it was a curse.

Quintus could feel that the man was nearly spent. 'Soldier,' he said harshly to Agnus. 'Pull yourself together. Report.'

'Sir.' Agnus made a half-hearted salute. But the water and the admonition had done their work, and he began to tell his story from the beginning. 'I was on my way back from the Germani with urgent messages when I was caught up in the storm.' He paused. 'I was coming to tell you that one of the tribes is holding Titus Flavius Pusio. He is a hostage.'

Quintus was speechless. This news should have galloped down the path with Caius, this news was more important than the massacre of a group of pioneers.

'Tell me, tell me all of it.' He shook Agnus, not meaning to harm him, although he saw the flare of fear in his eyes. 'Quickly.'

'The commander is safe — or he was when I left. They say he is an honoured guest. I did not see him, sir, so I do not know.' He shook his head. 'They were not fooled by the cloak. They want the eagle. They say they need its protection.'

'Protection?' Quintus asked, confused.

'From these men, this tribe that tears bodies to pieces. They are an enemy to all. The leader is called Dagaz. He claims to be a champion of the people, of what they call the *Klein-volk*. But the tribes fear him. I learned of him from the Germani. They think him mad.'

'Who and what is he?' Quintus demanded. 'And why this?' He waved an arm at the killing field.

'He is young,' Agnus replied. 'He is a warrior — a chieftain in his own right, but also of the blood of Maelu, the high chief who led the raid that stole our eagle from us.'

'The chieftain who wanted to be a Roman citizen?'

101

'The same. The supposed friend. He who led an alliance of tribes across the river. This Dagaz claims he is not of the Sugambri or Tencteri or Usipetes. He claims to be of all tribes and none. Though he says Maelo was his father, no woman is claimed as his mother, so he can ally with any tribe. But his only true allegiance is to Týr, whom he calls Tiwaz — the god's name in what they call the old tongue. Týr is the one-handed god of war and justice. Dagaz worships the dark side of him, which involves blood and death and a justice gained through violent action. They say he fears no-one and is a god himself.'

Quintus thought briefly. 'So is this meant as a curse or an act of worship?' He indicated the field and the pyre. Agnus could only shake his head in response.

Quintus took in the messenger's dishevelled state. 'What happened to you before you came here, Agnus? To your clothes?'

The legionary smiled. 'I demanded that the barbarians release the commander. I think I was too insistent, too haughty, too much of a Roman. I reminded them of their obligations. They laughed, then ripped off my tunic and caned me. Not a whip, you understand. I don't think they meant to hurt me — it was a thin thing they used, the sort of pliant branch a pedagogue might use on the backside of an errant pupil. It was meant to shame, to remind me of my place. There was no ceremony to it. They joked as they struck, then ran me out of their camp, their laughter following me like a flock of magpies.'

'They have no right,' Quintus said indignantly. 'You are a free-born Roman. Striking you is akin to striking Rome.'

Agnus indicated the bloody field. 'I think this sends a clearer message to Rome.'

The man speared on the track and the one nailed to the trees were both carried to the pyre. Only these two each had a coin beneath their tongue, obols for Charon placed by the capsarius. Sextus claimed that the Vestals would guide the others to follow these two, each with hand on shoulder, like a sighted man leading a line of the blind. It was an unsettling image, yet a comforting conceit. None of the men really believed it. Charon would only carry the dead for payment and, even if the Vestals paid, where would the boatman find the money if there was no tongue to look beneath?

'There are no fragrances, no herbs or spices to light the way,' said Tullius, with a sad shake of his head.

'I have a little oil,' Alba said. 'It is not much, but it will at least help the blaze.'

'We can show them honour,' Quintus added, pulling his cloak over his head. The legionaries followed suit, covering their heads whilst the flames grew.

Quintus gathered everyone in a wide circle. 'Men, this massacre is ours to witness. Only we saw the signs carved on the chests of these victims. The barbarity of this action, and these deaths, should make us hot to avenge them.'

A few heads were raised. Quintus answered the unasked question. 'Yes, we have a new enemy. A son of Maelo.'

This was a name that awakened memories for Alba, and any others who had served with the Larks, who had suffered the ignominy of losing their eagle to the tribal chieftain.

'We know little about him, except this.' Quintus stretched his hand out towards the rising smoke. 'We will find him, and we will destroy him.'

The men nodded vigorously, but also whispered prayers under their breath.

The two centurions put their heads together. 'We wait for Galba here?' Felix asked.

'We wait, though I do not think we will camp here. This place will be full of the ghosts of the dead. Though it is a flat and useful campsite the men, even hard-headed ones like Tullius and Marcus, know it to be haunted. Another suitable campsite will have to be found.'

'The trees are thinning,' said Felix. 'I don't think it will be too hard to find another. I could send men with the archers.'

'No,' Quintus said, after pausing to think. 'We only go when we are at full strength. I do not want to risk any more losses.'

'Agreed,' said Felix. 'I will post pickets.'

'Make it so,' nodded Quintus. He thought about sending another messenger to Galba, to tell him of the predicament of the commander, but decided it would not be worth it now. Galba would find out soon enough. His best runner was Agnus, and he was in no state to go anywhere. There was nothing for the men to do until the rest of the cohort arrived. Then they could take a force big enough to defend itself to find a new campsite. They had been punished severely for their complacent reliance on an 'ally'.

Some of the men had predicted betrayal. Tullius had openly questioned the faith of the tribesmen, and thought the trust foolish. He would have preferred to find his own way along the river. Sextus, similarly, had not seen the alliance blessed by the gods through any portents or interpretations. Others just accepted that sometimes friends, in pursuance of their own ends, could become enemies.

The trees were still dripping, but the pale sun had at least dried up the rocks that were scattered around. On these the men sat dolefully in little groups. They were not used to having nothing to do. Some wanted to hunt game, but Quintus would not allow it.

Galba should not have been far behind. Quintus' concern at the delay grew with every minute. He worried that the cohort had been attacked, but he could not risk sending men to find out.

As they waited, some men took to practising the standard sword strokes of the Campus Martius. Marcus and Tullius stood side by side, repeating the same movements. Across from them Crassus and Sextus went through a similar set of steps, somehow more smoothly and artistically.

Sextus, breathless, came up to Quintus. 'You should try it,' he said seriously. 'It chases away the demons.'

'*Quam mox oblivioni sunt horrores*,' Quintus said. 'How soon the horrors are forgotten.'

'Very profound.' Sextus put on a face of mock solemnity.

'Proculus, my brother, taught me this line of poetry,' said Quintus. 'He learned it from a girl. She quoted it to show that she had feelings, and could recognise suffering.' He smiled. 'My brother stole it from her and used it to impress other girls at sacrifices, games and executions, casting his eyes to the ground and pretending gravity whilst squeezing the girl's hand.'

'I do not know it,' Sextus admitted, with a shake of his head, 'although I would have found it useful.'

The watery sun faded behind the thin cloud so that it was no more than a patch of lighter sky. Mist gathered and swirled at the corners of vision, creeping up the hillsides and the tree trunks, wreathing the base of the pyre. To Quintus' relief a trumpet in the distance finally announced the arrival of the cohort.

The tramp of caligae and the rough voices of men could be heard approaching. A trumpet sounded again. Galba was clearly taking no chances, having the cornicen announce his presence as if he led an entire legion.

'Go, Agnus,' Quintus ordered. 'Wash yourself, drink some more water, and share some food with the men. Tell them I sent you and to give up some of their hidden stores. You will be needed as soon as Centurion Galba arrives, so you might as well be refreshed.'

The runner saluted and left. Quintus rose, ready to meet Galba.

XVII: LEMURES

Galba had split the cavalry into two, so that half rode at the front of the march, half at the rear. The front unit carried long spears, the ends decorated with floating pennants. The Cantabrian ponies trotted immediately behind them. In the middle of this front rank, Aquila rode with the eagle held high. To one side, the cornicen was also mounted, his great curved horn shining; to the other, a signifer flew the red bull of the cohort. Behind them, after the Cantabrians, the tall figure of Rufus carried the standard of Century One. Next to him was the imago of the emperor mounted on a pole.

Thus there were flags and standards and pennants in abundance, designed to convince the Germani that they were dealing with a legion and not just a depleted cohort.

Centurion Galba rode to one side, ahead of all the banners, in his red cloak and tall crested helm. Quintus approached his horse. 'All dead?' asked Galba, waving his arm at the disturbed earth and the fire.

'Yes, sir. Mutilated and killed. We built a pyre.'

'Of course. Good. What else?'

Quintus swallowed. 'Sir, the prefect has been taken hostage.'

Galba was shocked, although he looked more annoyed than concerned. 'At least I have his women,' he sighed. 'They returned to us before we set off with tales of their own. That is what delayed our departure.' He cursed under his breath. 'Who has the prefect?' he asked. 'What do they want?'

'Our erstwhile allies,' Quintus said, 'and they want that.' He pointed at the eagle wavering in the hands of the aquilifer as he dismounted. 'That is what they demand.'

Galba pulled over to one side to let the rest of the cohort through. Antonia Flavia and Lady Aurelia rode in the midst of the first group of cavalry, wearing military cloaks with their hoods up.

'I will have to tell them,' Galba sighed. 'Do we camp here?'

Quintus hesitated before replying. 'I think not, sir. The place is infested with lemures. The men will not wish to sleep amongst the ghosts of the dead.'

'Then beyond the next hill.' Galba turned around and held his hand up, addressing the decurion. 'Do not dismount. We have yet to find a campsite. Pass the word. The men here will lead.'

He leaned down from the saddle and spoke into Quintus' ear. 'It is a god-cursed mess. We will talk when we are settled.'

The members of the advance party formed up, Felix and Marcus chivvying them. Quintus moved to their head and led them out, regaining the track. The ground soon began to rise and, within a half hour, they were blessed with another plateau, flatter and broader than the one they had left. They stood aside to let the cavalry lead the cohort into the space.

Many orders soon rang out amongst the ring of trees that fringed the site, and men scurried to and fro, each with a specific job. Water was fetched, stakes were cut, ditches were dug. This would be a proper, defended, marching camp. A group were ordered to be quick and erect the prefect's tent, into which the women were hurried. They seemed to have lost their body slaves, but Quintus, concerned at least for Aurelia, called Jovan across and sent him to them.

'See to their needs,' he commanded. 'Your cousin, too, if you can find him.' He looked around the bustling site until he spotted Alba. 'Capsarius, check on the ladies as soon as they are settled. Make sure that they are not injured.'

Quintus hardly noticed the deserters. The two sorry figures were being dragged along, tied to the carts. One was Hirtis, still flabby despite his weight loss, and still managing to look sullen, if not quite defiant, his tunic hitched up to stop it dragging on the floor. The other, his companion, was thin and bony, as if suffering from a wasting disease. He looked half dead already, not bothering to lift his tunic, but letting it trail like a weed in a river. He would not, Quintus surmised, survive a scourging.

Hirtis, recalcitrant as he was, would probably survive, but this meant he was likely to face an even more painful death at the hands of his comrades. Though he claimed to have their loyalty, none had come forward to defend him, and none had offered him so much as a sip of water.

The cohort had marched past their hamstrung and silent co-conspirator, staked by a tree. They took in the warning. The two prisoners were taken from the cart and tied together. Punishment would be at the morning assembly.

Finally, all was settled. The two streets of the castra were laid out, though not as precisely as they would have been had the engineers still lived. The gates were positioned and logs on trestles spanned the gaps. Latrines were dug, the men ordered not to go to them alone. At each corner a raised area allowed a guard point, hardly a tower, but the best that could be achieved. A ditch was grubbed out to mark the perimeter, legionaries stationed in pairs at regular intervals along it. Tents were erected in lines. The standards were plunged into the earth by the commander's tent. Torches marked gates, corners and junctions.

A tripod was broken out, ready to burn the exta after the morning sacrifice. Fires were lit and the slaves were cooking food. The men ate and slept in relays. There were no games of knucklebones, no gambling, no wrestling or weapons practice.

The centurions pressed on the men that this was hostile territory — unless they were eating or sleeping, they were on guard. Though the officers wished for a better constructed, more permanent castra, time and daylight had been short. This would have to do.

Inside the prefect's tent a small brazier provided warmth, filling the space with smoke. Curtains were hung to provide some privacy for the ladies. Maxim and Jovan were both pressed into their service, though neither was trained as a body slave. There were clothes in the carts for the women to change into, but they struggled with fastenings and ties. They helped each other and, to the relief of the Macedonian cousins, dismissed the slaves to cooking and cleaning. By the time the women emerged, they looked much more presentable.

Maxim cooked a hot pulse flavoured with dried herbs. Jovan found a skin of wine. They also lit torches, so that flickering shadows played in all directions within the tent. The pair then stood, enjoying the warmth, until Quintus shooed them out, telling them to find something useful to do.

'Find Optio Crassus. He will employ you. I will call you when you are needed,' he said.

Cornus joined them and stood in the shadows, ready to record events. He believed that Titus Flavius would be rescued and would need to know how his camp and his women had been treated. Two folding stools had cushions put on them for the ladies. Galba claimed the third stool.

Quintus had not yet had time to give the full details of the slaughter to his superior. Galba had been busy informing Antonia of her husband's plight. She was stoical, deciding that she would tell her story first, then deal with the rescue.

Quintus squatted down to listen, as close as he dared to the warm skin of the Lady Aurelia. Galba — and a few others —

were aware of his trysts with the lady and turned a blind eye to them. Galba raised an eyebrow in warning and Quintus shrank back just a little, so that there was a definite gap between himself and Aurelia.

It was the Lady Antonia Flavia of the Menenii who began. She was no stranger to violence, being the daughter of the senator Menenius, who had been sentenced to death by Marcus Antonius and Augustus, when he was mere Octavius. She had pleaded her father's case personally and later helped him escape, a loyal slave in his clothes taking the death blow meant for him. Then, consorting with pirates and supposed traitors, she had arranged his escape to Sicily. She had used criminals and brigands and was not afraid of them.

Now, as she prepared to tell her tale, she sat up and squared her shoulders. 'We were bounced around as the slaves carrying the litter ran from the storm. Then we stopped suddenly, and I opened the curtains to see what was going on. A tree directly ahead of us was split and charred by lightning. One half of it had crashed down across the trail, flames leaping from it.

'I told the slaves to go around it. But the thunder and lightning flashes made them more alert to what the gods said than what their mistresses ordered.' She made a dramatic gesture with her hand. 'Then the litter lurched and we were flung to one side as it hit the earth. All I could see through the curtained gap was the rain and the burned shard of the tree.'

Aurelia joined in. 'It appeared that one of the bearers had been hit by a falling branch. We later found he had been killed outright. The other three could no longer lift the litter between them, so they just let it fall, then crouched down trembling. I suppose they were waiting for the storm to pass.' She spread her hands. 'We were trapped. We could do no more than them.'

Antonia continued. 'After an eternity, the storm abated. The thunder still echoed, but it sounded far away. The lightning no longer split the sky. But now it was dark as night in Hades. You could not see your hand before your face.'

She finished her wine, then held the vessel out to be refilled. It was a moment before the men realised what she wanted, there being no slaves present. It was Galba who leaned forward and poured from the jug. Antonia swallowed the contents gratefully.

'One of the remaining bearers, a Scythian, bolder than the rest, told us to wait. He said that he would fetch help. At first we relaxed and made ourselves as comfortable as we could — after all, we were still dry. Then the curtain parted. I could see nothing and assumed it was one of the slaves. But the face that was thrust in was not a slave, but a legionary.'

'A friend, we thought,' Aurelia added. 'A rescuer.'

'A soldier, yes,' Antonia said fiercely, slamming her empty wine cup down on to the table, making the jug jump. 'But not a rescue.' She held the cup out again. This time Galba knew what to do.

'You tell it,' Antonia told Aurelia. 'It was you he tried to ravish.'

The light from the brazier glanced off Aurelia's dark curls and high cheekbones as the two men expressed shock.

'A legionary?' Galba asked incredulously.

'And why would a legionary not think to rape a defenceless woman, probably with the excuse that he thought her to be an enemy?' Antonia rebuffed him sharply. 'I have seen it many times before.'

'One of ours? He must have been a deserter,' Quintus said softly.

Aurelia was both angry and on the verge of tears. 'One of ours,' she said finally. 'Though in the darkness I had no idea what he looked like — he could easily have been a native, had it not been for the tongue he spoke.'

'Do not tell it if it pains you,' Quintus advised. He would have put a hand on the lady's shoulder in comfort had he dared. Aurelia did not look like she would accept such attention.

'I will speak,' she said firmly.

XVIII: ACUS

There was a profound silence. Then Aurelia took a deep breath, steadied herself, and began.

'He said he was sent to find us, that he would help. I tried to leave the litter. It was on the ground, one of the legs held fast by a root or vine. He said that I needed to step out so that he could free the litter. I don't think he realised that there were two of us.' She sniffed. 'He sounded kind.'

Quintus wanted to enfold her in his arms, but he knew it would not be acceptable, so he merely murmured encouragement. 'Go on, lady.'

'I tried to step out, but the bastard could not wait. He grabbed me first by the arm, then, when I resisted, by the hair. He dragged me out of the litter and turned me around, pressing my head against the side of a tree.' She put a hand to her face. 'Here, it is still scratched.'

Quintus looked where she pulled her hair back. Angry red marks ran from her ear to her neck.

'Then he pinned me by the throat, the crook of his elbow stopping me from breathing, and squeezed my breasts with his other hand. It was sickening — his breath was hot and rank on my neck, his grunting vile in my ear. He tried to rip my dress at the front, but the material held. Though it stretched, it did not part and he was frustrated and angry. So he lifted the hem at the back and thrust his hand up from behind, laughing that there was more than one way to cook a goose.'

Aurelia swallowed hard at the memory. 'I could hear other voices, other men, and feared that here was a group of bandits.

I knew then I would be raped, and not just once. Then I heard Antonia's shout, and it gave me courage.'

She smiled across at her friend. 'My attacker was struggling to free himself from his undershorts. He needed a hand for that, so he loosened his grip. It was only slightly, but it was enough for me to reach into my hair.'

She mimed the action. Her hair was held in place by an acus — a long, sharp pin. 'I stabbed first at the arm that still encircled my neck, but that seemed to have no effect. Then I thrust blindly over my shoulder, hoping to catch something soft.'

She repeated the frantic stabbing with her free hand. 'I was rewarded with a high-pitched scream, but the acus was caught fast in whatever I had stabbed. I had to let it go. At first the arm around my neck tightened, and I thought I would choke. Then his grip slackened and I felt him fall. He died a coward's death, weeping and whining like a whipped dog.' She was triumphant. 'I found out that he wept from but one eye. I had stabbed him in the other.' She looked with appreciation and affection at her companion. 'It was Antonia who killed him. She stabbed him in the thigh.'

'I knew where to find soft flesh — my husband taught me, my father before him. Cut the great vein in the leg and the man dies. I was lucky.' Antonia smiled grimly. 'I was trying to stab him in the balls.'

Aurelia smiled at Antonia's bravery in using such language in front of the men. The soldiers could bandy crudities around as much as they liked, but ladies were expected to be prim.

'Another man looked inside the litter and found a second victim — me,' Antonia went on. 'But he never even laid a finger on me.' She gave her friend a knowing look. 'I travel with more than a knife. I always keep my father's gladius with me — it is precious to me. My father never took it to Sicily, since he was disguised as a slave when he fled, so it is mine. I used it to stab this fellow in the face.

'He fell back and, enraged, I followed him.' She cast her eyes to the ground. 'Stupid, I know, but I did not stop to think. Anyway, he yelled and ran. I don't know who or what he thought I was, but Aurelia says I was shouting and cursing fit to bring Jove down from his sky-seat in shock. That's when I saw that she was being assaulted by another shadow. That was the one I killed, opening his leg.'

'We stood back-to-back, ready to defend ourselves. I do not know how long we stood like that, but it felt like an age,' Aurelia said. 'We could still see nothing, not even the sky through the trees, and expected a blow to fall at any time.'

'Finally, dawn came and in the morning light we could see we were no longer under attack. The litter was still in one piece, trapped by a fallen branch. Beside it, a man lay dead, Aurelia's acus buried in his eye. I retrieved it for her.' Aurelia patted her hair to show that the pin was now back in place. Quintus looked sideways at her with a new respect.

'He was a rat-faced man with thinning grey hair and a deep scar below his remaining eye,' Antonia continued. 'One of our bearers lay dead also, the tall Scythian. He must have tried to fight them off with his bare hands. He was badly cut. Another lay crushed beneath a fallen tree.

'In the light, the other two slaves crept from hiding. They had every chance to run away, but they did not. Instead they followed the trail of the men who attacked us — deserters, I presume — back to where you were breaking camp. Perhaps I should reward them in some way.'

'I will make a note,' said Cornus, appearing from the shadows like a wraith, tablet in hand. They had all forgotten that he was there. 'It will be done.'

'It was your scream, lady, that alerted us, for we were already marching when we heard it,' Galba said, waving Cornus back into the shadows and offering Antonia more wine.

She accepted. 'It was your man tied to the tree. He held his arms out to us and made a horrible noise in his throat. I thought he was some sort of spectre. I did not mean to scream.'

'No ghost,' Galba said laconically, 'just another of the deserters, demonstrating what will happen to them when they are caught.' He turned to Quintus. 'Do you recognise the one they slew?'

'He was not one of mine,' said Quintus with certainty. 'There are none of that description in my century. Nor does it sound like a rabbit, so Felix will be relieved.' He reflected briefly. 'It does not really matter. He was one of ours. They all were.' He asked Antonia, 'Lady, how many do you think were in that party?'

'Three, maybe four. One dead, one injured — the other one or two ran.'

'So they have split up,' said Galba thoughtfully. 'Perhaps we do not have to fear them attacking us.'

There was quiet between them for a while, broken only by the muffled sound of the guard outside being changed.

'You ladies will wish to retire,' Quintus said, with a certainty that smacked of being patronising.

'Why?' Aurelia asked, an eyebrow raised.

'I am calling the messenger to tell me what happened to the pioneers.' Galba waved a hand at Cornus, who dipped his head in acknowledgement and left.

'Then you will speak of my husband's rescue. I think we would like to stay for all of it,' said Antonia. Aurelia nodded in agreement.

'So be it,' said Quintus. 'But prepare to be shocked.'

Cornus returned with Agnus then stepped back into the shadows. The runner had been waiting for the call. At Galba's bidding, slaves replaced the torches, which burned low, and fed the brazier. The smoke from both combined in the air like an indoor fog. Agnus was once more equipped as a legionary, wearing lorica laminata and a cloak, and carrying his helmet beneath his arm. Sweat dripped from his forehead and the end of his nose, but he did not dare wipe it away. He stood to attention, eyes on the back of the tent rather than on the ladies. He had never been in the company of such nobility before.

'You can stand easy, soldier,' Galba said. 'We are not on parade.' Agnus loosened his stance only slightly. He did not move his eyes from the point he had decided was a suitable focus.

Aurelia decided to tease him. 'I cannot see your eyes, legionary. How can I tell you are speaking the truth?'

The messenger dared to look down at the two ladies. Aurelia met his gaze, and she smiled softly and fluttered her eyelashes at him. Immediately he jerked his head back upright.

'Stop it, Aurelia,' Antonia chided. 'Let us hear his story instead.'

'Tell us what you witnessed,' Quintus ordered. He had noted the little exchange and did not approve.

Agnus looked at the two women, and then at Quintus, an unspoken question in his glance. He was unsure of how much to say in the presence of ladies.

'They know much already,' Quintus said. The messenger nodded.

XIX: DAGAZ

Agnus' chin snapped back up, and he began his tale. 'I was coming back to the camp as fast as I could to report the commander's capture, but the storm was faster. It outran me. At some point I tripped in the failing light. I hit my head and all went black. When I awoke it still rained, but not so fiercely. It was night and I could see no moon or stars. I had no idea in which direction to continue.' He ran out of breath, had to stop to breathe deeply, a sigh, really. He continued more slowly.

'I heard screaming. Roman legionaries were being corralled by horsemen shouting in barbaric tongues. I wanted to go to the rescue of the men, but they had been captured and stripped by the tribesmen. I wore no armour, and I could see I would be just another victim, so I climbed a tree.'

He looked ashamed at his actions, casting his eyes to the ground. Quintus was brusque. 'Better a witness than a body,' he said.

Agnus raised his head, and Galba gestured for him to continue.

'There was no attempt to kill them; they were merely forced to their knees. I realised that they must be pioneers — they had started to mark out a space with stakes. Many resisted, drawing weapons and trying to reach the enemy. Even these were not killed — they were just clubbed with the flats of swords or axe handles. Once the men were all in the middle of the space and disarmed, they were tied together. I would guess there were about twenty of them.'

'Twenty exactly,' whispered Quintus. 'One ran for help, but was brought down with a spear, so nineteen.'

'Then the strangest thing happened,' Agnus went on. 'The chieftain of the tribe — or so I took him to be — dismounted and issued orders. The captives were forced to disarm and had their armour cut from them. Their tunics were ripped open so that they were bare-chested. Then the tribesmen made a circle around their captives, and all knelt and lifted their hands to the sky. The name they called on was none of the gods of the Germani that I know. They called, "Dagaz, Dagaz," and the chieftain appeared to be accepting the invocation.'

'Preparations for a sacrifice — a religious thing, I would think,' said Antonia. When the men looked at her, she explained, 'I have attended many ceremonies for the Good Goddess, and I have been priestess at a few. You men should know the ritual that goes with a sacrifice.'

'Ripping clothes off and chanting names is not unusual,' agreed Aurelia.

Agnus stopped, not sure how much detail to go into as to what happened next. He looked to Quintus. 'Sir, you saw it. Should I share the details?'

Quintus looked to Galba for guidance. 'The sight was truly harrowing, sir. Perhaps the ladies should retire.'

'And perhaps not,' Antonia Flavia said firmly. 'I have been close to many deaths, brought about in many different ways. You will have to dig deep to shock me. Aurelia, would you care to retire?'

'I would not,' came the immediate reply. 'I too have seen mutilations, crucifixions and heads mounted on the Rostra. Let him say what he saw.'

Galba nodded consent. Quintus narrowed his eyes in disapproval, then turned to Agnus and said, 'Carry on, messenger.'

Agnus lowered his voice, only the crackling of the braziers competing with him.

'Once the chanting of the name stopped, the tribesmen became workmanlike, each group of them choosing certain legionaries to keep together. One seemed to be choosing by height, pushing any he thought too small back into the pack. The tallest man was taken to two trees at the edge of the clearing. He was stripped naked and his hands and feet nailed to the trees so that he was stretched between them. They tied something into his hair and to a branch above so that his head was fixed, facing the clearing. They did something to his face. I think an eye was taken. He screamed as they carved his chest.'

'His fate was to watch,' Quintus said. 'He kept both eyes but his eyelids were taken. We found him dead.'

Agnus sighed and resumed. 'Another seemed to be matching up the broadest. I have seen such matching done in the arena. I assumed that they were going to make them fight, but they didn't. The tall ones they took to where a set of long posts were hammered into the ground. They stretched them between the posts, in the shape of an X, tying them at wrist and ankle. One, a broad-shouldered man wearing the fur of a bear, brought out a curved blade and removed their tongues. The chieftain himself drew a small knife and offered it up to the gods — presumably for blessing — before carving patterns into the chests of these men.'

'Runes, we think, sir,' Quintus explained to Galba. 'Though we think we know their meaning, we have yet to divine their purpose.'

Galba nodded. Antonia and Aurelia sipped their wine, seemingly unconcerned by these descriptions of barbarity. Cornus scratched away in the background.

'Is he all right to carry on?' Quintus asked the ladies.

'Yes, yes,' said Antonia Flavia impatiently, then to Agnus, 'Go on, man.'

'Very well,' he said, taking another deep breath. 'Then they cut off the hands of the men, leaving their wrists tied, pulling the leather thongs that bound them tight so that they bled only slowly. Then they did the same with their feet, hanging both hands and feet from their necks. It will have taken them a long time to die. The other tribesmen, and their captives, watched this mutilation in silence. Small groups were taken away. I did not see what happened to them, but I found out later they had been staked to the ground, similar figures carved into them, and given slow and painful deaths.'

The atmosphere in the tent was thick and warm and sweat glowed on the scout's face. The ladies had both emptied their drinking vessels, but no-one moved to refill them. Galba sat still as a stone, Cornus silent, even the scratching of his stylus quietened. Agnus' shoulders slumped as he painted the picture.

'One man was tied between two horses, one arm to each; then the horses galloped to either side, tearing the victim in two. Another was given the same treatment, but his face was smashed into a tree. At least their deaths were quick. The remaining four men, also with their chests carved, were stretched between short stakes to form a star. They were laid on their backs, hands out and touching each other, feet splayed. They were stripped of armour, but not baltea and cingulum. They also left them with their tongues. Their screams were terrible.' Agnus paused, wiping the sweat from his forehead.

'What happened?' Aurelia asked gently.

'They rode over them, lady. Rode around them and across them, in straight lines and circles, tearing their flesh, pulling out their guts, smashing their faces to pulp. Arms and legs were broken and soft flesh gouged out — but they did not ride over the symbols. Those they left.'

He shook his head as if to clear it of the vision. 'They gathered up the weapons and the armour, wearing some of it and taking what might be useful from the pile of clothes.' His voice now hoarse, he concluded, 'There was one last act of barbarity. The tribesmen collected the heads, cutting them off cleanly with great knives or sharp axes. Some were almost untouched. Others had been smashed or broken. Still others had an eye gouged out. They seemed to argue over who should have which head, the chieftain demanding unmutilated ones. They laughed as they tried to fit heads into helms. They tied their trophies across their horses then, whooping and shouting, rode off.'

Cornus' stylus scratched a little longer, the only sound apart from the spitting of the brazier and guttering of the torches.

Antonia Flavia broke the silence. 'Drink, soldier,' she said, holding out the jug to the messenger. He hesitated, looking at his officer.

Quintus nodded. 'Not too much.'

Agnus took a draught and his breathing slowed. 'Do you have questions?'

'I think we had detail enough,' said Galba. He addressed the others in turn. 'Quintus? Ladies?' They each shook their head. Agnus put the jug down and waited to be dismissed.

'You did your duty, legionary,' Quintus said flatly.

'I relieve you of guard duty,' Galba added. 'Now, go and get something to eat.'

'One last thing,' said Quintus as Agnus lifted the tent flap to leave. 'Find me the slave Jovan — the Macedonian who served my contubernium. Send him here.'

A blast of night air came in as he went out, swirling the smoke around and cutting through the tense atmosphere. The two women began to speak at the same time and both Galba and Quintus reached for the wine jug, wordlessly agreeing to share it.

Galba took the first swig. 'Why do you need the slave, Quintus?'

'We may have Germani amongst the slaves — or their cousins. I want to know what those symbols mean.' He drained the jug. 'Cornus, find another,' he ordered the scribe, the only person present whom he could command. Cornus bowed and left with the empty jug.

Jovan entered and bowed low before the noble ladies. Quintus observed the respect but was impatient. 'Amongst the slaves, Jovan, does the cohort have any that speak Germani, that know of their customs? If we have, bring them here. If not, bring the closest thing we have — a Gaul, perhaps. The dead were marked with runes. We need to know what they mean.'

Jovan thought briefly before replying. 'The blacksmith at the castra hiberna was of the Tencteri tribe — Germani. When I brought horses to be shod, or weapons to be sharpened, he often marked his work with the runes of his race. He is still with us, I think.'

'Bring him,' Galba commanded.

As Jovan left, bowing again, Antonia Flavia addressed the men. 'How does knowing what the runes mean help us?'

'There was a reason they were carved. If we know the reason, we can defend against it.'

Once more the challenge of the guards could be heard at the door. Then Jovan was bidden to enter, this time leading a man almost as tall as Quintus, but broader. He had yellow hair and a yellow moustache that, braided and tied, sat atop a yellow beard. He wore a simple tunic, leaving his arms bare. The scars on them bore a remarkable resemblance to the pattern that Quintus had seen on Crassus, a blacksmith also.

'Does he speak Latin, Jovan?'

The man smiled, revealing a set of even white teeth. 'I can speak for myself,' he said. 'I know your tongue, though I understand more than I speak. What would you have of me?' Then, lest he be misunderstood, he added, 'I am a free man. I ply a trade.'

'You are no citizen,' Antonia Flavia said haughtily.

Fire sparked in the native's eyes as he turned angrily on the woman, saying something in his own harsh-sounding language. Quintus interrupted quickly, holding a hand up and speaking sharply in rebuke. 'Enough. We are friends here.'

Though Antonia gave him an ice-cold look and the big man bridled, Quintus' tone was enough to stem the hostility. 'What is this?' he asked the blacksmith, making the 'T' shape with two hands.

'That is the rune for Týr, the one-handed god called Tiwaz in the old tongue. He gave his hand to help bind the great wolf Fenrir. So it stands for sacrifice, but also for judgement. Týr is the god of justice and balance. The rune also stands for the fire of a warrior.'

'And this?' Quintus drew the two triangles on the floor. 'Is this Wotan?'

The man was thoughtful. 'Like the wings of a butterfly — no, this is not the rune for Wotan. That rune is Ansuz, very like the Roman letter F. What you have drawn is Dagaz. It is used to mean "day" or "dawn" or "awakening."'

'Awakening?'

'This tribe — or perhaps its leader — has awakened from slumber, and now fights. Perhaps for freedom from slavery and oppression.' He looked defiantly at Antonia. 'Its use is a source of great joy to the poor, the little folk, as it means new beginnings — perhaps the chance of a better life.'

Both Antonia and Aurelia made little disapproving noises. This time it was Quintus who glared at them. 'Their chieftain is called Dagaz,' he said to the blacksmith. 'Does that mean anything?'

The big man spoke seriously and quietly, as if afraid to be overheard. 'It means that is not his name. He has chosen it to represent what he does — like *centurion* or *orator* in your world. He represents an idea: justice and a new dawn. Dagaz is awakening; linked with the warrior rune, it asks Týr's help in making this happen.'

Once more, silence fell. Galba broke it, thanking the man brusquely and bidding him leave. The women looked to the two centurions for an interpretation.

'The men were sacrificed to Týr the god and to an idea of freedom,' said Quintus. 'By all the gods, I hate the thought of fighting an idea.'

XX: INIMICA ANTE PORTAS

Galba rose and stretched. 'Walk with me, centurion.'

'Sir.' Quintus also rose and both men left the tent, leaving the noble ladies behind in the company of Cornus. Two legionaries still stood guard at the door.

'Stay with the ladies, Cornus,' ordered Galba.

The freedman was about to object, affronted at being treated like a slave, when Quintus leaned across and whispered in his ear.

'I trust you to keep these ladies safe, secretary Cornus, and defend them. I can think of no-one better. Will you do it?' Of course it was a request, not an order, and one to which he would have to accede.

The two centurions put on their helmets and set off, purportedly to check on the guards. But this was a secondary duty; what they really intended was to make a decision on what to do in the morning. The fact that Dagaz was both man and idea had unsettled them.

The Lady Antonia also had to be satisfied, or she would undermine their authority with her own appeals to the men. Her priority would be the rescue of her husband.

'Don't be political, or diplomatic,' Galba warned Quintus. 'We need an honest assessment, however bleak.'

'Honesty, then,' Quintus said bluntly. 'Do we let him die?'

'Perhaps a little too frank,' said Galba, smiling humourlessly. 'I spoke more with Agnus. Our prefect is apparently neither prisoner nor hostage, but treated as an honoured guest. They seem to understand that if he was a prisoner this would dishonour him, so he is not.'

'Very diplomatic — and very clever. Still, the question remains: do we abandon him or rescue him, guest or not?'

'We cannot abandon him. The presence of the Lady Antonia will make certain of that, if nothing else.'

'Nor can we pay his ransom. There is no way under Jove's eye that we could give them the eagle.'

'The men would not allow it,' said Galba thoughtfully, 'even if we two thought we could get away with it.'

They reached the gate — a young tree stripped of its branches and lifted onto trestles across a gap in the ditch. A torch burned on either side. There were two men on guard. They spotted the plumed helmets and saluted smartly.

'A rescue, then,' Quintus said, as they crossed the space behind the gate, the beaten earth of the via principalis. 'If we fight them, we risk both him and our own men. If we could demonstrate overwhelming force, to show that we could not be resisted, we might avoid a fight.'

'We do not have enough men. The Germani must know that, eagle or no eagle, we are nowhere near a full legion. And we have used our "senator" enough. I don't believe Cornus will fool them anymore.'

'So you think we will have to fight?'

'I think so, yes.'

They reached the other side of the gate, where the two guards also saluted, and continued to walk in brooding silence. Absent-mindedly Galba reached out and cuffed the side of a legionary's head as they passed. Its owner jerked upright, initially ready to fight, then recognised the centurion.

'Stay awake, soldier,' Galba said, affably enough, but there was no denying the hard edge to his voice. 'Sir,' saluted the man, speaking unnecessarily loudly, causing a ripple amongst his fellow legionaries nearby as they realised they were under inspection.

They reached the corner of the castra and turned right along the next ditch. Another gate was at its centre, another road, the via praetoria, leading from it to the southern side. There was a raised mound at the corner, shored up with timbers. It was no tower, but better than nothing. The two men on it saluted. The word that the officers were about had spread rapidly.

The firmament above them was clear, all trace of the stormy weather gone. There was no moon and a thousand stars shone cheerfully above their heads. From time to time a bright flash winked into existence and rapidly faded. These flew singly, one after the other, each leaving a rippling wake as if a fish had swum across the heavens. The centurions stopped for a while, the men on guard near them becoming increasingly uncomfortable.

As they were about to move, a shower of stars burned across the dark canvas, leaving a set of silver furrows to mark their passing.

'What does that signify?' Galba wondered.

'I do not know,' Quintus replied. 'I do not have the power of divination. I am sure the augurs would interpret it to mean whatever the priesthood want it to mean.'

'A sceptic, you? I would never have guessed it.'

'I am as god-fearing as the next man, sir, and one of my companions is an expert at reading the stars.' Quintus paused. 'But too often have I seen stars and auspices interpreted to favour the reader. I do not think the gods smile on such corruption.'

'Would it be wrong to use the starfall to fire up the men? Would it offend the gods?'

'Truly, sir, I do not know. It could be dangerous — especially if the men think they are being fooled. I will consult Sextus and see what he divines. We might as well be informed. But I would not want to pretend anything that went against the gods.'

'Nor I,' said Galba, and Quintus noticed that he made the warding sign of the horns.

'Whereabouts is the commander being accommodated as a "guest"?' Quintus asked.

'The oppidum of this branch of the Germani, which Agnus says is nearby.'

'Is it well defended?' Quintus persisted.

'I am told that it is no Alesia but nevertheless a formidable task. Agnus describes it as longer than it is wide, raised on an oval hill and surrounded by both ditch and palisade. The tribe is not at war, and has not been for a long time, so the fortifications are not as strong as they should be. There are gaps in the palisade. The ditch has collapsed in places. Nevertheless, it is enough to protect against raiders. A frontal assault would have us winnowed down terribly. We do not have enough men for a siege. We have no siege engines or weapons, no onagers, no ballistae, no siege towers.' He stopped and turned to face Quintus. 'I do not think we could take it before they killed the prefect, but I cannot see another way.'

'We could build siege engines,' Quintus said slowly, with little confidence. They began walking again.

'We have few engineers,' replied Galba. 'And that would not save the commander.'

'There will be a way,' Quintus concluded.

They reached the south-west corner and turned again. Here the men on the raised mound made a great play of trimming the torches and looking alert.

The centurions nodded amiably at the two trumpeters, who squatted at the foot of the mound, polishing their brass instruments. Many cornicenes would be available to a legion. Even a cohort would have at least one in each century, along with a trumpet player and buccinators who played the raucous bass horn. Most of the cohort's musicians had been killed, and these were the only two on duty.

'And our other problem — Dagaz,' Galba said. 'How do we solve that?'

Quintus considered for a while. 'The man is a religious fanatic, but also a leader of men,' he said eventually. 'I do not think he is stupid enough to face us in open battle.'

'Nor I,' Galba said laconically. 'So how do we defeat him?'

Quintus thought for a moment. 'I don't think we do — not in the way you mean. I think we have to use guile. We must undermine his authority — prove him wrong somehow.' He sought for an opening. 'The starfall might be a way…'

Galba shook his head. He was more pragmatic. 'We need soldiering, not magic. He seems to have grabbed that for himself. If the starfall had any power, he will already have harnessed it. The fervour of his followers will protect him as long as they think he has a direct path to their gods.'

The summer night was short. The false dawn was already brightening the east with a line of milky white as Quintus and Galba walked back towards the commander's tent. As they turned, Quintus thought he caught a movement — a bird perhaps, or a night animal on its way home. Then he jerked his head and saw the sharp points of enemy spears.

'*Inimica ante portas!*' he shouted. 'Enemy at the gates. Sound the alarm.'

The two cornicenes did not hesitate. Both blew the long notes of action as Quintus and Galba shouted warnings and orders.

'Form up — defend the gates. Sound again.'

Men were urged into position by their fellows and their officers. This was a marching camp in enemy territory — they slept in their armour. In moments, soldiers were gathered at the ramparts, the raised corners and the gates. If they were attacked, they would fight. If not, they would keep watch and warn if the enemy came from other directions.

The tribesmen came from the east, with the morning light behind them. They had attempted to approach stealthily and at least partially succeeded. They had crept to within a spear's throw of the makeshift palisade before they were seen.

Shouting, they lifted their arms and their javelins flew through the air. They had the range right — none of the spears fell short. The line of the fort stood out against the black of the forest. The torches marked its limits and its gates — but they also showed the tribesmen where to aim.

XXI: VALE, GERMANI

The legionaries were armed and ready. Their shields were lifted to receive the spears, and their lower bodies were protected by the raised mound. Only at the gate was there any vulnerability, and here a line of overlapping shields was formed. Points thudded into the wood or bounced off the metal bosses of the scuta. Those javelins that did not find a shield passed harmlessly over the men, thudding into the soft ground.

Quintus knew that these Germani, superstitious as they were, never fought at night. But they had broken their tradition, or almost so, by attacking at first light, cleverly using the light at their backs whilst the castra was still in darkness. As the sun rose and dawn proper lit the heavens in myriad reds and golds, their advantage was gone.

Quintus had to admit that they had used the light well. He also knew that they had failed. If the first flight of spears did not kill or maim a good number of the defenders, then the attack was doomed. He looked along the front palisade to where more and more men were reporting. The other centurions, Felix, Marius and Furius Lentulus, could each be seen shouting, pulling their own men into defensive lines. Crassus had taken command of Century One and had them out of their tents and formed up, chivvying them into straight lines.

'The commander's tent, Crassus,' Quintus called to him and could immediately see him detail a group to join the guards that stood by it. The cavalry made sure that it defended the wagons. The Anatolians rushed forward, seeking orders.

'Bowmen,' Quintus shouted, 'loose arrows from the gate.'

The auxiliaries rushed to the gate and let fly. But the arrows flew over the heads of the attackers, as in spite of the failure of the first volley of spears, the tribesmen continued to advance and were already at the ditch. They screamed insults and battle cries, their axes, swords and round shields raised high.

The Cantabrians rushed to the gate wielding short barbed javelins and their deadly iron mákhairai, the curved blades catching the glint of the morning sun. These blades were the first to taste flesh, carving into arms, necks and shoulders.

'Javelins!' Galba had somehow managed to appear at the far side of the gate, his gladius raised high. 'Loose!'

The front row of legionaries, a line of around forty men, let their spears fly at the enemy. The attackers were close so they aimed low, screams of pain validating the tactic.

'Second row,' called Galba, and the front rank of legionaries ducked down to allow their colleagues free rein. 'Loose!'

The momentum of the Germani attack had failed already. The tribesmen realised they were not going to advance any further than the gate, that they were unlikely to be able to engage in hand-to-hand combat with the Romans. Those that tried to cross the shallow ditch and climb the bank were cut down easily.

Quintus saw that this was no great tribal assault, but a fairly small group. At the back of his mind it troubled him that so few thought it worth the risk of attacking.

'Marius, send men around,' Quintus commanded, gesticulating as he did so. There were gaps in the north and south palisades closed with tree branches. Marius saw what was needed and issued orders. Immediately his century divided into two columns of men, each around forty strong, who ran two abreast out of these gates, along the side of the ditch and onto the plain, a pincer movement.

Quintus stood to the right of his own century, who still fought those that came onwards. But it was no great number, no more than ten breaching the first line of defence, only to be cut down on all sides by Cantabrian and Roman blades. There was no joy in it, no challenge. Blood flowed freely into the ditch, which quickly filled with dead and dying. The legionaries had not even raised the bar of the gate. The attackers seemed to have no leader — at least none that stood out as commanding other men.

The two wings of Marius' century joined together at the rear of the Germani and locked shields. Under the command of their optio, Marcus, they stepped forward inexorably, a line of glinting metal. They bore down relentlessly on the attackers, Marcus calling, 'Step, step, step,' in an unflagging rhythm. 'Encircle them,' he ordered and the edges of the lines closed in. The Germani were forced into a tighter and tighter knot, in which the cold edge of the gladii could not fail to find flesh.

'Halt.' Quintus ordered, realising the battle was over. 'Sheathe your arms. Take them prisoner — we need information, not more bodies to bury.'

On Marcus' command, the men took two steps backwards. This did little but afford the enemy room to die. Many who were held up by the tightness of the encirclement could now fall. Others had space to raise weapons and were cut down before they could strike.

'Take some of them prisoner,' Marcus called. 'The centurion needs information.'

By the time all the legionaries had heard, there were few attackers left alive. The soldiers stepped back and lowered their blades.

Just three tribesmen remained untouched. They knelt with their arms outstretched, empty of weapons. In front of the gate there lay around forty others, either dead or deeply wounded and dying.

'Secure them,' said Quintus. He gestured at the pile of bodies. 'We need to know the reason for this.'

Of the defenders, just five legionaries needed the attention of the capsarius, and then not for long. Among the Romans there were no deaths, nor even any major wounds. Binding the broken wrist of one of Centurion Felix's rabbits who had tripped on a root was the most that Alba had to do, sending the man off with a stricture to watch his step in future.

The sun was high, the sky blue and cloudless. The flies were already massing, the smell of blood attracting them. They whirred and hovered around the dead. They nagged and bit and vexed the living. Slaves were called to strip the bodies of anything of value, including clothes and weapons. Others boiled pots on fresh fires for a breakfast of hot grain pulse and hard biscuit. The Anatolians retrieved their arrows.

The guards at the palisade were still vigilant. Legionaries continued to man the gates and the towers. The men not on duty cleaned their weapons but did not remove their armour, bloodstained or not. They were but a half-step away from being ready to fight again.

A bigger than usual scouting party, under Marcus, was sent to root out any further enemy. Another, a cavalry patrol also containing more men than would usually be the case, was sent down the hill under the command of the decurion. Neither standards nor horsemen had been brought to the action. Aquila had run for the eagle but Centurion Furius Lentulus had ordered him to leave it be, saying there were not enough enemy to warrant its presence. Aquila — along with many others — had not even engaged with the enemy. It was all over too swiftly.

Quintus and Galba stood at the top of the slope by the gate. They drank in turn from a waterskin, splashing their faces and necks. Both now had helmets tucked beneath their arms. They were plagued by insects and batted them away.

'I think we should move camp today,' Quintus said, as he waved the empty waterskin at a swarm of flies. 'Away from this pestilence.'

'We stay here one more day,' Galba replied. 'We can clear this ground. Do not forget the deserters, Quintus. We have punishments to mete out. Also enemy to interrogate. Pass the word.'

Crassus was within earshot. 'Pass the word,' Quintus called to his optio. 'We do not break camp today.' Crassus waved an arm in acknowledgement.

Quintus had not forgotten about the deserters, but had pushed them to the back of his mind. They would be punished at the evening assembly. The prisoners would be tortured for information, then die. It was their lot.

Galba ordered the slaves to drag the dead down the hill. At the foot of the slope was a marshy area that, in winter, was probably a stream. At least the remains would be out of sight — and would hopefully take the flies with them.

The valuables the slaves gained were a poor haul. As far as the officers could see, there was no gold or silver, nor heavy torcs or wristbands. There was no point trying to share the collection amongst the cohort. It was hardly booty. Even the weapons were of poor quality.

'Deliver all the metal to the blacksmith, weapons included,' Quintus ordered. 'He may be able to make use of it.'

The castra buzzed with activity. Fires were lit and the smell of food wafted across. As soon as the order to remain was given, the canvas at the base of the tents was rolled up to allow air in and guy ropes were tautened. The legionaries did not spare the commander's tent, rolling its sides up off the floor even though the women were still inside it. Secretary Cornus came out, ready to complain, but the job was finished and he ducked back inside, frustrated.

'The women,' Galba sighed as he saw Cornus. 'I had almost forgotten them. I will soothe them for now. You and your man who speaks their language will lead the interrogation of the attackers.'

Quintus nodded and turned to see where the prisoners were tied, stopping to survey the state of the camp. The guards were in place and vigilant. The tents were airing. The standards were fixed in the centre, the eagle flying high above them.

In the middle of the castra, close to the commander's tent, a group of men watched with heads covered as a legionary, cloak over his head, burned an offering on the tripod. It was the prerogative of the men to give thanks to the gods, to Jupiter Optimus Maximus and Mars for victory.

'Do you know what they sacrifice, capsarius?' Quintus asked Alba as he returned up the hill, covered in blood. He had been ordered to check that no more tribesmen lived — or at least none that were fit to give information.

'It is the heart of the enemy's leader — or so they have determined. I did not see them take it. Him there.' Alba pointed to the body of a broad man with white hair, the plaited beard and moustache of his people, and tanned limbs. His ribs stood out like wave-carved ripples in wet sand, and his arms looked thin and weak.

'Look at him,' said Quintus. 'This is no warrior leader. He died hungry.'

'Look at them all,' Alba echoed, casting his eyes over the bodies. 'They are no war band. Some are too young. All are underfed.' This thought prompted a change of tone. 'Sir, I need to ask — do we feed the deserters?'

'Water only,' Quintus said. 'We will punish them this evening. Why waste food?' He tugged his tunic down to help his belt to sit more comfortably. An unnecessary action, but one that those who knew him meant a decision had been taken. 'Today, the captives are our priority.'

XXII: DELICIA

Quintus ordered Alba to fetch him Caius, then walked across with the evocatus to the south-west quadrant of the camp, where the captives were held. They skirted the impromptu sacrifice.

'Caius, do not translate yet,' he said. 'I have an idea.'

The three Germani were tied to each other back-to-back so that each faced a different way. Quintus circled them, looking at them closely. Two were young and fresh-faced, barely more than boys. Like most of their people, they had yellow hair. One was old enough to have grown a scrubby beard and moustache. The other was younger, bare-chinned. The soft down on his upper lip and the pale hair of his people brought back uncomfortable memories of fair-headed Lux, Quintus' friend who had been killed by an enemy's spear. The third man was older, but just as skinny as the two younger prisoners. His moustache was long and both his hair and his beard were plaited. His face was lined, and there were shadows beneath his eyes. It was to him that Quintus spoke first, squatting beside him and smiling.

'Three of you live, not too many to crucify. Perhaps I will have crosses set up.'

The boy who could see him did not react, except to glare defiantly at his captor. The older man's eyes widened — a sign that he spoke at least some Latin.

'You speak our language,' Quintus said slowly and carefully.

'I understand a little,' the man replied haltingly. 'I understood *crucifigo*. We do not deserve that.'

'But you attacked a Roman fortress, threatened the lives of Romans. What other punishment could there be?'

The man's eyes misted with sadness. He spoke in his own guttural language, unable to think in a foreign tongue. Caius listened, asking the man to repeat certain things, then translated. 'Look at our dead. We have been punished enough. Our wives and daughters, their mothers —' he jerked his head towards the boys — 'told us not to try it. But what choice do we have?'

'Ask him if he would not have peace with Rome? Is this not a choice?'

'It is Rome that will not have peace with us,' Caius translated. 'We are just farmers, not warriors. We used to have mines and furnaces, used to work lead and iron. Iron that would compete with that of Noricum.' Caius added, 'That is an unlikely boast, sir.'

Quintus gestured for him to carry on. 'Just translate, soldier, as best you can.'

Caius turned back to his task. 'Now we have no mines, poor soil and few animals. We cannot pay tribute to everyone that demands it. Not without starving. We know hunger. Our children die of it.'

'And why is this the fault of Rome?' Quintus asked.

'Rome is one of those that demands tribute. It was Rome that drove us from our lands. Rome that gave our forges and workshops to another tribe. Legions came seeking silver and gold of which we have none. So they took slaves — young men who could work senatorial fields, young women they could train to serve. They were amazed at our colouring, our blue eyes, yellow hair, fair skin.'

The man shook his head as Caius struggled to keep up. He was becoming harder to understand as he became more emotional.

'They took my boy, a mere seven summers old, to train — not as a slave, they insisted, but an apprentice, perhaps to a smith or a potter. They hinted that he might even end up in the army, a soldier, a legionary. He might even serve great Caesar directly. They paid for him, but not enough.' He paused, then continued in a whisper. 'He was a dryad, spending all his time climbing trees, communing with the woodland animals, swimming, leaping rocks, skimming stones across still water.'

'You were done no harm,' Quintus asserted. 'You were paid.'

To his surprise, it was the older boy who still faced away from him that spoke. Quintus recognised the name of the emperor.

'What does the boy say?' he demanded of Caius. 'Does he insult our emperor?'

'Speak, boy.' Caius grabbed the youth by his hair, turning his face upwards. 'What do you say of the emperor?'

What the boy said was incomprehensible to either legionary. His voice dripped with scorn and he spat at the ground as he finished.

The older man continued as if he had not been interrupted. 'I found to my horror that my boy was sold as a *delicia*, a pet almost, made to wait on adults at dinner, naked or decorated with fruit or flowers. He was treated no better than a dog. But he grew too tall, too manly, too quickly. So they broke him, then sent him to work in the fields. He died a slow death. His friend escaped and brought me the news.'

'Again,' Quintus said, 'what does this have to do with your attack today?'

'It was your great god Caesar,' the man continued. 'He moved tribes around like they were crops to be rotated. We were sent south, like sheep to be put on new pasture. But people already occupied the land, already cropped the grass.'

'For the last time, why did you attack us?' he demanded, pulling the man's head sharply backwards.

'For that,' the man said in Latin. His watery gaze was levelled at the eagle stationed in its place above the other standards. 'If we deliver your eagle to the madman Dagaz, he and his followers will leave us alone. If we do this, he pledges to drive Rome from our backs.' He looked up, his blue eyes meeting Quintus' own dark ones. 'We are not fanatics. We have no loyalty to the supposed son of Maelo. He wants to resist Rome, to free all the Germani people. All we seek is our own freedom.'

'But you must have known that your attempt was doomed.'

'Our scouts brought us news. They said you marched behind a Germani tribe. That you were vassal to them. That you fled the wrath of Thor.'

'Vassals? Thor?'

'The tribe marched ahead of you. Thor is the thunder god. You fled from him into the forest. We concluded you were part of the other legion, the defeated one. That you would not fight. We saw women, slaves, fear of storms.' He paused. 'And an eagle, a device that could buy our freedom.'

Quintus ignored the litany of so-called evidence. He was more interested in the presence of other Romans. 'What other legion?'

The older boy tried to twist his head round and spoke in a harsh whisper, full of contempt. Caius translated as well as he could. 'He says the legion that lives in the forest like wild animals. That feeds on grubs and worms. That dare not go home to Rome, but is not wanted here. A legion of cowards and deserters.' The boy continued, not even trying to hide his disdain. Quintus understood nothing but the scorn. 'Caius, tell me,' he said through gritted teeth.

'Sir, he says most of the Germani are already free, and will remain so. Rome will never reach them. He cannot even count the tribes he knows, and there are untold numbers beyond them. The world goes on forever north, through forest and field and mountain until the sea itself freezes. "We inhabit it all," he says. "We are free. Free to attack and raid, free to steal, free to burn and batter. Free of the Roman yoke, and always will be."'

As Caius translated, the boy wriggled and squirmed, trying to loosen his bonds. Quintus struck him with the back of his hand, and the boy ceased moving.

'Nonsense,' he muttered scornfully, 'utter, god-cursed nonsense.'

'I will take you to these Romans,' said the old man obsequiously, 'in return for your eagle.'

'You will take me to these Romans,' Quintus said, 'in return for your life, and the life of this boy.' He indicated the younger of the two boys. There was a resemblance to the older man — the same eyes, the same shape of chin. If not a son, he was certainly family. 'If you choose death, you will both die slowly and painfully.'

The man lowered his head. 'I will take you to them,' he said softly, in Latin.

'Good.' Quintus pointed to the other boy.

'This one dies anyway. A warning.' He turned to Caius. 'Take this one elsewhere. I do not want him talking to the others. Stop his mouth, but leave him his tongue. Water for all of them, food for these two.'

Quintus sheathed his gladius and walked away as Caius called over comrades to help him move the prisoner, and slaves to bring water and pulse. He was troubled by what he had been told and found it difficult to believe. He also realised that he had not even asked about the prefect. He would return to that later. His immediate problems were a supposed lost group of soldiers and the threat of Dagaz. He intended to go in search of Galba, but realised he would be busy placating the ladies. He did not want to join them. He did not feel like conversation.

He heard a voice calling. It was Sextus who hailed him — he was coming from the direction of the tripod, and Quintus realised he must have been officiating at the burning of the tribesman's heart. He waved an encouraging hand as he walked across to the gate to see if the dead had gone. In the distance he could see the dust thrown up by the mounted patrol, the standards it carried identifying it. It was returning at a trot, not being pursued and, he gathered, having found no further enemy.

'The starfall, Sextus. Did you see it? Did it mean anything?'

Sextus had jogged across to join him. 'I saw it,' he said. 'It predicted the deaths of enemies. These men were doomed from the moment the stars tumbled from the sky.'

'So even their own gods do not protect them.' Quintus shook his head as he waved Sextus away.

XXIII: BON FORTUNA

Below the gate the slaves had been efficient. There were no bodies left, although the evidence of the action remained — most notably the long trail of blood that wound through the grass down the hill. The approaching cavalry would obliterate it. In addition, a fire smouldered fitfully.

A slave tended the fire and bowed his head at the centurion. Quintus did not wish to interfere with or interrupt what he was doing. Consciously, he moved away from him. Unconsciously, he made his way to where the animals were tethered. He was from farming stock, used to animals. He pulled some grass and offered it to the mule, his hand resting on its head.

'Am I being told lies, or is there more I should know?' he asked it.

'Sir?'

Quintus looked up. It was one of the Macedonian slaves.

'I am well, Maxim. Just faced with a problem.' Quintus smiled. 'I came to see if the mule could help.'

Maxim retuned his smile. He, too, talked to animals.

Though he did not mean to share information with a slave, Quintus found himself continuing to muse aloud. 'I am told that there are legionaries in the forest. That they are cowards and deserters. I am told that this Dagaz requires our eagle in order to free his people. We have rescued the commander's women, but now they are a liability. I am told our commander is held hostage, but I do not know where. They, too, want the eagle for his safe return. What would you advise?'

Though Maxim had been asked a question, he did not know if he should speak. Quintus encouraged him, waving a hand in the direction of the beast that stood mute between them. 'Speak freely. None but us and the mule will ever know it.'

'Master,' said Maxim, bowing his head, 'I was always advised that it is best to keep the women happy. Plan a rescue for the husband, the commander, and all else will fall into place.'

'You have a wife, Maxim?' Quintus asked without thinking.

The slave's eyes misted. He spoke in a whisper. 'A long time ago, master. In a different world.'

Quintus felt like apologising for the hurt he had caused, but his rank prohibited it. Maxim's head was now lowered, his slave mark clearly visible.

'About your business,' said Quintus brusquely, ashamed of his own stupidity.

In another life, Maxim the Macedonian ex-soldier would have been a friend. As Maxim bowed and left, the sight of him somehow reminded Quintus of his oath to his friend and mentor Ursus. He felt surreptitiously for the secret pocket that Jovan had sewn for him. He did this often, unconsciously. This was the place where he kept the will of Ursus and the copper armlet his friend had received for valour from the general's own hand. He gripped the metal and prayed that he would be able to fulfil his vow.

He returned to where the captives were tied. The older man and the younger boy were bound back-to-back; the other youth had been removed. Quintus took off his helmet and squatted down. He spoke quietly to the man. 'I think you understand me well enough.'

'Perhaps I do,' the man admitted.

Quintus spoke slowly and clearly. 'The youth will die, as a warning and an example. It could be quickly or slowly. Your boy here could join him. It is as easy to erect two crosses as one. Their fate lies in your hands.' He nodded towards the boy that remained silent. 'Speak true and this son or nephew of yours lives.'

'You are right. Sister-son,' the man admitted reluctantly. 'What do you want to know?'

'The tribe that led us here — that we were following — you know who they were?'

'A branch of the Raeti, sundered from the main tree. A mountain tribe who came to the foothills for peace. They are known as the Vindelici, I think.'

'And this is their land?'

'Disputed, as is much of our territory. Our main border is the great river. Other borders are —' he searched for an appropriate term — 'fluid.'

'Where is their city?'

The man managed a smile, the Roman was naive if he thought the Germani went to the trouble of building cities. 'There is no city. There is what we would call an oppidum, a fortified settlement.' The man's tone became optimistic. 'We can take you there.'

'What about Dagaz?' Quintus asked.

'He, too, has a base, hidden in the hills beyond the eastern bank — but not so well hidden that those who wish to join him cannot do so. My tribe — my family really, a mere sliver compared to the Suebi or the Tencteri — refused his offer of "protection". That is why he oppressed us.'

'Is this base where they would keep a hostage?'

'That or the oppidum, depending on who holds him,' said the man. 'I can help you if you spare us.'

'We shall see.' Quintus stood up, tucked his helmet under his arm, and pulled his tunic straight. He decided that now he wanted both Galba and the women to hear what he had to say.

The commander's tent was already busy. Quintus saw the back of the decurion as he dipped in under the flap. He followed him into the tent, catching the last of the report.

'We found no enemy, sir,' the decurion was saying, 'nor any sort of village or settlement. We found no further sign of anyone.'

Marcus was also reporting. He had scoured the land towards the riverbank without finding any further natives or any evidence of habitation.

'Their women?' Quintus asked out of curiosity, knowing that wives and children often followed tribesmen to battles, sometimes fighting alongside them.

'No sign,' the decurion announced, whilst Marcus shook his head.

'We keep up our guard, just in case,' said Galba, then turned to Marcus. 'Tell the men they can stand easy, optio. We leave in the morning.' The decurion was also dismissed. 'You, too, see to your mounts.' Both saluted formally and left the tent.

The ladies had not been present for the reports, but were only behind curtains. They had heard everything. They came forward and sat on the stools. Galba was already occupying the commander's chair. There was space for Quintus next to Aurelia, but he decided to remain standing, addressing himself to Antonia Flavia.

'Two things, lady. I think I have information that may lead us to the deserters.'

She nodded. 'And the second?'

'I am fairly certain that I know where your husband is being held. I think we could mount a rescue.'

'What about the renegade, Dagaz?' Galba asked. 'How is he to be punished?'

'With overwhelming force, sir,' Quintus explained. 'To rescue the commander, we need to take this fortified hill, this oppidum of the Vindelici — the tribe that first led us then betrayed us. That clears our way along this bank of the Rhenus. We carry on with our mission to meet up with General Drusus. He is marching this way with not just a legion, but an army. Dagaz will not be able to stand against him. When we report what he did, I am sure the general will wish to destroy him as much as we do. I have information from our captives. They can lead us to him, to his base.'

'So, *bon Fortuna*. Rescuing my husband becomes part of your mission, not a side issue.' Antonia Flavia spoke archly and looked searchingly at Galba. Clearly, Quintus thought, there had been discussions here.

'It would seem so, madam,' Galba said, without enthusiasm. 'The place where he is held lies in our path. Dagaz can wait. What about the deserters?'

'They could also lie in our path,' Quintus said. 'If they do not, we can hunt them later.'

'They will not go free?' Aurelia asked.

'On my life, they will not,' Quintus promised.

'Thank you, centurion,' said Antonia Flavia, though it was not clear to which of the men she was speaking. 'First we rescue my noble husband; the rest follows.' She rose imperiously. 'The Lady Aurelia and I would like to wash. Will you arrange for hot water and privacy?'

'And for someone that might pass as a body slave,' Aurelia added.

'Cornus, make it so.' Galba knew that the freedman would be within earshot. As ever, he was standing in the shadows.

'Sir,' he acquiesced.

Quintus and Galba followed him out of the tent.

'There is something else you should know,' Quintus said as they walked. 'The prisoners tell me that there are more than our runaways in the forest. There are other legionaries — a bigger group. I am not sure I believe them.'

'Nor I, centurion. It is a lie.' Galba laughed dismissively. 'If we find any, we will whip them and add them to our ranks.' He moved on. 'In the morning, we send scouts to the front, half a century at least, double the usual numbers. I think Optio Marcus could lead them. Then the other centuries can travel in a column, cavalry and pack animals to the rear. We have no carriage for the women; they will have to ride. They will need escorts provided by the decurion. I will not lose them again. Are our prisoners to be executed?'

'One of them deserves it. The others we will need.'

'I will deal with the deserters tonight — or at least, their comrades will. Your prisoner — do you want him whipped, or just crucified?'

'Whipped first, I think. Though our patrols found no-one, I cannot believe that our enemies will not be watching.'

XXIV: LEX EXERCITUS

The two centurions parted, Galba to his horse, Quintus making sure the orders and dispositions were passed on to the other officers. Quintus knew exactly what Galba intended for the deserters. Under the law of the army, the *lex exercitus*, the centurion had no choice. They would die.

Now that the men had been told to stand easy, they could take the opportunity to clean their weapons and armour and, if they could find a slave and hot water, wash their tunics and even their cloaks. Many fires had pots of water boiling on them, and the legionaries already squatted down in little more than undershorts and caligae. Some were being scraped clean by slaves with strigils. The camp itself was festooned with washing drying in the warm sunlight.

Quintus walked to where his old comrades were pitched, to a place of familiarity and friendship. He had been first a member, then the leader of his contubernium, and he still thought of this tent, these men, as his home. They, too, treated him more as a comrade than an officer, especially in private. They shared the shame of punishment and the pain of losing three of their number, popular men who had died bravely. But they embraced their replacements.

Now they had lost Marcus and Tullius to another century, whilst Rufus and Aquila had duties as signiferi. Vetruvius had deliberately avoided any sort of promotion and remained a gambler and womaniser but, like Sextus, a charmer. They had also lost Quintus and Crassus to the officers' quarters, but only when there were any.

In these small marching camps, Quintus and Crassus often chose to eat with their old comrades, sometimes to sleep in the tent with them. Marcus and Tullius, along with Piso the wrestler and Alba the capsarius, would drift back often to share food and comradeship. Sextus had the knack of always finding flesh of some sort — a chicken, a hare, sometimes a pig or a lamb. On good days, he also produced wine.

In Hispania, this contubernium had adopted the Macedonian slaves Maxim and Jovan as their own. These two had served the group since they had marched away from the legionary base of Lucus Augustus, and had been with them in Britannia and Germania. Whilst both had been soldiers in their former lives, Jovan was adept at many things — reading, writing and reckoning on behalf of the men, whilst Maxim was an excellent cook.

Quintus joined the group now, sitting on an upturned pot and placing his helmet on the ground. The slaves helped him to unlace his armour and he removed his own baltea and cingulum. He pulled his tunic over his head, handing it to Maxim to wash. The sun was high and hot, and it would dry quickly. Once the laundry was done, he would order one of the slaves to scrape his back. Rufus and Vetruvius, who had become fast friends, ribbed him about his rank and the state of the crest on his helmet. Rufus pretended that it was an animal and attempted to feed it hard biscuit. Vetruvius reckoned he could get it to do tricks and talked to it as if it were a puppy.

When Sextus returned and joined in, the jokes became coarser and the laughter louder. Quintus took it in good part. It was Jovan who became offended, and removed the helmet with a tart, 'I will comb the crest out, sir.'

'And feed it liver,' called Vetruvius.

'And polish its shiny arse,' laughed Sextus.

The jokes over, they fell to playing knucklebones and telling tall tales, feeling like a family once more. As the afternoon waned, sun-dried tunics were returned, clean and mended, armour was scoured and leather was polished. Most of those legionaries not on duty did not tighten the straps on their chest armour, but all wore it. There were deserters to punish and prisoners to execute. They knew there would be an assembly before nightfall. As the sun sank towards the horizon, the plaintive sound of the cornu rang out, ending on a long downward note.

It had been more than two years since the cornicen had last been told to sound this particular series of notes. Not all of the legionaries would remember it, especially not the new men, the rabbits. But Centurion Felix would be there to instruct them. All the men had to put on full armour and weaponry, including helmets and swords. They carried shields, spears and cloaks, but no packs or satchels. They must form a hollow square, a punishment square for a legionary punishment.

The men knew that they were to witness the chastising of the deserters, possibly even be involved themselves. No slaves, servants, auxiliaries or women would be allowed to watch. The deserters would be whipped, then beaten to death by their comrades — quickly or slowly, depending on their popularity and their crime. Desertion was unforgivable.

'Dress the lines,' Quintus barked, as the men hurried across to the space that, in a proper camp, would be between the porta praetoria and the tribunal. There was no tribunal, no alae for the standards and sacrifices, just the commander's tent in the centre of the castra. The men formed the square in front of it. Quintus ordered silence.

The day had not yet begun to cool. The air was still and sullen, not a whisper of wind disturbed it. Conversation was

154

muted, relegated to grumblings and quiet questions about what was happening. Sweat prickled on soldiers' foreheads and the backs of their necks, making focales damp. The flies had become lazy, indolent, crawling rather than buzzing. The sound of slaps that announced their deaths punctuated the assembly.

Though shadows were already long, it would be well over an hour before the sun finally set. By then the men would be dismissed back to their tents, readying themselves for the march the following day.

Quintus looked across at the commander's tent. 'Crassus, make sure that tent is sealed. The commander's ladies are in it. They are not permitted to witness. Keep the guard on it.' Crassus saluted and detailed men to make sure the sides of the tent were rolled down and pegged.

Galba was mounted, his helmet strapped to his head, his cloak pinned at his shoulder. The men parted so that he could enter the square. Aquila walked ahead of him, the head of the wolfskin he wore snarling above his helmet. The shining eagle was accompanied by the cohort standard. Even the imago was here. Each centurion stood with his own century, each forming a side of the square. They ordered the shields grounded, so that a solid metal wall faced the beaten earth of the centre. They commanded silence as Galba arrived, the shields closing behind him. The standards of each century were in place at the corners.

'Proceed, centurion,' commanded Galba.

Quintus waved an arm and, from the opposite side, the square opened to allow the two deserters to be dragged in. They were in a sorry state already, wearing dirty tunics, with no weapons, belts or caligae.

There was no whipping post; instead, they were each tied beneath the weight of a yoke, arms outstretched above their shoulders. They were very different. Hirtis, once corpulent, had lost some of his fat, but none of his swagger. He still held his head high. Bizarrely, one finger was lifted to make some legal point or other. Somehow, it seemed, he still believed that he had been unjustly taken. He was ready to defend himself and, indeed, began to speak. Quintus swung his vine staff almost casually, catching the side of the man's head. He staggered and dropped to one knee. It looked like he would continue speaking until Quintus raised his arm again in threat.

By contrast, the other deserter dropped to his knees and bowed his head. He was a younger man, thin, clean-shaven and with a full head of dark hair. If his comrades at least half forgave him, they might place an obol under his tongue for Charon.

'*Fustuarium*, Rufus,' muttered Sextus out of the corner of his mouth. 'We have seen it before in Hispania. It is not pleasant.'

Rufus did not reply. As a signifer he had a duty to the standard he carried. The imaginifer cast a dark glance at him. Being caught for chattering in the ranks would shame them both.

Galba took a tablet from one of the escort and handed it to Quintus, who read out the full name and tribe of the first deserter, then the punishment. 'From the legion, for dishonouring it, twenty lashes. The rest is in the hands of your comrades.'

Quintus signalled to the men of Century Two, and two soldiers stepped forward. They were part of a short rank that stood apart. They carried no shields and wore no cloaks or helmets. They were unarmed. Their victim would not receive the mercy of a clean death. There were seven of them waiting, the other members of the deserter's contubernium. The task of these first two was to rip the tunic from the back of the deserter, exposing the flesh. A knife slit the material and a hard tug tore it.

The deserter's broad back was criss-crossed with white lines — this man had been whipped before, and not just once. What for, Quintus did not know — but it could not have been anything serious, otherwise the man would not have survived. A serious offence involved the flagrum, the short whip that was furnished with metal spikes to rip the skin. These scars were clean and straight. Petty theft or disobedience, Quintus thought.

The men stepped back to allow the optio room to swing.

XXV: VESICA

It was the job of Marcus, as optio of the Second, to administer the punishment. He approached with the simple whip in hand, the short-handled three-tongued leather scourge, knotted at the end to help it travel, but with nothing else attached. The man remained on his knees, bowed down by the weight of the yoke. He raised one hand and Marcus moved his head to listen to him. Whatever he said, Marcus repeated it to Galba, who nodded to one of the legionaries.

A short length of leather was passed from him to the optio and Marcus thrust it between the man's teeth. He bit hard and knelt as upright as he could. An unpopular man, Quintus knew, would not be given the benefit of something to bite on. He knew that it did nothing for the pain; it was to stop the guilty man from shaming himself by crying out.

Marcus did not hold back, but nor did he show any enthusiasm for the task. He counted out loud as he struck. The first blow raised a red weal on the man's exposed back, the second another, and bright droplets of blood where the two stripes crossed. A third brought more blood. The man groaned but did not cry out. The crack of the final blow fell into absolute silence. After a whipping, a man's back was generally splashed with a mixture of water and vinegar, but this did not happen now. Why waste it on the dead? The man was still conscious. He spat the strap from his mouth — almost bitten through and bloodstained — and attempted to rise. No-one helped him.

Instead, Marcus waved across the man's contubernium. They crowded around him for a short time, then stepped backwards.

The man lay dead. That his death had taken little time was a measure of his popularity with his comrades. Instead of prolonging his end, one had placed a boot on his back and, with a twist and snap, broken his neck. Someone might even have paid his fare across the Styx.

The dead man's comrades had agreed to forgive him. Their decanus had come to Quintus with the request that the man merely be whipped, rather than executed. Quintus refused: the man would either die from the whipping or, if his comrades refused the task, by being nailed to a tree and left there. Fast or slow, it was their choice. If they refused to kill him, they faced a whipping themselves. They had chosen to kill him mercifully and now claimed the body, the ranks parting to let them through. It was their right to do as they wished with it. It would not stop the man's name being expunged from the records.

Hirtis was not so lucky. He found himself unable to stand, and witnessed the other man's sentence from a kneeling position. He had many enemies, even in his own tent. He was sly and nasty, as well as being a bore. The men of his contubernium carried many surface wounds on their backs — the results of Hirtis' meanness. He never justified his actions nor sought forgiveness, instead being — in his own eyes — right all the time. An expert on everything even when no expertise was required. He had gained a nickname, but not an affectionate one.

They called him *vesica*, the word for an empty bladder, a boastful man. No-one was quite sure why he had joined the legions. It was clearly not the sort of life he would have chosen for himself. Perhaps the people of his family, or his village, had sought to be rid of him and paid the recruiters to take him. Quintus knew of such cases.

Despite the yoke and the blow to his head, he was still claiming that he had been forced to follow against his will. What he was forgetting was that in *lex exercitus*, the law of the army, he had already been found guilty. It was not like the law courts in front of the Curia; there was no-one arguing for and against. He had fled and had been caught, and was therefore guilty. That was the extent of the trial.

He was part of the Third Century, to Centurion Marius' disgust. His contubernium waited for him as the others of the Second had done. On a signal from Quintus, the charge and sentence having been read over the top of his pleadings, two came and ripped the tunic from his back. They were not gentle.

Caius was the optio of Century Three and took the whip from Marcus. To him, this was an unpleasant job that had needed doing for a long time. Many of them, from Galba downwards, had attempted to turn this man into a soldier, but none had succeeded. They had given him many chances to redeem himself.

It was harder for Caius, as the victim was already low to the ground. The second blow caused Hirtis to both cry out and fall forward onto his face. By the time Caius had called 'thirteen', Hirtis had stopped crying out. Caius paused and bent down to the victim.

'Water?' Quintus asked, assuming that he needed to be brought round.

Caius shook his head and looked to Galba for direction.

'Continue,' Galba ordered, though it seemed clear that the man was dead. 'The sentence was twenty.'

Caius obeyed, the saggy flesh quaking under his blows like a jellyfish stranded on the shore. Though more skin was opened, little more blood flowed.

The men of Hirtis' contubernium had bound their fists with cloth. They intended his death to be long and painful, the result of many blows. When Caius reached twenty and fell back in with his century, the men were eager to be called forward.

They were disappointed. After just a few kicks, they realised Hirtis was gone. He was, indeed, an empty bladder, deflated and dead.

'Take the body,' Quintus ordered the contubernium. 'It is yours. Do with it as you will.' There would, he knew, be no coin for this man, no-one paying his fare for Charon's boat. He would wander as a ghost, telling his story to everyone he met, still believing he was in the right. His body, Quintus suspected, would be tipped into the latrine before it was filled in.

As the body was dragged off, Galba addressed the men. 'We have information from our captives,' he said. 'Our commander is held in an oppidum, a sort of fortified settlement somewhere between us and the forces of General Drusus. We strike camp at sunrise and follow the bank of the river in search of this place. When we find it, we take it and rescue the prefect. When we reach the general, we avenge ourselves on the renegades.' He did not mention Dagaz by name. He would not risk showing him respect that he did not deserve.

'One of our captives proved defiant,' he continued. 'He will be punished in the morning light so that spies of his tribe can see him die.' He looked at Crassus. 'Optio, be ready; he will be flogged before he is executed. We will leave him behind to send a message to his people.'

As he turned his horse to leave, Galba nodded to Quintus who, in turn, instructed the cornicen to sound the dismissal. Within minutes the area was once more empty.

Over the next half hour, men moved swiftly, changing duty with guards and sharing the story of the two deaths they had witnessed. In a corner outside the perimeter, a small fire burned brightly; the first man to die had earned a pyre.

As the false dawn brought a wash of pale colour to the eastern horizon, the camp was swiftly struck. The ditch surrounding the castra was filled in, the mound tumbled into it. The centuries formed up, standards aloft. There was no carriage for the women so, escorted by cavalry, they rode. They refused to travel in a cart like baggage, nor entrust themselves again to a litter.

Before they left, there was a brief assembly. The Germani prisoner who had defied Quintus was brought forward and, with little ceremony, flogged. He resisted crying out to begin with, but once the floodgates were opened, he wailed and sobbed. Legionaries carried him away as the cohort moved out.

The Cantabrians rode with the wagons, and the Anatolians marched at the rear of the legionaries. Where the commander's tent had been, a hole was dug and there now stood the trunk of a tree with a single branch at around the height of a tall man lashed to it. It was the best the men could find at short notice. The Germani youth was nailed to it, stripped naked with his arms outstretched and head lolling. He did not cry out anymore, but had grunted with pain as he was fixed in place.

As the centuries passed out of the clearing, Quintus gave a whispered instruction to his optio.

'Break his legs, Crassus, after the last of the wagons has left. It will quicken his passing and will be no less of a message.'

XXVI: CASTRA INCOGNITA

The captive uncle and nephew — whom Quintus still believed were more likely to be father and son — went ahead with Marcus and a much larger advance party than the twenty pioneers.

The prisoners were unarmed, but otherwise walked freely, unbound, each with a legionary as escort. They claimed the oppidum was large, but hidden — at least to those who did not know where to look.

Forty minutes behind this group the cohort marched easily on paths and beaten tracks, making good time, although it could only proceed as fast as the slowest wagon. Here and there were dark patches of wet ground — clearly in the winter this was more of a marsh — and the cohort was slowed as carts were manhandled across.

The day was once again hot, the sky containing only high clouds, thin, translucent and insubstantial. There were scattered oak trees that threw their branches across the track, providing welcome shade. The cohort stopped to cross a small stream, letting the horses drink and the legionaries fill their waterskins. The stream was wide, but with little more than a film of water in it, flowing shallow and noisy over polished rocks. The women followed the example of the cavalry and dismounted to lead their horses to the water, whilst the auxiliaries and Century Four, who had drawn the duty, remained on guard.

'Do we know how far it is to this settlement?' Antonia Flavia asked Galba, drawing him to one side. 'Is it a matter of hours or days?'

She could not contemplate the thought of it being any longer if her husband was truly there. Galba shook his head and repeated the question to Quintus, who had just finished splashing water on his face.

'The captives could only say that it is not far,' Quintus soothed her. 'But what distance that is in their eyes, we do not know.' He continued to wring out his focale and tie it back around his neck. 'I think it is days rather than either hours or weeks.'

A disturbance interrupted their conversation. Agnus, who was riding with the leading group, cantered towards them down the long slope. He had won a friendly contest with Crassus and now rode the black colt.

'Let him through,' Quintus shouted. 'What is it, Agnus?' The scout's breathlessness and haste made him fear the worst. 'Not an attack?'

'No, sir. No attack. We have found something strange — a settlement. But not the oppidum. It appears to be a Roman camp.' He paused and shook his head. 'Well, not a Roman camp — more a barbarian camp occupied by men in Roman dress. There are no streets, no watchtowers, no standards, no gates — but the men I saw through the trees appear to be Roman.'

'Dagaz,' spat Quintus, forming an immediate opinion. 'Wearing the clothes he stole from our pioneers.'

'It could be,' Agnus said hesitantly, 'but I saw little in the way of yellow hair and beards.'

'They do not all have the same colouring,' said Quintus dismissively. 'Did you see any evidence of the runes that seem so important to them?'

'No, sir, but I did not get that close. It was a glimpse through the trees.'

'How many, do you think?' Galba asked.

'Hard to say, sir.' Agnus turned to the senior man. 'Tens rather than hundreds, and they were scattered over a wide area.' His head tipped to one side and he sounded puzzled. 'They seemed to be at ease, sir. They mounted no guards or defences.'

'Then it must be Dagaz,' insisted Quintus. 'This is their land.'

'What do the captives say?' Antonia Flavia had been listening to the report.

'Nothing yet, lady.' Agnus glanced at Antonia, unsure if he was permitted to directly address her. 'As I left, the optio was taking the captives to look.'

'Do you think they have my husband amongst them?'

Agnus shook his head. 'I saw no prisoners, lady — but it is possible. I did not see all of their camp.'

'Go back with him, centurion,' Galba commanded Quintus. 'Take six of your best men. Find out if this is Dagaz or some other.' He made sure the Lady Antonia could hear him. 'Do not spook them, Quintus; our commander may be held by them.' Antonia Flavia inclined her head slightly, a gesture of thanks. 'Do not fight them until we have all arrived.'

Quintus immediately turned to his front rank. 'Sextus, Vetruvius, with me.' He looked to where two others stood. 'Aquila and Rufus, you know I would take you, but your place is with the standards.'

They nodded in agreement, although the disappointment showed on both their faces.

'Crassus.' The blacksmith stepped forward, eager to serve, but he too was to be disappointed. 'You must stay and take command of Century One. Again, you know I would take you if I could.' Quintus then called across the shallow valley. 'Caius

Sergio Nerva, evocatus and optio of the Third, Alba of the Fourth, report.'

Caius needed the permission of his centurion, but Marius was happy to wave him forward. Felix was perhaps less willing to release Alba — a capsarius was always useful — but he nodded his assent reluctantly.

'You will be mounted. Travel light but armed,' Quintus ordered. 'You can leave your satchels and packs, but bring spears and shields.'

They needed no orders to carry a gladius. It was with them always. They set off at a trot, following Agnus. The colt was spirited, and they had to ride hard to keep up. In time, Agnus gestured for them to slow down and pointed ahead to where a stand of juniper stood out on a low hillside. 'The optio is beneath those trees. I will tell him that you are coming.'

'We will wait for your signal.' Quintus nodded as Agnus urged the colt forward in a brisk gallop.

'Where does his energy come from?' Vetruvius asked as his horse took the opportunity to graze from a grassy bank beneath one of the solitary oaks. Sextus halted beside him. 'He must have a pact with Neptune,' he said half-jokingly, the sea god being the patron of horses.

Caius Sergio was also keen to catch his breath. He was the oldest of them, but unwilling to admit that he might be a little less fit. He leant his shoulder on the cool trunk of the great tree.

'Me and this cavalry nag need a rest,' he said, patting the horse affectionately.

'Not now,' said Sextus. 'Look.'

The silhouette of a mounted man waved them forward. 'Come,' Quintus said. 'The trees are not far.'

They set off, feeling the heat of the sun as soon as they were out of the shadows. One of Marcus' group came down to meet them and escort them in. 'The scout warned us of your coming, sir. The optio is this way.'

Marcus and his men had found a defensive position: a thick holly hedge fighting for space amongst the straight trunks of the juniper trees behind it. They had put this at their backs, and further reinforced the side of the position with cut branches of holly. It was basic, but effective. It was the highest point in the immediate landscape and provided a view across both the leaf-shaped valley that they had traversed and the more heavily wooded ground in front of them.

Quintus saluted and greeted the optio. 'Marcus, well met, old friend.' The two grasped each other by the forearm and briefly embraced. Quintus spotted the man who was Marcus' shadow, and greeted him, too. 'Tullius, well met.'

Tullius returned the salute, without enthusiasm but not disrespectfully. He was not about to embrace anyone. The twin scar he wore down one cheek made him look ever more dolorous. Marcus grinned at the reunion, and Tullius' face twitched, but he only managed a weak smile. Only the two of them sat in their makeshift fort; the rest of the party were spread as pickets around the trees.

Sextus also greeted the two evocati. 'Marcus, Tullius, good fortune to you.'

Quintus could not wait for further formalities. 'Is it Dagaz, Marcus? Can we look forward to avenging our comrades?'

'It is not,' said Marcus glumly. 'Tullius, fetch them here.'

Tullius left, swiftly returning with the two captives, the upper arm of each held in his strong grip. The boy hardly spoke, half-hiding behind the older man, who spoke clearly enough when ordered to do so. 'Not Dagaz, sir. Not even any of the tribes of the Germani. These men are Roman.'

'Tribesmen wearing Roman gear?' Tullius shook the man roughly.

'No, sir. They are of none of the tribes. They wear the wrong clothes, style their hair the wrong way, speak the wrong language.' He looked to Quintus and Marcus. 'I have heard them talk, sir. They speak the same tongue as you. They speak Latin.'

'So these are the lost Romans of whom you spoke?' Quintus asked.

'They are, sir.' The captive shook his head. 'They have moved from their previous camp, otherwise I would have recognised them sooner.'

'Who accompanied you?'

Two legionaries, middle-aged men who looked reliable, stepped forward. 'We did, sir.'

'And you saw for yourselves?'

'We did, sir. We could have walked straight into the camp without challenge. They are not prepared for battle. There are not even pickets posted.'

'How far?'

The legionary pointed. 'The hill dips where you see that dark line of trees. They are beneath it, by a tributary of the great river.'

'Go back the way we have come and report to Centurion Galba,' Quintus ordered Agnus, who was standing a little way behind the captives. 'Tell him that it is not an enemy camp, and he can bring up the cohort. There is flat land, wood and water here. The campsite will be paced out ready.' He looked at Marcus, who nodded agreement.

There was enough light left; the sun was still well above the western horizon. Quintus turned to Agnus. 'If I am not back when you arrive, tell Centurion Galba that I have gone to look at our strange natives, who appear to be Roman. Tell him I perceive no threat from them. I do not think we will have to fight.'

The four men who had travelled with him were keen to see the camp for themselves, as was Marcus, so it was a group of six who set out with the older captive, this time on foot. The boy stayed behind, Tullius under orders to kill him if there was any whiff of treachery. Tullius also undertook to make sure that the castra was marked out.

The group jogged across to the place the legionary had indicated, ducking down and moving stealthily over the last couple of stades. To their left, a river flowed down, the fullest that they had seen in a while. It fell noisily over a couple of steep drops before widening and bubbling over tumbled stones.

Reaching the ridge in silence, their progress further masked by the song of the water, they dropped and looked through the trees.

What they saw amazed them.

XXVII: STULTUS STULTUS

An area of the riverbank was partially cleared; they could see where trees had been felled or roughly cut off at the knee. There had also been many fires. The bigger trees, though their lower limbs were hacked off and their trunks were in places charred, still stood. Here they were mostly beech, with a few oak, but amongst them, high above the canopy, were stands of spruce. They had shed a great mass of green needles, which, like deep snow on a winter's eve, provided soft terrain and muffled the legionaries' steps.

The busy melody played by the water as it weaved its way between boulders and tumbled over cascades was punctuated by the grating sounds of men. The sharp fragrance of the needles was blighted by the rank smells of human activity. The sounds jarred discordantly with the natural music. Smudges of smoke lurked beneath the canopy and the distinct tang of charcoal revealed where trees had been set alight.

A noxious stench emanated from a crude uncovered latrine, mingling with the smell of cooking meat. A path made muddy by many feet led down to the water's edge. The watchers pulled back instinctively as a pair of comrades approached with waterskins. They laughed and joked with each other in Latin, clapping one another on the back. They also wore, as no native ever would, sturdy caligae on their feet.

One lifted his tunic and was about to piss when the other, waterskin already in the stream, shouted and roughly pushed him. 'Downstream! By all the gods, go downstream!' The other shrugged and, having started, moved the direction of the amber flow to the far bank, narrowly missing the bent figure of his companion.

'Indiscipline and stupidity,' Quintus cursed under his breath. '*Stultus stultus*. Utter fool.'

Because of the trees and the many bushes, it was hard to see how many men were camped here. There were no tents, but a number of rough shelters, built in the standard way that all legionaries were taught: one long branch wedged partway up a tree, in the crook between trunk and branch, with crosspieces leant against this spine. Some of the crosspieces appeared to be legionary spears.

Quintus estimated that there were fewer than fifty men in total — the addition of Marcus' and his own group might just about produce a century. He could see no standards or vexilla. There were also no crested helmets or hastilia, no sign of cornicenes or signiferi. The officers seemed to have either escaped or died. If these men were deserters, they had most likely killed them.

There were eight to ten horses, loosely tied to a picket line at the edge of the forest. No-one appeared to have charge of them. Quintus could see no mules, carts or provisions. For the most part the men he could see wore tunics, baltea and cingulum and, to his relief, still had their swords scabbarded in their baldrics. Without the fearsome gladius, the Roman legionary was at less than half his strength. Quintus knew that separating a soldier from his sword should be like peeling the bark from an oak — difficult, if not impossible.

Some wore lorica laminata, or parts of it, whilst a good number had clearly unlaced and discarded the regulation armour. Over some shoulders, there were cloaks, although a good few wore German furs instead. *So*, thought Quintus, *they have either fought or traded.*

He had seen enough. He signalled the watchers to move backwards and they wriggled away from their viewing points, not speaking until they were out of earshot of the camp.

'Well,' said Marcus, still amazed. 'Not even basic hygiene. What a tangled mess.'

'A mess, indeed,' Quintus agreed. 'But whose mess? Who are they, and where do they come from?'

Sextus offered an explanation. 'They are a remnant of the Alaudae, of the defeated legion. They can't be anything else.' His tone was dismissive. 'Deserters who are turning into a Germani tribe.'

'They lived through the winter,' sad Marcus. 'That in itself is amazing.'

Caius, Alba and Vetruvius were all of the Fifth. They had survived the disaster that was called Clades Lolliana, the total defeat of Legio Five by Maelo. Maelo was the chieftain of the Sugambri who had united many of the warring tribes in order to strike at Rome. Maelo had led not only his own people, but also the tribes of the Cherusci, the Suebi, the Tencteri and the Usipetes. Somehow he had persuaded all of their chieftains to join him and cross the great river when it was at its lowest. Maelo had tortured, crucified and beheaded the officers of a whole legion. And now Dagaz, their newest foe, claimed to be his son.

'Is Sextus right? Do you recognise any of these men?' Marcus asked the three legionaries of the Fifth.

'They are unshaven and dirty. I would not be used to seeing them like this,' said Alba, shaking his head. 'Unless they were of my own contubernium, or perhaps my own century, I doubt I would recognise them unless I had treated them for injuries.'

Vetruvius was equally noncommittal. 'There are none I would pick out — not from this distance. Perhaps if we were a little closer.' He was as scandalised as Sextus. 'I did not recognise either of the two fools in the river. The one who wanted to piss in the drinking water should be flogged.'

'The problem with the Roman legionary is that, apart from hair colour or shaving habits, they all look much the same,' said Caius.

'They carry different scars,' added Marcus. 'But you are right, from a distance each one could be described as a "big man" and "wide shouldered". On the whole, if there is no distinguishing feature, these men are much the same as bees in a hive.'

'The beekeeper would know,' Sextus said.

'But they have lost their beekeepers, their officers,' said Caius. 'I do think that I recognise at least one. One who might have been mistaken for one of the Germani. He was standing by one of the fires — he had fair hair, long moustaches, a broken nose and a battered ear. He's not from my century, but I would wager he has scars on his back. I think I have seen him whipped.'

'Any larks' wings?' Marcus asked, knowing that the Fifth had been raised by Divus Julius in Gaul, and adopted the Gallic custom of wearing representations of larks' wings on their helmets.

'I could not see,' said Caius.

Marcus turned his attention to the centurion. 'Do you think they are from the Larks, Quintus? Are they deserters?'

'Larks, yes, I think. Deserters? I don't know.' Quintus addressed the group. 'You four, stay here and keep watch on them. Run back quickly if they show any sign of moving out — although I think it unlikely. Keep yourselves hidden. I do not want them warned. I will send relief after sundown.' He turned to Marcus. 'You and I will report. I will consult Galba over what to do with them. At least they do not hold the commander.' He shook his head sadly. 'But if they are deserters, we have no choice but to execute them all.'

They set off back to the post beneath the juniper trees at a run. This was news that Galba needed to know quickly. Quintus did not think they had enough strength to take captive and then execute such a large number of men, deserters or not. He hoped that they had a good reason for being where they were, so that nothing would stand in the way of his using them to reinforce their own numbers. They had been short of men since the storms had scattered and sunk the cohort on its way from Hispania.

They were challenged by pickets as they approached the hilltop, but the passwords for the day still held, so they passed without incident. The little defensive position that Marcus had established was now a sort of command post, its holly walls strengthened, its approaches guarded.

Within it, Antonia Flavia and Aurelia sat on a low bench, made hurriedly and cleverly out of branches and stumps by legionary carpenters. Cloaks had been laid on it for comfort, but the women looked anything but comfortable. Though each held a cup of something, they were being ignored. Cornus, no longer a senator, stood in the semi-darkness behind them. Galba had his back to them all, issuing orders to officers and men, who scurried away to carry out their duties establishing a castra.

It had already taken shape. The camp had clear boundaries and a line of men were busy digging ditches. The juniper trees created a natural barrier, so were left alone, but other timber was brought in from the forest to make trestles on which to place the long branch that would be the front gate. Earth was being raised and shuttered to provide high spots to serve as watchtowers. Tent lines were established and a number of tents already erected, including the big one in the centre.

The information that the commander's tent was ready for the ladies was being delivered just as Quintus and Marcus arrived. Galba was detailing two legionaries to escort them to it, along with Cornus. Quintus noticed that Jovan was also in the party and smiled to himself. No doubt the Macedonian cousins had persuaded the ladies of their usefulness as cooks, if not as body slaves. Antonia stopped when she saw him. 'My husband, centurion?'

'Not there, lady. For certain. These are not even tribesmen.'

'Then we must make haste.' She turned to Galba.

'Agreed, lady. But we must solve this puzzle first.' He waved them on. 'I will bring you any information later.'

Reluctantly, she turned on her heel and left, allowing Galba to focus on Quintus.

'Well, what did you find?' he demanded. 'Not your Germani friend Dagaz, I trust?'

'No, sir. These are Roman legionaries. We think they are a remnant of Legio Five Alaudae — escaped from the clutches of the Germani chieftain Maelo.'

'Really? Escaped or ran? Are they deserters?'

'I am not sure, sir. They seem to be more lost than actively deserting. Our own deserters fled into the forest and may even have joined the enemy, but these are just … loitering.' He shook his head in bafflement. 'They seem like a herd that just moves to new pastures when the old is worked out. They seem to have no officers, so no leadership or direction. I think there is perhaps a story here that is not desertion.'

Galba harrumphed. 'How many?' he asked cautiously.

'Perhaps fifty or sixty,' Quintus estimated.

'Infantry or cavalry?'

'Infantry, sir. I saw no sign of cavalry, although there are a few horses.'

'Armed?'

'Sword and shield,' said Quintus. 'At least they seem to have retained their gladii. They have some spears, although some have been used to strengthen their accommodation.'

Galba sighed. He gestured towards the juniper trees behind him on the rocky outcrop. They had grown close together and their lower branches, heavily green, were intertwined. 'I cannot crucify fifty men on these,' he complained. 'And it would take at least three days to cut down enough timber from the forest. Even longer to scourge them all.' He lowered his voice. 'That is time we, and more importantly, the prefect, do not have. We cannot leave them behind us. We must bring them in, preferably without a fight. Once we've heard their story, we may have a better idea of what to do with them.'

'They could be re-sworn,' Quintus began hesitantly.

'Not if they are deserters.' Galba was grim. 'Deserters die.' Then he smiled. 'So they had better not be deserters, centurion, had they?'

Quintus understood. The problem had been handed to him. Either he brought them back with their honour somehow intact, so they could be re-sworn, or he did not bring them back at all.

XXVIII: AQUILA

Quintus saluted Galba and left. He needed to find Sextus. If anyone could devise a plan that would fulfil their aim, it was the rogue of the Suburra. He would also know which of the gods needed a sacrifice to ensure success.

'Mercury, of course,' Sextus laughed when asked. 'Or Laverna, although she is as likely to prove false to you as true. Mercury needs a goat or a lamb as an offering, neither of which we have, so a libation will have to do. He will understand.'

Quintus did not approve of the flippant way in which Sextus spoke of the gods, as if he was a friend of theirs. Being brought up by the Vestals certainly gave him the confidence but, Quintus believed, not the right. Tullius often muttered fervent prayers to counteract this disrespect.

Quintus mulled Sextus' idea over. If it worked, it would save a lot of fighting and might even allow the men in the valley to rejoin. If it did not, he would only have risked a few men, himself leading them.

He took the idea to Galba, who did not immediately approve. He certainly liked the idea of only risking a few men, but he did not like the idea of risking the eagle. In the end, he was persuaded that as it was not the eagle of the Ninth, his own legion, it could be used in the way Quintus suggested.

'We cannot wait here for you,' Galba said carefully. He had spoken at length with the ladies about the commander. His release was imperative. 'You understand that, Quintus?'

Quintus understood. The camp would be struck and the cohort on its way before the sun rose above the horizon.

Galba's responsibility was first to his commander and second, to his general. Ideally, the Germani captives would lead the cohort to the oppidum and it would be taken. The prefect would be rescued and the cohort would continue along the bank of the river to meet up with General Drusus. The legions of Rome would then wipe out Dagaz and his followers. But things rarely happened so smoothly.

Galba had conditions. 'Your optio will lead Century One in the meantime. You will have to catch up as best you can, when you can. If you can bring the lost sheep with you, so much the better.' Galba shrugged. 'If not, *sic vita*.'

There were four parties if the six Anatolians were counted separately. Quintus had twelve men with him, including a cornicen and the aquilifer. Both wore concealing blankets over their animal skin cloaks. Both had bare heads. The decurion led a group of ten, walking their horses. Around twenty of Quintus' own century concealed themselves behind this group. The Anatolian archers climbed and sat high in the branches, arrows pointed at the clearing. There were about forty men in total, as many as Galba would risk. Enough to put up a fight if necessary, Quintus hoped.

The needles beneath their feet muffled their tread. As they went out from under the spreading branches, into the grassland that opened between them and the tree-filled valley, the ground was wet with dew. They moved silently towards the camp by the river, cloaks wrapped tight to prevent noise and any glimmer of metal once the sun rose.

It was still dark when they set out, even the first pale glimmer of dawn was yet to appear. The sky was clear, the moon set, the pinpoints of the stars bright. The air was crisp and sharp, breath hanging on it in spectral threads. The swirling mist hid their feet so that they walked like ghosts, seeming to float above the solid earth.

Quintus' party went on foot, with just a single rider in their midst, the hooves of his mount muffled by the soft floor of the forest. That rider was Aquila, who kept the eagle swathed in cloth and held horizontally. He was himself bent low over the back of the horse. Rufus carried the standard of Century One, also out of sight. A few paces behind him, the single cornicen was ready to blow the alarm if there was any trouble. His first job was to convince the deserters that they had been discovered by Rome.

Quintus walked in the shadow of Rufus, half crouching. Caius and Sextus marched at his side, with Marcus and Tullius immediately behind. The optiones had removed their crested helms and hidden them behind their shields.

They were marked closely by the rest of the legionaries, who lay concealed. These men were ready to both raise the alarm and to rush into a fight if there was one. At a shout from any one of them, spears would be flung and swords raised in an attack that would rely mostly on surprise. The Anatolian archers would loose their arrows and the cavalry would also respond.

The horsemen were stationed just beyond the shallow valley in which the lost legionaries camped. The decurion had requested that they be allowed to deploy to the east, so that they could charge downhill if an attack was signalled. He led the troop round the shoulder of the hill, the riders at their horse's heads, gentling them.

Once in sight of the river and the camp, Quintus' party readied itself. The men split into smaller groups and strolled as if they were on a country ramble, so as not to reveal their discipline and organisation. Aquila slumped across the back of the horse as if he was weary. Some were challenged at the river, but not by any guard that had been posted for the purpose, merely by men who happened to be on the bank, filling waterskins, washing, and emptying their bladders. Quintus presumed the men thought his groups were either part of their own camp, returned from foraging, or new additions to their number. They did not seem bothered either way.

Carefully Quintus forded the river, the putative border of the camp, and was met with a scene of idleness and indiscipline. Half the camp seemed to still be asleep. Fires sputtered and men left tents and relieved themselves where they stood.

When all of his men had reached the far riverbank, Quintus barked an order and suddenly the band of weary pilgrims was no more. The legionaries threw back their cloaks and the signifer and aquilifer their blankets. The officers donned their crested helms and Rufus pulled his wolf's head up and raised the standard high. To the astonishment of the men in the camp, a shining eagle appeared above them, held tight by a wolfskin-cloaked aquilifer riding a tall roan stallion.

Quintus ordered the cornicen to sound his trumpet, the call that they had agreed. 'Sound the alarm, cornicen, as if the camp was under imminent attack.'

The cornicen put his lips to the curved tube of the cornu, blowing three short, shrill blasts, three long blasts, then an alternating panic of short-long, short-long, like the call and response of a pair of tawny owls. In the trees, the Anatolians drew back their arms and tautened the strings of their great bows. At the head of the valley the cavalry heard and mounted, then trotted into the clearing, displaying its own standards. As planned, the men hiding behind the trees also revealed themselves. The legionary force came together in a disciplined line, three deep, and marched forward.

On the ground it had the desired effect. The renegades dropped what they were eating or drinking, ran to grab spears and shields, crammed their helmets on their heads and drew their swords. This was all instinct — drilled into them by recruiters and junior officers on the Campus Martius.

This automatic reaction to the call was what Quintus was relying on. It gave way quickly to confusion. The men turned from side to side, ready to defend themselves, looking for an enemy that they could not see. What they could see was a force led by a standard, cavalry, the crests of officers, and an eagle.

It was the last that was most wondrous. The bronze bird, sharp-beaked, was tightly gripping the wreath on which it perched. Its wings were open, its head turned to the right, the side for victory. It no longer sat above the number and symbol of the Larks, but on a pole of Aquila's devising, its perch dressed with bright red ribbons. It was enough to make the men pause, giving Quintus the opening he needed. He shouted an order: 'I think we have their attention, cornicen. Blow the assembly.'

The note of the cornu changed, and the series of blasts for a general assembly rang out.

The men looked confused, but then confident voices emphasised the command. Marcus called on them to form up. Caius chivvied them into formation. Tullius glowered and straightened the lines. All the while, the eagle and the standard drew their eyes.

The Anatolians, for now, remained concealed.

Most of the legionaries in the camp formed themselves into rough lines almost before they realised what they were doing. Some were armed, but few armoured. By the time they were ready to complain, those still within their temporary shelters were being encouraged out by Quintus' men. A few resisted, but not many. They were silenced with a fist or the flat of a sword blade. The one that Caius had recognised was loudest. He received the hardest blow, a spear butt splitting his lip.

A small group on the far side of the ramshackle camp saw what was happening and, grabbing whatever they could, began to run, crouched low beneath the trees. Quintus saw them, pointed, and shouted, 'Archers!'

At once arrows whistled overhead and three of the men dropped. Another stumbled but carried on, helped by his comrades. He dragged a pinioned leg, the barbed shaft impeding his flight. A couple of men tried to lift the fallen. One they dragged a little way by his arms, but they were soon forced to abandon him. The rest encouraged each other on, dodging behind trees for cover.

'Do we follow, sir?' Caius called, ready to take a squad after them.

'Leave them,' Quintus commanded with a scoff. 'They look like the sort that will starve if left to their own devices.'

That appeared to be the last of the resistance. The deserters were cowed and overawed, especially now that they were aware of the archers in the trees. They were surrounded by legionaries, weapons drawn, the circle closed by a group of mounted cavalry. An imperial eagle, a god, looked down on them.

Quintus was pleased. The plan had gone as he had hoped, the deserters assuming that a much larger force had found them. Their deep training had worked against them. Although they had the advantage of numbers, it was not enough to beat the element of surprise.

Quintus prepared to address them, to offer them a future.

XXIX: AGMEN FORMATE

A cry from the branches above stopped him — a shout of warning from one of the Anatolians. Then an arrow whirred over their heads in the opposite direction to the earlier shafts. It vanished into the line of trees by the river. Splashes and shouts came from where it had flown as further arrows streaked over their heads.

A yell came from the archers. 'Germani! Germani!'

'How many?' Quintus shouted back.

'Many!'

'*Agmen formate*,' Quintus ordered. 'Form a square. Blow the command, cornicen.'

Marcus and Caius echoed the order as they pushed and pulled men into place. Both wore the transverse crest of the optio on their helmets, and each wielded a hastile in hand, excellent for shoving men into line.

All the legionaries had practised *agmen formate*, the formation of a hollow square — and many other shapes — on the Campus Martius. Its completion should have been smooth, but these men were from different legions; many did not know their place, and half of them had no officers. Some of the deserters looked like they might try to run, until Caius and Marcus wielded their staffs. Sextus and Vetruvius lifted their gladii, ready to stop them, with the legionaries to either side of them following suit.

But the men called out in their own defence. 'Weapons,' they shouted, pointing to the spears that helped support some of their shelters. Marcus understood and waved an arm in consent. At once the men ran and grabbed spears, helmets and shields, then returned to the square.

'Decurion, engage,' Quintus commanded, wanting to buy time. The cavalry at once turned to face the direction from where the noise was coming. The officer saluted Quintus and shouted an order to the cornicen.

'Sound the advance. Half-speed.'

The cavalry turned on the order. They set off towards the river at a fast walk, round shields firm on their arms, spears levelled, ready to draw their longer cavalry swords once the javelins were loosed. There were not many of them. If there was a horde of Germani, they would not survive.

But their bravery would give Quintus time to form a defence. Sextus used his sword arm to steer the newly armed men into the formation. Marcus used his hastile. Rufus had taken up position with the standard on the corner of the square that faced the river.

It had not taken long. The formation was not a perfect square, not a traditional quadratum — the terrain did not allow for that — but Quintus was happy with the shape. It was a rough hollow diamond, pointing to the river. He was pleased that there were no gaps in it. Vetruvius held the eagle for Aquila, and was about to help him to dismount.

'Stay on horseback, Aquila,' Quintus commanded. 'Keep the eagle aloft, and stay by Rufus and the standard if you can.'

Aquila was the only soldier mounted, and the eagle marked the point of the formation that would receive the first wave of the enemy. The hurried arrangement of the four sides meant the two forces had become inextricably mixed; some poorly armed deserters were on the outside of the hollow shape, some on the inside. The line of overlapping shields that should meet the charge of the enemy was not complete.

'Armour and shields on the outside,' commanded Quintus, walking rapidly around the perimeter of the diamond, dressing the lines by shoving and cursing the men, pulling those who were protected and fully armed from within the lines to the outside rank. 'We have a better chance of victory if our first defence is better armed than our reserve.' Marcus took note and was doing the same on the other side.

Satisfied, he took up position on the left side of the diamond, while Caius stood on the right. Quintus was at its point, facing the enemy, flanked by standard and eagle. They could hear fighting through the trees — war cries, the clash of metal on metal and the screams of injured horses.

A riderless horse, blood bubbling from its nostrils, ran out of the trees in panic and veered off along the valley, plunging into the trees, head tossing from side to side.

A huge tribesman stumbled into view after it, his beard and plaited moustaches falling to his bare chest. He bore the broken shaft of an arrow in his side, a bloom of red marking its entry. His bright patterned trews were stained with blood from the wound. He wielded a two-headed axe, needing both hands for it. Seeing the formation and the standards, he roared defiance and lifted the weapon high, striding towards Quintus.

He seemed to stop for no reason, as if his leg had sunk into a bog. He let the axe drop, then, lifting it again, revealed the reason for the halt. A long shaft now protruded from his chest, deeply buried. He looked at it in shock as he let the axe fall.

Quintus sensed movement behind him. 'No!' he shouted. 'Hold. He is dead already.'

The man shouted a curse of defiance — Quintus thought he recognised the name of the god Týr — then made a final attempt to lift his weapon even as another arrow punched into him, sending him reeling backwards. He fell with a crash, the axe useless at his side, a silence enveloping the glade after his body keeled over and hit the ground.

'Hold,' called Quintus again, the optiones repeating the order, ready to strike any man who broke formation.

Once more they listened. The sounds of battle moved towards them. The tension was broken by another horse crashing through the undergrowth, this one with its rider still aboard. It was a Germani warrior's horse, with a human head tied to it, bouncing grotesquely. The rider, weapons in both hands, guided it firmly with his knees around his fallen comrade.

The horse tossed its head and bared its teeth, ready to bite. Its rider called on his gods to protect him as he galloped towards the square, screaming the names of Týr and Wotan. His axe was held high and already dripping with blood, his bare chest streaked with red. In his other hand there was a long, curved sword. His shouts were loud, his war cry long, an unearthly noise that sounded as if it had its roots in the underworld. Arrows flew from above, but as if he was magically protected, they passed him by. He made straight for the point of the formation, bearing down on Quintus, threatening to cut the eagle from its pole, attempting to punch straight through the square.

Realising that the horse could not be halted, Quintus dropped to one knee in an effort to protect himself. He tilted his shield and braced it with his shoulder, digging its edge firmly into the forest floor. The men either side of him quickly did the same. The horse kept coming and tried to clear the barrier in front of it, its front legs pawing the air, its back legs scrabbling for purchase. Its momentum took it over the point of the diamond, landing in the hollow centre of the formation, twisting madly and blowing and biting at everything it could see. Quintus was almost trampled, but managed to keep hold of his shield and raise his sword.

The warrior on the horse's back struggled to keep his balance, whilst furiously waving his weapons. An Anatolian arrow skewered his right arm and his axe dropped. A legionary sword — one of many — slashed at his leg. Another thrust at his body as he was being dragged from his mount. The horse, maddened and terrified, raised itself onto its back legs.

'Let it out,' yelled Caius, seeing that the horse was now riderless and ready to bite or gouge anything that moved. The men at the rear of the formation hurried to make a gap and the horse bolted through. The men closed their shields behind it. At the front of the diamond, the two standard bearers once more stood shoulder to shoulder. Shakily, Quintus rose, shield firm, as more enemy, both on horseback and on foot, streamed out of the trees.

Arrows thwacked into some of the attackers, but others came on, throwing themselves against the iron wall, hacking at the shields, impaling themselves on levelled spears, all the while screaming their war cries. Some tried to burrow between the shields, even to climb over them. Their horses were encouraged to rear and kick, but the shield wall broke their charge like the ocean crashing on rocks as it reached the shore.

'Stand your ground. *Quadratum defende*,' Quintus shouted, and the men braced themselves against the enemy. Each legionary used first a spear, until it was embedded in an enemy too deeply to retrieve or until it snapped. Then he drew his gladius. Each sword struck time and again, finding victims with every thrust as it darted out between the shields.

Inevitably some Romans fell, cut down by a lucky or skilful stroke, or by the weight and ferocity of the mounts. The long swords of the enemy cut between shields where gaps appeared and tore at the skin that showed above the shield's rim. Those on horseback were able to slash downwards. The horses were themselves weapons, hooves and teeth seeking soft flesh.

The shield wall was strongest at the front of the diamond, but horsemen were already testing the other sides. If a legionary on the outside of the formation fell, another took his place at once, so that the shield wall, whilst it remained whole, gradually became thinner. It was but a matter of time before gaps would appear in it. Even so, it was the best defence against a wild charge.

Anatolian arrows had taken some of the first horsemen, and felled some of those on foot. Fallen bodies and injured animals created barriers to the charge. Where Quintus stood, the fighting was fierce, the enemy heedless of its safety or survival. They sought the standards that stood proudly next to him, Rufus on foot, the eagle raised up on horseback by Aquila. Marcus and Caius, at either side of the quadratum, echoed Quintus' words. 'Hold! Stand! Brace your shield!'

One bloodied warrior heaved a fallen comrade out of the way and, stepping into the space created, swung his sword in an arc that would have cleaved a ten-year oak in two. His target was Aquila's horse. But the blow never connected. From above and behind him, the long pole that carried the eagle, its end sharpened to a point, thrust down into the man's exposed chest. Aquila grunted with the effort as he pulled the standard free and sought another victim. The horse stood firm. The standard and the horse gave him a reach that his gladius could not match.

The horse, unlike the sword, was not his. Although he sat on it firmly, its flanks gripped tightly between his knees, he was only now learning its temperament. Clearly, it had been in battle before. Its ears were pricked and its eyes flicking from side to side, but it did not seem disturbed by the activity around it.

Inevitably, one side of the formation failed, a gap appearing that the remaining legionaries were unable to close quickly enough, and both Germani foot soldiers and horsemen screamed defiance as they attacked the inside of the square. Some legionaries took their chances and carried the fight to the enemy, striding alone or in pairs with an amicus. Marcus and Tullius fought with their backs to each other. Sextus and Rufus were shoulder to shoulder, protecting each other and the standard. They had been here before. Vetruvius fought at the right flank of Aquila's mount, and Agnus and Alba protected the other side.

The confined area inside the formation prevented the enemy from manoeuvring, meaning that every slash, every thrust, had the potential to be a killing stroke. As the intruders were cut down, Marcus and Caius shouted commands from either side and the square — smaller now — closed up again, those trapped within it ruthlessly despatched.

Some legionaries were caught on the outside. One, the man earlier recognised by Caius, could be seen protecting his smaller companion, but then he was set upon by another enemy. The two grappled, indistinguishable from each other, each with fair hair and long moustaches. The Roman lost his helmet and blood poured from a head wound. He struck the second enemy down, then turned as the first swung at him again. Quintus strode out to help, the shield wall closing behind him. He stepped in front of the man, who was big even for a legionary, and took the blow that was meant for him on his own shield. The force of it made him stagger and take a step backwards. The enemy followed through with a dagger thrust, the weapon held in his other hand.

Quintus ducked the blow, letting it scrape harmlessly off his shoulder armour. To the surprise of the Germani warrior, he grabbed the man by his beard and pulled hard, using the weight of the warrior's body to help him plunge his gladius deep into his chest. The tribesman pitched forward, groaning and clinging to Quintus to try and stop his descent.

The air left Quintus in a great rush as he landed on his back. The Germani tribesman collapsed on top of him as he managed to lift his shield in protection. There was another thud as the big blond legionary, at last cut down, fell on top of the pair of them.

Quintus wondered if he had a coin for Charon as darkness closed in around him.

XXX: CAPSARIUS

'Here,' said a voice, 'lift this one up. He is one of ours.'

Quintus could hear grunts of effort as something was moved above him.

'Cornelius Rubio,' the voice said. 'A sad loss to the Fifth. Add him to the pyre.'

'This one is enemy, sir.'

'Put him with the others.'

'There is one beneath him.' There was a pause. 'Sir, I think it may be the commander.'

Quintus had never thought of himself as a commander, so he did not realise the voice was referring to him. Suddenly, light and noise flooded in and he was able to breathe more easily as the weight of the dead Germani was lifted from him. He blinked in the brightness, trying to focus. Two strange faces looked down on him, then were thrust aside as the familiar face of Caius, evocatus and optio, appeared between them.

'Get him up,' Caius commanded, 'and fetch the capsarius.' He turned to Quintus and shook him by the shoulders. 'Are you hurt, sir? I have sent for the medic.'

Rough hands lifted Quintus, pulling him into a sitting position. He tilted his head and let out a long breath, running his hands over the parts of his body not covered by armour. He could feel no deep pain anywhere, but seemed to have blood on both arms and on his face. He went to rub his cheeks with the back of his hand but was stopped by a firm grip on his arm.

'No, sir. I will clean it,' Alba said as he moved Quintus' arm away and leant over with a wet cloth. Quintus smelt vinegar.

The capsarius sounded relieved. 'It is not your blood, sir. Or at least, most of it is not. Your face is uninjured. There is a cut to your left arm, but it is not deep, and a cut to your neck, also shallow. The blood on your face and other arm belongs to another.'

Gingerly, Quintus felt his body all over. No breaks, no serious wounds. There would be bruises of course, but they did not matter. He felt for his weapons and his armour. His gladius and scutum were missing, his lorica laminata dented. He reached for his helmet, hands coming to rest instead on his unruly hair. He realised that a legionary already knelt beside him, offering him the crested helm.

He took it with thanks, but did not yet put it on, instead asking the man, 'Did you find my gladius? I think it is embedded in an enemy.'

'That one,' the kneeling legionary shouted across, pointing to what had been the centre of the quadratum, where Quintus could see bodies were being piled. 'He may have the commander's sword.'

A few moments passed. There was some activity around the body, then a shout of triumph. There followed a series of grunts, then another legionary came running.

'Here, sir. He was trying to take it into their afterlife with him. He held on to it tight.' The man, whom Quintus did not recognise, grinned, showing black gaps in his teeth. He passed the sword across. 'I cleaned it on his trews, sir. He didn't seem to mind.'

Quintus nodded his thanks. He stood up and sheathed the blade, then finally turned to look around the clearing. In one direction a pile of enemy bodies was being relieved of anything of value. The giant he had stabbed was just the latest addition; his own sword was but the latest treasure found.

He squinted. There were at least two tribes represented here, possibly more. In a few cases the hair was tied in an elaborate knot, pulled to one side, a hairstyle he recognised as belonging to the Suebi tribe. He pointed out the intricate plaiting of another's moustaches to Alba. 'Tencteri, I think,' he said. Alba nodded before moving off to tend to others.

Quintus looked into the sun, shading his eyes, to see the aquila standard plunged deep into the ground. The sun was low and the eagle cast a long shadow. Next to it, casting a shorter shadow, the standard of the First Century of the Ninth stood proudly, though the pole had been broken. Nearby, the horse on which Aquila had sat was grazing on the short grass unconcernedly.

A legionary ran across to him. It was Sextus. 'Quintus, we thought we had lost you,' he said with unfeigned delight. 'Are you hurt?'

'Alba tells me that I will live,' Quintus joked. 'I look worse than I am. Most of this blood isn't mine.' He paused to look round further. 'Sextus, where are the enemy? Where is Dagaz and his Germani tribes?'

'Not here,' Sextus replied with a grin. 'They never were. There were not as many as we feared. Their first charge was their fiercest. We do not know who led them, but it was not Dagaz. No such chieftain is among the fallen. Agnus knows what he looks like and swears he is not here.'

'So we defeated them?' Quintus asked, still not certain.

'Look around,' said Sextus, waving an arm.

Quintus looked and nodded in approval. 'Prisoners?'

'None taken.'

'And our men?'

'We lost a few, Quintus. How could we not?' He pointed at the pyre that was being built on the far side of the glade. Many bodies were piled on it, laid as neatly as the men could manage.

'Any of our own, Sextus?'

Sextus knew what he meant. There was a difference between the renegade Romans, the extra men Quintus had been given by Galba and the men he thought of as his own comrades. 'None of our contubernales, I am fairly sure. I think I have seen them all. Marcus is organising the pyre, and Tullius is with him.' He rubbed his chin. 'None of the cavalry survived, or at least, none came back. Just a few riderless horses. Aquila has sent men to look. With you missing, the men looked to the aquilifer for leadership. We lost a good few of the deserters — many were neither armed nor armoured. A few tried to run but were cut down by the Anatolians. They did us good service, today, Quintus.'

By this time, others had spotted the tall figure of the centurion. Aquila and Rufus came across together. Rufus slapped him on the back. 'Macilentus,' he laughed, 'we thought you had left us.' Aquila was more restrained, congratulating Quintus on his good fortune and quietly giving thanks to the gods. He remembered thrusting the eagle into several enemies and seeing Quintus go down. He had managed to stay mounted and it was he who had rallied the men, telling them from his vantage point that no more enemy came.

'Did the cornicen survive?' asked Quintus. 'We will need him to call the muster once these tasks are complete.' He indicated the pyre. 'And find someone who can act as a priest — those men will need a prayer.' He looked round again and realised he was missing someone. 'Where is Vetruvius?'

'He is there.' Aquila pointed to where Vetruvius sat having his arm bound with a strip of cloth. 'You can rest, Quintus. All is as it should be.'

'Not until I know who they were, Aquila, and whether there will be more. Have guards been posted?'

'Of course,' replied the aquilifer, 'and messages have been sent to Centurion Galba and the cohort. I have despatched Agnus with an escort.'

'The deserters, have we secured them?'

'No point, sir. They fought. Those that ran did not get far — the Anatolians saw to most of them, and the wolves will get the rest. The survivors are working alongside our men.'

Sextus covered his head and offered a prayer for the dead. He then sacrificed a wood pigeon and pronounced its entrails auspicious. The pyre was lit and its thick smoke curled into the evening sky. Despite the assurances from Sextus that the Vestal Virgins would pay the passage of a soldier killed in battle, the friends and comrades of the fallen had found coins and placed an obol under each dead man's tongue. Charon needed payment and the men were not convinced about the Vestals.

There were more dead men here than Quintus had first thought. He counted over twenty bodies before he gave up. There was no scribe to record names and families. Cornus would be able to work out who had not returned of the Ninth, but the renegades would have to remain anonymous. It was up to the Flavian, when he was returned to them, whether they would be listed as missing in action or as deserters. It made a huge difference to their families and friends in Rome. It affected citizen rights, the standing of sons and the validity of wills. Quintus was pleased that it was not a decision that he would have to make.

Where the quadratum had stood, the ground was churned into black mud and the pile of native bodies received neither fire nor prayer, but were left for the animals of the night. Already a huge swarm of insects buzzed and crawled over them. Beyond this sight, a little further down the river, the horses that were uninjured were collected and tied. There were only a few of them. Many of the native ponies had galloped away into the trees. Most of the Roman cavalry mounts had not returned from their part in the action. The loss of the cavalry troubled Quintus, especially since they included the decurion, probably a minor nobleman, a member of the equités. Though legionaries were sent to search for them, they discovered no evidence of their fate. Whether captured or killed, nothing remained but riderless horses and bloodied ground.

At the edge of the clearing were some roughly made benches and tables — no more than branches pulled across or logs balanced on tree stumps. A number of injured men stood or sat around, and one or two lay on the makeshift boards. Alba could be seen moving amongst them, his hands and forearms stained red, a native cloak tied around his front to protect him from the blood and gore. The capsarius had helpers, amongst them Tullius, easily identified by his bald head and double scar. The helpers cleared the men from the tables when Alba had finished. They sat them on stumps or, in many cases, passed them to other legionaries to add them to the pyre.

Quintus set up a temporary command post further down the valley, in a glade he judged big enough to hold the men. He needed to make haste before darkness fell. He was determined to march the men at least a little way from the killing ground before establishing a simple marching camp, but he needed to muster them before he could do so.

XXXI: CINERES CREDIS CURARE SEPULTOS

A horse was brought for him, one of the surviving cavalry horses, a brown cob with a white blaze and three white socks. Quintus stroked its long nose, drawn to it by its imperfection, and mounted, for once needing the help of a legionary's bent back. From his raised position, he surveyed what was left of the camp. The temporary shelters had been used for kindling. He could see the river through the trees; it had already cleaned itself and ran clear between the muddied banks. Both the pyre and the pile of bodies were blots on the scene, the crackle of the flames mingling with the buzz of flies.

Aquila mounted up beside him with the eagle. Rufus stood to the other side with the standard, a hazel branch firmly splinted to its pole.

'We need to be away from here,' said Aquila. His wolfskin cloak was bloodied but otherwise undamaged. He, too, had escaped serious injury. 'Before the ghosts of the dead come seeking their killers.'

'Agreed,' replied Quintus. He leaned down to speak to a nearby legionary. 'You, soldier. Go fetch the cornicen to me — and tell the capsarius that he and his charges can ignore the call to assembly.'

The man saluted and left them. The cornicen came quickly. The man had taken part in the fighting but sustained only minor injuries. He had taken blows to his arms and his focale was tied around one of them.

'Is the instrument undamaged?' Quintus asked.

'I think so, sir, though I have not blown it. If it is intact and I still have the strength to blow it, it will serve.' The cornicen smiled up at the centurion.

'Call a muster,' Quintus commanded him. 'Nothing urgent, just the boring call of an assembly at the end of the day.'

The cornicen complied, the long and short notes of the cornu ringing out in a familiar pattern. The long, curved tube, though battered, still functioned. There was some movement amongst the men, perhaps surprised that they were being called to an assembly. Some still carried out tasks, fetching wood for the pyre, or relieving the dead of their possessions. Others squatted at the stream, washing blood from weapons and limbs. Several stood silhouetted by the red sky of the setting sun. They faced the pyre with their heads covered. These were men who had lost friends and comrades.

Quintus was about to have the call blown again when men started to move. He waited. As soon as some of the legionaries spotted the eagle, they pointed it out to others and all began to move towards it. A shout or two from Marcus and their speed increased. They started to form up in the clearing.

Quintus' own group — what remained of it — lined up on Rufus, who stood to one side with the standard of Century One. The men who Quintus referred to as renegades or deserters tried to put themselves into some kind of order. Many of them seemed to have no idea where they should stand. A number appeared to be without much of their basic equipment, including weapons and armour. Caius recognised some of them and began to organise them into columns. Marcus, no longer a man of the First, helped him. By the time the cornicen blew for silence, there were around fifty men lined up in two distinct groups. Those from Century One made up the bigger group, still tiny by legion standards. Seven rows of four was hardly more than three tents. The others were even fewer, lined up in twos. It looked like there were around twenty of them. To the side stood the cornicen, to the front Caius and Marcus and the two standard bearers. Alba remained with his charges, assisted by Tullius and one other. There were three legionaries still waiting for treatment and one on the table.

Quintus surveyed the men from his high position on horseback. He was not quite sure what to say. He had never been in this position before — formally at the head of a group of his own victorious men.

Rather than announce who he was, he decided to let his crested helm signify his authority. 'Well fought, men,' he said simply. 'I make no speeches. We march, we camp. In the morning, we gather again. We have regulars —' he looked at his own men, standing smartly in front of Rufus — 'and irregulars.' He looked at the column of twos.

'The status of the irregulars is to be determined. They are not prisoners, but may be deserters.' A raised hand silenced the muttering that accompanied this statement. 'They remain under suspicion until cleared. You, the regulars, will keep watch on them.' He turned to the trumpeter. 'Cornicen, sound the march — column of twos. Aquila, you lead, that way. We seek the rest of the cohort.' He pointed along the river, following the line that Galba would have taken.

As the cornicen blew, Quintus moved his horse to one side to watch the column go past. He was pleased to see Cornelius Appius. They recognised each other with a nod. Many men had cuts or bandages or even slings. He noted that most still had their spears and shields, and all seemed to have a baldric, gladius, baltea, cingulum and pugio. He suspected that some of those on the pyre were crossing the river with less than a full set of equipment. He was sure that neither Charon nor Mercury would mind.

Reaching the back of the column, he trotted across the clearing to where Alba still worked at his dressing station.

'Capsarius, are you close to finishing?'

There was now just one legionary left waiting for treatment. The one that had been on the table was being moved by Tullius and his assistant to the pyre. He had not survived surgery. One of the others had watched the surgery and decided that he could walk. He hurried to tag on to the back of the column, leaning on a comrade. There were ten to twelve others still dotted around the area. Some of them sat with their backs to trees, sewn up and bandaged. The others leaned against trunks or on crudely made crutches.

'There is no cart for the wounded,' Quintus told Alba. 'The walking wounded must bring up the rear, moving as well as they can. They must determine if they can march and catch up with the column. Tell them now.'

Alba moved around the dressing station quickly, urging patients to join the others if they could. Most were happy to at least try.

'There are a few horses for those who will survive being carried on horseback,' Quintus went on. 'If they won't survive and cannot walk, they stay here with a gladius.' He turned to Tullius. 'Tullius, make sure those left behind have the means to depart with honour, then bring the remaining horses.'

Tullius knew what he meant — and that these men would have to rely on the Vestals paying their passage.

Quintus turned his horse and rode back to the head of the column, greeting men he knew by name. There were many that he did not know, and the two groups had become mixed, the deserters of the Fifth with the soldiers of the Ninth. He shook his head. In the morning he must not only separate them but judge them. Reaching the front, he slowed to keep pace with Aquila. The eagle shone blood-red as the sun died. Rufus marched immediately behind the eagle, Sextus at his side.

'I suppose the rest of the tribes — Dagaz, too — will come down to bury their own,' Rufus said. 'They will be on our trail. They cannot be far away.'

'You may be right,' said Quintus. 'That's why I want to put at least a little distance between us. After what Dagaz did to the pioneers, they will not just bury their own, they will despoil ours. We should save the men from that sight.'

'*Et cineres credis curare sepultos*,' said Sextus, with a wicked grin and a shrug. 'And do you think that the ashes of the dead will care?'

'That sounds too high-flown for you,' Rufus laughed. 'Is it part of some sort of curse?' He looked around. 'Tullius is not here, so you can tell me.'

'You hear much growing up in the Temple of Vesta,' Sextus replied. 'It is from a reading of the poet Publius Vergilius. Part of his tale of the foundation of Rome by Aeneas was recounted for the Holy Sisters. It means that they can do what they like to the remains of the dead — their essence has already crossed into Elysium.'

Quintus nodded. 'I hope so, for I do not think they will go undisturbed when the Germani discover their own losses.'

It did not take long for Tullius to catch up with the horses. His task, unpleasant though it was, was not spoken of. He merely nodded an acknowledgement to Quintus, who understood. There were six mounts, one of which the legionary rode, one of which Alba rode, an injured man held in front of him. Two others had injured men thrown across them like sacks of flour.

'Marcus,' Quintus said, as he rode alongside the optio, 'take one of the mounts and Tullius and see if you can find us a defendable position.' He looked to the sky. The sun had gone. 'We have a summer hour, no more.'

He did not need to elaborate further; Marcus was much more experienced than him. He and Tullius pulled themselves onto the spare mounts with relative ease and set off at a canter.

The clouds were thin and tinged with red and gold. They promised another clear day on the morrow. Quintus estimated that it was the eleventh hour, so there was enough light left for the men to construct a reasonable castra.

As they crested a rise, Marcus and Tullius could be seen ahead, pointing to the east, telling Quintus to turn the column. He signalled the manoeuvre with his arm, Rufus magnifying it by waving the standard, and the column left the trod they were on and began to climb. It was a steep but short climb on rocky ground, skirting big boulders and stunted trees. The men could hear the muffled roar of fast flowing water, a noise that grew and let them know that they had once more reached the left bank of the mighty river, the Rhenus.

Quintus managed to persuade his mount to climb the last steep part of the hill and found himself on a small but flat plateau of short grass, sloping gently away from where he had stopped.

He moved the horse towards the edge above the sound of the river and carefully looked over.

XXXII: PRAESIDIUM

Far below, the river foamed over boulders and falls. The water had cut a path through shining white rock and ran in a gully that was both deep and wide. No trees had managed to establish a foothold at the top of the bank, although a few hardy colonists, holly and alder mostly, grew as thin and spindly trailblazers in the cracks further down. Quintus nodded approval.

The cliff provided an almost perfect defence. An enemy would have to descend steeply on the other bank, swim through the river and then climb to attack from the east. To the south the plateau also provided a defence, a landslip at some point creating a steep scarp, scattered with rocks. To the west, at the bottom of the slope, the trees grew thickly together, mostly spruce, but with a tangled understorey of holly, alder and bramble. It was only to the north that they would need to defend.

It was probably the shortest march any of the men had ever undertaken, but it was enough to take them away from the pyre and the ghosts of the dead.

'A ditch, there,' Marcus ordered, pointing at the side that needed defending. 'You archers, cover them whilst they dig.'

'Guard posts at each corner,' Quintus added. 'Fires if you have anything to cook. No-one is going hunting tonight.'

Caius and Marcus organised the men, shouting orders and pointing to where actions needed to be taken. Sextus somehow managed to join those giving instructions rather than taking them. Aquila and Rufus planted the standards and mounted a guard on them; Vetruvius watered the horses. Alba once more needed the help of Tullius to take the injured from horseback and lie them down, and to check the dressings and splints on the walking wounded.

The legionaries had filled waterskins earlier in the march, when it was easier to access the river. Some men always carried a pouch of grain or pulse, enough for themselves at least. Almost all carried hard biscuits, twice baked by slaves.

By the time the castra was complete, darkness enveloped it, its corners and gates marked by sputtering torches. Quintus looked on it with pride. 'Order and discipline,' he said to Aquila. 'These men are no deserters.'

There were few fires lit, the men assuming they would not be needed for warmth, but the temperature quickly dropped and places by them were sought. A third of the men were on guard, changing every two hours in the short night.

Quintus spoke to Caius and Alba, asking them to bring him a couple of the Larks, men they either knew, or at least deemed trustworthy. They, in turn, spoke with Vetruvius and Aquila, who had also been of the Fifth. Two men were chosen and brought by Caius to the centurion. One was an older man, with a scar beneath his eye, short grey hair above, a lined face and a stubbled chin. The other was younger, with long dark hair and smooth skin. Both were built as Quintus would expect legionaries to be built — tall, broad-shouldered and strong of limb.

'This is Aulus,' Caius said, indicating the older man. 'He has fought in many battles and has almost served his time. He was injured when the Fifth was under Marcus Agrippa in Hispania — he almost lost his eye.' He turned to the other. 'This is Cotta. His father was a shoemaker in the Suburra, so he bears the nickname Sutor. He came with the latest batch of probationers, joining us in Germania.'

'Sit,' Quintus said. 'You do not look like deserters. Then again, what does a deserter look like? The only deserters I have ever seen were being beaten to death by their comrades, a sentence called fustuarium. You will be familiar with it?'

The two men nodded glumly.

'Tell me what happened,' Quintus ordered. 'You do not strike me as cowards. Are you indeed deserters?'

'We are citizens, centurion,' the older of the two men said. 'All of us were lost. We were never deserters.'

'So why did you lurk in the enemy's forest? Why did you not return to your legion?'

Aulus looked at the ground, while Cotta became visibly impatient. 'It is no use protecting honour anymore, Aulus. We are broken, scattered.'

'Honour is more important, Cotta…' began Aulus, but the younger man interrupted him forcibly, addressing Quintus.

'It was the old man, sir. The ex-senator. He was reliving past victories. He was only visiting, not in command, but he was determined that we should fight. He boasted of the numbers he had beaten in Parthia, of his part in making Licinius Crassus into a great general.' He dropped his voice. 'I think in his dotage he must have forgotten Carrhae. But we did not have the men. We should have retreated to report the enemy's position and find the rest of the legion.'

'Legio Five Alaudae. The famous Larks?'

Aulus was bitter. 'That is us, sir. Larks on our helmets and elephants on our standards. Beloved of the divine Julius Caesar. Favoured by Augustus Caesar, with his friend Marcus Agrippa as our commander.' He turned his face to the standard, plunged into the ground behind the centurion. 'The famous Larks, sir. Lately commanded by the noble ex-Consul Marcus Lollius. And I think that is our eagle.'

'Tell me what happened to the famous Larks? How do I have their eagle?' Quintus asked gently. Of course, he already knew, but he needed to be certain that these men were genuine, and he wanted to know if they had been in the action when the eagle was lost.

Cotta took a deep breath. 'We were ambushed, sir. Betrayed. Our officers were slaughtered, and our commander fled. Our ex-senator initially ran, then insisted that our cohort — what was left of it — turned and fought.'

'It would have been an honourable death,' Quintus said.

'It was suicide. Many were cut down, and many died under the hooves of Germani horsemen. We should have broken off the action. We should have fetched reinforcements. We were on foot, in a column, and they were on horseback. It was carnage. They targeted the officers first, and we would all have died if the Germani had not abruptly stopped fighting. They obeyed a call from somewhere and suddenly rode off. We still do not know why.'

'Did the ex-senator fall? Where is he now?'

'He was taken from the field, sir,' Aulus muttered, still with his eyes on the ground.

'He was relieved of command,' said Cotta angrily.

Quintus was shocked. 'By whom? Who would have the authority?'

'The primus pilus, sir. The first-ranked centurion and another had been assigned to the senator by the commander. They stayed with him. They followed him when he first fled, thus they survived the massacre. Apart from the senator himself, they were the only senior men left. They took him from the field. He was on horseback, slumped across the saddle. They were on foot. They led the horse, one either side, into the forest. They were the last of our officers. We never saw them again. We were abandoned, sir, not deserters. Our officers, our general, our senator, all deserted us.'

The silence between the three men stretched out. The crackling of the fires, the murmur of conversation, the bubbling of the river, all seemed to be muted.

Eventually, Quintus asked, 'Is there any more to tell?'

'We were left, sir,' said Cotta, unemotionally. 'Surrounded by our own dead and dying. Many of the slain were headless. The Germani…'

'I know,' Quintus interrupted flatly.

'We collected up the dead bodies and burned them, a grisly and thankless task,' said Aulus. 'A small group of men, senior men, took charge. Though I am a veteran, I was not one of them. They were men of a certain stamp. I have never been a rule-breaker, whereas many others carried the marks of the lash on their backs. The big fair-headed man who fought with you, sir, a popular man, he was one of them. These men at least made the right decision, that we should seek to return to the fort. But a thick fog gathered that night. When it lifted in the morning, we were lost in the forest. We were trying to follow the river — we could think of no other way to find direction. But I fear we were moving further away from the fort rather than closer to it.'

'Then the winter came,' said Cotta. 'Snow and ice and winds colder than any I have ever known. We lost many men. We had to eat some of our own animals to survive.'

'Only in spring did we start to move again, to follow the river. But ever more slowly, as if we no longer cared,' said Aulus quietly.

There was shame in Cotta's voice. 'We became disheartened, unwilling to move quickly or be ordered about by men with no rank. There was fighting, and some men did desert. We were undisciplined, no longer Roman. That's how we were when you found us. Most of us were glad to be found. We were all glad to fight. At least we might die with honour, though I did not believe we deserved it.'

'We were glad to have you,' Quintus said quietly. In a louder voice, he asked briskly, 'Do you have any more to say? Your fate lies in my hands. I am ordered not to bring back any deserters.'

Cotta and Aulus looked at each other, then both shook their heads.

'You are dismissed, then,' Quintus said. 'Report nothing. I have not yet decided.'

Caius and Alba were waiting nearby in the shadows and now came forward to escort the men back to their comrades. Quintus wished that his amicus, Crassus, was present. He was always a sensible voice when decisions of such import had to be made. But he was still with Galba, leading Century One in Quintus' absence.

He pulled himself to his feet. They had been sitting on an arrangement of logs that, placed in front of the standards, constituted his praesidium. He walked through the camp, checked on the guards, spoke to comrades, then returned to his base and wrapped himself in his cloak to sleep.

The sounds of the forest — wind in the trees, animals in the night — were close, and the sound of the water closer. Quintus found his mind racing, full of visions every time he closed his eyes. Headless and crucified centurions, funeral pyres, injured men, a crimson eagle dripping blood — he could not sleep.

XXXIII: IUS IURANDUM

When the first rosy hues of morning lightened the sky, Quintus stood once more, wrapping his cloak tight around him, and sought the cornicen. There would be a dawn assembly before they continued. Galba had been clear: no deserters could be brought back to the cohort.

The cornicen spoke to Quintus. 'Some of the men have asked to speak with you, sir. They all know that you must decide the fate of these men. They seek to influence that decision.'

Quintus did not know which way these men would wish to sway him. Perhaps they were advocates for the death penalty, perhaps not. What he did know was that commanders usually received such delegations and listened to them if they wanted to keep the loyalty of their men. He knew it was his decision, his alone, but that did not mean that he could not listen to others.

'I will hear them,' Quintus told the cornicen. The man saluted and beckoned a small group of legionaries forward. Here were Caius and Alba, as he had expected, but also Aquila and Vetruvius and, to his surprise, Marcus and Sextus. Quintus bent his head to listen.

Marcus seemed to be the spokesperson. He stepped forward stiffly, as if on parade, and saluted, fist to heart. His armour and baltea and cingulum were polished, his hastile was at his side, and his optio's helmet, also polished, was tucked beneath his arm.

'They fought, centurion,' he said formally. 'Without them, we would all be dead. They are not cowards, sir. And they did not run from us when we found them. Some of their number — the true cowards — had already fled. Some tried to escape us, and they were rightly shot down by the archers. Our men will speak for the ones that are left.' Marcus waved an arm, encompassing the hilltop. 'In the night, each man of the Fifth has gained a sponsor, a soldier of the Ninth willing to stand surety for him. I stand guarantor for Aulus.'

'And I for Cotta,' said Sextus.

'You think they should be forgiven?'

'The loss of an eagle is unforgivable,' said Aquila, then raised a finger to make his point. 'But these were not the ones that lost it. We know what happened.' Quintus noticed that he did not go so far as to blame poor leadership; that would not be Roman.

'It is your choice, Macilentus,' said Marcus, dropping the formality. 'Make the right one.'

'I have made a decision,' said Quintus, then looked searchingly at the small group. 'I need a sign, a signal from the gods that what I decide is right.'

Sextus stepped forward. 'I can interpret the will of the gods. What have you decided?'

'The gods already know, Sextus. Let's not try to fool them. Read the auguries, tell me if my decision is right.'

Sextus pulled his cloak over his head. Although they were high up on a promontory, the forest still climbed to the east and the horizon could not be seen. The pale light of day grew, the change in light revealing that the sun was rising behind the trees. The soldiers were restless, ready to break camp. They expected to have been called by now. Usually the morning assembly was before dawn. As Sextus looked towards the forest, searching the skies, a flurry of rooks rose and fell, settling quickly. It was not much, but it was enough.

'Great Jupiter approves,' he told Quintus in a voice that was more confident than he actually felt.

Quintus did not respond, but merely turned his head to the cornicen. 'Blow, soldier,' he said. 'Call the assembly.' The cornicen lifted the long, curved instrument to his lips. Before the first note had died away and long before the call was finished, the men were lined up, the Ninth on Rufus and the standard, the Fifth in much better order than the day before.

Quintus sat atop his horse, and Sextus stood by his left foot, cloak still drawn over his head. Quintus had done the same with his own cloak. The decision was blessed by the gods and had to be delivered with respect.

'Men of the Larks.' He did not need to raise his voice; the men were eager to hear. 'I do not have the power to forgive you.'

The assembly became even quieter, the noises of the forest sounding loud in comparison.

'So I have put my decision to the gods. Only Jupiter Optimus Maximus can forgive you. The augur has read the signs.' He indicated Sextus. 'The gods approve.' He paused. 'You will be re-sworn.'

There was no cheer, just a great collective sigh of relief. Sextus breathed easily once more. He had divined correctly.

Quintus continued. 'Jupiter, first and greatest, has sent a sign that you should be readmitted. You will swear the *sacramentum* and the *ius iurandum* with me. You will swear on the rescued eagle of the Fifth.'

Aquila lowered the eagle towards the men, so that those closest could place their hands on either the symbol or its shaft. Each man touched the shoulder of another, so that all were connected.

The men of the Larks once more became regulars, sacred to the gods, as they spoke the oath of brotherhood: 'I swear that I will never leave my comrades through fear, or flee from danger; that I will only leave the ranks to pick up a weapon, to kill a foe, to save a comrade or to rescue a standard. On my life and by Mars and great Jupiter.'

As soon as it was over, Quintus uncovered his head and ordered the men to march.

The column set off once more, keeping the river to its left. They marched south, after first negotiating the rough descent from the high ground on which they were camped. Alba saw to his charges, none of whom had died in the night.

Quintus knew that his cavalry horse would make the slope easily. But he did not think he could steer the beast down, so he dismounted.

As he led the horse, he noticed that something had lifted. There was no longer an air of despondency about the men. There were conversations and jokes, many of them ribald and rude. There were light-hearted insults being thrown around. In short, everything you would expect from a section of the Roman army. The legionaries of the Ninth were glad to have saved their comrades of the Fifth. For the renegades, the re-taking of the *sacramentum* and the *ius iurandum* marked a new start, the past forgotten.

Mounted again, Quintus trotted up and down the column, talking to those that he recognised.

'Sir,' laughed Aulus, 'the archers think you are a god.'

'How so?' Quintus asked.

'I think perhaps my translation is not good. I am explaining to the Anatolians what happened for us to be accepted back. I think I may have misled them over the augur's sign. I have some of their tongue, and they some Latin.'

'How do you come to speak their tongue?'

'I spent time in their part of the world twenty years ago, serving with Marcus Antonius beneath the rugged Taurus Mountains, protecting the Tetrarch Amyntas from his enemies.'

'You had better put them right,' said Quintus, with mock solemnity. 'I will accept no sacrifices.'

Aulus saluted. No-one asked him where he was when Antonius went to Egypt, no-one on whose side he had served in the civil wars, in whose legion he had fought at Actium. Also in the past. Also forgotten.

At the foot of the slope the forest ended abruptly and the ground turned into a series of gentle hills, rolling ever upwards, curving away into the distance like soft waves on a shore. The strength of the light made Quintus blink. He knew that the reflections from the men's shields and armour would be visible for miles.

The land had been cleared for agriculture, and worked fairly recently. Big trees had been cut down and their trunks laid in lines to provide windbreaks — a difficult task. Brush and bramble had populated these lines. They ran north-south across the land, parallel with the river, so at least the column would not have to cross them. Quintus worried that they might provide cover for an enemy. Wiry saplings grew along them, springing up on the plain. A few thin streams ran away to the west. The path became wider and he ordered Rufus to signal the men to make a column of four, allowing the legionaries more chance to talk.

This was a perfect battlefield, gently sloping, one wing protected by the great river, the other by the low hedges. Before and behind there was forest in which to hide cavalry, auxiliaries or other reinforcements. Once committed, there was no means of escape for an army except back the way it had come. This was the sort of landscape that a Pompeius or an Antonius would have sought in order to fight a battle on his own terms, moving legions and cohorts as if they were pieces on a game board. Unfortunately, he had no such pieces to play should an enemy force appear before him. It made him nervous.

Quintus dismounted near the front of the column, bending down to test the soil and let it run through his fingers. In his blood, he was a farmer rather than a soldier, and he found the quality of the soil poor and sandy. Perhaps that was why it had been abandoned. On the far side, the forest once more filled the landscape. He was keen to be back within their shelter.

As he pulled himself back onto the horse, he spotted a flurry of dust beneath the horizon. He raised an arm to stop the column, ready to order them to form a square to repel the enemy, but the dust resolved itself into just four shapes. Four horses came on rapidly, but not at the sort of gallop that would betray a charge. He watched until he was certain that there were no more, then gave his orders. They were crossing one of the shallow streams.

'Order a rest, Rufus. Water the horses and let the men eat and drink if they wish. This is no threat, but post guards nevertheless.'

XXXIV: KÖNNEN WIR DIR VERTRAUEN

As the horsemen came closer, Quintus recognised Agnus, the messenger. He was accompanied by a Germani tribesman and flanked by two legionaries. The two sat upon their mounts, the spatha, the long sword of the cavalryman, at their side, round shields strapped at their back.

'Centurion,' Agnus shouted happily. 'I have found you.'

'I was never lost,' replied Quintus as he and Agnus dismounted.

They clasped arms and then Agnus stood back and saluted. 'I thought you might not have survived the action. You were still missing when Aquila sent me to find Galba.'

'Buried beneath the dead, but not yet among them,' Quintus grinned.

'I am glad of it. I warned Galba about the tribesmen who attacked us, as ordered. It explained our delay and alerted him to possible danger. But he was more concerned about the Germani in front of him than those behind. He thinks he has found the commander. The ladies are keen to see a rescue attempt mounted.'

'And these?' Quintus indicated the other three riders.

'These two are my companions and protectors, keen to find out if their friends in the cavalry live still. And this one you know; he is our guide to the oppidum.' He pointed to the boy clad in trews and a plain tunic, unarmed. 'Your men have orders. We have a fight waiting for us.'

The Germani boy made a sort of salute as Agnus pointed to him. He looked unhappy, eyes downcast. Of course, he had seen his cousin flogged and crucified, so he had no love for these men.

'Welcome,' Quintus said to him. 'How is your father? *Vater*?' He had heard the word used before.

The boy said something Quintus did not understand and pointed to the sky.

'Is his father dead?' Quintus asked Agnus.

'No, sir. He thinks you are referring to Wotan. They call him the Skyfather.'

'Why would I…? Never mind.' Quintus shook his head, then looked at the boy, at his pale hair, his smooth cheeks, his lack of the beard that clearly marked out manhood in his tribes. 'You are still young,' he said, not unkindly. 'You will learn to live with Rome in time.'

The boy hung his head. He clearly didn't understand what Quintus was saying to him.

'Dismount,' ordered Quintus, accompanying the command with a gesture. The boy slid off the horse. 'Give the horse to the legionary and wait there.' He pointed to a spot. Agnus, seeing that the boy did not understand, took the horse's reins from him and pointed to the same spot. The boy, sulking, stood where he was told.

Quintus looked at his men, squatting on the ground and chewing biscuit or dried meat. At the edges of the group there were guards posted. 'How urgent is the message? Do we need to go now?' he asked.

'Not at once, sir,' said Agnus. 'Centurion Galba plans to attack at the dark of the moon.'

'Attack who?'

'The Germani. In their fortress. The prefect is held a day's ride away, sir, in the oppidum of the local tribe — possibly the Vindelici. It is in a crook of the river, less than half a day's march below where Galba is camped.'

'He plans to take it?'

'He believes it to be the headquarters of a federation of local tribes. He thinks the fort may even harbour Dagaz. There is a chance for the commander to be out and safe before our men attack.' He indicated the Germani boy. 'This lad is to show us how to enter secretly and lead us to where Titus Flavius is likely being held. Your orders are to rescue the commander before the cohort crushes the Germani.'

'Centurion Galba trusts him?'

'As far as I can tell. Of course, he still holds his uncle.'

'He has no choice, really.' Quintus was philosophical. 'Either we go in blind or we trust him. Of course he might betray us. I am not one to note the waxing and waning of the moon. How many nights until the men attack, Agnus?'

'Including tonight, his freedman calculates four, sir,' Agnus replied.

'Not urgent, then,' Quintus said, 'but I want to be off this plain.' He looked to the other riders, speaking quickly but respectfully. 'I regret that your decurion died in the action with the Germani. Most of your comrades also fell. They died bravely, defending their brothers; they were given a pyre. I can say no more to offer you comfort.'

The two horsemen saluted and looked at each other. 'We suspected as much,' said one, waving a spear in the direction of the men. 'There are few horses here, it would seem, and even fewer of our comrades.'

'They died as Romans. They are in Elysium.' Quintus said. There was a pause, then the other cavalryman asked, 'May we join the men?'

Quintus nodded. 'They will welcome you. They will tell you how well your comrades died. I will keep the Germani boy in my care for now. Agnus, send me Caius. Tell him to bring food and water for the prisoner. We will move as soon as the horses have drunk enough.'

Agnus and the two cavalrymen dismounted and walked the four horses across to where the others were being watered. It was a shallow stream, peppered with many small boulders, but it was enough. They would hear the tale of the battle from fellow soldiers.

Caius brought food and water. The youth received the waterskin and hard biscuit from him without any show of gratitude. Indeed, he flinched as Caius approached him.

'Why does he fear me?' Caius asked Quintus.

'Do you ever look at your reflection?' Quintus smiled. 'You would frighten the gods themselves.'

Caius had the look of a ruffian about him. His stubble seemed to be permanent, never growing into a beard. His broken nose and the prominent veins that betrayed a life of drinking did not help. He shrugged. '*Sic vita*,' he said. Such is life.

Quintus gestured for him to sit down. 'Caius, I will need your skill,' he said. 'This boy speaks even less Latin than his father.'

'What is his purpose?' Caius asked. 'I thought the father, or uncle or whatever, was our guide.'

'His father is with Galba. Galba has found the oppidum of these people. He thinks he has found Dagaz. We thought the chieftain was behind us, a part of the group that attacked us in the forest. But either he has passed us — not impossible — or Galba is wrong and he is not in the oppidum.' Quintus took a long draught from his own waterskin and sighed. 'Dagaz is more dangerous out than in. He could catch the cohort between the oppidum and the forest, a hammer and anvil.' He paused. 'This boy is to tell us how to enter the oppidum stealthily and rescue the prefect. I don't know if we can trust him.'

'*Können wir dir vertrauen, mein Junge?*' Caius asked harshly in his own version of the captive's language — *can we trust you, boy?* The boy said nothing and merely sipped from the waterskin and chewed the dried meat. Caius shrugged. 'Time will tell,' he said.

The legionaries were ready to leave on Quintus' command, Caius taking charge of the guide at its head. Quintus thought the column was looking more and more like a real Roman unit; the soldiers' backs were straight, their manner disciplined and confident. He reminded himself that he should arrange a sacrifice of thanks for the return of the Larks to the ranks.

They crossed the open ground quickly and reached the edge of the forest. They were climbing higher and higher, and could see the shadowy outlines of great mountains on the skyline ahead of them. A line of grey, that could have been cloud, coalesced into something more solid, reflecting the setting sun on its peaks, even as the valley fell dark. Quintus whistled through his teeth, either these mountains were close, or they were a long way away and very imposing.

The pioneers found good ground, with the river to the east as protection, the forest to the south and one of the long hedgerows to the west. The guards, once posted, had an uninterrupted view of the plain running gently downhill to the north. The soldiers suspected the night would be cool and banked up the fires. Quintus called Sextus to assist with the evening's sacrifice.

'Clementia,' Sextus said without hesitation when asked which of the pantheon should receive the sacrifice. 'Divus Julius took her with him to the heavens — or so the Senate decreed. She is both goddess of mercy and redemption. These men of the Larks have redeemed themselves.'

'What does she require?' Quintus asked warily, afraid that it would be something unlikely and unavailable.

'If I remember rightly, two turtle doves would be sufficient, or a lamb,' Sextus said. After a pause, he added, 'The forest is full of loud and ungainly wood pigeons, easily brought down by the archers. One of these will be enough.'

'You are sure?'

'Certain.'

'Then tell the Anatolians to make it so. You will collect the necessary stones and oil and sacrifice it at the evening muster.'

Numerous pigeons were shot down, but only one formally sacrificed. After the sacrifice, Sextus declared the exta favourable before burning them.

'We have a special mission,' Quintus announced from his makeshift platform. 'We are going to try and release the commander, then destroy the fortress that holds him.'

The men nodded with enthusiasm. They enjoyed fighting. The mood in the camp was light. The sacrifice was favourable and there had been no punishment detail. It always lifted spirits when no-one needed to be flogged. Quintus was one of the few commanders who recognised this.

XXXV: HROLF

To the legionaries the Germani boy was a curiosity, a tall, long haired, smooth-faced Germani youth, wearing strange clothes. For many, this was the closest — unarmed — that they had ever come to one of the numerous tribes that lived along and beyond the great river.

They stood him up to admire his height and felt the fineness of his hair between their fingers. They turned him around on the spot and pinched his arm muscles before grunting approval. They compared their caligae with his foot coverings. When they felt the rough material of his tunic and trews, the boy swiftly showed that this was enough, pulling away, baring his teeth and lifting his fists to fight.

The men smiled and gentled him, making attempts to speak his language. They pointed to parts of the body and repeated sounds to try to learn 'head', 'nose', 'leg' and 'arm'. The boy, after they had stopped poking and prodding him, grew more confident and warmed to the attention. He was fascinated by the heavy studded caligae worn by the soldiers and part fascinated, part disgusted by some of the things they ate. When he indicated a desire to hold a sword or dagger, he was quickly and firmly rebuffed. Caius remained as his shadow and chaperon, helping with the language whilst learning more of it himself. The men tried to learn his name.

'Hrolf,' the lad said. The men thought he had misunderstood and was making an animal noise, but he repeated the sound, pointing to himself. 'Hrolf, Hrolf,' he insisted.

'He sounds like he is barking like a dog,' Cotta laughed. He pointed to himself and said his name slowly and clearly, then pointed back to the Germani boy.

'Hrolf,' he replied, hand on his chest.

The men laughed. So be it. Some managed to pronounce a version of the name that they could wind their tongues around.

In a semi-circle facing a fire, Quintus sat with his own contubernales Marcus and Sextus, along with Caius of the Larks and the aquilifer. Caius brought the Germani boy with him, his new friends waving him farewell and calling 'Hrolf' after him, as if they were temple dogs in the night.

There was still pigeon meat cooked by the Macedonian slaves, posca and — thanks to Sextus' sorcery — heavily watered wine. The boy ate the meat with relish, but turned his nose up at the smell of the wine and spat out the posca — the rough mixture of water, vinegar and poor quality wine was not for everyone.

'Water it is, then,' Quintus said, passing over his own water skin. As the boy drank Quintus addressed the group. 'As I explained at the muster, the message from Centurion Galba is that we are to rescue the commander. We need to decide how.'

'They have found Titus Flavius?' Marcus asked.

'Yes. He is being held in the town or fortress of a local tribe, the oppidum that Galba seeks to attack. Our traitorous former guides are either of this town or allied with the tribe that lives there. They are, apparently, a mountain tribe, a branch of the Raeti — not a tribe that we have heard of before, not one of the alliance that rode with Maelo. Galba has intelligence that Dagaz is there also so, if he takes the town, we rid ourselves of more than one enemy.'

'He is being held hostage?' Marcus asked.

'We are told that he is being held as a "guest" inside the town,' Quintus replied. 'This boy is to show us a way in and to take us to him.'

'But we do not know if he can be trusted,' Caius interjected. Unaware that he was the subject of the conversation, the boy was washing down a piece of pigeon breast with water. He had not been allowed an eating knife, so he pulled it apart with his teeth and fingers.

'We do not,' admitted Quintus, shaking his head. 'But Galba is still holding his father; we hope that will be enough. Without him, we are blind. We do not even know how to find the town, let alone a way into it.' There was a long pause as each of the men appraised Hrolf. As he realised that all eyes were on him, the boy lowered his meat nervously.

'Caius, ask him where this town lies,' Quintus ordered.

Caius, using a mixture of sign language and Gaulish and Germani words, asked the boy the question. Hrolf nodded in understanding and put the remains of the bird on a rock next to him. Leaning forward, he smoothed a patch of the sandy earth in front of the fire. Using a stick, he drew a winding line with a collection of pointed shapes at its bottom end. He pointed at the snaking line and said, 'Rhein.' He then indicated the pointed shapes and said, 'Alpen.'

'This is the great river,' Caius said, 'and at its end, I think, a range of mountains.'

'Perhaps those cloud-capped peaks that we can see in the distance,' said Marcus.

'Where are we?' Quintus asked, waving an arm to indicate the group and pointing at the rudimentary map.

Hrolf understood and made a mark with his stick. He made another mark further down, in a distinct horseshoe bend in the river. 'Oppidum,' he said.

'It is a fortified settlement,' Caius said. 'We cleared out many of them. It is a sort of headquarters for a tribe, although I have known them to be abandoned and rebuilt elsewhere. It is not a town as we would understand it. Alesia was one such settlement — Divus Julius took it when defeating Vercingetorix and the Celts.'

'That was not easy,' Marcus said. 'It took several legions and a long siege. The place was on a hilltop and properly walled, protected with both a palisade and a ditch.'

Quintus nodded in agreement. 'Show us the oppidum,' he said to Hrolf.

For the next hour the boy drew various crude pictures in the dirt and the men peppered him with questions. The boy had a little Latin and Caius was busy learning some of the local language. He sent Jovan to fetch Aulus to join them. He had traded with tribesmen on behalf of the Fifth. Sextus had also learned a little from the traders at the winter fort. With the help of these two, the information flowed more quickly.

The oppidum seemed to sit in a peculiar bend in the river, protected on two sides by the water. An outcrop of rock stopped the course of the river, turning it east until it found soft ground again and resumed its valley and its northward course. The people used the rocky hill as the base for their settlement, whilst on two sides the river served as a natural defence.

Before reaching the rock it flowed quickly, tumbling down from the foothills of the looming mountains. Hrolf scrawled a drawing that showed rocks in fast-flowing water and another that could represent nothing but a series of waterfalls.

Once turned it flowed east for a while, along the side of the rock and against the edge of the oppidum. If they interpreted correctly what the boy said, there was a bridge over the water that led to a way into the fortification from the south. He drew some lines that might indicate ploughed fields, alongside shapes that definitely indicated trees. The men laughed and understood when, his illustrations and words having failed, in frustration he made the noise of a pig, turning up his nose. It seemed that pigs occupied the cultivated land and rootled for acorns and hazelnuts in the forest that bordered it. There must be a route out to it through the palisade and across the ditch.

'There are many farmers here,' Aulus explained. 'Some of the clans are not warlike at all, but work the land. They don't fight unless provoked.'

'They are not all naturally warriors — they are farmers and herdsmen, but have been forced to defend their fields and flocks against other clans of their own people,' Caius added.

'The tribes that live by fighting are the ones who raid, steal and enslave women and children,' Aulus went on. 'We think they live further to the east, deep in the forest, and raid seasonally — especially when the weather is poor or game is scarce.' He smiled crookedly. 'I imagine a fat pig would suit them just as well as a wild boar.'

'There is movement of tribes across the land,' said Caius. 'Some of those raided choose to move out of their way and merely find different land to cultivate.'

'We have today crossed areas that seem to have been cleared for cultivation, then abandoned,' Quintus observed.

'Those who farmed there will have been driven off by their more aggressive cousins,' Aulus said. 'Divus Julius tried to stop all this infighting by settling the tribes on suitable land.' He laughed. 'But even a god could not civilise these people.'

The other men made non-committal noises. They would have nodded in approval but were not sure whether the statement could be considered a criticism of the god. Sextus opened his mouth to speak and then, seeing the dark look on Tullius' face, decided against it. He, along with everyone else here, knew that Caesar's policy had failed mainly because he had moved tribes to land already occupied by others.

'I admire the fighting spirit of many of these Germani tribes,' Caius said carefully. 'But surely it would be better if it could be harnessed for the benefit of Rome.'

'It has been done successfully elsewhere,' said Quintus. 'Illyricum, Macedonia, Asia, the new provinces of Hispania and Tres Gallia. They have all provided auxiliaries. Look at our Cantabrians and Anatolians. Some have even provided us with legionaries.' He turned to the men of the Larks. 'Wasn't Legio Five itself raised by Caesar in Gallia Transalpina?'

The men nodded. They knew that the larks' wings on their helmets were a reflection of their Gallic foundation and heritage. They were proud of them.

'So are these people farmers or fighters?' Sextus asked.

'Both,' Caius said. 'They farm unless threatened, then they fight. Dagaz may have threatened them, or they may be in league with him. They certainly oppose Rome.'

'Then we will have to fight them,' said Quintus flatly, 'and we need more detail.'

XXXVI: TUTUM EST. VIDE

Quintus turned back to questioning Hrolf. When asked to describe the town, the boy drew the shape of an olive, with lines to show it was raised high on a mound. A finger dug into the dirt marked out a ditch all around it. There were dwellings inside but also dwellings scattered outside it. The men concluded that not all of the people lived within the oppidum itself, and some would only enter it for protection from attack.

The boy drew a route for them that appeared to go through these settlements, and then crossed the cataracts to gain the pig field. Quintus could not see how his men could pass through unnoticed. He demanded further details.

'He says that if the town is threatened, there will be no people in these dwellings,' Aulus said.

'And the waterfall?'

Caius and Aulus again questioned Hrolf. This time he drew a recognisable picture of a waterfall with a number of stick figures standing on its edge.

'There must be a causeway of some sort on the edge,' Sextus said, 'a line of rock or stone.'

Quintus quickly drew a stick figure of a horse, but Hrolf shook his head vigorously. 'No,' he said, 'no, dangerous.' He rubbed the flat of his left hand against the back of his right, then parted the two suddenly.

'It is slippery,' Sextus said. 'That is what he is trying to say.'

'But men can cross on foot,' concluded Quintus.

Further discussion went on long into the night, the slaves banking up the fire as necessary and bringing more drink. Having established what the oppidum looked like, and where it was situated, Quintus now needed to know how to enter it secretly. He needed to know how to cross into the field of the pigs, how the bridge and the entrance were guarded, and where the commander was being held.

Hrolf's lack of Latin and the Romans' limited knowledge of the Germani language made this part difficult. Even simple concepts like 'up' and 'down' were hard for them to explain to each other. Finally, late into the night, Quintus decided that, even if he did not have all the information he needed, there was no more to squeeze out of the boy.

Once more unable to sleep, he checked the guards, his mind turning over plans and possibilities. By the time he wrapped his cloak around himself and lay down to rest, the sky was already noticeably lighter. If what Hrolf had told them was accurate, not even a full day's march would be needed for them to reach the oppidum. The moon was a mere sliver, lingering pale in the sky. If Galba planned to attack at the dark of the moon, the rescue must be mounted tonight.

Quintus found his seer and asked, 'Are we too late, Sextus? Is tonight the dark of the moon? Will Galba be attacking even as we attempt the rescue?'

'There is a final splinter of moon to rise tonight,' Sextus reassured him. 'Galba will attack with the dawn the day after tomorrow.' He smiled, turning his eyes to the cheerless sky. 'Come, Quintus, even you know that the moon does not take heed of the weather.'

The legionaries, around half a century in total, along with auxiliaries and slaves, formed up in a column and left the overnight camp behind. Quintus, Aquila and Rufus rode at their head, the eagle and the standard of Century One held high. The remaining cavalrymen, a sorry number after the fight in the forest, brought up the rear, guarding the few wagons the column still possessed. These, pushed by slaves and pulled by mules, dictated the speed of the march. Legionaries took it in turns to fall out and help with their progress.

The day may have been overcast, with the threat of rain in the air, but the men's spirits were high. There were many trods and tracks through the forest, so the men could sometimes march in a column of two, sometimes a column of four.

Cotta ran up the column to Quintus. 'The men ask for permission to sing, sir.'

Quintus agreed readily. To his surprise, he found himself the subject of their bawdy lyrics, the singers even using his nickname, Macilentus, and referring to him as many versions of an amber stream. The verses were crude but not unflattering. He knew that only a popular commander would receive such treatment.

They broke out into a glade, which gave a clear view of the dull sky above. The glade was ringed with giant specimens of spruce and larch, reaching for the heavens, walled in by battalions of spindly birches wrapped in vines. The patch of sky that could be seen was punctured all around its perimeter with many branches. The forest floor was dotted with tree stumps, and piles of fallen timber sat at the edges of the glade.

Quintus was nervous. This was clearly a spot that was visited, in which case it could only be the enemy that came here. He looked at Hrolf nervously, fearing they had been led into a trap and raising his arm to order a halt. Rufus signalled the same with a dip and twist of the standard. The cornicen raised his instrument to his lips. 'No noise,' Quintus said quickly, putting a hand on the cornicen's arm. 'Rufus, have the men ready to fight if necessary, but make sure they stay quiet. We are in the atrium of the enemy.'

Hrolf, fearful, spoke quickly to Caius. 'He says it is safe,' Caius reported to Quintus. 'He does not say why.'

'It could be the season,' Aquila guessed. 'Perhaps wood is not felled here in summer?'

Hrolf spoke directly to Quintus, using simple Latin and pointing away from the glade. '*Tutum est. Vide.*' It is safe. Look.

'Marcus, with me,' Quintus ordered, both of them following the boy.

Hrolf led Quintus and Marcus to the edge of the glade, where the trees parted to reveal another path, this one wider and manmade. They could hear the rushing of the river through the trees.

A few steps down this track and, to the east, what looked like a great walled town rose up out of a forest-clad hilltop.

'Oppidum,' said Hrolf simply.

Although it was big, the oppidum was well hidden. Both the folds of the land and the tall trees that grew in the hills and valleys served to hide it from prying eyes. Seeing it now through the gap in the trees, Quintus turned to Marcus, who stood beside him. He was impressed.

'We could have ridden straight past it, within a javelin's cast.'

'Not even a very well thrown javelin,' joked Marcus. 'Well hidden, indeed.'

It was the scale of the thing that took Quintus by surprise. Its size had not been apparent from Hrolf's description. The scrawling in the dirt had been unable to convey anything but its shape and where it was situated in relation to the Rhenus. Quintus had pictured something as large as a winter fort — a small village at best. What loomed in front of him was much more extensive than he had imagined.

The hill on which the settlement sat was steep-sided and bare, though tall trees grew close to its base. It had been cleared of anything that might provide cover and was covered in short grass. A wide ditch ran along its base. Halfway up its slope, a wooden fence had been raised. Above this, at the top edge of the hill, there was a substantial palisade. A timber wall stood, tall and solid and, as far as Quintus could see, unbroken as it curved away westwards into the distance. The thatched roofs of buildings inside poked out above the top of the fencing, and columns of smoke indicated that there were others that they could not see. Though so much less than a city, this was so much more than a tribal village.

From this angle they could see no way into the oppidum. No bridge appeared to cross the ditch. Quintus could see, over to the east, that the flat area at the base of the hill had proved too tempting for some of the inhabitants. There were simple dwellings here, and animal pens with cattle in them, along with patches of what looked like vegetable gardens. Perhaps, Quintus thought, the settlement, big as it was, had grown too small for its inhabitants.

From Hrolf's drawings Quintus knew that the river must run along the two sides of the hill that he could not see. He could hear its roar, muffled by the distance and the lie of the land.

From this viewpoint, neither he nor Marcus could see a way to attack the oppidum, at least not without siege engines and ballistae. The closeness and vastness of the structure made them unconsciously drop into a whisper.

'I can see why a siege was needed at Alesia,' said Marcus.

'There seems to be no other way to dislodge them. It is too massive, too well-defended.'

'And yet our boy here says there is a way in.' Marcus clapped Hrolf on the shoulder.

The three of them returned to the glade. Quintus wanted to address the men but, now he knew how close they were to the enemy, he did not want to raise his voice. They did not know how far any pickets or outposts would be from the oppidum, nor whether these areas were patrolled. The boy was little help, even with the intervention of Caius as translator. According to Caius, Hrolf appeared to be saying, 'It depends.'

If the people knew that they were under threat of attack, then there would be pickets; if they thought they were safe, there would not. Of course, they had no way of knowing whether or not the Germani were aware of their presence or that of Galba. From where they had viewed the oppidum, they could see no Roman force. Galba might be camped directly outside the front gates for all they knew.

There was, the boy said, a 'porta' — a minor entrance, not the main gate. This was the way in. Hrolf claimed it would be unguarded.

Quintus decided to risk but a few men; this was a rescue attempt, not an attack. He sent a legionary for his horse and mounted, gesturing for the men to come closer. Those at the front would repeat his message to the others. 'We can see the oppidum. It lies just beyond these trees.'

A murmur of anticipation travelled through the gathering. Quintus let it die down before continuing. 'Our task is to rescue the commander and then join Centurion Galba and the rest of the cohort to take this settlement. The first part does not require all of you. Those who are left behind must be ready to join forces with Galba should our mission fail.'

This time there was grumbling mixed in with the murmurs.

'You men who remain, the eagle stays here. It stays with you, as does the standard of the century. I do not like to leave the standards behind, but I cannot risk them on this expedition. Our mission will rely on stealth, furtiveness, soft tread. It is about secretly entering and exiting without a fight. It is no place for an eagle. No place to risk an eagle. It could easily fall — once more — into the hands of the Germani. It is your sacred charge.'

Aquila agreed with Quintus. The eagle projected power and presence and charisma, it was about shouting the pride and strength of Rome to the heavens. Quintus' mission, by comparison, was a whisper.

'I will send for those men I need,' Quintus said. 'The remainder can rest, but light no fires and make no noise. Mount a double guard and wait for our return.'

'And if you don't come back?' Aquila spoke directly to Quintus, but made no attempt to keep his voice down. The men would have heard.

Quintus matched Aquila's volume. 'Wait as long as you dare, but if we are not back by first light, march for the oppidum. Join Centurion Galba. The aquilifer will lead you.'

Quintus did not like to leave Aquila and Vetruvius behind, having seen their fighting skills. But he would not try to separate the aquilifer from the eagle, nor from his amicus.

Quintus dismounted and swiftly issued orders. 'Marcus,' he said, 'you are with me.'

Tullius, of course, came with him. With Marcus, he was leaning heavily on the older man's experience and expertise. With Tullius he knew he had an efficient and ruthless fighter. He called to his other contubernales, Caius and Rufus, whom he thought would have followed even if he had not chosen them.

'Rufus, deputise another to carry the standard. I need you with us.' Rufus nodded assent, and Quintus continued, 'Caius, I need you for the language and to keep an eye on the boy. He may yet decide to betray us. Agnus, you may be needed as messenger, Alba, you as capsarius.'

Hrolf, unarmed, would lead them, walking between Quintus and Caius.

XXXVII: NOVEM

Novem — there were to be nine of them in this rescue party. Sextus approved. He considered nine to be a lucky number — or at least was willing to make a case for it. 'There are nine muses, and nine twists in the river Styx,' he said.

Tullius was less convinced. 'There are two consuls, six Vestals, seven hills of Rome and twelve labours of Heracles,' he muttered.

'Nine stars in Taurus, and the symbol of our legion is the bull,' countered Sextus.

'A stretch,' Tullius replied sulkily. 'But I am happy to believe it is lucky if you do.'

The men who were to stay behind made themselves as comfortable as possible, squatting in circles and talking softly. A guard was mounted on the perimeter and the paths. To those men chosen the day, still grey and overcast, dragged on as if the night would never come. They were eager to be on their way.

The men of the rescue party sat in a circle of their own and used dirt to dull their shields. Alba and Agnus were tasked with making a rope out of twisted vine strands. Quintus knew they would need to cross the river at least once, and if they were roped together, they would be less likely to lose someone.

As they worked, they listened to Hrolf rehearse the way in which they could enter the oppidum, and where they should go once in. He drew pictures on the ground until there was no longer sufficient light to see them.

Quintus forbade fires and torches due to fear of discovery, but also to aid his men in adjusting their eyesight to the dark.

The moon, the thinnest of crescents, would provide no light, and the sky, overcast as it was, had extinguished the stars.

He waited as long as he dared. Then, when he judged it dark enough, the party set off.

They wore no helms and wrapped their cloaks tightly around their armour. The cheek pieces of helmets would restrict their vision and light could bounce off them, betraying them to the enemy. They moved lightly, carrying no throwing spears or satchels. Their shields they kept, the faces of them darkened. They ran at an easy pace along the forest track, following the boy's lead, their footsteps quiet on the leaf-strewn floor, their bodies bent over to make them smaller targets for any prying eyes. They needed, Hrolf explained, to pass the oppidum completely on its western flank.

What little light remained was dying, flickering through the trees to their right. To their left, the oppidum loomed, a dark and forbidding silhouette, tinged with a blood-red light. Quintus, thinking death a more likely outcome than success, whispered a heartfelt prayer to Ceres, his own household protector. It was true dark by the time the group reached the bank of the river. Not even a glimmer came from the last of the old moon — either it was not yet risen, or the thick clouds obscured it. A few stars had managed to wink out but not enough for anyone — Sextus included — to recognise any constellations.

The trees were thin here and, at times, it was difficult to pick out the track from the scrubland to either side. The grass was wet and slippery with the constant spray blowing across from the waterfalls.

The noise of the river grew louder as they approached, a roar like a wild animal, but constant. Now it could also be seen, water cascading downwards with a luminescence that needed no other light as it tumbled down the craggy hillside. Quintus could see three separate cataracts rushing down to where the water foamed at the level of the bank, three wide steps of deep blackness each punctuated by a sudden boiling line of foam and then a whitewater plunge to the pool below. The water between the falls was black as pitch, its surface unruffled, its depths unknown.

In the last of these stretches of inky water, a large stone sat, flat-topped and soaked with spray. The river flowed up to it and around it, but not over it. In the winter, it would be underwater.

'Are there more of these?' Quintus shouted over the roar of the river. 'Caius, ask him.'

Caius pulled Hrolf to him and spoke into his ear. When the boy replied, he told the men, 'We cross here. There are more stones. He says it is safe.'

'Then he goes first,' said Sextus.

'No, he could betray us,' said Marcus.

'I will go first,' Agnus offered. 'I have good eyes and I am the lightest.'

'Most likely to be carried away then,' Tullius muttered.

Quintus waved Agnus forward. Alba brought over the vine rope.

'Wrap the rope around yourself and tie it tight,' said Quintus. 'Each of those that follow will turn it around their wrist. Take care, soldier. I will send Hrolf directly behind you. Keep watch over him on the other side. I will go next. I will be right behind him.'

Agnus tied the rope around his waist. He then hoisted his shield onto his back and stepped gingerly onto the stone. It measured about half a pace across. From here he could just see the further edge of it, then a gap of dark water. He could not tell how wide this gap was. He stepped onto the shiny surface and looked from side to side in trepidation. On one side, the waters poured over the edge and fell vertically into the pool below, the noise of their arrival competing with that of the other cataracts. On the other side, he could not determine where the black waters finished and the next stone began.

He shuffled forward and felt around with his foot, at first finding nothing then, with relief, making contact with the next stone. It felt solid when he tested it carefully by pressing down. He offered a silent prayer to the nymphs of the river before transferring his weight across. Both stones stayed steady. The gap between the stones was wider than he had expected, easily wide enough for a person to fall into. He shuffled across this second stone in the same way and again felt outwards with his foot. As he touched the next stone, he smiled to himself. This would be an easy crossing in daylight.

Quintus saw that Agnus was making progress and pushed Hrolf forward onto the first stone. The boy understood and wrapped the rope around his wrist. He began to make his way across. As soon as the stone was free, Quintus reluctantly stepped out after him.

'Alba, you next,' he shouted before he stepped again. 'Then you, Sextus. Then the rest. Marcus, bring up the rear.' He relied on the evocatus to defend them if necessary.

Quintus did not have far to go before he could no longer see the bank. He could barely make out the smaller figure of the boy ahead of him and was acutely aware that one small slip or a tug on the rope and either or both of them could be in the water. At this point they were all extremely vulnerable. If there were any guards posted they would be dead in an instant. He comforted himself with the thought that at least the dark hid them from potential enemies.

There were ten or twelve stones in the line that spanned the top of the waterfall. Quintus lost count after the first few, concentrating instead on keeping his footing. To begin with he could see Hrolf in front of him, but the boy was light and quick on his feet and unencumbered with weapons and armour. He was forced to loosen his grip on the rope, letting it run through his hands, as Hrolf was so much faster than he. The boy vanished into the night.

In the almost tangible darkness, Quintus' whole world became the roar of the water, the cold touch of the flying spray and the solid feel of the stone beneath him. He grasped the rope as if it alone could save his life. To his right, the waterfalls fell noisily; to his left, a dark chasm threatened, bubbling white as the river reached it. He did not like the sensation of fear — the tingling caused by not being in charge of his own fate. He knew that the boy could lie in wait for him and push him in easily, or pull on the rope. Like Agnus, he placed his trust in the gods.

It was with relief that his foot at last felt soft ground, and he let out a great sigh. 'Agnus,' he called.

'We are here, sir.'

A shout from behind confirmed that Alba needed him to move aside so he could gain the bank. Sextus was immediately behind him. The men were crossing much more quickly than he had.

'Turned out to be as easy as the boy said,' Sextus grinned, although Quintus noticed that he gave a little squeeze of gratitude to the bulla he wore around his neck

The others followed. It was an easier journey knowing that others had gone before, but it was still heart-in-mouth territory for each step into the dark. The men were glad to be on dry land.

'This is but the first part of our enterprise,' said Marcus, the last to arrive.

'And possibly the easiest,' warned Quintus. 'Do not be complacent. We are now in enemy territory.'

The men's night sight enabled them to make out the shadows of each other in the dark.

'Column of two,' said Quintus. 'Marcus, bring up the rear. Although I fear no attack from that quarter, I still think we should be wary.' Marcus nodded in agreement.

Quintus turned to their guide. 'Hrolf, lead on to the next crossing, the bridge.' He gestured to help the boy understand, and he nodded.

The others formed up into pairs so that all stayed close together and set off across the rough ground. Underfoot it was uneven and wet from the spray of the waterfalls, and what might have been the start of ploughed furrows caused them to trip and slow down. They were irregular furrows, and short.

'The hogs have been allowed to root here,' said Quintus, remembering his family's farm. He walked beside Hrolf, and turned to address Sextus and Rufus behind him. 'Take care, the hogs may still be here. Pass the word.'

The noise of the river no longer drowned their speech, but continued as a constant rumble in the background. Quintus could not raise his voice any louder for fear of being detected. This next crossing might be guarded, though the boy had insisted it was not. He was adamant, and Quintus reluctantly believed him.

Though they could not see far to their right, Quintus felt as if this side was closed in. He thought that there was forest here, and that would be the most likely place for pigs. As they moved awkwardly over the broken ground, the noise of the river behind them diminished, but now flowing water could be heard ahead of them. A different sound, not the mad rushing of water downhill but a softer note, the muffled music of water running quickly but in a deep place.

'It is the other river crossing,' said Quintus. 'Spread out. Draw your weapons. We move stealthily. There could be guards here.'

The oppidum now loomed above them, massive and forbidding, even darker than the sky, blocking it out. There were no lights to be seen on this side. They reached the riverbank and began to feel their way along it, seeking the bridge.

Rufus found a post driven into the earth. 'No sign of any guards, but here is a post,' he reported. 'There is a beaten track leading away from the river.'

At the same time Tullius found a similar post. 'One here also,' he said. 'Two paces or so between them. Quintus, this is where your bridge should be.'

XXXVIII: PONTO NOX INCUBAT ATRA

Of course there were no guards. Quintus cursed his stupidity. Who needed to waste manpower on guards when you could just pull up the bridge? He guessed that it would not be solid, but slats tied with rope, the rope then fixed to these posts and pulled taut. Horses would not cross it, but people would not mind and cattle, goats and pigs could be persuaded. At the end of the day, the ties could be undone and the bridge pulled to the opposite bank.

'You knew this,' Quintus accused Hrolf angrily.

Hrolf shook his head vigorously and beckoned furiously to Caius. Caius bent his head to listen.

'He says he did not know. He says that the last time he was in this place, there was a bridge here. People crossed it. Animals crossed it. But this was in daylight. He has never seen it at night. He insists he did not know.' Caius tilted his head upwards so that he could look Quintus in the eye. 'He is in fear of his life, centurion. I do not think he could lie now. He is scared witless.'

Quintus cursed. There was no way back apart from the way they had come. Quintus was both disappointed and angry. Disappointed to have failed before even entering the oppidum; angry at wasting time and risking men on a mission that could barely find a beginning.

'Down,' warned Tullius suddenly, ducking. He pointed to where a couple of lights now bobbed briefly above the palisade before vanishing again.

'I do not think they are looking down here,' Quintus said dispassionately. 'We are no threat.'

The men sat on the edge of the ditch, looking down into the depths of the waters flowing far below.

'*Ponto nox incubat atra*,' whispered Sextus.

'More poetry?' Rufus demanded. 'What is it this time?'

'Publius Vergilius again, my friend: *black night sits brooding on the deep.*'

Tullius, clearly unimpressed, hawked as he polished his gladius on his tunic. He was no lover of poetry.

Quintus suddenly realised that the boy was missing. 'Where is Hrolf?' he asked.

'Betraying us,' said Tullius darkly.

'*Adsum*,' said the boy, hurrying back to the group. 'I am here.'

'What are you doing?' Quintus asked.

'Looking,' Hrolf said in Latin, then beckoned Caius to him.

'He says he can get across and throw the rope back to you,' said Caius. 'He says come and look.' The boy pointed excitedly at a spot further down the stream.

This section of the defences was not part of the natural course of the river; this ditch was manmade. It was cut in a wedge shape, the top wider than the bottom. Where Hrolf pointed Quintus could see that the distance narrowed, that someone light enough would be able to jump to the other side. Here, there had been a landslip, and the opposite bank was lower than the one on which they stood. With luck, a man would be able to cross and scramble up the opposite bank. If they missed the leap, or missed their footing, they would plunge to their death.

From the other side, the vine rope could be attached to the bridge and thrown back over, and the bridge pulled across. But why would Hrolf, a Germani prisoner, an enemy whose father was still being held captive, do this for them?

'How can we trust you?' Quintus asked, taking the boy by the shoulders and looking him in the eye.

The boy understood and grinned. Clearly he knew they had no choice.

'We cannot trust him,' said Marcus. 'It is a stupid idea.' Tullius nodded in agreement.

'What else do we do?' Quintus asked. 'Go back the way we have come? Fail miserably?'

'If he betrays us, we are no worse off than we are now,' said Sextus. 'The occupants of the oppidum cannot attack us across the bridge if the bridge is not there. And I hardly think an enemy will try to attack across the stepping stones.'

'At worst, we join the pigs in the forest,' Rufus said, 'then work our way back to Galba.'

'We should at least try.' Agnus felt junior to the veterans and the contubernales, but dared to at least offer an opinion. Alba held the rope out to Hrolf.

Quintus knew that this was the only course of action that gave them any chance of success. All of the men trusted Quintus. So it followed that they trusted his decision to at least let the boy try.

They made their way across to the point where Hrolf had indicated he could cross. The boy draped the rope around his shoulders. On his feet he wore leather wraps, wound around several times and tied at the ankle. He untied these and shoved them into his belt. He then set off, facing away from the edge, lowering himself carefully until only his head and arms remained above ground level.

'Steady,' said Caius gently, in the boy's own tongue. Hrolf's head tilted and he managed a grin before vanishing over the side. His hands seemed to slip at the same time, and suddenly there was none of him to be seen.

Some of the men strained forward to peer over the edge, expecting to hear a splash as the mission failed. But even in the dark they could see that the boy was no longer there.

'Gone,' said Agnus, disappointed.

'I knew it was a stupid idea,' said Tullius, who had stayed back, along with Marcus and Rufus.

'*Adsum.*' The boy's voice came from deep in the ditch, a muffled hoarse sound, announcing his presence, letting them know that the mission had not yet failed. Quintus looked down, narrowing his eyes in an attempt to focus, but he could not see him. Hrolf was not clinging to the bank.

'Look,' said Sextus, whose eyes had caught movement. 'He is on the other side.'

The other legionaries looked up, searching the opposite bank. There a dark shadow clung on like some sort of giant frog, just above the swirling waters, barely visible against the dark side of the ditch. Hrolf could only be clinging on with his fingers thrust deep into the soil and his bare toes sunk into the bank.

His cheek was pressed against the cold earth, which explained the muffled voice. That and the distance that the boy had fallen. Hrolf must have let go as he dropped, turned and jumped all in one go and now was splayed on the far bank. There was no way that he could ever reverse the move and return. At the moment, it seemed that neither could he move. There was only one way he could survive.

'Climb,' urged Quintus, though he said it quietly, more in hope than as a command.

Curiosity had taken charge of the three chief doubters, who now also leaned forward.

The boy's left arm moved, his hand feeling upwards for a better grip. The movement was not a success, and the rest of his body slipped downwards a good handspan. There was an audible intake of breath from the watchers.

'*Adsum*,' the boy's voice drifted up. A reassurance, although it sounded less confident than it had before.

This time his left foot moved, his toes digging into the bank. The toehold must have felt trustworthy, because Hrolf then straightened his leg so that his whole body moved upwards. A handhold for his right hand, reaching far above his head, proved good.

His right leg moved upwards and found a toehold of its own. In two smooth moves, Hrolf had gained half the height of his body. The rushing waters no longer looked to be a danger. The boy rested, catching his breath, then moved again. Though the bank was crumbly, he dug in to find holds, or entrusted his weight to the roots of the few spindly trees and shrubs that attempted to grow at the top of the bank, threading down towards the water below. He climbed until his hands reached the top of the bank.

Gaining the top was difficult and hazardous; there was only a very thin stretch of ground between the oppidum and the ditch. Part of the bank had crumbled away. There was no room to kneel or stand, even if he could have pulled himself up. He now had to move sideways two or three paces before a ledge opened out. His best bet would be to haul himself up at the bridge posts. The legionaries watched him move, powerless to help.

Quintus silently willed him on. It seemed that the boy took an age to reach the spot where he could finally grasp the post and haul himself out of the ditch. When he did, pulling himself over the lip on his belly, it was all the men could do not to applaud. Hrolf scrambled awkwardly to his feet and crouched to gain his breath.

Then he stepped cautiously between the bridge posts.

'You four. Go,' Quintus ordered, his gesture including Marcus, Tullius, Sextus and Rufus. The contubernales understood and ran to the bridge posts on their side, ready to receive the rope. Across from them, Hrolf stood tall and raised his arms in triumph, then began to unwind the rope.

He tied a complicated knot in one end of the rope to weight it and fixed the other end to one of the posts on his side. Drawing his arm back, he flung the rope towards the opposite bank. The legionaries did not even try to grasp it. They could see it would fall far too short, the rope snaking out and the knot making a disappointing splash in the water below. It was a long way short, and they were immediately concerned.

Hrolf reeled it in and tried again. Once more, though it appeared to be well enough thrown, it found the surface of the river. This time it came nearer.

'It is too short,' said Rufus, with a curse. 'This is all a waste of time.'

'Have faith,' encouraged Sextus. 'The gods are with us so far.'

'Third time lucky,' Marcus said unemotionally. Tullius just grunted.

'Third time lucky,' Sextus agreed. 'Fortuna be with us.'

They watched the boy bend down and do something, but could not work out what it was. Then he straightened up and gave the rope its third chance to reach the other side. Quintus saw what he had done as Marcus, almost falling into the ditch, grabbed the long stick that Hrolf had thrust through a much reduced knot. Marcus was ecstatic and pulled on the rope to secure it, eliciting a cry of panic from the boy as he was tugged towards the river.

XXXIX: A CAPITE AD CALCEM

Caius spotted what had happened. 'He has the rope around his wrist,' he hissed urgently. 'Do not pull him in.'

Marcus realised and let the rope go slack, other hands reaching for the knot and undoing it. Now the rope spanned the ditch, Hrolf sought to attach it to the bridge, which was no more than a collection of slats, rolled up at the side. Between them, the legionaries took the weight of the bridge as Hrolf fed it out over the ditch. It turned out not to be heavy and they were able to pull one side of it across and tie it off, the other dangling temptingly. Again, it seemed as if they faced failure until Quintus slapped himself on the forehead with an exasperated, 'Of course.'

He picked the stick up from where Marcus had let it drop and, lying on his belly, used his long reach to hook the other side of the bridge and gradually tease it towards them. Sextus grabbed the rope end whilst his centurion wriggled backwards away from the edge. Marcus and Rufus pulled the sides taut and wrapped the ropes around the posts.

They had barely finished when Hrolf, clearly delighted, ran across the bridge. Anyone heavier would have plunged the structure into the river. The rope in Marcus' hand tugged and he cursed the boy.

'By the gods, barbarian, can you not wait?'

Hrolf grinned at the veteran. The others congratulated the boy on his feat. Sextus clapped him on the back whilst Caius, against all propriety, hugged him.

'Tell him that it was well done, Caius,' said Quintus.

'He knows, sir. Look at him. He is purring like a cub that found a lioness's teat.'

'*A capite ad calcem*, happy from head to heel,' smiled Sextus. Hrolf sat grinning as he tied his foot coverings once more.

'We move on to the rescue?' Tullius asked unemotionally.

'We move on,' Quintus said. 'Across the bridge one at a time, I think. No need to put unnecessary strain on it. If we succeed, we will need it on the way back.'

Carefully they each crossed the bridge, making sure that only one of them was on it at a time, waiting until the man ahead had reached the other bank before stepping on to the slats himself. The simple structure swayed with each step. There was, of course, no parapet or even a rope at waist height to grasp, so their progress was slow and careful. Marcus was the last to cross.

Quintus signalled the men to gather round and they stood in a rough circle.

To the east, deep in the woods, a solitary wolf howled. An answering howl came from even further away. An owl hooted, and then the land was once more silent.

'The wolf is a good omen,' said Sextus confidently. 'Lupus suckled Romulus.'

None of them dared ask about the owl. All knew what its cry meant. They just hoped that the death it predicted was none of theirs.

'Stay in pairs up the track,' Quintus said. 'Hrolf and I will lead. Caius, you stay close in case I need your skills. Marcus and Tullius will bring up the rear. We stay silent, and we deal with enemies when we must. They seem to think the river is sufficient protection on this flank of the oppidum, so I do not anticipate guards until we reach the palisade. You will have drawn blades by then.'

They followed a well-trodden path that, to avoid steep climbs, curled backwards and forwards across the hill. The first barrier, around halfway up, which they feared was guarded, turned out to be broken fencing and large stones. It was enough to provide a defendable line, but no barrier to anyone climbing. Clearly there had been no attack from this direction for a long time. They kept going.

Quintus gathered them together before the last turn that would take them up to the palisade. They knew this would be manned, so they crouched low to the ground to look at the imposing structure.

The palisade fence was much taller than a man, and stretched round the hill. They could see that a gate was pierced into it at the top of the track.

'Quickly,' Quintus ordered. 'Beneath the timber, right up against the side. Go.'

The men moved in single file, keeping low. Quintus pushed Hrolf ahead of him.

'Shields,' he added, the order being passed down the line. The men lifted their blackened shields above their heads, making them even less visible. Caius pulled Hrolf beneath his shield. The height of the palisade meant that once the patrol reached its base, the men were no longer visible to any of the guards. The defenders would have to lean out and peer downwards into deep shadow. They would only do this if they suspected a presence, so it was imperative to keep quiet.

They crept along the palisade's foot, like a giant metal-skinned centipede. At the head of the beast, Quintus could see a flicker of torches that, regularly spaced, marked the top of the defences. At least the gate was not guarded. It was a single leaf, square and sturdy, with no way to open it from the outside.

The boy at once flinched away from the angry looks directed at him. He spoke to Caius.

'He has only ever seen it open,' Caius translated.

'Here,' said Sextus, who had been studying the door. 'There is a way in.' The men crowded closer as he explained. 'With gates and doors, people spend time and effort on locks and bolts and forget the hinges. These will cut.'

The door hung roughly on two hinges of leather. There was a gap between the gatepost and the timber of the gate through which the straps could be seen.

'Cut them,' Quintus ordered, and at once pugios flashed out and began sawing through. It did not take long. Quintus gathered them close. 'You two, stay here and guard our exit,' he told Agnus and Alba. 'Keep the boy with you.' He then detailed the others left, right, centre. 'The boy says the commander will be in one of the smaller huts; it will be one with a single door and no window. Find it. Silence anyone who discovers you.'

They pushed at the door and it opened a crack. Another shove and there was enough room for them to slip through. Still pressing their bodies to the palisade, they entered the settlement.

The way that Quintus deployed the men was different to most strategies any of them knew. They were Roman soldiers, trained men of the legions — they should be facing the enemy front and centre, shield to shield, drawing their swords in unison. They felt more like thieves than legionaries, especially as it was deep night. There were no fires burning outdoors and the only torches were those that marked the top of the parapet. They scuttled between the huts like rats in a threshing yard.

It was inevitable that they would be discovered. Rufus and Sextus were the first. They almost bumped into a man, perhaps a warrior, perhaps not. They did not wait to find out, lowering his body to the floor as the life seeped from it. The others also silenced enemies that night or, as Tullius muttered to the gods later, murdered them. None were guards, and none were armed.

The oppidum appeared to be at peace. There were no watchers on the inside, and if there were watchers on the palisade they had their eyes turned outwards. People slept soundly.

Almost all of the huts were without windows. Each had straight sides and a domed roof of thatch, along with a doorway covered with skins. In the huts that the legionaries investigated, pulling back the hide coverings, there were few people. They guessed that most slept in the longhouse that stretched across the centre of the settlement.

In the huts were some of the very old, some sick, some with babes in arms. Tullius disturbed a mother breastfeeding a newborn. He put his finger to his lips and withdrew, muttering a prayer to Juno to protect both himself and these two, even as she retreated into deeper shadow, pulling a covering over her head.

Quintus and Caius took a single torch from an empty hut and continued to search. 'Here,' whispered Quintus as they came across a dwelling with a solid door, a sturdy bar of timber across it. Lifting the bar, they prised the door open and looked inside.

Quintus was not the first to find the commander, nor did he have the honour of freeing him from his captivity. No-one did. The single torch revealed the prefect's stiff body.

It was no honour to be captured, it brought shame and humiliation. Titus Flavius Pusio had already stumbled on his way up the *cursus honorum*, had already failed to make praetor or aedile, had already been a disappointment to his more noble-born wife who expected to be the consort of a consul. Now he had made it to the top of the ladder in one wild leap, his honour and future name assured.

He had not been ill-treated, that much was apparent. When Quintus held the light close, he could see no yellowing bruises on his face, no features that had been cut or disfigured. Flavius' shiny breastplate with his family crest was still buckled to his chest, his lower arms and his shins still protected with bronze, his baltea and cingulum intact. Neither his crested helmet, nor his paludamentum, were anywhere to be seen. His gladius was missing, and they could see no sign of the weapon he had used to reach Elysium. He had clearly thrust upwards beneath his breastplate, so that the tip of the blade should reach his heart.

The wound was not recent; the body was stone-cold and the blood congealed and black. His face looked like the sort of wax death mask that would be at home in a noble atrium. Quintus could not work out why he had not been moved, had not been buried or burned.

'We need to take him with us,' he whispered urgently to Caius. 'We will need the help of the others.'

Caius understood the need for a proper funeral, but as he turned in the doorway to find his companions, a noise made them both start. First it was geese cackling and complaining, then dogs barking, then angry voices.

'We are discovered,' Caius said. 'We are going to have to leave him for now, unless you want to fight six against a village.'

Briefly, Quintus thought of what a heroic stand that would be, then checked himself and moved for the door. The light in his hand caught a glint on the prefect's finger.

'I will at least take his ring to his wife,' Quintus said. He grabbed the ring and pulled.

'Hurry,' called Caius urgently. 'They are coming closer.'

Quintus' blade was quickly in his hand and a bloodless cut released the ring. 'Sorry, sir,' he said, slipping the ring from the finger and onto his own hand before careering out of the door.

They heard the crackle and rush of torches being lit. The shouting, the barking of dogs and the honking of geese grew louder. Once or twice a different sound intruded, a more desperate sound — someone had been found dead.

The two of them ran for the gate through which they had entered, hoping that the others had made it. They were not the first. Sextus and Rufus appeared just ahead of them. Marcus and Tullius were already the other side of the timber, ready to push it closed. Behind them, a swell of anger and indignation was growing like a tidal wave.

'Run!' Quintus yelled.

XXXX: MORTEM IPSE SIBI

The men needed no further urging and set off down the winding track. Moments later, the gate burst open and an angry crowd emerged, screaming defiance. It was preceded by snarling dogs and lit by many torches. Spears whistled over the heads of the fugitives and stones and curses were thrown. The pursuers ignored the track and began to scramble straight down the bank. If they were to escape, the Romans had to do the same.

They slipped and slid, running so fast that they could barely stay upright, heading for where they knew the bridge to be.

Hrolf was fastest of them and crossed first. Not only was he the smallest and lightest, but he carried nothing. The others had shield and armour and weaponry. Quintus expected the boy to vanish into the dark. It looked like his captors were about to die, so here was his chance to escape.

Instead the boy stood by the gatepost, frantically waving the others on, urging them to follow.

The boy slapped Agnus and Alba on the back, then urged Rufus and Sextus across. Quintus ran across last. He pointed away from the bridge. 'Go, Marcus, Caius. Shields, there,' he commanded sharply. 'Not you, Tullius. I need you and your sword.'

The evocati understood and immediately organised the others At once there was a line of protection, shield edges overlapping, across the end of the bridge. Sextus grabbed Hrolf by the arm as he passed and pushed him behind the shields.

Six shields was not many, but better than none. They were only just in time, as spear after spear, and even a few axes, bit into the wood. Quintus crouched behind his own shield at the side of the bridge. He knew that Tullius' gladius would have the keenest blade — he spent many hours sharpening it. 'Quickly. Cut the rope that side.'

At the other post, Tullius bent down and chopped away at the twisted twine that held the rope bridge in place. Quintus did the same. There were two slavering dogs already on the bridge. As it moved they stood still, uncertain, legs splayed. Then they ran back the way they had come.

When the pursuers saw what was being done, their shouts became angrier. As the first of them stepped onto the slats, a young man, his face contorted with rage, Quintus' rope parted and the bridge turned and twisted, throwing the attacker downwards. Another, an older man, just as angry, with a two-headed axe in his hand, just managed to stop himself, lurching backwards with a cry. The young man grasped the bridge as he fell, but his weight just pulled the other rope taut, making it easier for Tullius to strike down and cut it. As it snapped apart, the bridge writhed backwards, like a snake whose head was cut off, leaving the man dangling over the river, knocking against the bank.

'Back!' Quintus shouted. 'Join the wall.' They each took up station, extending the protection. Missiles continued to be thrown, but the legionaries backed away in formation, step by step, Marcus calling the pace. They held their shields in front of them, the axes and javelins thudding ever more lightly into them.

Quintus judged the moment when the barrage stopped. He dared to look and saw that the spears were falling short, that axes were no longer being thrown. The mob was lit by many torches, spreading along the bank, looking for places to cross. But the bank on their side was lower — they would not be able to repeat Hrolf's feat, even had they anyone as agile as he. Only their curses would make it across to the other side.

Quintus was surprised. There were few men here, few warriors. Most of the torch-bearers were women, recognisable by their ankle-length skirts, short capes and bound hair. Some held dogs on leashes, some threw missiles, and all encouraged the others. Those casting spears were beardless youths, boys no older than Hrolf, or old men, slow-moving and white-haired. Though they still made a lot of noise, there was no way that any could cross. The legionaries stood up and drew their breath.

'Was it worth it?' Tullius asked sulkily. 'We killed a few. We made an enemy.'

'We found the commander,' said Quintus.

There was a brief pause as this information sank in.

'Then where is he?' Rufus asked. 'Did we leave him behind?'

'He is dead.' Quintus said. 'By his own hand. *Mortem ipse sibi.* He was in the hut where he fell.'

'Why?' Rufus asked.

'Perhaps they are waiting for the warriors. There seemed to be none in the settlement. We should have been discovered long before we were,' Caius said.

'I found no fighting men,' Tullius said slowly. 'Only women and children and old men. And babies. I do not kill babies.'

'They must have a use for him,' Sextus suggested. 'Some sort of ritual sacrifice, perhaps.'

'With a dead man?' said Alba.

'These are barbarians,' said Rufus. 'Who knows what they plan?'

'Where is our barbarian?' Marcus asked. 'Did he run? Hrolf,' he called.

'*Adsum, dominus*,' a small voice replied from behind them. The boy was still with them.

Quintus hid his surprise. 'I have the prefect's ring,' he said. 'At least I can prove his death and hand it to his widow.'

There was a silence. The mission had not been a complete failure. Now all they could do was return to the rest of the group and lead the men back to Galba, to help him take the oppidum.

Looking back at the bridge, Quintus could see that the inhabitants were starting to return up the hill. The track was dotted with torches. A few lights still explored the bank, no doubt looking for a place to cross.

'We return,' Quintus said. 'There is much of the night left. We go back to Aquila and the others, then join Galba. Galba commands the cohort now. Caius, tell the boy we need to find those stepping stones.'

'Just follow the noise of the cataracts,' Sextus said, deeming it obvious. Rufus slapped him on the back. 'I did not want to cross those again,' he said, a smile in his voice even if it could not be seen. 'They are more dangerous than the Germani.'

They turned their backs on the oppidum and began to walk swiftly across the broken ground towards where they knew the waterfalls to be. Hrolf led the way, although all could hear the water.

Darkness once more enfolded them, the pinpoints of light on the side of the oppidum rapidly diminishing, the angry shouts fading into the night. Shortly, it was as if the raid had never been. Quintus felt the ring on his finger. It was real enough. Once more their talking dropped to short sentences and low tones — dark seemed to have the effect of muting conversation.

'Why would the prefect kill himself?' Rufus asked.

'The stigma of capture,' said Sextus. 'That is all I can think.'

'For his honour,' said Marcus simply. To him, as to all the evocati, it was obvious. The shame of being captured would be too much to bear, too much for Flavius' wife to bear. The prefect would never have been able to return to Rome. To offer his own life to the gods was the only way in which his honour and name could be restored.

'The stars, the gods, aligned against him,' said Sextus. 'He could not help what happened.'

'He should not have let himself be taken. He should have fought to the death,' said Marcus harshly. 'That is the Roman thing to do.' He had once been a captive himself, but had been tricked and drugged whilst injured. Had he been taken in battle, he would have killed himself.

'It is easy,' Tullius added. 'Yesterday he was a captive. Now he is a hero.' He did not feel there was any more to say.

They trudged on over the broken ground. Suddenly, a light sparked in front of them. A single torch. Then another, and another. They winked into life like stars in a cloud-strewn sky cleared by the wind. They formed a semi-circle that blocked the way to the rushing waters, a sound that they could now clearly hear.

'The warriors. They had to be somewhere,' Quintus said. 'Shields.'

The legionaries were already automatically forming a line, the blackened faces of their shields overlapping. Each man gripped his gladius, pointing it forward. The halos of light cast by the torches burnt into their eyes.

The central torchbearer walked forward. He was an unfeasibly tall warrior, a Germani. He wore a Roman helm and, on the arm that held the torch, a single bronze arm guard — also Roman. The light bounced off his otherwise bare arms. His trews were cross-tied with leather thongs, his jerkin covered with a Roman breastplate, once the pride of a cavalryman. The lights in the arc behind him slowly moved forward.

The leader held up his round shield so that the writing on it could be seen — a rune. Not the T rune for Tiwaz or Týr, but to Quintus' horror, the D rune for Dagaz. Was this him? How had he found them?

'Hrolf,' he called, suspecting the boy had led this monster to them.

'He is here,' said the giant Germani in heavily accented Latin, thrusting the boy forward. 'We have your spy. He will take a long time to die.'

Quintus blinked rapidly, willing his eyes to adjust. He could not sense a larger force standing behind, ready to intervene. There was no noise, no deeper shadow, no shuffling of feet. There were just these men — twenty, perhaps. A match, but not an impossible one.

'Flanks,' Quintus called, but even as the men moved, they realised that it would be too late. The line of torches had already shifted so that they were now at each side. They were also getting closer. The Romans would be surrounded imminently. Their shield wall bent around so that the flanks were covered — but there was no way that they could protect all sides.

Quintus dared a glance backwards and saw there was no danger of an attack from behind. The hill was clear of lights and once more still and peaceful. *Still*, he thought, *no doubt the oppidum's warriors will be leaving by the front gate and marching round to cut us off.*

'We can fight our way out of this,' said Marcus. He and Tullius were next to Quintus. 'I will not allow us to be captured.'

'There are not so many of them,' said Caius, from the other side. There was a trace of amusement in his voice. 'We might even win.'

'The boy?' Agnus began.

'Is not our concern,' said Tullius flatly. 'He may have even led them here.'

'He was in our charge, under our protection,' said Quintus. 'In all honour, he is our concern.'

Tullius grunted noncommittally. Quintus was his superior, so he would not express dissent, though he disagreed.

Marcus had no such qualms. He spoke out. 'Our duty is to Rome, not to a foreign tribesman, boy or not.' He loosened his shoulders in readiness. 'We must fight.'

XXXXI: AUT VINCERI AUT MORI

Caius had grown fond of the Germani lad. He was annoyed enough to step out of line.

'Put him down!' he called to the leader, in Latin first, then the local language. He took a half-step forward with his sword raised. 'Pick on somebody your own size.'

'And who would that be?' The leader wore a round shield on his left arm, and in this hand held the torch aloft so that he stood in a circle of light. He was a giant of a man, as tall as Quintus but as broad-shouldered as Marcus. In his right hand there was a short throwing spear. This did not prevent him from holding the boy tight. His arms rippled with muscle and he wore a spatha, a cavalry blade, on his left hip. Stolen, thought Quintus, as was his armour and centurion's helmet.

'I will fight you for the boy,' Caius insisted, taking another step forward.

'Close that gap,' Quintus hissed at him. He did not hold with heroism. He did believe in duty, however. As Caius stepped back into line, the centurion turned his own shield to one side so that he faced the Germani.

'He will not fight you. I will,' he said firmly. 'Not just for the boy, but for our freedom. I beat you, you let us go.'

'And if I win?'

'The boy is yours. My men will make their own decisions. Caius, make sure he understands.' Caius clarified where necessary.

'They follow your orders,' said the Germani.

'I can only tell them to fight or die. It is the Roman way. *Aut vinceri aut mori*. We win or we die; either is honourable.'

'So be it. When I have killed you, I will kill them all. Slowly.'

'*Sic vita*,' said Quintus, shrugging.

The man wavered. 'I do not trust you. I think I will keep the boy and kill you anyway.'

'Caius, tell him in his own tongue that he is a coward, that when he slaughtered our men they were few and he was many. Tell him he now threatens a mere youth, an unblooded boy, rather than face me like a man. Be quick.'

Caius stumbled over the words, but by the grunts of indignation and anger that came from the giant, and the low growls that came from the torch holders, he had made himself understood.

'I will fight you to the death, Roman. I do not fear you or your gods,' the giant said.

'Swear by yours,' said Quintus. 'Swear by Týr and Wotan that you will free us if I win.'

The giant spat and spoke dismissively.

'Caius, what does he say?'

'That the names of his gods should not even be known by you, let alone spoken. That you befoul their greatness by putting them in your filthy mouth. That he will carve the names of these gods into your living flesh. That if you win, you will deserve your freedom because his gods will have abandoned him.'

'Then we have an agreement,' said Quintus unflinchingly, full of determination. 'We fight.' He took a step forward, whilst the men closed the gap in the shield wall behind him.

The giant let the boy go, pushing him towards the Romans. He stumbled, then ran, clinging to Caius for protection. Caius, fond as he was of Hrolf, shrugged him off. The boy cowered behind the men.

The Germani leader settled the shield on his arm as he handed the torch to one of his men. The circle was now complete but, as Quintus had surmised, there were no more than twenty of them, so the gaps were wide. Tullius had turned around, choosing to watch behind them. The giant drew the long blade from his belt and tested its edge against the air. It whistled softly. He held it up and muttered a dedication. Quintus lifted his gladius into the air and did the same, invoking Mars and Jupiter Optimus Maximus out loud, with a whispered, 'Ceres, protect me,' to his own patroness.

They squared up to each other on the rough ground, Quintus ready to dance and dodge as he had been trained.

Without preliminaries, the giant wielded his long sword. It bit hard into Quintus' shield. It could easily have cleaved it in two had the centurion not made a quarter-turn as he stepped forward. This meant it glanced off, but not totally harmlessly. The blow was struck with sufficient power to force Quintus onto one knee, his long scutum held awkwardly above his head. A second blow now would make the fight short indeed. But the long cavalry sword was designed for swinging from a horse, and its arc took the Germani off-balance. By the time he had righted himself and once more raised the blade, Quintus was back upright, planting his feet firmly.

The Germani grinned and swung the sword again, not downwards this time but across, again finding the shield, this time chipping a great splinter of wood from it. He held up the sword and said something harshly, at which his men laughed. Quintus took a step forward, using the boss of his shield as a weapon to turn his opponent. He then countered with a swipe of his gladius, aiming for the man's neck.

The blow was batted away with the round shield with what seemed like little effort. The man grinned again. He thrust his shield hard towards Quintus' face. It made a sickening noise as it made contact, not as hard as it might, as Quintus instinctively pulled his head back. Still, blood flowed freely from his nose and lips and down his chin. He wiped the back of his hand across his face and tested his jaw. His nose might be broken, his lip was split and his teeth were definitely rattled, but the wound was not serious. His jaw was intact, his sight clear.

Another blow to his shield clanged off the metal boss and he was once more forced onto one knee, leaning backwards to avoid the next swing. The long blade swished past, this time just making contact. A thin line of blood appeared in Quintus' neck above his focale. He sensed movement behind him and angrily thrust his sword arm out.

'No. Stay where you are. The gods will decide.' His voice was thick and hoarse, but still carried authority. Though he could not see who it was who had moved, he heard the shields clink as the men shuffled back into line.

Instead of administering the killing cut, the giant stood back, wickedly confident. He looked around the circle of torches for approval, and his men responded with appreciative noises. The runes had been carved into the chests of the pioneers whilst they lived. Perhaps he wanted to do the same to Quintus.

But his confidence was misplaced. While he was distracted, Quintus lunged forward and drove the point of his sword into the man's left leg, into the meaty muscle above his knee. It was no more than a flesh wound, but the sting was real and the blood flowed copiously. The giant yelled more in shock than pain and turned once more to his opponent.

He and Quintus stood back now, panting with exertion, one with a throbbing leg pain, the other struggling to breathe, sucking in air through his mouth in great gulps. They eyed each other up. Quintus hoped that he had taught the man to respect him. For his part, the tribesman bristled with anger. Warily, they began to circle each other, Quintus with blood soaking his chin and focale, the giant with a red stain spreading across one leg of his trews.

The Germani leader did not follow the rules of the Campus Martius. Or the daily routines of active service when the optiones ground the new men, the probationers, into the dust, sweating and cursing.

Where an opponent in training would usually sway and step, looking for an opening whilst ready to duck an attack, this man looked like he had staked out his ground and moved slowly and purposefully. Legs astride, the Germani warrior crouched side-on, his shield held close to his body, presenting the smallest possible target. The shield, covered in hide, was metal-rimmed, and could break skin and bone. But it was also lightweight, so that he could move it quickly into place. He looked at his cavalryman's blade and grunted something in disapproval.

'He curses the sword, Quintus!' shouted Caius. 'It is not his choice of weapon.'

'It is not his weapon at all,' mumbled Quintus, spitting blood from his mouth.

The giant feinted left, then, with a step to the side, turned his body and swung. Quintus had read the move and now spun around himself, to catch the Germani in the side with his shield boss, the full weight of his body behind it. The warrior let out a grunt of pain and, with a torrent of furious exclamations, pulled the helmet from his head and threw it aside. Quintus knew that one of the drawbacks of the helm was that it limited vision. In a Roman battle line, this made no difference — a legionary had no business looking anywhere but ahead — and it kept your head on your shoulders. But in this sort of one-on-one fighting, it mattered.

The giant was relying on his strength, rather than skill. His attempt at a sidestep had not worked, so now he decided to batter Quintus into the ground. Again and again, he struck the Roman's shield with the spatha. Quintus could do nothing against the barrage but defend himself, down on one knee, his shield held firm.

A clang and a curse and the sight of the giant's blade reflecting the torchlight as it went spinning to the ground told Quintus that his shield boss had got the better of the spatha. He dared to look and saw the Germani had turned, seeking his spear. For a moment, his back was to the centurion.

Quintus thrust upwards, into the back of the man's thigh. Blood spurted and drenched his arm. There was little resistance to the blade as its point broke the surface of the skin and its razor edge cut through the flesh. The big man grasped his spear and turned, not yet realising that Quintus had dealt him a death blow. This was no flesh wound; this was one of the killing cuts discovered by great Caesar's battlefield surgeons.

The Germani dropped to one knee. He began to call on his gods, but his breath failed him. With a huge effort, he pulled his body upright, using the javelin as a support. Quintus ignored the movement and stepped forward, lifting his blade to give the death blow. The man's neck was exposed and he would die swiftly. As Quintus prepared to strike, Dagaz grasped the shaft of the spear, bent his arm and hurled the weapon. The centurion swerved to one side, but he need not have bothered. The deadly blade was not aimed at him, but past him. His momentum was such that his gladius completed its swing, cutting the Germani's throat and releasing another torrent of blood.

Dagaz died with a crooked smile on his face. Quintus turned to see Hrolf tumbling backwards silently with the spear embedded in his chest.

'No!' Quintus screamed, falling to his knees beside his victim.

XXXXII: MORTUUS EST?

There was a deep silence following the cry, broken by an owl hooting in the distant forest, its mate responding mournfully from further away. Sextus and Quintus shivered. Minerva had claimed not one, but two victims. Caius held the limp body of the boy in his arms.

Dagaz was dead, and Hrolf with him. He had bound the boy to him in the most enduring way. They trod whatever path led to their own afterlife together. The thought made Caius shiver.

The evocatus pulled out the spear and readied himself to use it for his own defence, planting his feet firmly. The other legionaries braced themselves for the inevitable attack. Instead they watched as the lights, one by one, were extinguished, hissing as they were plunged into the ground. There were what sounded like a few curt commands, then nothing. The body of the chieftain was left on its knees where it had fallen.

To the surprise of the Romans, no spears flew, and no axes were raised against them. They crouched behind their shields, battle-ready.

'Caius, *mortuus est?*' Quintus asked, pointing at Hrolf.

'He is dead, sir,' Caius said. 'The spear went right through him.'

There was nothing else for Quintus to say. He considered Hrolf to be one of his own, and he did not hold with losing any of his men. But he could not spare time to grieve for the boy.

Marcus asked, sword tip pointing at the chieftain, '*Mortuus est*, Quintus? Is *he* dead?'

'He is,' nodded Quintus.

'I think his men have gone,' Marcus said in wonder.

'So do I,' said Quintus. 'I can hear nothing. Anyone?' The rest of the men, still in their protective circle of shields, muttered agreement. No breathing could be heard, no sound of movement. It seemed the troop of tribesmen had melted away into the night.

Marcus was still wary, but they had to move. 'I think we can dare to break the shield wall. Move outwards slowly; four paces should be enough. See if you can find any of those torches. They may have left them behind.'

The men fanned out carefully, still with swords in hand and shields raised. The enemy had fled.

As soon as he could, Alba rushed across to Quintus and began to untie his bloodied focale.

'Leave it,' said Quintus harshly, batting him away. 'It is only a flesh wound.'

'I will be the judge of that,' Alba said. 'Stand still and let me see. The giant's shield has made a mess of your face.'

'Here,' said Rufus, 'a light.' He blew on the torch he had picked up. There was a glimmer still in it and with his encouragement, it grudgingly flared to life. Tullius and Agnus also found usable torches. As Alba examined a reluctant Quintus, they lit them from the one Rufus held aloft.

Satisfied that it was but a scratch, Alba moved on to Quintus' face, dabbing at it with the focale. His ministrations stung and Quintus could not stop himself from yelping as Alba tested the state of his nose.

'It will not spoil your good looks,' Alba said. 'It is straight enough — and your lips will mend. There is dirt there, though — you need to wash it. And your tunic is soaked with blood…'

'Thank you, capsarius,' said Quintus automatically, already turning away to assess their situation. He did not think there were further injuries, and was not about to unbuckle his chest armour to find out.

Sextus, Marcus and Agnus stood over the fallen Germani warrior. He had died on his knees, his chin rested on his chest, which was drenched in more blood than it looked possible a body could hold.

'You should take his head,' Marcus said matter-of-factly. 'It will prove to his people that Dagaz is no more.'

'It is not him,' said Agnus quietly but firmly, shaking his head. 'I am sorry, Quintus.' He lifted up the head by its long, fair hair. 'Remember, I have seen him. This man is very like him — same colour hair, same shield — but certainly not him. Somehow, sir, we have gained nothing.' He let the head drop.

'He never said he was Dagaz,' Sextus observed slowly. 'He just never denied it.'

'No matter,' said Tullius unemotionally. 'One dead Germani is much the same as another.'

The men grunted agreement, although Quintus was clearly frustrated. 'I would have liked to kill the man who inflicted such harm on our comrades.'

'What was the point of this attack?' Rufus wondered. 'This was not all the men of the oppidum. Where are they?'

'I don't understand, either,' Quintus said. 'Perhaps it was a tactic to delay us. They could have discovered Galba's plan. Perhaps their other warriors are on their way to cut off our retreat.'

'But why vanish into the night?' Rufus asked.

'I think the torch holders were more old men and boys, not warriors. Only the giant came to fight — and he expected to win. Their job was done, or so they thought.' Quintus paused.

'They held us here for as long as they thought necessary. They thought we were a larger force and they could stop us reinforcing Galba. No-one would be stupid enough to attack a town with a handful of men, would they?'

He looked around the circle of faces in the torchlight and saw many of them break into grins.

'It will make a good story,' said Agnus.

'They may not have held us for long enough. We may still have time,' Quintus said.

The sky was cloud-covered, moonless and starless. What night-sight they had was for now destroyed by the torches. They had no way of knowing how long it was until dawn.

Quintus turned to his diviner. 'Sextus, can you tell anything?'

'The time of day or night, no,' Sextus said, pointing. 'But the sun rises beyond the river — over there — and I sense no light yet. I can do no better than that.'

'You can make a guess.'

Sextus paused, then said, 'Two hours, perhaps three.'

'So we may yet have time to find Aquila and the others before they join Galba,' Tullius said.

'We may,' said Quintus. 'If we are fast enough.'

Everyone gathered where Quintus stood, next to the Germani corpse with the broken sword. Everyone except Caius. He stayed with the boy, holding him in his arms, muttering words over him, words that he hoped might take him to his own underworld. He knew Hrolf could not enter unless he was armed, so he lowered the boy to the ground then took the spear and placed it in his pale hand.

'Caius, you can do no more. Leave him,' said Sextus, not unkindly.

'There is one thing I can do,' Caius muttered, taking a handful of earth to sprinkle on the corpse.

'We need to make haste,' Quintus said. 'We need to run.'

Rufus went ahead with his torch; Agnus lit the middle and Tullius the back. They followed the sound of the rushing water and found the stepping stones easily. This time they crossed with more confidence. They were amazed that no enemy waited to topple them from the stones, that the people of the oppidum had not yet reached here. On the far bank, despite Quintus' protests, Alba called a halt.

'A brief stop only, sir,' he said. 'I need you to splash your face and neck with water. I need to know if there are other injuries.'

Quintus obliged, the icy water at first stinging, then refreshing him. Alba looked closely by the lights that were held for him.

'Nothing more,' he said. 'Your armour is not punctured. Most of it must be the enemy's blood.'

'Then there is nothing to stop us running,' grinned Quintus. 'Come, let us beat the sunrise and find Aquila.'

They were used to making haste, there was a sort of more-than-double-time jog-trot that the legions of Divus Julius had developed. He was famed for the speed with which his men covered the ground, arriving in places long before they were expected. But this was different. This was a proper run.

They retraced their steps through the damp and slippery scrub that bordered the river. The trees were thinly scattered and loomed at them out of the dark, forcing the torchbearers to dodge and swerve. The broken ground was uneven and treacherous with roots and brambles, but Quintus did not let this slow them and, breathing heavily, they began to climb.

The ground, as it rose, became more even, allowing the men to open their stride with more confidence. The trees grew more numerous, until they were once more deep in the forest.

Within the trees, the track was wide and obvious, the men's steps muffled by the leaf litter.

They had no idea when dawn would break, or how many hours they were from daylight. Between the branches solid black turned to charcoal and the edges of the tree trunks now stood out starkly against the sky. The first sounds of birdsong began to grow. Sparrow and wood pigeon, they were relieved to note. No owls.

'It is getting lighter,' Quintus said as he dropped back to run alongside Sextus.

'Colour has not yet returned to the leaves,' Sextus said. 'The sun is not yet risen.'

'Was that the last of the old moon last night? It looked like it.'

'I am sure of it,' Sextus replied. 'It was barely visible. Tonight will be the dark of the moon.'

'Then we may have time. Galba attacks with the dawn. It will be easy; there are no fighters in the place.'

'It may not be as easy as we think.'

'What is it that augurs badly, Sextus? The owls? The manner of the boy's death? The manner of the commander's death?'

'Just a feeling,' Sextus said. 'Do not worry. It may not come to pass.'

Of course, this did not reassure the centurion. Unconsciously, he made the warding sign with his hand.

They continued in silence at a steady pace. A thin morning mist began to swirl around their feet as they climbed. Birds began to call more energetically to each other. As the sun rose, the colours started to return to nature. They were close now, but Quintus was increasingly worried that they would find an abandoned camp.

Out of the gloom, a legionary stepped across the path with a blade. '*Quo vadis?*' he demanded.

'*Frater*,' Quintus replied with relief as he held up a hand to stop the patrol. *Brother*. At least his luck held so far. If there were pickets, Aquila was still here. It was Vetruvius who challenged them.

'So, you have made tesserarius,' Rufus laughed. 'Well met.'

'Is that so?' Quintus asked, raising an eyebrow. Vetruvius, like Tullius and Sextus, never sought promotion.

'No, sir. Just a picket. I am still a common soldier.' He stepped aside, waving his drawn sword. 'Proceed to the camp.'

'You should come, too,' said Quintus. 'We are not being followed. The enemy has emptied their fortress and cleared the land of warriors. I can only think that they are fighting elsewhere.'

Vetruvius put his fingers to his mouth and whistled. Two more legionaries appeared, Aulus and Cotta.

'Did you find the commander?' Vetruvius asked as the men fell in alongside Quintus.

'We did,' Quintus replied. 'But that is a story I should tell Galba and the prefect's wife first.'

Vetruvius saw that Titus Flavius was not with them. Quintus left him to draw his own conclusions.

Within minutes they were at the edge of what, to the uninitiated, would look like chaos. But the legionaries recognised it for what it was — a marching camp being disassembled. Tents were packed on carts; the few animals had bundles tied to them. Smaller campfires were extinguished, wisps of smoke rising from them, while a large fire burned in the centre. Legionaries were filling in the ditch by piling the earth rampart into it.

The eagle could be seen alongside the century's standard, guarded by the man Rufus had deputised. With Quintus' permission, he went to reclaim his post.

Aquila came down the slope in the opposite direction. 'Ave, centurion,' the aquilifer greeted with a fist to his heart.

'Ave, aquilifer.' Quintus returned the salute.

Aquila looked at the company and asked, 'No commander?'

Quintus shook his head. 'No guide, either,' he said. 'He fell to his own people, to one I thought was Dagaz.' He lowered his voice. 'I did find the commander, but too late to help. You are ready to leave?'

'Almost. Do your men need rest?'

'They will be ready.'

'Then I will have the cornicen signal as soon as the rampart is destroyed.'

'So be it,' said Quintus. 'We go to join Galba.'

Before it was fully light, the men marched from the glade.

XXXXIII: VOLCANALIA

Galba was clearly angry. He stomped towards Quintus, smacking his vine rod across his palm.

'Ave, centurion, what news do you bring?' He gave Quintus no time to reply. 'No commander, I see. And more damned renegades. As if we don't have enough renegades to deal with.'

Quintus leaned down from his horse, trying to make sure only the centurion heard. 'No commander, sir. Dead by his own hand. I have his ring. I should tell his wife.'

Galba lowered his voice. He did not seem surprised. 'I feared as much. You should tell her, yes — and before anyone else does.' He waved a hand. 'What about these others you bring? Deserters? Runaways?'

Quintus was quick to defend them. 'No, sir. They are sworn to the legion.'

'Really? Their god-cursed comrades refuse to fight for us.' Profanity did not suit Galba. But here was the reason for his anger. 'I've just had a deputation, centurion. Quoting the lex something-or-other, demanding not to fight tomorrow. Two evocati, no less. Veterans of Hispania under Marcus Agrippa, who they dared to tell me was "a good commander and a religious man" as if I was not!'

Quintus was shocked. 'These men are keen,' he said, waving an arm behind him. 'They fought at our side. Many died.'

'Their comrades less so. A religious thing,' Galba shook his head. 'Not your fault, centurion. Report to the commander's tent as soon as you can. Your news will not wait.'

He stomped off, muttering curses under his breath.

Quintus turned in the saddle and shouted, 'Join your contubernales, and find billets for the Fifth.' He addressed the trumpeter as he dismounted. 'Fall out the men, cornicen.' He then turned to Aquila, who dismounted beside him. 'Why would any men refuse to fight?'

'I think I know,' said Aquila. 'Did you see the men bathing as we rode in?' Quintus nodded. 'And your optio, the blacksmith, wearing nothing but his belt and apron?'

'What of it?' Quintus demanded.

'Sir, I think today is Volcanalia,' Aquila explained. 'There are many drying their clothes, lighting bonfires in honour of Vulcan, and sacrificing in the flames any small animal they can find. Even now, Crassus has his tunic drying in the sun.'

Quintus looked around at the camp. A group of men appeared from the river, where they had apparently been washing tunics and undershorts whilst they wore them. A fully armed soldier watched before and behind the group, a necessary caution in enemy territory. The men reached the tents and began to strip off their wet garments, hanging them from guy ropes to dry.

'If today is Volcanalia, the tenth, tomorrow is the ninth before the kalends of September,' said Aquila. '*Mundus patet.*'

Quintus had to think for a moment. His knowledge of the religious calendar was hazy, apart from the festivals belonging to market days and to his own household gods. Finally he clicked his fingers in realisation. '*Mundus patet,*' he said. 'I had clean forgotten. The opening of the gates of Hades. But surely this no longer carries any weight?'

'It does with some,' said Aquila. 'Especially the Fifth. Forty years ago, the Dictator raised the legion from tribesmen, non-citizens. It was the first of its kind. We have tried to prove ourselves worthy ever since. Yet twice we found ourselves on the wrong side — the losing side — in the civil wars. Our priests and augurs blamed not just ill luck, but our failure to properly observe rites and holy days.' He added caustically, 'Though now citizens, we were insufficiently Roman.'

Quintus smiled grimly and raised his eyes to the eagle. 'So the gods are capricious with you. Losing that will not have helped.'

Aquila clearly did not like such reminders. 'It is dangerous to guess what the gods do or do not wish,' he said. 'So, out of respect for them, the men of the Fifth will fight furiously and victoriously after tomorrow. They will fight to the death. But not tomorrow.' He shook his head. 'I could not make them even if I wished to.'

'So that was Galba's deputation,' said Quintus.

'It was,' said Aquila glumly. Then he brightened. 'But what is a day anyway? Surely we can wait a few hours to attack with good omens, lucky portents, behind us?'

'The oppidum is empty at the moment, Aquila,' said Quintus. 'We could find only old men, women and children in it last night. The warriors are away fighting somewhere. Tomorrow we could take it. Maybe even with just the men of the Ninth. It might not still be empty after tomorrow.' He unlaced and removed his helmet. Only then could the full extent of his injuries be seen, the bruises dark and angry. 'Fetch me Optio Marcus and Caius of the Fifth,' he commanded the nearest legionary.

Marcus came first. He looked on Quintus' face with admiration. 'It looks well, sir,' he grinned.

'I would return the smile, my friend, if it did not pain me to do so.'

Marcus laughed.

'I need your advice,' Quintus said. 'Many of the Fifth will not fight tomorrow. Religious reasons, I understand.'

'I heard,' said Marcus. 'Word passed quickly.'

'Do we not have enough men without them?' Quintus asked. 'Men of the Ninth? We have seen inside the oppidum. It is ours if we move quickly enough, while it is empty. We should attack now, at once, before their fighting men return. A single charge would overrun the place. We could take it and hold their own oppidum against them.'

Marcus was looking at the ground and slowly shaking his head.

'What is it?' Quintus demanded.

'Our men will not fight whilst their comrades pray,' he said reluctantly. 'It would offend the gods.'

'Will none of them fight, Caius?' Quintus demanded as he approached. 'Not even the evocati?'

'The evocati are more determined not to fight than any,' said the gruff veteran. 'Many have seen the results of defying the gods. The gods were with us when the legion won its elephant emblem at Thapsus. Though I was but a probationer, I was on the right side. I chose the wrong side at Actium and the gods had me discharged, along with all those whose loyalty could be questioned.'

Marcus nodded his agreement. 'It is a highly inauspicious day, one of the few on which the pit of Hades is opened and the spirits of the dead can reach out and ensnare the spirits of the living…'

Quintus interrupted with a curse. 'So we sit here whilst the enemy fortifies himself because of a superstition?'

He was so annoyed that he almost did not notice how Caius and Marcus shied away from him. Calling anything to do with the gods 'superstition' would be enough to bring their wrath upon the heads of all associated with the blasphemy.

Quintus sighed, taking in his comrades' unease and making the sign of the horns to ward off evil. 'We can do nothing. It is the will of the gods. Caius, find the Germani guide. Tell him of the death of the boy. Let him know he died well.'

'He had also become our friend,' ventured Caius.

'I am not sure that will sit so well, but you decide.'

Caius saluted and left.

'I need to share my own news with the ladies — before camp gossip reaches them,' Quintus said sadly. 'Marcus, make sure the Fifth have billets — and that they do not suffer for their decision. It is the will of the gods.'

The patrol had entered the camp from the north, marching through a well-guarded gate at the porta decumana, and along the via praetoria. The castra was properly laid out, the streets were straight, the tents orderly, the commander's tent central. Galba was lodging in one of the smaller tents, having given over the bigger pavilion to the two ladies. Flanked by two of the other centurions, Felix and Marius, he came to greet Quintus as he approached.

'What happened to your face?' Felix asked as he came near enough to see the extent of the bruising.

'A brief explanation, centurion,' Galba said. 'The noble ladies are waiting.'

'A fight,' said Quintus flatly. With what he could manage of a grin, he added, 'I won.'

'Details later,' said Marius. 'Galba has shared your news with us, but not with the ladies. They are waiting inside.' A legionary guard hurried to pull back the flap of the tent.

He and Galba found the Lady Antonia Flavia Menenii sitting on a low stool, the Lady Aurelia next to her. Both wore clothes that had seen better days, frayed at the edges and not as clean as they might be. Their hair had been styled after a fashion, but certainly not by a professional. But still they tipped their chins upwards and raised their eyebrows haughtily to speak to a mere soldier, centurion or not. Galba took up position to the back of them.

Someone in the shadows breathed quietly. Quintus guessed it was the ever-present Cornus, freedman scribe of Titus Flavius.

Or perhaps even now a free citizen, if the commander had left a will that said as much.

XXXXIV: SEXTUS

Quintus stood to attention and looked round. Of course there was nowhere to sit. He had his plumed helmet beneath his arm and his red cloak over his shoulder. His face was a mess of blue and yellow bruising. In addition, he had not been shaved in several days, and his hair was longer than he generally wore it. He nodded a greeting to the ladies, his gaze lingering on Aurelia.

The Lady Antonia wasted no time. 'You have been in a fight?'

'I have, lady.'

She had no further interest in that, and moved on to what she really wanted to know. 'Centurion Galba tells me you have news of my husband.'

'He did not tell you, lady?'

'No, he said it was up to you to tell me. As you have returned without him, I am assuming the news is not good. Did you fail to find him?'

Quintus took the prefect's ring off his finger and handed it wordlessly to the lady. It was gold, thick and heavy, with a raised carving in white stone that gave it its use as a signet.

Antonia opened her palm and he dropped it in. She looked at it unemotionally and asked, 'Did he give this to you as a token?'

Quintus shook his head.

'So you took it from him — or perhaps from one who had taken it from him.'

'From himself, lady,' Quintus said, though he forbore to mention that he had been forced to cut it from the finger that wore it.

'Then he is dead,' she said frostily. 'He would not have allowed it to be taken otherwise.' Her eyes betrayed her matronly stoicism, glistening with unshed tears. 'How?' she asked.

'He died honourably, lady, by his own hand. He could not bear to be taken and could not stand being caged, and that is only right. I took the ring not from him, but from his cold body. His spirit had long since departed.'

'Did you close his eyes?'

'Of course, lady. And I gave him a coin for his passage.' Quintus wasn't sure why he was lying about such details, except that he hoped to comfort her. Aurelia had one hand on Antonia's lap whilst the other made a gesture which brought Cornus out of the shadows with a jug of wine. She took the jug from him.

Antonia looked across. 'Pour a little on the floor, Aurelia, in honour of his memory.' Cornus stepped back to allow room for the libation, then produced two goblets.

'The men, too,' Antonia commanded, and the freedman reached for two more vessels, into which Aurelia poured the drink. 'To a safe journey to join his ancestors,' Antonia said, raising her glass. 'He has made his name.'

Galba and Quintus also raised their goblets and drank. Quintus desperately wanted to comfort both ladies, but his presence was now an embarrassment to them.

'Go, centurions. You, too, freedman,' Antonia ordered. 'Leave us to our grief. Send in the slave; he must find us a suitable sacrifice to Father Dis. For now, he will be our cupbearer.'

The man summoned was Maxim, the contubernium's own, pressed into service as a body slave.

'Of course,' Quintus said to Galba outside. 'A slave will see and hear nothing.'

They walked away from the tent, Galba leading the way to his own fire. It was much less grand than the commander's pavilion, but at least he had it to himself.

'You are commander, now, sir,' said Quintus as the pair of them squatted on their heels by the fire, each with a cup of posca.

'I am not of the equités,' Galba said, shaking his head. 'I am a common legionary, raised up and promoted. I have no wish to be a magistrate of any sort and have taken no steps on the *cursus honorum* — and at my age I never will.' He smiled as they drank. 'How did you find him?'

'The Germani boy, Hrolf, led us across stepping stones and a bridge to a back gate through which we slipped into the oppidum. He had an idea where the prefect would be held, and bid us search windowless huts. We found nursing mothers, children, grandfathers, and finally the body of the commander. It was clear he had taken his own life. We would have brought his body away, but the alarm was raised — dogs and geese.'

'So the inhabitants did not discover you?'

'They almost did. Some youths and old men had to be silenced before the alarm was raised. There seemed to be no fighting men.'

'There are now. They are returning,' interrupted Galba resentfully, but he gave Quintus no chance to question him. 'Go on.'

'Once the animals were awake, we fled, leaving the Flavian behind. I took his ring to prove his death. We ran down the hill, cutting the bridge so we could not be followed. We were stopped by a force of Germani, led by one who I thought was Dagaz. But it was not him — a witness to the massacre of the pioneers confirmed it.'

Galba gestured for him to continue.

'To let us pass, he insisted on single combat. I beat him.'

'Though not without some damage.'

Quintus pointed to his face. 'This was the boss and rim of his shield.' He pulled down his *focale* to show the angry red line across his throat. 'This was the tip of his blade — a stolen Roman cavalry sword.'

Galba grunted and nodded appreciatively. 'Good wound, almost fatal, but not quite. Clearly *bon Fortuna* was with you.'

'Clearly,' agreed Quintus, 'but not with the commander.'

'I am sorry for Titus Flavius, and for his widow, but I am not him. I will not aspire to his position.'

'Yet you will command us?' Quintus asked tentatively.

'Of course.' Galba laughed. 'Until the most noble Augustus says otherwise, or until I take Mercury's hand.'

'We will need an assembly, an official handover,' said Quintus, and Galba agreed. But they were given no time to consider what must be done as Maxim ran up to them, seeking permission to speak.

'The Lady Antonia Flavia summons you again, *dominus*,' he said, then added, his puzzlement apparent, 'She says that you should bring with you a thief.'

'A what?'

'A thief, sir. I am not sure what she intends.' He bowed his head and waited.

'What do you think, Galba?'

'I think there is no way to explain the intricacies of a woman's mind,' Galba smiled. 'I would take her a thief.'

Quintus decided to find out first what sort of thief she required, and what she might wish to steal. He looked forward to once more being in the company of Aurelia, to have a chance to rekindle their romantic relationship. The legionary guards parted the tent flap for him, but Aurelia was not there.

It was Antonia who received him, with just Cornus standing at her side. She sat on a small folding chair, the commander's own seat present but empty. Quintus looked around for stools or chairs for himself, but again there was nowhere to sit.

'Stand at your ease, or whatever it is that you do,' said Antonia, waving a dainty hand. 'Let us not stand on ceremony. Where is the thief?'

'Lady, I was not sure what you required.'

She gave him a knowing smile. 'Come, centurion. This is a Roman legion. I am sure it has more than its fair share of criminals, including thieves. Or tricksters, pranksters, persuaders, men with silver tongues.'

One name immediately flashed into his head. 'I know of one such,' he said.

She spoke over her shoulder. 'So modest, Cornus. Two legions now represented here, and he can only think of one such. What paragons must the Ninth and the Fifth recruit.' She turned her eyes, devoid of emotion, to Quintus. 'Who is he, centurion?'

'Pupillus Sextilius of the Esquiline tribe, lady. Known as Sextus.'

She waved imperiously at the scribe. 'Find him, Cornus, and bring him here.' The freedman dipped his head in acknowledgement and ducked out of the door.

Quintus found himself alone with the lady, and this made him nervous. He shuffled his feet.

'You seem uneasy, centurion,' she said.

Quintus fixed his eyes to the floor. 'I am not used to being in the presence of nobility, lady.'

She shrugged and allowed herself a little smile. 'My companion the Lady Aurelia tells me you are from agricultural stock, centurion?'

'I am, lady.' His neck reddened, the flush creeping up his cheeks as he realised that the two women shared intimate information.

Antonia did not notice or, if she did, feigned indifference. 'Then your household gods must include Ceres?'

This he could answer. He lifted his chin and looked at the lady. 'She is chief of them. Ceres is my patron and protector.'

'I need her help.' Antonia gave him a softer look. The corners of her eyes glistened. 'Will you intercede with her for me?'

Before he could answer, the door flap opened again and Cornus appeared with Sextus.

'This is he,' said Cornus importantly.

'I am legionary Pupillus Sextilius,' said Sextus. 'At your service, *domina*. What do you wish of me?' Somehow he had managed to find a shave and a haircut in the camp. He was smooth-chinned and looked impossibly young. He gave Antonia a knowing smile. He was used to being summoned by ladies, especially noble ones.

Antonia recognised the look and her expression grew faintly amused. 'No, legionary, not that. I hear you have other skills.'

Sextus had the good grace to redden. 'As you wish, lady,' he said.

'I need a thief, Pupillus Sextilius.' Antonia's tongue ran softly round her lips. The use of his name was an intimacy that made him colour further. 'A trickster, a scoundrel. One whose patron is swift-heeled Mercury.'

'He is my protector, and I his champion,' said Sextus, his voice hoarse, lacking its usual easy confidence.

'I knew it. These are the two that I need, Cornus,' said Antonia, turning to the secretary. 'Ceres and Mercury.' She looked at Quintus, suddenly businesslike. 'So, as I understand it, the gates of Hades are opened at sunrise on the morrow?'

'They are, mistress,' Quintus replied. 'It is, unfortunately, the least auspicious of all days on which to fight.'

'Yet it is the most auspicious day to take a wandering spirit by the hand and help it across the river, is it not?'

Sextus realised what she wanted. 'You wish to secure your husband's passage to Elysium, lady?' Before she could reply, he turned to Quintus. 'If so, sir, tomorrow would indeed be the most auspicious day to do so.'

Quintus nodded, finally understanding. 'The opening of the gates of Hades. As Ceres is my patron, I can intercede with her to help Titus Flavius make it across the river. As Mercury is yours, you can ensure he takes the commander's hand.' He turned to Antonia, once more a picture of composure. 'Indeed, lady, as we will not fight, it is the best use of such a day as tomorrow.'

Antonia brushed her hand against the freedman's tunic — a gesture of affection and trust that, to Quintus, demonstrated that they spent too much time in each other's company.

'Cornus knows of a rite that will work,' she said. 'This evening, your soldiers will build a pyre. Once the gates open at sunrise, I will sacrifice a sow and feed it to the flames. My husband's ring will represent his body. Ceres will receive her portion and help my husband's spirit to consume his share. You, centurion, who found his ring, will ask for it to be so.' She turned to Sextus. 'She will also, with your blessing, young thief, place his hand in that of Mercury, to ensure he reaches

Elysium.' She paused. 'Cornus assures me it will work … and if it does not, we will have done all we can.'

'It will be as you wish,' said Quintus, formally. She thanked them graciously and waved them away.

'A pyre, a pig and a prayer, Sextus,' Quintus said as they ducked under the flap. 'It sounds Egyptian to me.'

'Perhaps,' said Sextus, seriously. 'But I understand her. Although the body would usually be with the pyre, this way she can at least appease the gods — and know that she has done all she can to ensure that the Flavian has crossed the river safely.'

'Only the gods themselves know if such a thing will work. But it will comfort her,' said Quintus. 'I will issue orders for the pyre and a pig, captured from the forest. The prayers we must supply ourselves. I will have to tell Galba what is to happen.'

XXXXV: MUNDUS PATET

'It sounds cultish to me. Is this what they do when they worship the Good Goddess?' Galba was not alone in being mystified by those women-only secret rites. They had been the subject of a great scandal only a few years back, when a man disguised in women's clothes had sneaked in.

'That I could not say,' said Quintus. 'All I can tell you is that it is what the lady wants.'

They sat in the afternoon sunshine, still strong although summer was nearly at an end. Galba was pensive as he finished his drink. 'Your wounds. Your fight. It was definitely not Dagaz?'

'Legionary Agnus says not. I thought the man I fought —' carefully Quintus touched his face — 'was him. But it was not, and though we thought we were surrounded and outnumbered, when my adversary fell, his own warriors — if they were even warriors — melted away. He promised that, if I beat him in single combat, that is what would happen. I did not believe him. He took his revenge on our guide, spearing the boy as he died.' He was thoughtful. 'I would not have had it so.'

'*Sic vita*,' said Galba, dismissing the boy from his mind. 'This legionary, is he reliable?'

'He is. Agnus is the one that witnessed Dagaz torture and kill our men. He says this man was like him, but not him.'

'So where is he?' Galba wondered.

'He was not in the settlement, nor was he defending it. He must be away fighting elsewhere.'

'So he could still be at our backs?'

'It is likely, sir,' Quintus concluded.

'What do you think was the purpose of this single combat? What did it achieve?' Galba asked.

'I think it was to delay us. I think they thought us a larger group. I think they wanted to hold us until their fighting men returned. In this they failed.'

'Perhaps not,' said Galba glumly, shaking his head. He waved the slave forward with the jug of posca, and their cups were refilled. He sipped, then sighed. 'As I said, warriors are returning. We should have attacked today, this morning. I did not realise. The deputation of the Fifth came to me too late. Now we must wait.'

Quintus nodded. There was nothing he could say. The gods would have their way.

'It looks like your own mission had mixed fortunes,' Galba said. 'You look like you've been trampled by an elephant, and yet you have gained more men. Your soldiers from the forest — definitely not deserters?'

'Definitely, sir. They were leaderless men of the Fifth, their officers killed or kidnapped. They were seeking their legion rather than trying to desert. We were all attacked. Some ran — they are deserters, although the archers stopped many of them. Given the chance, the others stood with us and fought. As did the cavalry, many of them falling, including the decurion.' He paused and sipped at the drink. 'At least I hope they died. We could not find their bodies.' He shuddered at the thought of what might have happened to them had they been captured. 'Many men died, of the Fifth and the Ninth.' Silently, he tipped a few drops of liquid on the floor. Galba followed suit.

'The men of the Fifth fought bravely and honourably,' Quintus continued. 'I have re-sworn them to the legions. They all took not just the *sacramentum*, but the comrades' oath, the *ius iurandem*, each sponsored by a man of the Ninth. They have sworn by great Jupiter, but I will also vouch for them — with my life if necessary.'

'So be it,' nodded Galba. 'It is a shame. The oppidum was almost empty of fighting men and ours for the taking, yet we cannot attack.' He looked heavenward. 'I know, it is the will of the gods,' he intoned quickly with a sigh. 'Tomorrow we will spend the day training and planning. By the following day, the oppidum will be armed against us. Yet still we will take it, centurion.' He raised his hand to stop Quintus interrupting. 'There will be exercises and drills; there will be foraging and strengthening of fortifications. There will be an assembly tonight and another tomorrow.' In irritation, he added, 'Apparently there will also be, great Jupiter help me, a funeral without a body at the opening of the day. Set your men to building a pyre.'

Word travelled quickly. They were not to fight on the morrow — a great relief to those who knew the significance of the day. Some said that they were disappointed, although all at least claimed to respect the rights of their fellow soldiers. It was difficult not to agree with them. If the day was inauspicious or in any way unlucky, they were reluctant to take the risk. On any morning if the augurs read the haruspices and they were poor, they would stand down.

When omens and portents were ignored, the gods felt slighted and disasters happened. As children, they had been told the story of Claudius Pulcher's chickens and the ensuing Carthaginian victory.

The evening assembly was a muted affair. Knowing they would not fight, and that the day still belonged to Vulcan, the men sought permission to attend in less than full uniform. Galba angrily denied it.

Thus, as the cornicen signalled the assembly, those celebrating Volcanalia pulled on damp linen and needed slaves and comrades to tie their lorica laminata. It was not how they would have ended the day's festivities in Rome.

Galba and his escort climbed the platform, beckoning the standards to follow. He would look better standing beneath the eagle.

'I am not here to make a speech,' he said, standing with his helmet under his arm, as usual. 'I am here to confirm that the prefect, the noble Titus Flavius Pusio of the equités, has joined his ancestors, and that, for now at least, I command.'

He paused, waiting for a reaction. He knew he was popular, but not universally so. He believed in harsher discipline than the Flavian had ever meted out. There was no sound of dissent, but no general rejoicing either. That was how it should be.

'I also mourn those others who have fallen honourably.' He paused again, to allow private prayers for lost friends and comrades. 'I welcome some of you back, and others who I have not seen before. Centurion Quintus tells me that the men of the Fifth are re-sworn.' He lifted a clenched fist high. 'On behalf of great Jupiter and of Caesar Augustus, we accept them.' This time there was a cheer.

'What you have heard is correct,' Galba continued. 'We will not yet attack the oppidum. The augurs tell us the day is cursed. But make no mistake: there will be work and training. It is no day of rest.' He turned to Quintus. 'Centurion.'

Quintus had been put in charge of the punishment detail. Even in enemy territory, or during times of religious celebration, there were men who answered back to officers or were discovered showing disrespect.

'Step forward,' Quintus commanded the first of the sinners. A whipping post was already driven into the ground, and the man was tied to it by his wrists, his back bared. 'For petty theft, six lashes.'

The soldier's back carried scars of a previous punishment. He did not even cry out as Caius administered the simple leather whip.

'Step forward.' The second offender's back was unmarked.

'For disrespect to the most revered Caesar Augustus, *divi filius*.'

A murmur went through the ranks. For this he could be put to death.

'Twenty lashes.'

The man had to be brought round twice with water flung at him, and was carried away by his fellows.

'He was lucky not to have been castrated or crucified,' said Marcus.

Quintus was sanguine. 'He was probably drunk, took a bet and was egged on by his fellows. When he thought that no-one was looking, he took a piss on the imago. Luckily for him, he hit only the pole where it was fixed in the ground. Had he splashed the face, his fate would have been worse. It was a joke, nothing serious.' He shrugged. 'Dismiss the men.'

The officers gathered together to plan the assault. Unlike great generals like Scipio and Pompeius they had no maps or models, no strategists or advisers, not even a table on which to lean. Instead they squatted on camp stools outside Galba's tent, drawing diagrams in the dirt before the fire.

They were faced with a fortified township on a hilltop. It was big, bigger than the Roman's own winter fort, and the hill itself was steep. Halfway up was the first defence, a wooden fence

— not large or substantial, but enough to slow down an attacker and sufficient to stop any cavalry.

Above it, on the crest of the hill, was a more substantial palisade, with a ditch in front of it. The heads that could be seen bobbing above the top of this fence revealed that a walkway ran along it.

The only point of entry was the gates, hung beneath a bridge that connected with the walkway, so that the occupants could defend from above. These were approached via a narrow road, bounded on either side by steep mounds of compacted earth.

Messages came in hourly from the men in the observation positions. It was clear that word had spread and men, armed men, were returning to the oppidum. 'There were places where the fence looked broken, and where the ditch was filled in,' Quintus said hopefully. 'It even looked like there were dwellings up against it.'

'No more, I would think,' said Furius Lentulus, shaking his head. 'Not now they are warned. No doubt even now the fence is being rebuilt where there were gaps or weaknesses.'

Reports told them that fences and ditches were being repaired, and that the buildings near the gates were emptied and knocked flat. That animals were being driven inside.

'It has to be the gate,' said Felix. 'Or we need to batter down the fence itself.'

'Then that is what we do,' said Quintus. 'We have carpenters, we have timber, and we have an entire day at our disposal.' He looked optimistically at Galba. 'We should have ballistae made, and siege towers, and catapults. If we were with the legion, we would have such things.'

Galba was sharp. 'We are not with the legion — not yet.'

'We have a blacksmith, sir.' Quintus was thinking of Crassus. 'We must have carpenters.'

'Rope?' Galba asked.

'Some in the carts,' said Felix.

'And more could be made using saplings or ivy or honeysuckle…' Quintus was allowing his enthusiasm to get the better of him.

'The hill makes siege engines useless,' said Galba slowly. 'And we do not have the materials to make ballistae. But we could make catapults to fling stones at the gates. And a battering ram.' He paused. 'We will make sure the carpenters are busy, and then we will take this place.' He looked around at the four faces, lit unevenly by the flickering flames, Quintus' bruises looking angry. 'Our orders are to join with General Drusus as soon as possible. This oppidum lies in the way. Also, we need vengeance for the commander's capture and death. That will not wait.'

'There's Dagaz, too,' Quintus said with venom. 'We need more forces to defeat the man who tortured and killed our pioneers. He — and his gods — should be destroyed.'

The men nodded in agreement. They would storm the fortress at first light, but not tomorrow.

'Today or tomorrow, either would have been easier,' Marius said under his breath.

Galba said nothing, but looked at Marius disapprovingly. He did not need reminding of the difficulty caused by inauspicious days designated by the gods.

'We cannot control the caprice of the gods,' Felix said cheerfully. 'We must just accept what we are given. A frontal assault it is. At least it will be over quickly.'

They all knew that a frontal assault would be faster, but that it would almost certainly lead to many more deaths and injuries.

'Make sure the men have deposited their wills with someone trustworthy,' Galba instructed. 'Centurion Quintus, you will take mine. I have no other to entrust it to.'

Quintus nodded. It was an honour to be so chosen by his commander. 'Sir,' he ventured. 'We may be able to do something tonight. The unlucky day has yet to start.' He paused, a puzzled look crossing his face. 'When *does* it start, I wonder?' He called across to Jovan. 'Jovan, find Sextus and bring him here.'

The slave ran off, returning quickly with the legionary. Quintus dismissed him, then turned to his comrade. 'Sextus, this day of ill omen tomorrow, *mundus patet* — exactly when do the gates of Hades open and when do they close again? Did not the Lady Antonia say sunrise?'

'She did, sir. As far as I know, they open at dawn and close at the setting of the sun.'

'You are sure?'

'As I can be. Shall I ask to see if anyone knows better?'

'No,' smiled Quintus. 'I am happy with your expertise. It means we have time. We can put ourselves in a better position.' He looked around at his listeners. 'We will know if we have done wrong when we read the haruspices in the morning.'

XXXXVI: IDEM FACERES

Quintus waved Sextus away. The augur had provided exactly what he had hoped for. He addressed Galba. 'If I may, sir?'

Galba nodded his assent, not quite certain what it was that Quintus intended. Hurriedly, Quintus barked orders to bring to him the junior officers. As each arrived, he told them that the priests had confirmed the unlucky hours were from sunrise to sunset, and that outside of those hours, they could be ordered to fight — and if not fight, certainly to work. The men should not rest until they were told that they could do so.

'Pass on the information,' he told them, 'and expect to work tonight.'

Century Four had its orders first. It could be seen running down to the track to block any further arrivals. Felix ordered them split into two groups: one would dig a deep trench across the road, while the other would guard the men whilst they dug. In addition, Anatolian archers covered the approach.

If the gates of Hades did not open until sunrise, these defences could be finished so that, by morning, a deep ditch and a line of stakes would prevent any more tribesmen from coming along the road. Quintus guessed the tribesmen would gather out of range of the archers until there were enough to mount an attack. Either that or they would seek other ways into the oppidum. The archers, Anatolian auxiliaries untrammelled by Roman religion, would keep them in check. Century Four would stand guard. Only they would be aware that, if attacked, they would withdraw.

Quintus then called on Furius Lentulus. 'Send Marcus across the river with a troop to close off the rear approach. He knows the way. Tell him to take as many as he needs to destroy the bridge if they have repaired it. Stealth is not needed now, so they should take lights. In fact, use the torches to burn the bridge if it is back in place. That will stop them from using it. He can leave a token force to guard it, though I think without a bridge they cannot cross.'

Century Three was next. 'Marius, I need your optio, Caius, if I may. Tell him to bring the guide to me. Your men should start cutting timber. Tell them to take care, Marius. We do not normally cut timbers in the dark.'

In a matter of minutes, there were only the two officers left. Galba allowed himself a smile. Quintus would have smiled also, but moving the muscles of his face was still painful. He managed a lopsided grimace.

'I will leave you to your tribesman,' said Galba. 'I will have to tell the ladies what is happening, then I will join Marius.'

Caius passed Galba going in the opposite direction, and wondered what was happening. After the evening assembly, it was a time for cleaning equipment, telling stories, gambling, eating and drinking. It was not usually a time for activity — certainly not at this level. He came with the sad-faced man, the Germani guide whose relative Hrolf had been killed. He knew of the boy's death, and of who had caused it. Quintus invited him to sit down in the place vacated by Galba and offered him food and drink.

'Caius, tell him that tomorrow we honour Father Dis, our guardian of the shades of the dead, and will not attack the oppidum.'

Caius said, 'I will try, sir. But that is a lot to say.'

'As long as he knows we do not fight tomorrow for noble reasons, not cowardice or fear.'

'That is easier, sir.' The optio smiled, and he and the man conversed in a mixture of Germani, Latin and hand gestures.

'He asks if you will besiege it, sir. He sees the ditch being dug.'

Before Quintus could respond, the man spoke in broken Latin. 'You will not starve them out, nor keep them from the river.'

'I did not think we could,' said Quintus. 'They have taken cattle and pigs inside. If they cannot feed them, they can eat them. And there is a side to the hill that we cannot assault, where the river runs. I do not think we have time to change the course of the Rhenus. Although this man should know it has been done — by Rome.'

Quintus and Caius knew that Divus Julius had taken Alesia in this way, building a wall around it so that nothing could leave, then another, even longer wall, so that nothing could enter. He had also altered the course of the river. His army had camped safely between the two walls and waited. It had taken a long time, and led to many deaths on the part of the inhabitants, attackers and defenders. Vercingetorix's own brother had almost overturned the defences — but not quite. Eventually, the Romans had been victorious.

'Tell him we storm the fort, that we do not besiege it. Ask him if there are any weaknesses.'

A few moments later, Caius said, 'He says not, though if he knew of any, I am sure he would not say.'

'Is Dagaz within?' Quintus demanded.

The man spoke, but the vigorous shaking of his head had already revealed his answer. 'He thinks not,' said Caius. 'If he were Dagaz, he would wait until you are hammering at the gates, then attack your rear. He would not come down the road, but across the river, across the stones.'

The tribesman tilted his chin up, the firelight making his eyes gleam. In clear enough Latin, he said, '*Idem faceres?' Would you not do the same?*

Quintus nodded. Of course he would. Now he was aware of the river crossing, he would deal with it.

Crassus did not stay with Century One, even though he was their optio. As a blacksmith, he had knowledge needed by the men building siege weapons. He put his head together with carpenters and other smiths and they worked out what they were able to produce given the materials at hand. Ballistae were quickly rejected. They were hard to build and slow to reload. Onagers required too much rope and had too many complex joints. They chose to build simple catapults, driven by the torsion of twisted rope strands and easily reloaded. They would not be huge and would be mounted on wheels, so that soldiers could reposition them. They also set men to making ladders.

Carts were lifted up onto blocks and their wheels removed, which carpenters fitted to the makeshift axles they fabricated. A simple frame was constructed, with a firing arm and a sturdy wooden brake. Crassus organised groups of men to make quantities of each part, all to the same design. These did not need to be carpenters, just men who could hew wood.

The winches needed to be more refined; they could not snag, and had to carry the ratchets made by the smithy. Here both carpenter and blacksmith worked together. Other groups built the machines and knocked in the pins required to keep them together. Slaves twisted the ropes around, providing the power. Legionaries tested them for reliability and range. Other men worked throughout the night, collecting ammunition. They dug up stones and stacked them in readiness.

'Take stones from the river crossing,' Quintus ordered, glad of the Germani's insight. 'Make sure there is a deep channel that the enemy cannot cross.'

Though the men struggled, needing trenching tools and levers as well as muscle power, they complied, and in time the river could no longer be crossed, as it rushed to fill the spaces where the stones had been. In addition they collected anything that might burn — the shavings and sawdust from the carpentry; small twigs and branches; dried grass — and bound them together with pitch into balls that, when lit, could be thrown. In case they needed to cross trenches in front of the lower fence and the palisade, they gathered and tied thin sticks in bunches, fascines, stacking them up ready for use.

The work went on by torchlight and firelight long into the night, the sounds of timber being cut and hammered and split echoing in the forest. Near the river a forge burned bright and sparks flew as hammers rang and slaves worked bellows. There were loud hisses as hot metal met flowing water, and the smell of burning on the breeze. Numerous slaves passed between the shadows, carrying waterskins to the sweating soldiers. The grunts and groans of physical labour accompanied the sound of pegs being hammered into joints. With all the fire, muscle and shouting, it was like a vision of Hades brought to life.

Vetruvius and Rufus were building the prefect's funeral pyre.

'I suppose it does not need to be too grand,' Vetruvius said to Quintus when he went to check on their progress. 'After all, I believe we are burning a pig and a ring.'

'It needs to be grand enough for Titus Flavius Pusio, soldier,' Quintus replied sharply. 'Prefect, commander, member of the noble order of knights, whose even more noble wife will be present.'

'Of course, sir,' Vetruvius replied, though without conviction.

'It will be the best pyre a pig has ever had,' Rufus muttered.

'A noble pig,' said Vetruvius scornfully, at which point Rufus told him to hush, before he said enough to earn a whipping.

Quintus then went to check whether Sextus had managed to secure the required sacrifice.

'The sow proved difficult,' Sextus reported. 'But the Anatolians have managed to wound a boar. It is a poor-looking thing, not much more than a piglet, but the best they could find.'

'We should be grateful to them,' Quintus said. 'I will find them a reward from somewhere.'

'Will the Lady Antonia sacrifice it in front of the pyre?' Sextus asked.

In Republican times, the wealthy of the city had sacrificed a sow before the pyre, cooking and sharing its meat between the mourners, the spirit of the dead body and Ceres. This was going to be something different.

'It must burn on the pyre, Sextus. It represents his body.' He hissed urgently into his ear. 'It must be right, Sextus. The Lady Antonia must be convinced that his shade has crossed the river. Can you make it so?'

'I can make sure he finds his rest,' Sextus insisted. 'If he crosses safely, there will be a portent.'

Quintus inclined his head with relief. He was as superstitious as the next soldier, but he at least knew that portents could be manipulated — Consul Marcus Antonius was also an augur and famous for it, using flights of birds and shapes of clouds to suspend the senate and undermine its power.

Sextus continued to outline the ceremony. 'The pig will be sacrificed next to the pyre, but not opened. I will place the ring in its mouth. I will bless it with oil, water and wine while it lives, so there is no need to check the exta.'

Quintus nodded. He understood. No-one wanted to find an inauspicious liver or unlucky kidney. He approved.

'It will burn,' Sextus said. 'Ceres will take her portion. I have told the lady that the family's portion will be taken by Mercury, who will grasp the Flavian's hand.' He smiled wickedly. 'No bacon for dinner, I am afraid.'

'Is that all?'

'That is all — the ceremony will be when the gates first open, before they are crowded with the manés of the dead,' said Sextus.

'Will it be small and private, or will the centuries bear witness? What does the Lady Antonia Flavia wish?'

'I think she would like the respect of all the legionaries, without having to ask for it.'

Quintus understood. 'Agreed,' he said.

XXXXVII: LAPIS MANALIS

Just before dawn, Galba ordered the cornicen to sound the assembly.

Gradually, the sounds subsided as the men, dirty and weary, gathered before the tribunal. Torches ringed the gathering. Marcus had returned in the night, but left a group of men marking the place where the bridge, now ash and cinders, had once stood. Felix and his troops still guarded the road. Their night watch had been quiet, but as the sky paled, the Anatolians shot at two small groups, who seemed unaware that the way was guarded.

The men lined up by century, standards to the fore, curious to see that to the right-hand side of the tribunal stood an unlit pyre. None had shirked duty in the night and all carried the marks of hard labour. Some, including Crassus, bore the black marks and small burns that came from working a forge. His teeth glowed white in his soot-streaked face; clearly he had been enjoying himself.

Galba mounted the tribunal platform. He nodded towards his left, where an area was marked out containing stone and the wooden tripod, lit by torches. The legionary acting as the priest, his head covered, completed a swift sacrifice. For Father Dis it should have been something black, a lamb, perhaps, or a ram. Quintus squinted across. In the uncertain light he deemed that it was black, but was a bird rather than a beast. A jackdaw perhaps, hopefully a raven. He watched as the shadowy figure of the priest opened the body and spoke swiftly to Galba before flinging the exta on the tripod, where they sizzled in the fire.

'The haruspices are good,' the priest said.

Galba turned back to the men and, as true dawn broke across the horizon, spoke clearly. 'The haruspices tell us that we have done no wrong to work through the night.' He pointed to the growing light in the east. 'See the sunrise. The augurs and scholars tell us that now, on this day, the gates of Hades are open. *Mundus patet.*'

He paused as his words dropped into the silence, then announced, 'Today we do not fight.' The men knew this already. 'We mourn. We honour the commander with a pyre. Today is an auspicious day for making sure his shade reaches Elysium.'

There was some muttering amongst the men, but a general acceptance. A pyre sounded like the right thing to do, even without a body. Who knew what ancient traditions these nobles kept?

For a funeral without a body, the pyre was magnificent. The legionaries stood to attention, sweating in the increasing heat of the day as the two ladies approached.

The Lady Antonia Flavia and the Lady Aurelia, dressed in the black clothes that Cornus had managed to find for them, came from the pavilion. They wore flowing dresses and their heads were covered. Four legionaries flanked them, banging sword hilts on shields in a slow rhythm. Preceding them was Quintus, head covered, lit torch in hand. Behind came Sextus, swinging a smoking censer. It was an impressive — and appropriate — procession.

The pig, trussed upside down on a pole and carried between two slaves, had been stunned or drugged. It lived still, but neither wriggled nor squealed. Antonia Flavia climbed onto the tribunal platform and gave a brief eulogy. It should have been a son or an heir giving the speech. She should have been wearing one of the ancestral masks of the Flavii. But it was the best that could be achieved. What she said was no more than a list of Titus Flavius Pusio's noble ancestors, so many times tribune of the plebs, so many aediles and praetors, and at least one consul. She then expounded on his major virtues, his *pietas*, *fides* and *gravitas*, his *honestas* and *auctoritas*.

She asked Ceres and Mercury, Janus and Father Dis, to allow the shade passage to the Elysian fields. A nod to Sextus and he blessed the animal with oil, then slit its throat and quickly laid it on the pyre, the ring beneath its tongue. Antonia took the torch from Quintus and put it to the kindling at the base. Sextus, on her signal, lit the other side.

There were no public prayers, no lamentations, no tearing of clothes. The pig would be quickly consumed; it was not big, so there would be no feast. The ring could make someone a rich prize — enough to buy freedom or a farm perhaps. But none would ever know where it had gone, and none would ever be stupid enough to admit to having lifted it. If it was not in the ashes delivered to the Lady Antonia, it would be because it was with the Flavian in Elysium.

A flight of rooks, wheeling noisily above the trees to the west, provided Sextus with his portent and confirmation that Flavius' shade had been escorted and accepted. His death mask would join his other noble ancestors in the atrium of his town house.

'I am told there are no punishments today,' Galba said to Quintus, allowing himself a brief smile.

'A rare feat,' Quintus agreed quietly.

'Keep it so until sunset and I will let this funeral stand as the day's only assembly,' said Galba. 'At sunset the gates of Hades once more swing shut. The *lapis manalis* will again cover the pit and the inauspicious hours for fighting will have passed.' He paused, then raised his voice, so the men could hear. 'We will attack and destroy this oppidum in the morning! We will avenge the prefect!'

The soldiers cheered. This is what they had wanted to hear — a proper fight, rather than a long siege, where they might suffer as many depredations as the besieged. Their battle would be violent and deadly, but mercifully short.

Galba continued, 'The orders for the rest of the day are to finish your tasks in preparation, to loosen your muscles for fighting and to grab what sleep you can when the sun goes down. The night will be short.'

The legionaries would first break their fast, then return to work or exercises. Quintus' contubernales ate hot grain pottage and flatbread baked in the ashes of the fire. Jovan ground wheat and Sextus found enough oil to make the dough. Maxim foraged some wild garlic, which added much-needed flavour.

On the Palatine at sunset, the black stone that kept the manés — the spirits of the dead — in check would once more be rolled across to cover the pit said to lead to the realms of Father Dis. Until then, the day was an unlucky one. The men felt it.

It turned sultry, with the sky overcast, oppressive and heavy. It was the sort of atmosphere that made people tetchy and short-tempered. Quintus broke up a fight near the construction area, his vine rod cracking over a soldier's broad back. The man cursed and turned, ready to take on another opponent, then grinned when he saw who it was.

'Sir,' he said. It was not quite disrespectful enough to warrant further chastisement.

Quintus recognised the man. It was the wrestler. 'You are a long service veteran, Piso. You should know better,' he scolded.

'So should he,' Piso said as he pointed to the youngster he had floored — one that Quintus did not recognise. He still had hold of the man's wrist, twisted upwards to pull the arm painfully straight, his foot on the man's shoulder. 'Ask him.'

'I am not interested.' Quintus dismissed them both. 'Let him go, Piso. Get up, you. And get to your work, both of you.'

As they scurried off, he turned to find Marcus approaching. 'An argument?' the veteran asked.

'They are tired,' said Quintus. 'The weather is not helping.'

'I have just broken up two fights, and stopped a soldier from beating a slave half to death,' Marcus said. 'The slave was taking out his ire on a mule.'

'They need to stay out of trouble until sunset,' said Quintus. 'Otherwise it will be assemblies and punishments. I do not wish to be party to insubordination.'

Marcus nodded in agreement. 'Little things climb onto the backs of other little things, and soon we have a mutiny.' He laughed softly. 'And we are not General Caesar.'

Divus Julius had quelled the mutiny of the Tenth Equestris with a single word, dismissing the legionaries from service as *quirites*, 'citizens' rather than *Romani*, 'citizen soldiers'. They had begged him to reinstate them.

'They are cursing any little piece of fortune that feels like ill luck,' Quintus continued, 'things they would usually shrug off. A tunic snagged on a branch and torn, a spark or brand burning the skin, the rope of a tent causing a trip, a comrade lacking skill, a slave not responding fast enough… I think some of them wanted to fight today. I think some of them see the pyre as an affront to the gods. What can we do?'

'They need to drill, Quintus. The catapults are all but complete, the forges are cooling, the ammunition stores are set. Let the slaves tidy up whilst we drill the men.'

Quintus agreed. They had been hard at work, yes, but on tasks that did not really provide feelings of satisfaction. Drill exercises would bring discipline back to the ranks.

The legionaries were quickly set to exercises: throwing the heavy pilum, unarmed combat and sword and shield play in pairs. Marcus called out the moves and supervised the training. He encouraged the men, and laughed with them when they made a mistake, not at them. Two of the centurions, Quintus and Marius, watched the optio. The other two were absent. Felix was once more with the patrol by the road. Furius Lentulus had taken a party of men to relieve those guarding the rear approach.

At the winter camp, it had been just the rabbits, Century Four, that drilled; now it was all the members of the cohort, including the new men from the Larks. Officers were exempt, unless specifically called on or volunteering themselves. Caius, Rufus and Aquila, all junior officers, were on the training field by choice.

The brooding atmosphere lifted as the men threw themselves into the exercises. The moves became smoother, swifter; there were fewer mistakes, then none. Anger and frustration dissipated, frayed tempers were mended, and comradeship was restored.

Although deep into the afternoon Marcus had called a halt, many of the men still continued their exercises. As the sun sank, the sky turned blood-red and black. Many of the men saw this as a good omen, a portent of victory.

Sextus appeared beside Quintus. He had managed to dodge the drill.

'Does the sky bode good or evil, augur?' Quintus asked only half seriously.

'A lion loose in the Suburra, heading for the Comitia; the shaking of the earth; the call of an owl in daylight; a slave's hand miraculously unburnt by fire — these all foretold the death of great Caesar. The portents from the heavens were less clear — although I did hear a tale of a bright light in the sky.' He looked at the retreating backs of the legionaries, many with friendly arms around comrades' shoulders. 'The men have decided what this means,' he said. 'Let it stand.'

Quintus nodded. 'The stone is back in place,' he said. 'The sky no longer lies open. The gates are closed.'

'The men feel it,' said Marcus. As he spoke, a light breeze came from the east and seemed to blow away the last vestiges of ill luck and bad feeling.

XXXXVIII: PER IOCEM

The men gradually wandered back to friends, fires and food, each group to its own tent.

Although Quintus could have claimed a tent for himself, he preferred the company of the men of his contubernium. After sunset, the tale of the raid and Quintus' single combat with the Germani warrior was told to those who did not witness the fight.

To his embarrassment, it far outgrew the facts in the telling. Three of the contubernales had not been present for the raid, but the others took turns adding on ever more imaginative details. Whilst Hrolf, sadly, was all but forgotten, outrageous estimates of the size of the warrior, the length of his sword, and the time he took to die all vied with each other across the fire. It was already taking on the trappings of a legend. The men clearly believed that a good tale was worth embellishing.

'How many did you fight?' Vetruvius laughed, through a mouthful of hard biscuit. 'Was it a whole tribe or just half of one?'

'With bruises like that,' said Aquila, also chuckling, 'it must have been at least an entire tribe, if not more.'

Marcus defended his friend weakly against this onslaught. 'Though I could not see in the dark,' he said, 'Quintus will have fought honourably. I am sure of it.'

Quintus tried to laugh along with them, but it pained him to do more than crack a smile. Instead he dropped his head to concentrate on his food.

Suddenly, he let out a yell, jumped up from his squatting position and stepped backwards, almost colliding with a tree.

He dropped his spoon and only just managed to keep hold of his bowl. He realised almost at once that he had been tricked, but not quickly enough to hide his initial reaction. The laughing men could therefore claim their jest was a success.

Quintus put his fingers gingerly into the liquid left in the bowl and fished out the object that had startled him. He had expected it to be soft and squelchy, but it was hard. Other than that, it was a totally lifelike human eye.

The joke was elaborate, difficult and, if truth be told, not very funny. It had been thought up by Rufus, and the others had endorsed it. Instructions were given to Jovan, with reassurances that he would face no punishment or strictures. The item was checked and inspected, with much hilarity, then cached against the day when it could be used. It was a piece of polished wood, a knot that looked so much like a disembodied eye that Rufus had immediately had the idea of using it in a jest. Maxim made dyes and Jovan painted it to look even more lifelike.

Before the men's evening meal, Jovan had fixed the false eye to the bottom of Quintus' bowl with a paste of flour and water, knowing that either the heat of the pottage, or the action of Quintus' spoon, would free it. As planned, it had risen to the surface and stared out at the butt of the joke. Quintus held it in his hand now, amazed at its likeness to the real thing. It had almost winked at the victim, performing better than the men had expected. They congratulated themselves — it was funnier than any of them had anticipated.

Quintus took it in good part, retrieving his spoon from the ground. He looked suspiciously at Jovan, knowing that he must have had a part in it.

'*Per iocum*, *dominus*, a jest,' Jovan said sheepishly and busied himself with tasks that took him further from his master.

'You are forgiven,' Quintus said, then made a grand gesture with his spoon. 'You are all forgiven.' He tucked the eye away in his tunic. 'But know that you have started a feud, and there will be retribution.'

'I am paying you back,' Rufus complained, although smiling. 'Remember?'

'Granted,' Quintus allowed, remembering the practical joke he — and others — had played on the redhead, luring him into squatting in a patch of thorns and nettles to relieve himself. 'You and I are even.' He waved his spoon threateningly again. 'But the rest of you…'

There was general laughter and, for Maxim and Jovan, relief. Not all officers had a sense of humour.

Later, a more serious debate commenced, about wills and who should hold them. The night before a battle, the soldiers traditionally needed to place their wills in safe hands.

'Our wills should have been held by each other,' said Vetruvius, pointing to himself and Aquila. 'But we instead put them all into the hands of our decanus.'

'Who, along with the rest of the contubernium, did not survive,' said Aquila.

'So your wills were lost?' Quintus asked, unconsciously fingering the tattered will of Ursus, which he kept in the secret pocket. The will that laid deep obligations on him. 'You should write another.'

'I should,' said Vetruvius with a wry smile. 'I have family in Tarentum — an ageing father, a sister, a niece and nephew. I am sure they would benefit from my accumulated wealth.'

'It is not about wealth,' Sextus chipped in, 'it is about honour.'

'Very well, I can count and calculate,' said Vetruvius, 'necessary skills for a gambler. But I never learned to write much more than my name.' He shook his head sadly, making his luxuriant dark hair bounce. There was no shame in this. Many of the infantry would not have received more than a basic education, some not even that.

'Jovan can write,' said Quintus. 'He will take down the necessary words.' He called across to the man tending the cooking pot. 'Maxim, fetch your cousin. Tell him to bring wax and a stylus.'

Jovan arrived shortly, ready to take down details. 'Your full name, first,' he said, stylus poised.

'Lucius Cornelius Vetruvius, of Tarentum, near Brundisium.'

'By Jupiter, a noble Cornelii,' exclaimed Rufus, laughing as he clapped him on the back. 'I did not know. We are indeed honoured.'

'I claim no great ancestry,' Vetruvius said, his smile white in his tanned face. 'It is not in doubt that I am a citizen. I am three generations a Roman. Still, I am also a Cornelii, as was my father and my grandfather. In my grandfather's time there were suddenly many Cornelii.' He chuckled. 'My grandfather did not start his life with such a noble name, but was one of the ten thousand slaves and indentured workers set free by the dictator Sulla in reward for their support.'

'Sulla the fortunate,' said Sextus. 'Of course, Lucius Cornelius Sulla Felix. He gave you your name, his name.'

'Do not worry. You are in good company. I am of the noble Junii,' said Rufus, bowing low, 'for much the same reasons.'

'My father, if he lives still, farms a little land given to veterans by the General,' said Vetruvius. 'Most of his neighbours are Cornelii.'

It had happened often, so that the ancient families of Rome were spread far and wide. The comrades laughed and teased

Vetruvius about who he might choose as a noble wife, then turned on Rufus about his hair.

Crassus returned from the forge, stripped to the waist, wearing just his baltea and cingulum. The thick curly hair on his head was echoed on his chest, softening the lines of muscle. Like all legionaries, Crassus trained on a daily basis, either practising stroke and counter-stroke alone, or running, or working his body up into a hot sweat with physical challenges.

He joined Quintus, who told him about the jest and showed him the wooden eye.

'How come you missed it, my friend?'

'I have been forging an arrowhead for the battering ram, a great fist of metal,' Crassus replied with pride. 'It is finished and ready.'

'Good, good,' said Quintus. 'We will need it.'

A silence grew between them, each lost in his own thoughts about the planned assault.

'We are in noble company.' Quintus explained the discovery of names. 'Amidst laughter and friendship. These are good omens.'

'We have come a long way since we shared a cloak in the mud,' Crassus said at last.

'In disgrace,' said Quintus, clutching Ursus' treasures once more. 'Don't forget that. In disgrace.'

Crassus nodded, but did not reply. He would rather remember the warmth than the shame. Soon they would turn in. Tomorrow they would fight.

XXXXIX: AUGUSTUS, DIVI FILIUS

It seemed to many that they had hardly closed their eyes before the cornicen blew, this time a different note, an instruction to take up positions for an assault. Today the oppidum would be taken, or the cohort destroyed. The men were therefore roused from their rest not to an assembly, but to arms.

After early promise — a line of gold and red on the horizon — the day barely dawned at all. The pale light was smothered by cloud. It was dull and oppressive but warm. Flies and small biting insects were seeking living food, and there was a hint of rain in the sultry air.

The men did not strike the camp. Either they would return to their tents and carts victorious, or the tents and carts would no longer need them. Two legionaries, unlucky in the draw, were tasked with guarding the ladies in the pavilion. Should the enemy arrive, their job was to kill both women, then fight to the death themselves.

The first sounds on the air were the gentle wheezing of horses and the music of their jingling harnesses. The cavalry, what few there were, could be heard settling themselves onto the backs of their steeds, adjusting weaponry, talking quietly to the beasts, then trotting forward. Their own vexillum went before them, gently rippling — unusually, a single banner, all the rest having fallen with their comrades in the deep forest.

The Astures and Cantabrians mounted with less order, talking and laughing softly, but with less attendant noise — they had no saddles or harnesses. They rode on the bare hides of their mounts and controlled them with firm knees and a rein. They followed the new decurion and his sparse force whose job was to protect the wings of the attack, to make sure that no enemy could outflank the infantry.

The sound of the cornu came next, the three short and two long blasts that told the men to move. Signiferi waved their standards in well known patterns in echo of the sound. Optiones and centurions shouted orders and instructions.

There followed the heavy tread of many pairs of caligae, as the legionaries obeyed the order to form up and move out. The first part of each century marched eight men wide, shoulder to shoulder, shield to shield, so that no gaps appeared between the men. A gap, an arm's span, was left to the next rank behind. Each man carried both heavy throwing spears and light javelins for closer combat.

To the flanks, the cavalry and the auxiliaries rode, Astures and Cantabrians now mixed together. Spaced at intervals, in front of the formations, each centurion, now returned from other duties, was mounted, accompanied by the century's signifer. The smooth red cloaks worn by the centurions contrasted sharply with the rough black wolfskins of the signiferi. In the centre, Galba was framed by the eagle on one side, and the imago of the emperor on the other, with the cohort standard directly in front of him. Aquila, fresh-faced and fair-headed, tall and broad, wearing the wolf's head over his helm, carried the eagle that Galba knew did not belong to his legion.

'Never mind,' he excused himself. 'It does belong to Rome.'

Next to the standards, the long, curved tube of the cornua reflected the light, one cornicen at either end of the line. Caius and the Germani tribesman walked beside Galba's horse, ready to serve.

The disposition spread the legionaries over a wide front. Galba was hoping that this would show the might of the

Roman troops to the enemy and that the sight would force them to surrender. Quintus was aware of this, and knew it to be a forlorn hope. The oppidum was now stronger, better manned, than it had been when he and his comrades had infiltrated it.

After these ranks came the Anatolian archers, tall men with tall bows, all bearded and long-haired, with both combed and fashioned carefully. They wore undecorated round metal helmets and thick leather jerkins, but little other protection by way of armour. They carried quivers of the same material over their shoulders. They had been loyal to Rome for a long time, many of them veterans of Marcus Antonius' campaigns beneath the snow-capped Taurus mountains.

Behind them came a line of catapults, trundled along on their wheels, pulled by mules and guided by legionaries. For now, the ladders and the battering ram — carrying Crassus' proud addition — were out of sight at the rear.

Galba waved Caius and the Germani forward. Caius called out in the foreign tongue, prompted by whispered advice from the man when necessary. The legionaries did not understand the words, but did understand the message. They caught the name of Galba, of Titus Flavius Pusio and of great Augustus, Divi Filius. They understood the message to be, 'Look at us: we are the might of Rome. You cannot resist. Stand down.'

Quintus smiled to himself. This might be a tactic that worked if you had overwhelming force, cavalry and siege engines. He worried that the Germani might know their true strength. Quintus was not even sure that the soft voice of Galba, however clearly he spoke, would carry to the main entrance of the oppidum.

Here the shoulders and heads of men could be seen moving on the bridge that followed the line of the palisade, spanning the space above the gates. The gates were firmly closed.

The message did reach the first opening, the one in the uneven wooden fence that ran all around about halfway up the hill. The men behind this barrier jumped up and down, waved their spears, and shouted. The gaps in this fence, that a couple of days ago had looked like broken teeth in an ancient's mouth, were now sealed up. Apart from the place where the track went through, it was complete. In places, shoulders, heads and spear points showed defenders in place.

The gap through which the track ran was no longer open. It was not sealed with gates, but blocked with the trunks and branches of trees, piled one on top of the other, their still green foliage bearing witness to how recently they were felled. Recently enough that they must have been cut down whilst the funeral was taking place, when even the observers were forced to leave their posts, under orders to assemble.

Quintus cursed softly. It was not the only time that he would rue the nature of superstition.

The warriors behind the fence responded to the Roman challenge. Their voices carried down to the legionaries. Quintus listened briefly, then called to Caius, 'Anything intelligible?'

'Mostly insults, sir. A great deal of stuff about who our fathers might be, and who has lain with our mothers and sisters. But mostly they boast that their gods are stronger than ours.' Caius grinned. 'It is for the most part defiance and a wish that we would withdraw, for which they suggest many imaginative ways.'

Quintus turned the head of his horse and moved to draw level with Galba. The movement was obviously noted by the

Germani, as two spears whistled out from behind the barrier and landed, quivering in the ground at his horse's feet. It was the same roan he had ridden before, trained and calm. It ignored the twin thuds.

'At least they do not have the range,' Quintus said to Galba, looking down at where the spears had landed, missing the cohort's signifer by an uncomfortably narrow margin. To his credit, the man had remained immobile.

'Those may have been to test the range. The next may fly a little further,' said Galba. 'If they will not surrender, I suppose we will just have to attack. But we cannot deploy properly until that first entrance is breached.'

'I will take men to open it,' offered Quintus confidently, turning his mount back towards the soldiers. Galba saluted in acceptance.

Quintus issued orders rapidly. 'Bring up the catapults, ready the missiles, bring up torches. Archers, forward and ready. Century One, forward to my mark. Rufus!' As he called the signifer forward, he pointed to a spot on the ground, level with the two enemy spears.

Rufus understood, ran across and marked the point with the standard of Century One. The bare pole had become something of a talisman, and the men had resisted replacing any of the discs or decoration stripped from it by the enemy. It was superstition again, and Quintus had been tempted to scoff at it until he met the cold gaze of Tullius and heard the soft spoken arguments of Sextus. The *manus* was still there, the hand, and Crassus had replaced the name of the cohort with a metal plaque, but there were no discs beneath, only threads of red cloth attached to either side of the new plate. This, Quintus was told, was lucky.

Orders were repeated and reinforced by other officers. Crassus, as optio, led the men into position, using his hastile to mark the spot opposite Rufus, plunging it firmly into the ground. Though they had shields and helms, they were both exposed. They knew that the transverse crest on the helm of Crassus and the wolf's head on that of Rufus picked them out as officers and therefore targets. They were not afraid. They looked at each other and grinned.

'Decurion,' Quintus called across to the cavalry on the left. 'I will need horses to pull away the timber. Bring rope.' As the newly promoted officer saluted, Quintus slipped from the horse's back. 'And take my mount,' he added. 'I am better on foot.' The officer saluted again and grabbed the horse by its reins. He shouted a command to his men and at once ten mounts, some of the cavalry, some of the auxiliaries, peeled off from the flank.

The catapults were trundled into the gaps between the centuries, with men loading them and aiming them at the enemy. As legionaries moved and machines were put in place, more spears whistled through the air, but none reached the men. None even reached as far as where the first two landed, the line marked by the optio and signifer.

The first injuries to the Romans came from sharp stones and flints, flying almost invisibly through the air, propelled by slingshots. One man took an unlucky hit in his eye and was quickly moved to the rear and replaced. Some others were hit on their bare arms or legs — none seriously. Galba rode his horse slowly across the front of the squares, urging the standard bearers and trumpeters to follow. They took up position on the right of the formations, out of range of the slingshots.

Galba was afraid more for his horse than himself. Even if the small missiles did little damage to the beast, they had the potential to spook it, to make it throw its rider. For once, in spite of the sultry heat of the day, Galba's helmet was firmly on his head.

Beside him, men held their shields just a little more carefully, the tiny missiles clanging off them like summer hail on a tiled rooftop.

'It is time,' Quintus said.

L: GLADIUM STRINGE

On Quintus' command, the Roman attack commenced with a bombardment. Century One marched forward, halting at the invisible line marked by the standard and the optio's hastile.

First, the heavy pila — the broad-headed spears — were flung by the front ranks, some finding only the timber of the barricade, some, from the sudden screams and bodies jerking backwards, finding the enemy. Once the first rank had thrown theirs, they gave way in a well-rehearsed manoeuvre to the second rank. Quintus had ordered only these two ranks to throw, keeping the others in reserve. This would not be the only action this day.

Behind the spears, the Anatolians strung their bows and many arrows sped overhead, some burying themselves in timber or earth, some in flesh. Quintus encouraged them to continue firing, to force the defenders to take cover rather than retaliate. Each catapult, loaded with rocks, then hurled its payload at the target. These mostly bounced from the fence or the ground although, again, a few passed over the barricade and killed or injured tribesmen. One or two breached the fence, knocking palings out where it was obviously already weak. Softer ammunition was used next — softer, but flammable. The cogs on the catapults were wound back again on ratchets until taut, then loaded with ammunition that was set on fire. A torch provided the spark and the burning balls were quickly released, tracing a smoky trail through the air before landing in splashes of cinder and flame.

The spears and stones threw up dust and caused confusion. The arrows brought pain and death from the sky. The fiery balls broke up as they hit the barricade or the palisade either side of it. Parts of the fence began to burn. Some men were hit by them and could be seen running and heard crying out in agony.

Quintus knew that the defenders would not be distracted for long, so they had to act now. 'Forward Century One, at the double. Close-order.'

The men broke into a trot, careful to keep their shields together. Close-order meant just that: no space between their shields, no way for an enemy missile to penetrate.

'Decurion!' Quintus shouted to the cavalry. 'Follow the infantry. We need to be quick. Pull down the barricade. Break the dam.' The officer slammed his fist to his heart and led his troops, lying low along the backs of their horses, into the wake of the infantry. Each man now carried a turn of rope slung over his shoulder.

Ahead of them the men were mostly veterans. They had done this before. They moved now as if they were joined together at the hip, jogging up the hill, the barest of gaps between them, shouting encouragement and instructions to each other.

'Javelins!' Quintus yelled at the men, and at once a storm of light spears flew through the air, the men parting briefly enough to throw, then quickly closing up again. This volley forced the defenders to once more duck for cover. Those who were not fast enough were pinned or spun around by the force of the weapons.

'*Gladium stringe!*' The order to draw followed. Swords left sheaths in a metallic whisper that echoed down the lines. Quintus pulled out his own blade and joined the century on the end of the first rank. Rufus and Crassus also drew, finding themselves places near the front.

The infantry ran swiftly along the beaten track and up the hill, heading straight for the blocked gate, bracketed now by two columns of swirling smoke. The defenders, attacked by spear and boulder, arrow and fire, were not given time to regroup. Many fell in the first seconds of confusion as the front rank reached the barrier, hitting it as one with the force of a single blow. The tribesmen had not expected a direct charge, and certainly not one conducted with such discipline and ferocity.

The legionaries climbed or leaped over the timbers, wielding swords and shouting war cries at the Germani. The names of many gods were in their mouths, mostly Mars and great Jupiter, whilst some called on the Great Mother, the manifestation of Rome herself. The name of Týr was defiantly called out by many of the defenders.

Quintus was one of the first over the barrier, stepping onto one of the trunks, then clambering over the remaining branches, leaping from the top and thrusting as soon as he landed. Still he remembered the drill, hard-baked into his training: go for soft flesh, eyes, armpits, belly, thighs, groin. Aim to prevent men taking further part in the fight; that was easier than trying to kill them.

That was how he was trained on the Campus Martius. Stab, don't slash; remember, the shield is a weapon as well as a defence. Move quickly, move smoothly, never hesitate. His gladius struck again and again in short stabbing motions, whilst his shield boss became a battering ram.

To the other side of the barrier the cavalry and the mounted auxiliaries pulled up. They dismounted and quickly tied ropes to the timbers, then urged their mounts to pull the barricade down. It groaned as the animals heaved at it.

The initial resistance weakened. The remaining defenders were already a good two paces from the gate and the legionaries of Century One continued to push them back. Quintus was in the centre. Germani wielding axes and spears fell before him, their blows avoided or glancing off his armour as he turned his shoulder or danced aside out of the way. He wore metal wrist guards, a recent gift from Sextus — probably taken from a dead man. The guards were weapons in themselves as well as protection, and they were now covered in the blood that ran down his sword.

He did find time to glance around, briefly. He glimpsed the bright beard of Rufus, so knew that Sextus could not be far away, and the solid form of Crassus, still shouting encouragement to the men. As swiftly as he had noted them he dismissed them from his mind, determined to take down as many tribesmen as possible.

Behind him the creaking sound of timbers under strain joined the other noises, as the horses, coaxed and cajoled by their masters, began to untangle the logs and trees of the barricade from each other. A cracking noise made Quintus glance back in that direction, to see one tree already being dragged away down the slope. The rest of the obstruction was already tumbling — the horsemen had taken this tree from its centre and, like a keystone knocked from an arch, it had loosened all the others. Already the bare earth could be seen where the barricade had stood.

Quintus found himself stabbing thin air, and was able to pause and breathe. He realised that the tribesmen's numbers had not just thinned, but that the defence was broken. Germani were fleeing up the hill, up towards the main gate, which he could see was swinging open to receive them. The red cloaks and bright helms of his own men could be seen following, scattered across the short grass and the beaten track that cut through it.

'Back!' he yelled, seeing the danger. 'Come back!'

A broken rabble of soldiers would present an easy target for the enemy. Even now he could see individual legionaries being cut down in their haste to pursue. Risking his own life by showing his back to them, he called down the hill, 'Cornicen, bring them back!'

Galba heard and echoed his command. 'Quickly! Sound the stand-to!'

The notes of the cornua rang out. Quintus thought for a moment that the men were too engrossed in the heat of battle to respond. Then he saw men slow, call out to each other, and turn to come back down the hill. A couple of them fell to enemy spears, thrown from the palisade. Quintus saw one fall then rise again — perhaps he had done no more than trip. Another remained still on the ground, a spear sticking out of him. At what remained of the barricade there were few defenders left to fight. There were many injured tribesmen and some who knelt in surrender, giving up their arms.

Quintus had no qualms about ordering that no prisoners be taken. It was not possible. 'Give the defenders the mercy of death,' he said unemotionally. 'Then clear them and the rest of these logs away so that the cohort can come through.'

From his position five or six paces above the fence, Quintus looked first down and then up the hill.

Below him, the dead were being moved to one side and the last of the logs and trees were being dragged out of the way. Legionaries threw earth on fires and kicked down the fence where it smouldered still. There were already parties, no doubt ordered by the optiones, collecting unbroken spears. Others stacked the stones that the catapults had flung, ready to be used again. The Anatolians moved across the ground, retrieving arrows.

Galba and the colour party — the standard-bearers and the trumpeters — were already trotting up the hill, the other three centuries falling in behind him. The cavalry and catapults were following. Behind them were several long ladders, carried by men at each end. In the centre was a single tree trunk, shorn of branches and needing eight men to carry it. The front of it carried a roughly cast fist, a great metal construction with knuckles, courtesy of Crassus, perfect for a battering ram.

Above him, Quintus watched the remainder of the tribesmen run up and through the tall, half-open gate, the dark mouth closing as the last of them vanished inside.

Though the gate was shut, the way to the oppidum was now open and a direct attack could be launched. The sun had not yet climbed too high. There was plenty of time.

Galba led the rest of the cohort through the gap at a trot. Standards and the bronze-beaked eagle were placed where all, including the enemy, could see them. The catapults were dragged into position, the ammunition brought up and piled ready for use. Century One was commanded to form up on the right so that Quintus could count his losses. Rufus and Crassus joined him, Rufus with the bare pole of the 'lucky' standard, Crassus reunited with his hastile. One of the other officers had plucked it from the ground as they came on and returned it to the optio. The men of Century One lined up as they had done before, leaving gaps for those missing.

Some were absent with injuries, including he who had received the first of the sharp flints in his eye. Though the flint was buried deeply, the man had pulled it out himself in an attempt to relieve the agony.

'He should have waited for me,' Alba said. 'If he had, he might not have lost his eye in the process. He is back in the camp.'

'Can he fight?' Quintus asked the capsarius.

'Not today,' said Alba. 'But in time, yes.'

Others were grouped to one side, still waiting for Alba's attention. The capsarius was busy checking and binding wounds, adding concoctions to some of them to assist healing, tying others tightly to stop them from bleeding. A few legionaries he declared unfit for further combat, in spite of their objections. However keen a man was to rejoin his comrades, Alba would not let him do so if he judged his presence to be a liability. Efficiency came before emotion.

There were also some who had met their death. To Quintus' amazement, the century had lost just four men.

Two were lying on the hillside between them and the oppidum, one with a spear sticking out of him, still rocking gently from side to side. The other was seemingly sleeping, curled up in a foetal position, with a pool of blood spreading from his neck.

One had been taken down at the barricade by a lucky strike that had cut his windpipe. He lay face-up next to the charred fence, his eyes open and his face bone-white. Another lay partly across him, speared in the back.

Quintus looked at the face of the first man. 'Is that the man who was whipped for offending the image of the emperor?' he asked Rufus.

'It is, sir.' Rufus replied. 'I suspect that he was trying to redeem his honour through an act of bravery.'

Quintus was annoyed. 'Just the sort of thing to get a man killed. Who is the other? Was he running away?'

'I am guessing his amicus, sir. I believe he was trying to save him.'

'Turning his back on the enemy — foolishness!' Quintus shook his head. Such men were no great loss.

LI: TESTUDO

Galba dismounted, as did the other centurions and mounted men of the cavalry. The hill was too steep for a cavalry charge, and probably too steep for any sort of horsemanship. In addition, the track by the gates narrowed between two shallow trenches, leaving little room for traditional manoeuvres.

The Cantabrian and Asturian auxiliaries stayed mounted. They made it clear that their ponies could navigate the slope, demonstrating how easily they climbed and turned. Quintus acknowledged their leader, and passed on the message that they would have a job to do. To the cavalry decurion, he passed the order that they hold themselves in reserve.

Galba lifted his palm to some of the legionaries yet to come through the gate. 'Keep that hidden!' he shouted to the men approaching the gap with the battering ram. 'Keep it down behind the fence. And the ladders, too. Keep them out of sight.'

Quintus looked at his commander quizzically.

'This is going to look like a siege, centurion,' Galba said. 'In reality, we are going to storm it. The longer they think it is a siege, the less they will expect a frontal attack — therefore, the better for us.'

Quintus nodded and carried on, now ordering the catapults into position. They were wheeled, protected by men with shields, to positions higher up the hill. The dead man with the enemy spear sticking out of him gave them a good idea of the limit of the defenders' weapons. The catapults had a greater range and were placed out of reach of spears thrown from the palisade.

The fascines were also brought up, the tight bundles of twigs being unnecessary for the first assault, as the trench in front of the fence did not continue across the track. Though not required for their intended purpose, they were useful for building temporary protection for the catapults and were stacked in a semi-circle around them. They would be deployed to fill the trenches by the gates. The ammunition came next and was stacked ready for use. Some men were also ordered to light fires, so that burning balls could be thrown. Fuel for these was brought up from the wood.

The barrage was not started until Galba had, once again, demanded that the barbarians surrender to the might of Rome.

'Life and liberty,' he promised, through Caius and the captured tribesman. 'You will be allowed to live and to leave in safety with all your families and possessions. We could even forge an alliance. But you must stand down. You must surrender.'

They could all hear that the response was laughter and a hail of insults. Amongst the tirade, the translator heard something else. 'They believe they will be relieved,' he said to Caius. 'They believe that reinforcements of their own people are on their way. They mention Dagaz by name.'

'If he comes, he will not be allowed to live,' Quintus said, remembering the fate of the pioneer party.

The translator dared to express an opinion. He needed Caius' help, but the gist of what he had to say was clear.

'They are Germani, sir. This is their land. Their own gods protect them here. They are confident that they can absorb this sort of bombardment forever. They have plenty of food and water. They believe that help is coming.'

The dialogue was clearly at an end. As soon as enough ammunition was brought up the catapults were put into action, stone after stone crashing against the palings of the fence. But it was built well, and was cleverly designed, not quite vertical, instead leaning outwards slightly — enough so that the full force of the missiles was not felt. The timbers not only repelled the stones, but were seasoned and hard enough to prevent fire taking hold.

Quintus looked at the catapults and the fence, accepting that it was unlikely that the machinery bothered the defenders. This palisade was a great deal more substantial than the one the Romans had just stormed. However much it was attacked, it would stand.

The defenders laughed and taunted the Romans from on top of it, waving spears and axes. Some of the younger men and boys even dared to bare their backsides to the invader, to show their contempt. Quintus ordered the archers to target them — an arrow in the arse would soon stop their laughter. But they were out of range of the bows, and jeered all the more as the arrows fell short. This angered Quintus, who ordered the catapults' aim altered. For a while, the missiles skimmed over the top of the palisade, forcing the defenders to withdraw. At least the fleshy insults vanished. But it was not an efficient use of either catapult or ammunition, so he relented and had the catapults readjusted to batter the timbers.

Relays of men were swapped regularly between the catapults and the waiting centuries. Other groups were sent to collect more rocks, more wood for the fires. The remaining men stood at ease, but in formation, ready to attack when needed. Legionaries were used to this. It was part of a soldier's duty to be ready in a field or on the edge of a battle, waiting for instructions.

The sun crawled across the sky and began to drop towards the treeline. Quintus did not want a second day of keeping up this barrage. Nor did he want to be in this exposed position overnight. He was about to order the ladders and battering ram brought up when the defenders played a wicked trick.

Above the gate a terrible spectre appeared. The eerie white face of the prefect stared sightlessly at the Romans. His body must have been supported by tribesmen, or propped up on a framework. One or two of the men were taken aback and made the warding sign of the horns, but all knew that the prefect was dead, and that even his shade had been helped across the river. This was but a body, a shell. They had witnessed the pyre, and they believed in the portents.

'It is but an apparition!' Quintus shouted. He grabbed one of the legionaries by the shoulder. 'Knock it down,' he hissed in the man's ear. 'Knock it off that wall. It was never here.' He did not want to put the widow through a second funeral. It was now apparent why the Germani had preserved the body, but as far as he was concerned the prefect was gone. Departed, his shade ferried across the river Styx in Charon's boat.

It took three legionaries and four javelins to dislodge the thing. They had to risk their lives, running forward until they had the range, then throwing the heavy pila. Even then the body only fell over, rather than falling back — but at least with spears in it the tribesmen could no longer support it. The legionaries — all renowned for their spear-throwing — looked at Quintus and shrugged. They had done their best.

'Well done,' Quintus mouthed, vowing that the body would be shifted as soon as they breached the gates.

Galba was pacing up and down, going from one catapult to another, encouraging the men at them. He expressed his disgust at how Titus Flavius had been treated with contempt.

Quintus intercepted him. 'Sir, we are getting nowhere,' he said. 'This palisade is better built than that paltry fence, and we are having no effect on it. We have yet to knock out a single paling. We have not even pushed the enemy from their bridge.'

The 'bridge', where the palisade and the step ran above the gates, provided both a lookout for guards and a firing platform from which to rain down missiles. It successfully forced any attackers into a narrow defile bounded by shallow trenches with the enemy above them. It was into this that Quintus wanted to go.

'Sir, it is time we forgot the pretence of a siege, and showed them what Roman legionaries mean by storming a city.'

Galba sighed. 'I had hoped to avoid casualties, or at least minimise them. A siege would have achieved this. Storming the oppidum will not.' He put up a palm to stop Quintus interrupting. 'I agree with you, centurion. We need to take this place today, and by force.' He finished on a more pessimistic note. 'Although we have fewer than four full centuries of foot soldiers, little cavalry and but a few auxiliaries.'

'And an eagle, don't forget the eagle,' Quintus said. 'It is worth a cohort on its own.'

'I agree,' said Galba. 'The eagle will lead. Bring up the ladders.'

'The ram,' said Quintus. 'Not the ladders, the battering ram.'

'What are you thinking?' Galba asked.

'What would you use to breach a wall, to bring an enemy to heel? What weapon would you choose?' Quintus asked. 'Humour me.'

'A tower, a ramp, a mine? Perhaps a ballista?'

'A ballista, I think,' said Quintus. 'One big enough could pierce that fence, open those gates. What we need is a bolt, an arrow — a sharp point to punch through, a shaft to follow, and a fletching to keep it straight and true. And we need it to fit into that space there.' He pointed to the track in front of the gates. 'A formation of men with an arrowhead leading, the battering ram protected by shields. It is similar to two formations I have seen rehearsed on the Campus Martius. It just means combining them. A sharp point made as a wedge or triangle, and behind it, infantry in column, with the ram. It would work.'

Galba shook his head. 'There is no enemy on the Campus Martius, and if it is the formation I am thinking of, it needs cavalry to guard the column, otherwise it would be fatal.'

Quintus' mind was racing. He had already seen other possibilities. 'A shallow wedge formation, each amicus protecting the other and the brother beside him. Shields at eye level. They protect themselves and in turn they protect the column. A rank of eight; those on the outside safeguard the flanks. Those in the centre propel the ram. Those between these two protect the formation from being attacked from above. If we first fill in the trenches, the auxiliary horsemen can add their protection. I said I would find a job for them.' He crouched down to scratch a diagram in the earth.

'The eagle leads,' said Galba. 'I will be with it, at the side of the iron fist. You must explain the formation to the men. Keep them in line and the shields high. It will be a sort of *testudo*, a turtle. If they lose their discipline, they will die.'

Quintus saluted and turned on his heel. 'Bring up the ram,' he ordered. 'And the ladders.'

They would not really try to storm the palisade with the ladders, but placing them as if they were would provide a distraction. He could use them to draw men away from the gates.

'Take the ladders to either side,' he ordered. 'Be ready to raise them.'

He called Crassus to him and explained the formation, the way the ram would be protected. To his relief, Crassus at once understood. The first part of the manoeuvre would be a variation on '*cuneum formate*' — a wedge. The second would be a column, the battering ram at the centre.

Suddenly, the hillside had purpose and energy. Ladders were being taken to the east and west sides of the gate, along with groups of men, seemingly prepared to scale the fence. The auxiliaries' ponies were busy dragging the tightly tied bundles of reeds up the slope in clouds of dust, darting in to drop them in the trenches then swiftly turning away, dodging any missiles that came their way. If this were to be a siege, then earth would be thrown on top of them and tamped down. As it was, the surface was still rough, but no soldier would fall into the trench. The Cantabrians and Asturians then held their ponies in place level with the track, ready to protect the flanks of the formation from any sorties. The legionaries formed up behind the catapults, which, over the heads of the horsemen, kept up the battering of the walls with renewed ferocity.

The jeering from the palisade redoubled as the battering ram was seen, many spears being thrown in its direction, but it was kept, for now, out of range. Crassus issued the order to form a wedge, then adjusted it to Quintus' requirements, until he declared himself satisfied. Aquila placed himself by the metal head of the ram, whilst Galba took up position on the other side. The men behind were ready not just to batter, but to work in relays, changing places with others so that it was always fresh muscles wielding the ram.

Galba, horsehair crest waving in the breeze, could be seen at the apex of the formation, with only one man beside him: Aquila, the eagle held high. Between them the metal fist glinted, ready to do its work.

The eagle cheered the men, whilst the disrespectful treatment of their dead commander's body angered them. Both gave them determination.

LII: LUGUBRI SONO

The curved instruments of the two cornicenes were battered but still serviceable. Their owners stood to one side at the rear of the position, prepared to convey orders. The first command, for the legionaries to arrange themselves into the formation, was given by the trumpet. The point of the 'arrow' was, after all, a variation of the wedge, so to blow the order '*cuneum formate*' was appropriate.

The construction of the rest of the 'arrow' — the non-standard part of the formation — involved those officers who understood what they were doing chivvying men into position.

Quintus and Crassus posted themselves to either side of the arrowhead, where the triangle swept back from the point and turned to join the shaft.

Crassus placed his hastile in the care of Alba. He did not expect to have to use it. There would be no retreat. These men would win or die in the attempt. When all signalled they were satisfied, the command for the cornua to sound the advance was given and the human ballista bolt was deployed.

At the same time, men of Century Two took the ladders forward and swung them up onto the palisade to either side of the gates, the archers and catapults providing cover. Legionaries stood on the first few rungs, looking as if they were ready to ascend. The other centuries also took up attack positions, as if they were going to storm the fortification, with the mounted auxiliaries guarding their flanks.

The defenders, seeing the soldiers preparing to scale the palisade, did what the Romans hoped that they would do and split their forces, men rushing to push the ladders away, or to fling ammunition down on the attackers. It would take them a while to realise that this was a ruse, that no Roman was actually climbing a ladder beyond its first few rungs.

On the command, the shape solidified and men lifted and angled their shields to protect its sides. Those legionaries within, where the battering ram waited, held their own scuta flat above their heads, edges overlapping. On the sounding of another note, swords were drawn in readiness before, on the final short command from the cornua, the men moved forward in a quick march, staying in step and together. They repeated a pulsing chant as they came on, just four beats at a time, emphasising the first beat: *one*, two, three, four; *one*, two, three, four — calling on Fortuna and praising mother Rome, great Jove, blood-red Mars and Father Dis.

As soon as they were within range of the defenders, the first spears and stones began to hit the front of the wedge. The shields held, although some of the lighter spears managed to fix themselves in their leather hide. Some men dared to reach across and strike away those that were stuck, knocking them to the ground, then quickly ducking back behind the shield wall. Within a few moments, the front of the formation was close to the gate and beneath the bridge, so that spears could no longer be aimed at its front. Instead they, along with other ammunition, clattered from its metal roof.

From within the testudo, the sound of the chanting changed to a two-note long-short pattern. The shields rattled as if the beast were a scaly monster quivering its backbone. Then, to a final shout and with a crash that reverberated down the valley of the river, the battering ram announced both its presence and its purpose.

The metal fist bit into the timbers, rocking the gates on their hinges. It caused the men on the palisade to redouble their efforts against the column. Men above the ladders set off to support their comrades, but as soon as they did, legionaries began to climb. This forced the defenders to return, against their will, to their positions, to try to cut down the ladders, push them away, or spear the attackers. They were partially successful — some legionaries were killed and at least one of the ladders was tipped sideways, but the others remained.

At the gates, the ram was swung again and this time splinters flew, as one of the planks gave way, parting with a crack. A third swing saw two planks broken, and the fist caught fast, biting into the timbers. The men freed the battering ram by turning it, then pulling it out. With a grinding and creaking noise, it brought great chunks of the gate with it. The hole was now wide enough for the Anatolians, some of whom were stationed at the rear of the formation, to pepper it with arrows, hoping to find victims behind it.

Three more times the ram was hauled back and swung forwards, striking the middle of the gates, which shook and cracked and groaned. Wood fractured and shards flew as hole after hole was punched. Finally the fist went all the way through, breaking the horizontal timber that barred the gates on the inside. Drunkenly the gates swung backwards, helped on their way by the legionaries of the arrowhead pushing against them. The bridge across the gap trembled, then loudly cracked at the centre, throwing men from the step into the path of the legionaries. These men did not long survive.

The movement also dislodged the remnants of Titus Flavius. The corpse fell, tumbling to the ground with a sickening thud.

'Back!' Quintus shouted the order, and the narrow column retreated, its job done. It took the battering ram with it, out of the way. 'Crassus!' he shouted and pointed. The optio immediately understood and, crouching low, dragged the prefect's body from where it had come to rest.

More commands were shouted. There were blasts on the cornua and a few curses, and the men moved from the ladders, from the field and from the testudo, instead forming up ready to march into the oppidum. Crassus quickly placed his gruesome charge, as reverently as he could, in the trench nearest to him, covering it with reeds.

Through the gates the cohort advanced. Galba, crested helm on his head, rode in the centre. The aquilifer, in his wolfskin cloak, rode to his right. He held the eagle high, where it shone brightly, catching the light. To his left was the imago of Augustus. Immediately behind flew the bull standard of the cohort. One column, eight men wide, eight shields held edge to edge, formed up behind these three. At intervals a gap marked the end of one century and the start of another. In each gap rode a centurion, waiting for the order to march.

'Centurion!' Galba called to Quintus, who stood at the front of Century One. 'Be ready to take the men in. They are defeated. I must ask for their surrender. There are women and children here.'

'Of course there are,' said Quintus, impatient with his commander. 'The Germani wives and daughters fight alongside their brothers and sons.'

Galba had been like this in Hispania, ready to extend mercy where Quintus thought none should be offered. He shrugged. His decisions were seldom foolish and in time had earned him the respect of the men.

'This is their home. This is where they live. I know it comes as a surprise,' said Galba amiably, and with a rare touch of humour, 'but not every nation spends its entire life in armour marching from one battle to the next. Some nations, some tribes, settle down and raise families.'

'They are not Romans,' Quintus retorted. 'Romans, even those gifted land and slaves, return to the colours. They would rather fight than farm. Witness our evocati!'

'Our task is to bring civilisation, centurion, to shine light in dark places. I will offer them freedom.'

'Sir,' Quintus responded without enthusiasm. He knew that this was the noble thing to do, but he was still angry at the way the enemy had treated the body of his commander. 'Not alone, sir,' he added, waving forward half of the first century and its officers, including himself, Rufus and Crassus.

Galba dipped his head in acknowledgement. He did not object. A flourish from the trumpets, a signal from the standard, and the march began, the rhythmic sound of the legionaries' caligae shaking the ground. They passed through the wreck of the gate under the bridge, now empty of defenders.

'Hold,' Quintus ordered as the last of the men entered the oppidum. 'Hold, but be ready.'

The men heard and stopped, but remained poised. What Quintus noticed was the tribesmen stepping backwards, lowering their blades, as if ready to give in. But they were looking towards the longhouse behind them.

From that direction a tall man walked. He wore trews held to his legs with criss-crossed leather, a tunic and jerkin and a cloak — a red cloak. At first Quintus thought it was the sagum he had traded in place of the eagle, then realised that this was fuller, richer, better quality. It was the paludamentum of the commander, the property of Titus Flavius Pusio.

The man had plaited moustaches tied with bright braid and a beard combed and styled like the tail of a horse. It too was decorated with braid and metal, possibly silver, glinting temptingly. He was bare-headed and wore no armour. His hair was tied in a knot on his head, not unlike those favoured by the Suebi, but there was enough of it left to almost reach his waist. He was heavily armed, carrying spear and axe, one in each hand. A sword and a dagger were sheathed at his side. The spear carried a long black and red pennant.

'He is either a chieftain of these people, or a shaman or magician of some kind,' Quintus said to Crassus. 'Keep the men alert. There may be a trick here.'

There was silence from the Germani as the man approached. They backed away, leaving him the space. As he came closer, into the killing ground before the gates, he theatrically raised the axe and spear in the air, then reversed them, so that the spear pointed to the ground, its pennant dragging in the earth, and the axe was held downwards, gripped by its shaft, as if he might offer it to the Romans.

'I am still not sure if it is a negotiation, or a surrender,' Crassus said quietly.

'Treat it as neither,' Quintus replied.

Galba was less cautious. It seemed that he had decided to treat it as a friendly gesture. Aquila was still to his right, the eagle held aloft. The cohort signifer sat to the other side, the bull of the Ninth tattered but recognisable. Galba reached behind and took hold of the standard's shaft, gently prising it from the fingers of the signifer, who was reluctant to let it go. Aquila made a point of moving the eagle to his other hand, so that it could not be easily reached.

'We bring you peace,' Galba said, raising the standard as his horse stepped carefully over a dead tribesman. 'Peace and freedom, liberty and the chance to serve.'

Quintus wondered if the man even understood. The chieftain looked down at the ground as if he was ashamed or shy, and took a half step forwards, bending the knee of his leading leg. Galba saw this as an act of submission and moved the horse a step closer, opening his arms wide in welcome, the standard in one hand, the other showing an open palm. Unconsciously, the legionaries lowered their swords further in anticipation of a truce, an end to the fighting. It seemed as if they, and the Germani defenders, held their breath.

Suddenly the chieftain raised his head and yelled a single word: 'Týr!' Then he lifted his spear and threw it, full tilt, into the man who sat, arms open in friendship and welcome, less than three paces away. The metal point of the weapon, from this range, had no trouble penetrating Galba's chest armour. The force of the blow lifted him from his horse. He toppled backwards, landing heavily. He tried to rise but subsided to his knees, losing his grip on the standard and letting it fall. The chieftain took two steps forward and put his foot on the black and red image of the bull. He swung the axe. His intention was to remove the Roman's head, but in this he failed as Galba fell further, already dead. Instead of biting into his neck, the axe blade struck the side of Galba's head, carving a deep gash, from which dark blood spread.

There was an audible intake of breath from the watchers, then Aquila reacted first, riding forward and plunging the shaft of the eagle into the chieftain.

A silence filled the space where chieftain and centurion had fallen. Quintus was stunned at the betrayal. 'Pick up that standard, signifer,' he ordered. 'Quickly.'

The standard bearer began to dismount to retrieve the sacred image, but already spears flew towards him and his hand never grasped the shaft as the life fled from him. Aquila managed to reach down and grab it before turning towards the gate. The defenders advanced and at once the fighting began. Quintus, incensed, drew his blade and raised his arm high.

'Cornicen!' he shouted to the nearest signaller, ready with his curved trumpet over his shoulder. 'Sound *lugubri sono* — the mournful note.'

The cornicen sounded a long note that rose and fell three times.

'They say that no enemy ever hears the mournful note twice,' Quintus said to his amicus.

'Why would they?' Crassus was grim.

Although the men heard the cornu, some still looked to Quintus for confirmation. He was their officer now. 'As commanded,' he said bitterly. 'This place is yours, everything in it. When you have ransacked it, burn it.'

The men, screaming their anger, needed no further reinforcement. The rest of the cohort, responding to the trumpet, marched unstoppably up the hill and into the settlement.

Anything they could gain would be theirs, everything except people. There would be no slaves. There would be no captives. There would be no survivors. This was what the mournful note meant. At once they renewed their assault on the enemy, with ferocious determination.

LIII: CARTHAGO DELENDA EST

'Crassus!' Quintus shouted across as they were overtaken by the other centuries marching into the oppidum. 'The Flavian's body, Galba's too — put them in the chieftain's house. Then burn it.'

Crassus saluted and grabbed help from other legionaries. He pointed out where he had hidden the body of the commander, then they picked up the corpse and ran to the longhouse. Other men lifted the fallen centurion, pulling the spear from him. He ordered men to also bring fascines from the side of the track as kindling.

The legionaries fanned out, but on a command from the optio, they parted for the strange cortege. Finding a table within the building, the men laid the prefect on it, arranging his body as best they could. Galba was placed alongside. They surrounded the table with bundles of reeds, which they set alight. The two commanders would share passage across the Styx.

As soon as they were out, it was the first house to catch fully on fire. Its roof collapsed inwards in a shower of sparks, forcing a torrent of flame to shoot briefly out of the doorway. The Lady Antonia would never see the body of her husband again.

The other huts were set alight in turn. Even the palisade itself was knocked down and burned.

There were animals in the oppidum — far too many to take back to camp. The birds — ducks and geese and chickens — were released. Some would find their way to the river and freedom, some back to the camp, where legionaries would be grateful for the meat. Most would fall prey to foxes and wolves.

In one stall, Sextus found a bull and, after seeking permission from the nearest centurion, led it away by the nose. He wanted to pull it away from the flames and sacrifice it to great Jove — Jupiter Optimus Maximus — a fitting offering for the king of the gods who had granted them this victory. He managed to drag it out through the remains of the gate before it tossed and jerked its head, escaped his grasp and gained its freedom. Maddened, it fled down the hill, bellowing. Sextus let it run, reasoning that it would not go far.

The butchery continued well into the night. The buildings burned brightly, the light of the deadly flames bouncing off the tall shields and bright helmets of the Romans. There was no joy to this killing, no exhilaration. There were no war cries, no invoking of the gods. This was slaughter — methodical, emotionless slaughter. All were despatched with heartless efficiency under the order of the mournful note.

Both men and women fought fiercely, but once the legionaries were inside the oppidum, the outcome was never in doubt. Some legionaries fell, but not many.

A few of the occupants tried to flee down the hill to the river, but the bridge was burned and the far bank patrolled by even more Romans. They threw spears at the Germani as they tried to cross the water, and cut them down if they gained the far bank.

Quintus was a part of it. He had legionaries marching to either side of him, as the four centuries fanned out to face the semi-circle of natives. A volley of spears was thrown first. Then the deadly work began in earnest.

Quintus closed his eyes briefly but tightly. When he opened them, he had pulled a thick curtain across, so that what he saw was separated from what he knew. He and his century marched forward, cutting and stabbing, making the enemy fall back before them. In his mind he was scything wheat in a sun-filled field, in a line with his father and brother and their slaves. The sky was blue. The birds were singing.

In the end, nothing was left alive.

As the fires began to die down, and the last moans of the injured were extinguished, the mournful note was sounded again — a long tone that rose and fell once. This was the other half of the order, this time meaning *stand down; the destruction is finished*.

The legionaries, sweating, blood-splattered and soot-stained, formed up in front of the remains of the gate and marched away from the charred and smoking oppidum. Although they were entitled to anything they found, they came away mostly empty-handed. This was a poor settlement. There were no fine swords or spears, the jewels the women wore were polished river pebbles, and the torcs and hair ornaments of the men were bronze or iron, not silver or gold.

Some legionaries talked in subdued tones; many were silent. There was no triumph here, no pleasure taken in the death and devastation.

Galba, dead by duplicity, had become another commander felled by an enemy that had refused to acknowledge it was beaten, an enemy that had kept resisting. Quintus did not understand how Rome's civilising influence and powerful gods could be rejected.

Lugubri sono, the command he had given, was the right one, Quintus told himself. Galba would have given the same order had he lived. He would not have needed the added incentive of seeing his current commander murdered. Titus Flavius himself would have given that order with no qualms. It was meant to strike terror into an enemy. It was a lesson from which the next enemy should learn — surrender or suffer the same fate. The smouldering oppidum would also serve as a memorial to the commander and to Galba.

Neither the auxiliary horsemen nor the Anatolian archers were part of the sack. Nor were the few cavalry that remained, or their horses. All the legionaries were on foot, including the centurions, the signiferi and the aquilifer, who had fought using the standard as a weapon in one hand, his gladius in the other.

They all returned to the camp, some dragging the catapults, which Quintus ordered to be taken back to the castra. They could not be left behind. The battering ram was pulled away by horsemen, to be taken down to the riverbank. The fascines had been used to stoke the fires, so could not be retrieved. The auxiliaries were set the task of deliberately scattering the piles of stones.

The battering ram was used as the base for a pyre near the ford. The remains of huts and hovels and animal pens were added as fuel, along with the fence itself. The ram was cut into eight pieces by sweating legionaries wielding axes, then the logs were arranged to form a square. Inside the square, flammable material was packed, then a platform constructed on top. Legionaries found their comrades and took them there, laying them out side by side. They found coins for Charon if they could; otherwise, they relied on the Vestals to pay the fare. Most had never seen the round temple of the Virgins tucked away by the Regia in the Forum, but they knew the guardians of the flame had promised to pay the soldiers' way.

Quintus stayed away. He would find out who had died when the morning assembly was called. Cornus would have the roll.

Once back in camp and dismissed, some legionaries went straight to their tents and slept, others down to the river to bathe. Some, Tullius amongst them, made sure their weapons and armour were in good order — no chips or nicks or weaknesses. Crassus took himself off to the forge, where Rufus volunteered to work the bellows. The work was something that would help them to forget. It was close to the pyre and, on seeing the forge lit, men came with swords and daggers and armour, needing the blacksmith's attention.

Some returned to camp and sat with companions attempting to lift the grim mood with the help of posca and sour wine. There was no moon, and the stars wheeled overhead. At least the morning's daylight would bring better humour, and they could march away from this place. It would be a memory, and would quickly fade once it was no longer in sight or sound or smell.

Briefly, Quintus managed to put the events of the day out of his head. He felt almost good, squatting with his comrades. Marcus said little, his amicus Tullius even less. The solid figure of Piso, Marcus' wrestling opponent, tried his best to break through the mournful atmosphere, telling stories of his long past in the service of the legions.

But the wine was too strong for Quintus; it was not sufficiently watered, and now his head throbbed gently but persistently, and the cloak of depression was spread heavily across his shoulders. He had taken off his helmet, for it seemed to make his headache worse.

'Galba never liked wearing his helmet,' he said listlessly, brushing the crest on the helm that was set on the ground next to him. He longed for morning as he chewed on a tasteless strip of boiled something prepared by Maxim.

'I will do my rounds,' Marcus stated, and rose to his feet. Tullius also stood. Piso made to stand, but Marcus waved him down. 'We two are enough,' he said, then indicated Quintus and Sextus. 'Keep these two company.'

Marcus and Tullius left the comrades to talk and drink by their fire.

'Marcus takes his duties as an optio seriously. After all, was he not once a centurion?' Piso said, as they left. 'He could be a centurion again.'

'They will not converse,' Sextus replied, with a wry smile. 'Although they are inseparable, they barely speak to each other. Tullius is naturally taciturn. Marcus is never keen to break the silence.'

Quintus nodded, although he was hardly listening. He turned to Sextus. 'Did you catch the bull?'

'Not yet. But I will,' Sextus replied. 'Piso will help.'

Piso nodded. 'A sacrifice to Jupiter will raise the men's spirits.'

They were sitting outside the tent, the embers of their fire glowing. Quintus pulled his cloak around his shoulders; it was nearly morning and the air had the first tang of autumn about it. There would be a mist on the river. Quintus sat with his knees to his chin. He looked at his feet and spoke softly to no-one in particular.

'I do not feel bad about it. In truth, I do not feel anything at all.'

'That is how it should be,' said Piso, putting a hand on his shoulder. 'Sometimes things are just … necessary. Rome has done a lot worse.'

'*Carthago delenda est*,' said Sextus, quoting Cato the Elder as he poked the fire with a stick. *Carthage must be destroyed*. There was not a legionary who did not know the phrase; there was not a

Roman boy who had not shouted it at his playmates as a threat when they were play-fighting with wooden swords. 'And it was,' continued Sextus. 'Destroyed totally, with thousands of its people killed, and thousands more sold into slavery.' He looked up and at the other two, both of whom had their heads down. 'But it did not raise its head again. It had to be so.'

They were all aware of the litany of sieges, annihilations and mass executions, from Africa to Asia, from Gaul to Macedonia, from battlefield to battlefield, besieged city to besieged city. Carthage, Syracuse, slave rebellions. Uxellodonum and the cutting off of survivor's hands; Munda and its rampart of human heads. There were many others. Piso had seen examples himself, taken part in them.

'I know,' said Quintus sadly. 'It is merely policy — and a just policy, for they would do the same to us. Look at what Maelo did to the officers. Look at what Dagaz did to the pioneers.'

'It was not your fault,' Piso said kindly. 'It could just as easily have been anyone wearing this.' He picked up Quintus' helm and turned it over in his hands, then placed it on his head. 'Look,' he said, 'it could just as easily have been me.'

'But it wasn't. It was my decision,' said Quintus, smiling weakly at his comrade's foolishness.

A noise to one side made them all lift their heads and half rise.

'A fox,' suggested Sextus, settling down again.

'Or Jovan coming to tend the fire,' said Quintus, throwing the remnant of what he was chewing into the embers.

'I will go and see,' said Piso, pulling himself to his feet.

Quintus and Sextus could hear an exchange of words, Roman to Roman, but not friendly — challenges and counter-challenges. Suddenly, Piso staggered, a strangled noise in his throat.

The tip of a long crescent-shaped blade protruded from his chest, and a knife glinted as it caught the firelight, appearing from behind his head, slashing above his focale and across his throat. The surge of blood from his neck met the bloom from his chest as the deadly weapon was withdrawn from his body. He fell face down, his arm scattering the ashes as it hit the remnants of the fire.

The untied helmet slipped from his head and bounced uselessly on the ground.

LIV: ACUS REDIT

Before his death, Piso had loosened his lorica laminata for comfort. The enemy had clearly marked him out, drawn by the senior centurion's helmet that he had been wearing on his head.

The long blade had entered beneath Piso's armour at the back, and curved its way up through his belly. It would have killed him without the knife to his throat. Quintus could see the sword, blood-stained, in the hands of a tribesman, bearded and moustached. He held a round shield marked with a rune in his hand and wore a round helmet on his head, fair hair escaping from it. Quintus and Sextus drew their swords at once and leapt up, ready to fight. Quintus lunged for the enemy with the point of his gladius, but the man sidestepped and then vanished into the camp, from where the clash of weapons could be heard.

The enemy clearly now saw no need for stealth. Out of the forest came a series of yells and ululations, war cries and challenges, the name of Týr foremost amongst those called out. Quintus reached down and scooped up his fallen helmet.

Together he and Sextus ran towards the place where the sound of battle was loudest. Many other legionaries were rolling out of tents as the noise from the forest grew. First light had turned the sky pale, but the sun had not yet risen. In places torches were lit and could be seen moving.

'Follow!' Quintus shouted as he ran towards the river, towards the racket. 'Arm!'

Within moments there were ten or twelve legionaries with him, more arriving all the time. The other centurions came running with their own men. They found the enemy by following both the noise of battle and the fallen bodies of their own men. Around the castra it looked as if many had been taken by surprise, sitting around fires, even sleeping.

Soon there were more than a hundred men fighting. The legionaries could not manoeuvre as a unit but had to fight one-to-one with the enemy. At close quarters the short, solid gladius was more effective than the long swords that opposed them. The auxiliaries, alerted by the noise, also arrived, and many enemy fell to the deadly blades of the mákhaira, the single-edged weapon of the Cantabrians, and to the long knives of the Anatolians. Quintus could not work out how the camp had been infiltrated. There should have been guards.

A lull in the fighting allowed him and Sextus to catch their breath. They stood back to back, panting. 'Where are the guards?' Quintus demanded.

Sextus was about to reply but a realisation hit him. 'The women!' he yelled. 'They will target the women.'

Quintus agreed: the noble ladies would be the choicest target for the enemy. They turned towards where the commander's tent was pitched.

There was fierce fighting in front of the entrance to the pavilion. The two legionary guards seemed to be in combat with at least two tribesmen each. Quintus and Sextus waded in to help, pushing back the enemy, making thrust after deadly thrust. The guards were injured, but not dead. They had done their job. No enemy had passed them.

The dawn light had grown in the few moments since the first alarm. Now Quintus and Sextus could see that many individual fights were already over, with men lying injured and dead. Hoping to find the ladies, they stepped through the flap of the commander's tent.

A torch smouldered on the floor, about to set light to material near it. Sextus kicked it away, then stamped on it quickly, sparks flying. Another torch sputtered to their left. Quintus picked this up and blew on it, illuminating a scene of carnage.

The far side of the canvas was open to the elements, a great slash indicating where it had been cut. Stools and the commander's desk had been overturned, and curtains had been ripped down. The rushes on the beaten earth floor were trampled and wet with blood. The open tripod braziers were toppled and would have set fire to the tent had not the combatants rolled on them. Glowing coals threatened to set light to the rushes and the bodies until the legionaries smothered them.

There were at least five bodies here, and no movement.

The soft glow of true dawn fell through the tear onto the wan face of the Lady Antonia Flavia, which stared at Quintus with sightless eyes. Little more could be seen of her. Lying across her body was a Germani warrior, his face hidden, the bearskin on his back dark, his legs, in cross-gartered yellow trews, splayed out behind him. His sword, a long cavalry blade, lay near his outstretched hand. His fallen shield bore the rune of Dagaz.

Next to these two lay the Lady Aurelia, face down and still, recognisable by her tumbled hair and blue dress. Beneath her lay a dead Germani. A long, thin knife plunged deep into his neck had killed him. It was still there. His shield bore the rune of Týr.

'They did not pass the guards,' said Sextus, holding the torn canvas aloft. 'Those others attacked them as a distraction whilst these men sought out their prey.'

A dead legionary lay face down. He was helmetless and dressed in a native tunic, but his gladius and caligae gave him away. Quintus turned him over with his foot.

'A deserter,' he spat. 'A Roman. One of those who ran from us. He was working with the Germani.'

Other faces appeared at both the doorway and in the gap held open by Sextus. Felix was one, Alba another.

'Felix, bring men and move this out. Throw it to the dogs.' Quintus kicked the body of the deserter in disgust. 'Shift these two outside also.' He indicated the Germani. 'Alba, see if there is any life in the women.'

Alba and others turned the Germani in the bearskin cloak over. He was clearly dead. Blood ran down his face and stained the complex knots of his beard. Protruding from his eye was the acus of Antonia Flavia. Quintus recognised the decorated end of the long hairpin, its shaft buried deep into the Germani's brain.

They dragged him outside and laid him face up on the earth. In the meantime, the capsarius bent over Antonia and examined her. Her dress was ripped from throat to waist, and purple marks from gripping fingers stood out on her neck. Alba was certain she was dead, but went through the motions. He peered closely into her eyes and listened for a heartbeat.

'She is dead, sir,' he reported, then looked her up and down. 'She did not die from any blow of sword or spear, nor from strangulation.' He saw the quizzical look on Quintus' face and explained, 'Her eyes, sir. Her eyes would start from her head if she was strangled. She was choked, yes, but not killed that way.' He bent down and lifted her head, then took his hand away from her hair and showed it to Quintus. It was covered in blood. 'This is what killed her. Her head was smashed on the earth, or something firmer — perhaps the desk or a brazier. Him landing on top of her will have forced her to the ground.'

Quintus was unemotional. Antonia Flavia had defended herself and paid with her life. The acus had been the two ladies' salvation before. At least she had kept her honour.

Aurelia had also fought her assailant. Her clothes were ripped and her shoulder bare. Clearly she had made the tribesman who attacked her angry, and he had stabbed her to death. There were many wounds.

'He stabbed her a lot of times, sir,' Alba said softly, 'in a sort of frenzy. I could not say which wound killed her.'

'You do not need to,' Quintus said. 'That she is dead is enough.' He added in a whisper, 'Once we were friends, if a noble-born lady can ever be said to be friends with a mere soldier.' He raised his voice. 'Take them out and lay them somewhere safe. Handle them with dignity.'

Soldiers carried the bodies out. The women were picked up with care, whereas the tribesmen and the deserter were dragged by their heels. Quintus looked around at the devastation with sadness, then realised with a start that the tent was not quite empty. Another body was revealed by the growing light. Cornus, the secretary, lay face up towards the back of the pavilion.

'He must have tried to save them,' said Sextus, going over to the freedman.

'He was no fighter. He never has been,' Quintus said. 'Our Macedonians would have put up a better fight. At least they were once warriors. Move him out, too.'

Sextus signalled to another legionary and together they began to lift Cornus. To their surprise, a sound escaped him, a long exhalation.

'He lives,' said Sextus excitedly, calling to the capsarius. 'Alba, see what you can do.'

'Bring him into the light.' Alba examined the scribe but could find no wounds, no blood. He felt along his arms and legs. 'There are no breaks, no cuts. There was a blow, here.' He pointed at an angry purple and black bruise on the freedman's temple. 'I have seen this before. It is like death but not death.'

'I have seen it also,' Quintus said. 'More than once. He may recover. Rufus was like this once. Lay him somewhere safe, and cover him to keep him warm.'

Alba called over another legionary and together they took the insensible scribe out.

Only Sextus and Quintus were left in the tent, the door flap open, the tear in the other side looking like a knife wound. The canvas fluttered in the morning breeze.

'How could I let this happen?' Quintus asked. 'I should have protected them better.'

'Deserters,' said Sextus. 'They must have fooled some of the guards — or at least fooled them long enough to kill them.'

'What could they want? The tribesmen could not hope to defeat us; there are not enough of them — even with the deserters.'

'The women — as captives or hostages.'

'Or just revenge,' Quintus said flatly.

They went out of the pavilion into the castra, astonished to find that the blue sky was clear and unaffected by the deaths. The sound of fighting had not ended, but it had moved further away, down towards the riverbank. A legionary, a shoulder and one leg covered in blood, ran towards them. Two others were immediately behind him.

'Agnus!' exclaimed Quintus. 'You are injured.'

'Not my blood.' He indicated his shoulder, then grinned, pointing to his leg. 'This is, but it has been seen to.' His leg binding was already bloody. 'These men want to carry me,' he went on, indicating the two that were behind him. The men were of his contubernium. Agnus was popular, especially with his close comrades; he made them laugh.

'Take him,' commanded Quintus.

'I have something to show you first,' Agnus insisted. 'Come with me.'

He hobbled around to the other side of the commander's tent and hovered over the dead Germani, the one in the bearskin. 'This is Dagaz, sir. No doubt about it. This is the son of Maelo that I saw with the pioneers.'

'You are sure?'

'Certain,' Agnus insisted, as he lost his balance. The men were waiting and caught him.

'Take him,' said Quintus again. 'Find the capsarius. Make sure he survives.'

This time Agnus did not resist and was carried away, one man supporting each arm.

Quintus looked at the man on the ground with wonder. 'So this is the man who wants to free all the tribes. This is the idea of liberty,' he said to Sextus. He spat on the ground in contempt. 'Nothing more than a raider and a rapist.'

LV: SEMPER HONORATUM HABEBO

'Come on.' Sextus encouraged Quintus away. 'There is more fighting yet to be done.'

They ran down the hill to the riverbank, only to find that the fighting was all but over. The men tending the pyre, along with those working the forge, had proved an unexpected foe for an enemy who had believed all of the Romans would be in the camp.

The attackers had crossed the river in simple boats. Now they fled the same way. Crassus and Rufus led the charge and threw burning brands into the craft, setting light to some of them. They could see more boats on the eastern shore, but the tribesmen were already abandoning them and fleeing into the forest.

Although some boats were still intact, pulled up on the bank, Crassus decided not to risk a pursuit. Quintus agreed with his decision. 'We could be trapped over there,' he said. 'They may have reinforcements. We would certainly not have any. Anyway, their leader is dead. I think they will scatter.'

A few tribesmen were captured, disarmed and corralled by legionaries with drawn swords.

'Find out what they know,' Quintus instructed Caius, who had fought by the bank. He turned to Crassus. 'Is the forge still working?'

'It is,' said Crassus.

'Then make nails. Find out what they know, then crucify them. Let them face the river as they die.'

Crassus nodded and saluted, fist to heart. 'Sir,' he said. 'It will be done.'

Quintus and Sextus returned up the hill to the camp. It was quiet now, with a few men detailed to collect the bodies of the dead for burning. Though he was not sure it was necessary, Quintus, out of habit, posted guards. Marcus and Tullius were not at the river. He would have seen them. Nor were they amongst the dead. They were missing. He and Sextus began to look for either of their comrades.

In time, at the far north west corner of the camp, they found them, partially concealed by cut brushwood. They moved the timber gently. Tullius lay face up with his throat cut clean across. His baldric was still over his shoulder, his gladius still sheathed. His pugio was still in its scabbard in his belt. He had been surprised, killed from the rear. Marcus lay next to him. He had at least bloodied his sword on the enemy. He lay in a red puddle.

A closer examination revealed that Marcus lived still and the blood belonged to another, a gory trail leading to a legionary who had crawled away to die.

'Another deserter,' spat Sextus in disgust, seeing the dead man's caligae and baltea, his military issue sandals and belt betraying him.

Marcus breathed shallowly, the pulse in his neck weak.

'Find Alba,' Quintus ordered. 'Tell him that this man is his priority.'

The capsarius came running, along with legionaries keen to help. Marcus groaned as they began to lift him.

'No,' said Alba, sharply. 'Do not move him yet. I need to examine him.'

There was a wound to Marcus' ear that had bled copiously. His sword was still gripped tight in his right hand, whilst his left arm lay at a strange angle.

'The joint at the elbow is twisted or broken,' Alba said. 'But nothing has pierced the skin. I must put it back where it should be. Best that Marcus is not awake when I do so, for it will be painful.'

He had the legionaries stretch Marcus out on his back, then knelt on his upper arm, whilst twisting the lower arm back into place. Marcus, even in sleep, groaned loudly. The capsarius bound the injury with strips of cloth, keeping the elbow straight with a short plank of wood. 'He will need prayers, Sextus. A sacrifice to Apollo will help. A raven, perhaps, though a wolf would be better.'

'A raven,' said Sextus, 'I think the archers could manage a raven.' A thought came to him. 'You,' he ordered one of the legionaries, 'go and find either the signifer or the aquilifer and borrow their cloak. Tell them it is to help save their brother.' He turned to Alba and Quintus. 'If we wrap him in wolfskin, that could be almost as good as sacrificing a wolf.'

Alba did not disagree, and Quintus nodded assent. Quintus looked all around where the two had fallen, but could not at first find Marcus' helmet with its optio's feathers. He found it at last with the deserter, no doubt hoping for a trophy.

'They saw his crest,' he said to Sextus. 'They targeted him because he was an officer.'

'Just like Piso. He was wearing your helmet,' Sextus said, without thinking. 'The blade that killed Piso was meant for you.'

Once more, a wave of guilt washed over Quintus. 'I know, Sextus. It brings me no comfort.' He turned his face to the sky in despair. 'Great Jove, what have I done for you to make this so difficult? Why can I not keep them safe?'

In Hispania, Marcus had accepted Tullius as his amicus when the cohort faced disgrace. Marcus had lost his own partner,

Ursus, to a brutal and unwarranted execution. Quintus carried the man's will. Tullius had lost his amicus at the same time. His had been scourged and crucified, though he was innocent of the charges laid against him.

'So much injustice.' Quintus shook his head.

Sextus tried to comfort his friend. 'I know of your vow, Quintus. You have done all you can. If Jove wills it, you cannot save them. I know of Ursus, and his wife and child.'

'Hardly a child anymore. He — or she — will be ordering the slaves around by now,' said Quintus. 'The boy will be wearing his manly gown before I can deliver his legacy. What about Tullius? You seemed to know of his burden.'

Tullius hadn't smiled since the skirmish in the mountains of Cantabria.

'He had demons following him,' Sextus said. 'In that action he took the chance to kill the centurion who ordered his friend executed. None knew but he and the gods to begin with. He told me later, a burden shared. Had he been found out, he would have been crucified himself.'

'Make sure he has a coin,' Quintus said sadly. 'More than an obol, a silver denarius if possible. Speak to Cornus when he wakes. I am sure he can manage it.'

Sextus nodded agreement. 'At least a silver denarius will go some way to ensuring he can step on to Charon's boat — if the Furies, especially Tisiphone, will let him go.'

They moved Marcus and laid him carefully on a board across two trestles. He rested on the wolfskin cloak that Rufus had given up in hopes that this would hurry his recovery. His moans at least proved that he lived. Only time would show whether or not he healed.

To Quintus, the rest of that morning seemed never-ending. He thought that it should be raining, or misty, or at least dark and bleak, but instead the sky remained bright blue and the sun shone down innocently, though with little warmth.

He did not want to rush the funerals, nor prevent those who wished to do so from giving eulogies. He wanted to look his best, so enlisted Jovan's services to shave him. The slave usually borrowed Tullius' blade for this, as his pugio was always the sharpest. This would be the last time he could. Quintus had to say the words himself over his comrades. He would also try to say something appropriate for the ladies.

On the other hand, he made a promise to himself that they would be away from this place as soon as possible, preferably not too long after noon. He did not wish to spend another night here, with the ghosts of both the Germani and the Romans wandering unchained in the dark, along with, possibly, the Furies seeking a victim.

At once, anyone who was not directly involved in mourning a comrade was set to work pulling the camp apart. The extra deaths meant that they were even more short of manpower, so this order included both the auxiliaries and the slaves. Each time they camped, there seemed to be less and less to load, fewer and fewer pack animals and carts. Some of the tents had been destroyed in the action, including the prefect's pavilion. Legionaries tried to take it down, with a view to mending it, but the wind caught an exposed edge and tore it beyond repair. Its canvas was used as a cover for one of the carts rigged up to carry the injured. It was into one of these carts that Marcus was placed.

The dead deserters could be punished no further. They would definitely not be honoured with a pyre or a eulogy. He would not allow it, and nor would their betrayed comrades. He consigned them to the swirling waters of the Rhenus. He did give permission for their comrades to take from them anything they wished, by any means that they wished. He did not watch what happened with them, but later heard their remains being tipped into the river.

The pyre for the noble ladies was tall but nowhere near as magnificent as it would have been in Rome. Alba found some of their clean clothes in the pavilion and covered them over, so that their wounds could not be seen. He did not dress them, as he could not bring himself to undress them, but arranged the garments so that they looked clothed. Jovan and Maxim, acting as their body slaves, offered to complete the task, but Quintus demurred, preferring to leave the handling of such noble bodies to the capsarius. Alba had to work quickly as the bodies were no longer warm, nor soft, but beginning to stiffen.

Cornus, awake again with no more than a bad headache, helped to dress their hair and clean their faces. He had little memory of what had happened, apart from a vague picture of noise and violence and the shock of a blow that had sent him reeling into darkness.

Sextus, of course, looked spotless, even down to his fingernails, making Quintus shake his head in wonder. He acted as the priest, making a sacrifice and saying a prayer to Father Dis, asking him to accept the two women and let them join the Flavian in Elysium. The sacrifice was a wood pigeon. The bull, intended for Jupiter Optimus Maximus, had not been found.

'Perhaps it swam the river, like Io swam the Bosphorus,' suggested Sextus.

'It will be in the forest,' said Crassus dourly. 'Free.'

'Can you find some of that poetry for me to speak? Some of what you quoted?' Quintus asked Sextus softly. 'I have little to say, but would not shame either of the noble ladies.'

'Publius Vergilius?' Sextus knew that Quintus had, at one time, been deep in the affections of Aurelia, that she had even been amorous towards him, but he did not think an expression of love would be appropriate. He thought for a while, then said, 'There is a verse, from the same poem — "*Quem semper acerbum, semper honoratum habebo.*" I think it refers to the death of Queen Dido. It seems right for a noble funeral.'

Quintus was joined by Felix, Marius and Furius Lentulus. The other centurions all had a part to play representing their own centuries. As the pyre was lit, Quintus spoke the names of the ladies and their noble lineage as far as he knew it, remembering that Antonia was of the Menenii. He described their Roman virtues of bravery and ferocity in the face of the enemy. Of *dignitas*, *pietas* and *virtus* — dignity, duty and honour.

He ended with the line of poetry Sextus had quoted: 'This will always be a bitter day, a grief that I will forever honour.'

LVI: DOMUM SERVAVIT. LANAM FECIT

The pyre for Piso and Tullius, the veterans, was no less tall than that of the noble ladies. The two comrades were burned together. Sextus, in spite of his insistence that the Vestals would pay, wanted to be certain that Charon would take them, especially Tullius. He found a silver denarius for each.

There were many coins in the commander's tent. Cornus knew where they were — in two leather pouches, concealed. The stash was not the pay for the troops — even though they were owed much. Cornus said it was to bribe local officials and informers. Quintus entrusted it now to Aquila, probably the most respected of the men.

The smoke from the pyre of the two evocati joined that of many other pyres, where legionaries burned their fallen comrades with less ceremony. Quintus said the eulogy for Tullius and included Piso in it, although he had not been of his contubernium. For Tullius, he remembered his name and lineage — Proculus Tullius Surus of the tribe of the Suburrana. He spoke of his service of over twenty years, starting as a probationer in the Sicilian Wars. He recalled also the stern but loyal nature of the man. It was customary to make a joke about a departing comrade, but Quintus found this impossible. Instead he spoke of what he knew.

'Proculus Tullius was a natural soldier,' he said. 'He did not really pay attention on the parade ground, or on the march, but could perform manoeuvres as ordered perfectly. He could do all that was ever asked of him. Though it often looked like he was in a world of his own, he was ready to snap into action on an order or a signal, to respond to command, instantly vigilant.' Quintus thought of the many times that he had seen Tullius, quietly humming to himself as he honed his blade or scoured his armour. Then he remembered the Furies, and the demons that must have populated his dreams, and wondered why he had not bothered to befriend him more. Marcus had, but was not here to speak. Sextus had, too. It was he who had asked the Anatolians to shoot down a raven, so that a sacrifice could be made to help Marcus heal. It was he who had pleaded with Mercury to share the offering and take Tullius' hand.

'He called himself Mal Fortuna,' said Quintus.

'I know,' Sextus replied. 'Perhaps he was unlucky. But he saved Marcus more than once. At least his scars will now no longer trouble him.'

'Nor the itch of his wolf-bitten ear,' said Quintus. 'I sent the earring on with him. Sadly for Jovan and my chin, I send on his pugio too.'

They stood side by side. Quintus paused and put his hand on Sextus' shoulder. As the priest, he was cowled. Quintus wanted to see the truth in his dark eyes, so gently moved his head around.

'Will he be allowed across, Sextus?' he asked.

'I have done all I can,' Sextus replied, lifting his eyes to look into those of his centurion and friend.

'Have I done enough for Piso?'

'You have done all you can.'

High in the heavens the smoke from the pyre mingled with the grey smudges that still rose from the destroyed oppidum, its remains like jagged black teeth on the nearby hillside. They had been thorough. The ground trembled with a hundred pairs of beating black wings as crows and magpies took their fill. Above was nothing but smoke and cinders.

Quintus gave an involuntary shiver. He would be glad to be away from this place, with what was left of his men. There was not even two thirds of a cohort, no noble member of the equités, only a few cavalry, some auxiliaries and some slaves.

There was no commander except him, this by the unanimous agreement of the other centurions. He smiled bitterly; they almost had more vexilla than men to carry them — the eagle, the imago, the cohort image of the bull, the standards of the centuries, the long banners of the cavalry, the pennants of the auxiliaries.

He called for Agnus. The man limped on his bound leg, but the binding was no longer bloodied. 'Can you ride?' Quintus asked him.

Agnus nodded. 'The colt is gentle with me.'

'Then scout ahead. Take Vetruvius and four of the auxiliaries with you for protection. I trust your eyes. Find a place to camp, away from the sight of the oppidum — hopefully not occupied by an enemy.'

He strode through the camp with Crassus, hurrying the men along in their tasks. He refused to spend another night here. By mid-afternoon, the camp was cleared. At this time, judging by the position of the sun in the cloudless sky, they would normally stop and begin to make camp. Not today.

Instead they assembled in a column, ready to move out. As usual, a bonfire of unwanted timber and other equipment that could not be carried burned behind them. Scattered around it were the cooling pyres, wisps of white smoke escaping the ashes. Marcus gradually regained consciousness and despite the pain in his arm wanted to walk. He was still groggy. His first question to the capsarius was, 'Where is Tullius?'

Alba pointed sadly to one of the piles of ash, the top of it gently blowing a trail like a horse's tail on the breeze. 'His death was a brave one,' he said. 'He may even have saved you. Centurion Quintus has honoured him and spoken for you.'

'He is gone?' Marcus asked, incredulously.

'He is,' Alba confirmed.

Marcus shook his head gently. 'I thought him indestructible,' he said sorrowfully.

Quintus addressed the men from the back of a horse. He had not asked for it, but it was the commander's roan on which he sat. 'An hour's march,' he announced. 'An hour will be enough. We will leave these ghosts and these memories behind. Scouts have already ridden out, looking ahead. They will warn us if it looks like we need to fight.'

As the cornicen sounded the advance and the cohort began to march, Quintus carefully placed two polished round stones near the pyre of the ladies. He had already left two by the pyre of Tullius and Piso. On each was inscribed the names of the legionaries, the number of their legion and the method of their death — 'died in battle' — along with a single word to describe what they had meant to their friends. For Piso, 'wrestler' was written, for Tullius, 'steadfast'. Crassus had used his blacksmith skills to help incise the letters. Many other legionaries left similar stones in memory of comrades.

Quintus left a single stone for both the women, though truly more in honour of Aurelia than Antonia. Crassus carved it for him. He could not put what he really wanted to say, so instead he wrote the customary words that memorialised the traditional virtues of a Roman wife and mother, though he did not know if either had children: *Domum servavit. Lanam fecit.* 'She kept house. She span wool.' He smiled softly. He thought the women would appreciate this. Neither had ever showed anything other than contempt for matronly virtues.

Their shades would know what he meant.

LVII: URSUS MAJOR

The cohort, hardly worthy of the name, marched parallel to the river and towards the wreck of the oppidum, high on the hill. It looped west around it, then back north following the track that led to the river crossing. It passed the trenches dug by Felix and his men to prevent reinforcements, then followed the route taken earlier by Quintus and the raiders. Instead of crossing at the stepping stones, the column veered further west, keeping the river on its left.

The legionaries marched in almost total silence, only the tramp of their caligae, the sounds of the beasts and the creaking wheels of the carts providing a ghostly accompaniment. Many of them looked fearfully at the smoking ruin and repeatedly made the warding sign of the horns whilst muttering prayers to various deities. There was no sign of any enemy.

When the oppidum and the scenes of the other attacks and actions fell behind them, the level of conversation began to swell. It grew slowly at first, in whispers, then became more bold. Quintus noticed that men were starting to talk more freely behind him, then that insults and jibes were being flung from one soldier to another. There was, at last, even laughter.

Quintus sighed with relief. 'Listen,' he said to Rufus, who carried the standard beside him. 'It is starting to return to normal.'

'It will be normal when they sing,' replied Rufus tersely.

They marched on for an hour or so. Though the talking continued, there were no songs.

Quintus sent a runner down the line a few times to check on Marcus. The responses the first two times were polite. 'He is well, sir,' the runner assured him. The third time, the runner came back with the reply, 'He would like some rest, sir, so in the name of the gods, please stop bothering him.' Quintus grinned. Marcus being cantankerous was a good sign. Clearly he was getting better.

It was already dusk when Agnus and his escort rode up. 'To the west, sir. No more than half an hour.' He turned the head of the black colt and fell in with the cohort.

Quintus wheeled the column in the direction given, halting where the ground, almost flat, ran gently down to the river. He would not normally have left it this late in the day, but wanted to be sure that there was no trace of the action. There must be no sight, no smell, no sound, no noise of marauding animals — nothing to remind the men of an experience already fading. The river was slower and wider here. Trees were thick on the far bank. On this bank the forest parted. They could camp by the riverside.

'What do you think?' Quintus asked Rufus conversationally. 'It does not look like farmland.'

'Unlike you, I am no farmer,' replied the redhead. 'I am a city boy. I was born in the Aventine, and lulled to sleep by the sound of the Tiber, not by the bleating of sheep and goats. So I have no idea.'

Quintus was disappointed. He really wanted to talk about the merits or otherwise of the ground they were on. It helped to drive away the ghosts. Even though Rufus was clearly not interested, he persisted. 'It looks barren, windblown. It could make rough grazing, perhaps for goats, but not crops, not barley or wheat.'

'If you say so,' Rufus agreed. 'It certainly looks barren.'

A cold wind blew now from the east, a wind with a bite to it. They could see that beyond this plain the ground continued to rise.

'That is a mountain wind,' Rufus offered. 'I can tell you that from my time in the Picos mountains of Hispania. It has an edge that only mountain winds have.' He smiled up at Quintus and added, 'It is why these tribesmen wear trews.'

The ground was good for driving in stakes and tent pegs, even if it was not so good for agriculture. The pioneers, some new to the tasks, marked out the camp. It was constructed swiftly, everyone having a job to do.

The night was clear, enough stars shining for Sextus to attempt a reading or two for those who believed the constellations could guide their fate. Here and there in the camp, sacrifices were made in memory of comrades, or to appease gods. Quintus shook his head at all of it. The mounting losses of the cohort made him doubt that they had the favour of the gods, whatever they did, although he did try to pick out the shape of Ursus Major, the Great Bear, in the star-filled sky. He failed, and had too much pride to turn to Sextus.

Instead he sought out Crassus, knowing that he would find him with the animals. He always spoke sense, and his belief in the gods, whilst firm, was also pragmatic. Crassus described the relationship between mortals and gods as two sides of an uneven contract.

'How is he faring?' Quintus asked of the blacksmith, who was stroking the sleek coat of the black colt.

'No longer afraid of his own shadow, nor of noise. He makes a fine mount, though I think he will have but one master,' Crassus said, slightly disappointed that it was not him. He understood that Quintus had not come to inquire about the horse. 'Stroke him a while. He will accept affection from anyone.'

For the next half hour they talked about nothing, ate some dried meat and drank some of the prefect's wine, well watered. Later, for the first time in what seemed like a whole age of the world, Quintus rolled into a tent and slept the night through.

The next seven nights were, unbelievably, much the same. They marched, they camped, they slept. Sometimes it was fine during the day, sometimes overcast. From time to time it rained. Sometimes the stars were clear, sometimes clouds obscured them. They were not attacked, by either animal or tribesman. Their routine became established and settled. Their efficient construction and destruction of the camps became more polished. Marcus recovered enough to walk, then began light exercises, drills that other veterans joined him in.

Quintus made sure that the guards remembered they were still in enemy territory, and stayed alert. Agnus, with Vetruvius and the auxiliaries, rode ahead to scout for danger. He would have run, but for his injury. On horseback they ranged further. Sometimes they were missing for a whole night.

On the morning of the eighth day since leaving the oppidum, Agnus arrived back in the early light. He was taken at once to Quintus. He had news. As they sat by the fire, the camp vanishing around them, Agnus asked, 'Did you see the sun rise, sir?'

'I did, legionary,' Quintus replied, baffled. 'What of it?'

'It rose ahead of us, sir. The river has turned a great corner and we are now heading east, not south.'

Quintus stopped what he was doing. 'You are sure? We have turned corners before.' The river had such bends and sweeping meanders in it that it was never clear in which direction they were heading. It has taken them every way but north, never quite curving back on itself. But it had always come back to south. 'East, you say? For certain?'

'Not just this morning, sir. The last two mornings also, and on the road ahead of us. We are marching east.'

Quintus nodded thoughtfully. 'Anything else?'

'There may yet be a great bend coming back south, but I think not. There are mountains in its way. Bigger mountains than any of the hills we have passed. Cloud-wreathed peaks, some of them either a long way away or very tall. I think very tall.'

'They must be the high mountains of the Alps,' Quintus declared. 'There are friendly countries there, and enemies, too. Noricum, Raetia, Vindelicia.' He thought for a moment. 'Through the passes, my friend, lies Italia and Rome. Home. This is the way Hannibal Barca brought his elephants. This is the way Divine Julius marched to Alesia. This is the way home.'

Agnus nodded in mute agreement.

'More practically, this is where General Drusus will have crossed,' Quintus went on. 'We cannot be far away from meeting up with him.'

'Perhaps that is why there have been no attacks on us,' Agnus offered eagerly.

'Perhaps. But we cannot drop our guard. I have been in mountains before, Agnus. They are dangerous places. Full of spots for ambush. I lost many friends in action in mountains in Hispania.'

Agnus nodded again. 'I do not think that these peaks lie in our path, sir. Unless we wish to make it so. The river seems to flow in the valley in front of them. The mountains on the right bank are more like hills. As long as there is a riverbank, we can continue.'

'General Drusus could have crossed the river. If we miss him, and reach the passes safely, we can do nothing but head for home.'

Quintus allowed his mind to wander. He half hoped that they would miss him. Then he could take the men home, arriving with the information on Britannia and the Druids for the emperor, and with the rescued eagle of the Fifth. All of them would be decorated heroes, with pensions and farms. He shook his head to clear it of such notions. Briskly, he asked, 'So, we continue to follow the river, but now east?'

'Yes, sir. But there are hills and crags growing near to it on this bank. I think we may have to cross from time to time.'

'The river is the only guide we have. Even if our Germani guide was still with us, this would be well out of his territory. Along the river we must march, and cross it if we must.'

The river was no longer as wide as it had been, and yet still seemed placid, flowing in gentle arcs. Sometimes it split into even smaller streams, with islands in the middle. At these places it was easy to traverse. With the far bank but a stone's throw away, crossing was not difficult. All the legionaries could swim, as could the horses. Equipment that had to be kept dry was wrapped in oilskin or kept high above the water.

One night they camped on the left bank, another on the right, determined by the terrain that Agnus found as he rode ahead, and by the ease of crossing the water. What worried Quintus most was that hills, great and small, rose up on both sides, and often forest marched right down to the water's edge.

'General Drusus could pass in the opposite direction behind a mountain, or in a forest,' said Agnus, 'and we would never know.'

'If that happened, we would have no choice but to continue through the high passes,' said Quintus, smiling to himself. 'If that is the will of the gods, so be it.'

That night, the constant murmur of the river was joined by the howling of wolves. All across the far bank, where the trees grew sparse on the high ground, the noise continued throughout the hours of darkness.

'What do the cries of wolves mean?' Quintus asked Sextus, as they passed a jug of posca between themselves in front of the fire.

'The wolf is Rome. It is us; it is our strength,' he explained, wiping his lips. 'Ever since the she-wolf suckled Romulus and Remus. Without the wolf, there would be no Rome.'

'So it is a symbol of good fortune, not bad?' Quintus took the jug back. The posca was no substitute for wine, being sour, but it did a better job of keeping men alert.

'It is,' Sextus said reassuringly.

Finally the wolves ceased their howling, and instead, out of the ensuing silence, an owl called mournfully into the night. It was close. It was on their side of the river. Another replied to it. This was even closer, in the trees behind the camp. Quintus shuddered. He knew that owls betokened death; they had foretold that of Hrolf and the giant. 'That is not so good,' he said.

'An owl was the harbinger of Divus Julius' death,' Sextus said. 'Perhaps a Caesar is dying somewhere. I don't think they have ever bothered with the common man.'

Quintus laughed. 'There is nothing more common than us, so we should be safe.'

But in his heart he was not so certain. Hrolf was not noble. Unlike Sextus, who rolled into the tent, he did not bother trying to sleep. He knew that he would not be able to. Instead he sat and watched the fire die to embers as the rose hue of dawn began to grow in the east. There were leaves already changing colour on the trees; the season had turned almost without them noticing. It was going to be a cool morning. He wrapped his cloak tightly around himself.

LVIII: OPPIDUM

Quintus' vigil was accompanied by the familiar sounds of the camp. There were men coughing and snoring, men talking softly, a game of chance being played somewhere, an argument flaring and petering out somewhere else. He heard the sounds of the animals breathing and the soft tread of the slaves as they went about their breakfast preparations.

Jovan approached him and asked after his needs, but he waved the Macedonian away, waiting for the cornicen to signal the start of the day.

Hoofbeats and shouted challenges reached him before the trumpet sounded the reveille. Horsemen were arriving at the gate. Within minutes Agnus appeared. He looked in a hurry to deliver his news.

'Jovan, water!' Quintus called the slave across. 'And food of some sort.' He saw that Agnus had been riding hard, that his face was flushed and sweat still stood out on his forehead. 'Send Maxim to see to the horses. It looks like they might need some care.' He turned to the scout, who was drinking deeply from the skin that Jovan carried.

'Your news, Agnus. What have you found?' He could not stop himself from adding, 'Could you see the passes? Could you see the way through to Italia?'

Agnus was excited and spoke quickly, his words tumbling over each other. 'Sir, we found another one of their cities, set on a low hill, but it was all but empty. A few chickens, a few old men and women — that was it. The gates stood open.'

'Slow down,' said Quintus, taking the waterskin from him and giving it back to Jovan, who ran to refill it. He motioned for Agnus to sit down. 'An abandoned oppidum?'

'Yes, sir,' Agnus confirmed, gratefully settling on the tree stump that was offered. 'We followed the river, as ever crossing tributaries that flowed in our path. We swam the horses through a particularly wide one then stopped to rest them on the far bank. Soon afterwards we found that we had water running on both sides. To our left the river flowed south; to our right, it flowed north. Either there were two rivers, or the Rhenus made a horseshoe turn around the hill.'

'And the oppidum within it?'

'Yes, sir. But empty. The mist sat thickly on the hill, so we dared to approach stealthily on foot. That is when we found that the gates were open, that there was barely a fire burning inside. There were no warriors, Quintus, no-one to fight.'

'Were they going to come back?' Quintus asked cautiously.

'I think almost certainly not.' Agnus shook his head. 'Everything of worth had gone. The door to the chieftain's house — the longhouse — was open. A few old men slept inside. Outside there were no animals, save a few scrawny chickens and the odd mangy dog. Even the door coverings had gone.'

'How big?' Quintus asked. 'A city indeed?'

'I would put each side at around a thousand paces, sir. We explored some of it, but could find nothing but the old and the infirm. We came down the hill for the horses, in order to explore it further, but when a wind blew the mist away we could no longer rely on secrecy.'

Quintus nodded in understanding — although he thought that, had it been him, he would have explored more. 'How far away?' he asked.

'An hour at most, and that includes the river crossing.'

Quintus spoke to Jovan. 'Find the other centurions and bring them here. Impress on them that speed is essential. Bring the cornicenes also.'

Felix and Marius came together, talking softly, Furius Lentulus two paces behind them. They were joined by their optiones, all except Felix, who left his second behind to help supervise a disciplinary matter. Aquila, as aquilifer, also joined the council, whilst Agnus stayed to repeat his message. Sextus, of no rank whatsoever, was also somehow present. The two cornicenes stood at a distance, awaiting orders.

Once Agnus had repeated his tale, Quintus pulled his tunic straight and said, 'Unless you have reasons to object, we march on this oppidum as if we were a fully armed legion, and they were a defended settlement. If it is as Agnus says, we will march straight in — and camp there for the night. If it is not —' and here he shot a glance at Agnus from beneath his brows — 'then we find ourselves in a fight. We cannot assume it is abandoned, whatever Agnus has said. We cannot leave it if it is defended.'

They all agreed readily enough, though Felix thought it might be a trap.

'We just do not know,' said Marius. 'There could be no-one there, or there could be the whole of Germania.'

'We have no choice,' Quintus said, with a shake of his head. 'If it is the whole of Germania, we will have to fight them.'

Marcus shrugged; to him it was obvious. He was recovered enough to be part of the discussion. 'If it is Germani, of course we will fight them. We cannot leave them to ambush General Drusus.'

'At least we would die with honour,' said Furius Lentulus. 'We would die fighting. I would rather that than be surprised, or picked off by the enemy, or, even worse, captured and enslaved by the barbarians.'

'They do not enslave the men. The men they kill,' said Sextus, quietly. 'If it is the Raeti, they kill all the men and boys. They even use magic to divine if pregnant women are carrying boys. These they also kill.'

'How do you know such things?' Felix demanded.

Sextus tapped his nose as if he keeping a secret, whilst Crassus just shook his head. 'We heard tales when we traded Norican iron,' he said.

'All the men need to know,' said Quintus firmly, 'is that if they die, they die with honour.' He stood up. The council was over. 'No assembly,' he told the cornicen. 'As soon as the camp has been demolished, have the men form up to march. I want us away whilst dawn is still fresh in the sky.'

The camp, as usual, was demolished with little fuss.

This morning, as the men formed up by century, Quintus was able to announce, 'There are no punishments, no floggings or demotions. We have two choices this day. Victory or death. Not far from here lies either an empty oppidum, a town whose warriors have fled at the mere sound of our tread, or the might of Germania — an unholy alliance of many tribes, lying in wait for us. I know which you would prefer.' This raised a cheer from the men. The thought of battle pleased them, the thought of plunder even more.

'We march in a column of four, cavalry on the flanks. The Cantabrian auxiliaries will ride ahead — they will act as both scouts and forward skirmishers. The archers will stay at the rear, to cover the wagons and slaves. We can spare no legionaries for this. This oppidum is an hour's march away, no more. Move out.'

Despite their diminished numbers, it was still an impressive display of military strength that set off under Quintus' command. At its tip, Aquila was on horseback, flying the eagle. To either side of him rode the tattered black bull of the cohort standard, and the imago of Augustus, carried by the third imaginifer since the image had arrived at the winter camp. After what had happened to its previous carriers, it was a brave legionary who took on the duty. It was extra pay, of course, but, as Sextus was fond of pointing out, double nothing was still nothing. They had not been paid in many a long month.

Behind these three symbols of power Quintus rode, high-crested and red-cloaked. Beside him marched Rufus, with the standard of Century One, the pilum and manus standard that had lost its discs to the Germani. The bare pole was now a source of pride. To the other side marched one of the two cornicenes that had survived. The other was halfway down the column, marching with Centurion Marius of Century Three. From here the cornicen was ready to repeat any orders from the front.

In the centuries behind Quintus, other standards fluttered, and the vexilla of the cavalry marked the edges of the formation.

The men were in high spirits, as they always were before a possible fight. Rufus smiled up at Quintus. 'They sing,' he said simply.

The track was for the most part stony and uneven, but the men covered the ground swiftly, keen to meet the enemy. It twisted and turned with the river, sometimes dropping into small valleys, almost to the level of the water. Then it was wet underfoot, and both horse and man splashed mud up their legs. At times it also narrowed so that the column had to reform, the cavalry trotting on ahead. It was at these times that

Quintus was particularly conscious of the rocky heights to his right, wary of possible ambush. But for now there were few trees, few hiding places.

They crossed the tributary with little fuss, with guards posted to keep a wary eye on possible attacks. The banks were muddy but the water only shallow. It was probably at its lowest level and would certainly be a more formidable barrier after spring rains.

The mist had burned off and the oppidum was visible for many stades. There was no movement on its palisade and, as Agnus had reported, a dark gap where its gates should have been. Although there were a few wisps of smoke indicating inhabitants, there was no sign of activity beneath its walls. Whilst the legionaries would be disappointed if it was empty, it would suit Quintus. Here would be a fortified place to rest, to decide on his next move. As he rode up the hill, he spoke to Rufus. They had both realised the oppidum was, indeed, abandoned.

'I was not aware of the vastness of the country, nor the extent of the great river,' Quintus was saying. 'I thought that by keeping to the left bank of the river, we would be bound to meet Drusus coming the other way.'

'But…?' Rufus encouraged him.

'But, there are many paths and many rivers,' Quintus replied. 'Many different ways that the general could have taken. If we do not find him before we reach the mountains, we go through them, over them.'

'That must be soon,' said Rufus. 'Before winter, before autumn even.'

As they rode through the gates unopposed, the eagle and the other standards dipping under the bridge that connected the gateposts, Quintus decided, 'From here we can send patrols in all directions to see if we can find the general.'

A dog barked at them. A couple of old men turned their backs on them. A little group of skeletal chickens ran from them. There was no opposition here. The men were disappointed. They tramped inside in silence.

'Fall out,' came the order. 'Close the gates. Secure the oppidum. For now, this is our camp.'

'The ancients still here?' Crassus asked.

'Put them all in the chief's house. Caius, interrogate them. Any information would be valuable.'

Once inside the empty citadel, the men could hear a low rumbling in the distance, as if an avalanche was taking place. It gradually became louder and louder.

At first, the legionaries thought it might be an enemy, approaching on horseback, a great herd of horses or cattle traversing the valley. But it went on too long for any of these, and it came no closer. Some, who had heard such things before, thought that they had once more reached the sea. That here, high in the hills, a hidden ocean rolled and grumbled. It could be the sound of waves crashing upon the shore.

Rufus was born in the Aventine, down by the Tiber. He had heard the river when it was in flood, and when it was low in the summer. He knew the sound. 'It is the river,' he stated. 'It is running over gravel and stone, shallow but fast. There will be rocks and rapids.'

Leaving the men to round up the remaining inhabitants and begin to make the oppidum more like a camp, Quintus set off on horseback with three comrades to see if Rufus was correct. With the advantage of his height, he saw the spume that marked where the waters fell. 'It is more than rapids,' he declared. 'It is a waterfall — a great torrent of white water stretching across the river. There must be a lake above it.'

They rode up through the trees. There was an animal trod to follow, which no doubt tracked down to the water's edge at some point. But not here. Here was an outcrop, a stretch of bare rock from which the spectacle in front could be viewed.

From this vantage point, the riders could observe the whole expanse of the wide waterfall. Jagged rocks stood up in the centre of it, splitting the flow into two main channels and narrowing it, the water turning white as it was forced through the gap. To the left, its path was still partially blocked by stones.

Here it cut deep clefts between many sharp rocks, tumbling angrily between them. Those outcrops that remained must have been made of harder material, obsidian or granite, and the water could wear them down only gradually.

To the right, the gap was deeper, allowing the water to plummet downwards so hard that it rose back up again as angry foam. The legionaries had not realised how much the trees masked the sound. From here it was impossible to hear anything else, impossible to even shout to one another above the tumult.

There would be no need to creep up on an enemy; the torrent would mask all noise. This was the perfect spot for an ambush.

LIX: RAPAX

Quintus returned with the patrol to find the camp already looking more Roman than Germani. There were two straight streets, one stretching from the main gate to the chieftain's longhouse, the other at right angles to it. These were the inevitable result of many pairs of tramping caligae as the legionaries erected tents and repurposed buildings for stables and stores. Others they pulled down for firewood.

The carpenters repaired the gates, so they could once more be swung shut.

Though some requested it, Quintus was reluctant to allow the men to go and look at the falls, even in groups and armed, reluctant to let them wash and swim in the waters downstream. He did not want to lose another man, and the noise made by the cataracts made it seem too dangerous.

'Once we are certain it is safe,' he prevaricated. 'There will still be enemy nearby.'

The cohort standards and the eagle were fixed in the ground where the two roads crossed, near the entrance to the longhouse. Within, the legionaries herded the few people who were left. There were no more than ten of them, all ancients except for two children, who were clearly suffering from some wasting illness and unlikely to survive another winter.

'Has the capsarius seen them?' Quintus asked.

'He has,' said Caius. 'They are not long for this world.' Caius had tried to speak with a few of the prisoners, and now he was keen to share his knowledge.

He and Quintus stood at the door of the longhouse, the shadows of the standards falling on them as the men busily completed the fort. There being no need for a ditch or palisade, the task was finished swiftly. There was a well, and the water in it appeared to be sweet, but they tested it on the prisoners nevertheless. In the meantime, a few men were allowed to collect water from the Rhenus. They were ordered to stay on the south side, the side from which they had approached, rather than visit the site of the falls.

Caius continued, 'Centurion, I do not think the patrols you plan are necessary. More than one of these tribesmen has told me the same story, and I am therefore inclined to believe it.'

Quintus was interested. 'Go on.'

'They say their people abandoned the oppidum because they heard the tramp of a great army. Then their scouts saw it. A cloud of dust above, as big as a thunderstorm. Animals were fleeing before it. The land was left barren behind it. An entire nation, they say, or words to that effect. It seems that either they — or I — do not have the words to express the number of men they witnessed, the size of the army.'

'Was it us they saw?' Quintus asked.

'Not us, no. They could not count the pennants and flags, the number of horses. They talk of many trumpets and tubas and cornets. They say that behind the soldiers came many carts. The men ate up all the grain in the land and killed all the animals — like a plague spreading across the terrain. They even speak of more than one eagle.'

'So more than one legion,' Quintus said. He hoped that this was General Drusus and his army. 'Did they come from the east, through the high passes of the Alps?'

'That is the strange thing,' said Caius. 'Apparently they came from the south and west, from the opposite direction to the mountains.'

Quintus shook his head. This was not possible. Drusus had to come through the passes. 'But this army caused them to flee? To abandon the town? It is so near?'

'It is. They could not stay here. They could see that it would be hopeless to defend. They have cousins on the north bank in another oppidum, three or four days away, called something like Scharten or Zarten. That is where they fled.'

'Might they return with these cousins? Should we be wary?' Quintus asked.

'This is the thing, centurion.' Caius had clearly saved his best revelation until last. 'I think not, for they say this army of Romans is still here. They put it at no more than a day away to the south.'

'Drusus,' Quintus whispered. 'It must be him. We have found him at last. But we must be sure. A deputation must go — men to represent the cohort.'

'The eagle?' Caius asked.

'No, it stays here, lest they think of us as some sort of raider or thief. No, we send the cohort standard, a centurion, an optio and no more than six men. Enough to carry a message. Not enough to pose a threat.'

'Will you go yourself?'

'Again, no,' Quintus said, after a pause for thought. 'I am torn, but I am — at least for now — the commander here. I will stay and meet the general at the head of my command — if it is him.'

In the morning, as the dawn broke, an assembly was called, the long note of the cornu ringing around the underpopulated oppidum. The four centuries that were drawn up, though bolstered with the remnants of the defeated Fifth, were sadly incomplete. Each at least had a centurion, an optio and a signifer. Each had its own standard.

Quintus had no tribunal platform, nor did he require any centurion to shout his words for him. He knew that speaking softly made the men listen. 'Men of Legio Nine Hispania,' he began, a designation that was almost forgotten by the men, but one that made them stand just a little straighter. 'If our information is correct, the legions we seek are less than a day away. If it is indeed the general, son of Augustus, then you will all soon be back under the yoke of a proper commander.'

He allowed himself a smile as many of the men shouted that he was a proper commander. He shook his head at them. 'There will be no more slacking or dodging duty.'

Again they laughed; neither Quintus nor the other centurions had allowed discipline to become lax. Punishments had still been meted out regularly but — the men acknowledged — fairly.

'Today I will send a patrol, a deputation, to see if these are, indeed, our people. If they are, tomorrow we march to meet them.'

The men shouted their approval, but he had one more surprise for them. 'You might even be paid. Cornus has all the records.' This elicited an even greater cheer.

The deputation that set out grew slightly from the original plan. It included two centurions and two optiones. Felix and Crassus represented the new men and a recovered Marcus and Furius Lentulus the evocati. Alongside them they carried the tattered and faded bull standard of the cohort, once sharply black on red, but no longer. Two of the survivors of the cavalry accompanied them. These took two of their own vexilla, long pennants that carried impressive battle histories. Their decurion had fallen when the camp was raided. They had not chosen another.

The group gathered together the best of the equipment left to them. A deputation in threadbare cloaks or battered armour would not impress. Slaves were set to sand-scrub the lorica laminata of the infantrymen and the breastplates of the cavalry. Quintus himself looked sadly at his own sorry state. Despite the efforts of Jovan, his crest had been sorely damaged by an enemy blade and bloodstains lurked on his cloak, tunic and armour. Neither eagle nor aquilifer went, nor the imago of the emperor. They were not going into battle. The deputation set off optimistically at a trot.

Quintus waited for their return with apprehension. Around him, the rhythm of the camp continued unchecked, and the standard chores and guard duties were undertaken. Once they were finished, the more experienced men started to practise their sword strokes and tactics in a square of beaten earth they designated the training area.

Quintus joined them for a while, long enough to break sweat, but his mind was not on the exercises and he found himself drifting back to the palisade and the bridge above the gate, now closed. It was cloudy, with no trace of blue in the sky, and a cool drizzle fell softly, blurring the horizon. It was almost evening when Sextus joined him.

'Have you said a prayer, Sextus? Have you sacrificed?' Quintus demanded.

'I have burned an offering, Quintus. We have little left to sacrifice unless you want to send out hunting or foraging parties.'

'I am praying that we do not need them. I am praying that our men return with good news. Are there no omens?'

'I can interpret the birdsong for you, if you wish,' said Sextus, smiling and gesturing at the grey skies, 'or read augury from the shape of a cloud.'

Quintus gave him a sideways glance of disapproval. He was never completely sure whether Sextus was being serious. Having lived with the priestesses, he was insufficiently respectful of the College of Pontiffs.

'Look!' Sextus pointed excitedly. 'There is your answer. That dust must signal the return of the deputation.'

The cloud in the distance resolved itself into the shape of horsemen. The group that rode up to the gate was slightly larger than the one that had left. The additions were two centurions on caparisoned mounts. They looked like they had just come from a triumph, or if not that, at least from the quaestorium with everything newly issued. They were sharply shaved, their armour shone, and they sat on well-kept mounts with glistening coats.

Furius Lentulus, his face barely visible behind his beard and hair, his armour scratched and his cloak faded, saluted and went through the formalities. Quintus had issued the passwords himself. He called down, 'Does home lie through a mountain pass?'

'Only if that pass leads to Rome,' Furius Lentulus replied. 'I bring tidings, commander, and guests.'

One of the polished centurions spoke. 'Why are we exchanging passwords with a vagrant in an abandoned oppidum?' His voice, coloured with a mixture of humour and disdain, carried to Quintus.

'Because we are Rome, and I command here,' Quintus replied clearly and confidently. 'We are of the Ninth Hispania. Who or what are you?'

The other centurion, a younger man, was more diplomatic. 'Your pardon, commander.' He bowed his head quickly then announced, 'We are of Legio Twenty-one Rapax, under the command of noble Varus, part of the army of Tiberius, son of Augustus, son of a god.'

'Not Drusus?' Quintus was surprised enough to drop the formalities. 'Not Decimus Claudius Drusus, son of Augustus?'

'He is further north and west, in the mountains,' said the older man, adding tetchily, 'Are you going to open the gates?'

Quintus shouted down and the gates slowly parted, revealing the mixture of castra and oppidum within.

The sight caused the visitor to once more forget his manners. 'By Jupiter and Mars, what are you?' he exclaimed. And then in a different tone, partly awed, partly accusatory, he went on, 'And what is that?' He pointed, open-mouthed, at the shining figure of the eagle, sitting on its unadorned pole with its wings outstretched and its head facing victory.

'And that?' The echo came from his companion as he spotted the imago next to the eagle.

'They are our standards, of course,' said Quintus. 'Though I admit the eagle strictly belongs to the Fifth.'

'To the emperor, more like,' said the older centurion. 'That eagle of the Fifth was thought to be lost for good.'

'It is a long story. I will tell it in full when we have joined forces with you.'

'You would join us with this remnant?' It was the older man again.

Quintus was immediately annoyed. 'Yes, with this remnant,' he snapped, then took a deep breath and added more calmly, 'They are no remnant, my friend. They are trained Roman soldiers; they have all spent time on the Campus Martius. They have marched here, and they have fought and defeated the enemy. They can follow orders. There may be few of them and they have lost commanders and officers, but I would bet their courage against a horde of tribesmen any day. They may not be as shiny and fresh as when they set out, but that's because they've spent more time defeating enemies than polishing kit.' He ran out of breath.

The older centurion spoke quietly to mollify him. 'You are right to be angry, centurion, and I am rightly chastised. You have *auctoritas* here, I can see it. Your men give it you. Of course you should join us. Tonight is possible…'

'In the morning, after the assembly, if you would be happy to wait out the night.'

LX: TIBERIUS

Quintus brushed the dirt from his tunic as best he could. His armour was dented and, in places, stained black with blood. They had not had the time nor the leisure to thoroughly clean everything. In a last-minute attempt to improve his appearance, he licked his palm and rubbed his face, feeling the stubble on his chin. He would have liked to have been washed and shaved, but there had been no time. The centurion had told him it was now or never.

The guards on the pavilion were themselves centurions, probably senior to himself, but he was able to respond correctly when they asked the question set by the tesserarius.

'Should Phoebus rise in the west…'

'The world is upside down,' he replied, remembering what the messenger had told him.

With deference, one of the two relieved him of both gladius and pugio. 'They will be returned,' he was told.

The other centurion pulled back the flap of the tent.

Inside, it was as if he had walked into the atrium of a noble family. It was light, but that was because one side of the tent was rolled up, open to the elements. This was the side that faced the tall mountains. Even so, he could see the backs of legionary guards not ten feet away.

The tent walls were patterned rather than plain, and beneath his feet was beaten earth and fresh rushes. He was about to bow to the tent's chief occupant when he realised that he was looking at a mannequin — a wooden dummy wearing the armour of an imperial general. The breastplate, showing the torso of a Heracles or Achilles, shone brightly. The helmet with its white horsehair crest was on top. The armour looked to be gold, though he thought it could not be. He did not dare to look any closer.

The servant who met him wore a plain tunic — a slave or freedman. He was about to push past when he realised he was wearing military boots. Confused, he stepped back, then looked straight into clear, unflinching eyes. *This is General Tiberius*, he thought, *and I am a dead man.*

'I think you may have found the one you seek,' said the young man, a smile flickering across his lips. His cultured accent would have betrayed him on its own, but there was something else — a bearing, a confidence, an authority.

Quintus noticed that rarest of things — the man smiled with his eyes as well as his lips. His eyes were set wide above an aquiline nose. His face was round, rather than long, his chin small. His curly hair was cut short at the front of his head, left longer at the back, a fashion of Rome with which Quintus was not familiar.

'Sir,' Quintus said meekly, not knowing any other title with which to address not just a general, but a member of Caesar Augustus' family. He was awed. This was the man who, at the age of thirteen, had ridden the trace-horse of Caesar's imperial chariot in the triple triumph that commemorated the end of the civil wars. The man who had saved Rome from starvation by securing grain from Egypt. The man who had brought back the eagles lost by Licinius Crassus. And yet he was still young.

Looking at him, draped in simple cloth, Quintus guessed that he did not do a disservice to the beaten outline of the breastplate hung nearby. He was, of course, not as tall as Quintus, but was nevertheless a tall man, well built and fit. He held his arm forward for Quintus to grasp, wrist to elbow, then put his other hand on top, making the gesture more personal.

Quintus could not help but notice the chunky gold ring, carved with a symbol of the college of augurs, the lituus or staff used in interpretation. Its worth he could only guess at. Certainly it would have paid the wages owed to his cohort companions, possibly even to the whole of the Ninth. He kept his head bowed until Tiberius released his arm.

'Sit,' the general said. 'Take wine.'

There was a sturdy desk, behind which sat a curule chair, covered with the pelt of an animal. Nearer, there were several stools, camp issue by the look of them. Tiberius sat on one and clapped his hands, signalling to Quintus to seat himself opposite. A slave appeared with a wine jug, silver, not leather, and a tray on which sat a ewer of water that appeared to be made from crystal. There were three silver wine cups. Quintus looked at the general quizzically, and he clapped his hands again.

From the shadows emerged Aquila, carrying the eagle of the Larks. It was no longer on its pole, but its outline was clear under the red cloth. Quintus immediately thought he had been betrayed, and looked hard at his comrade. Aquila shook his head slightly and silently mouthed a denial. Tiberius gestured for Aquila to sit and join them, a hidden hand gently taking the eagle from him. Aquila sat.

'I have seen eagles before,' said Tiberius conversationally. He waved away the slave and poured the wine himself. He offered both cup and ewer to Quintus. 'As you like it.'

With uncertain fingers Quintus took the wine cup and added enough water to make it about half and half.

Tiberius smiled with approval. 'I take it no stronger,' he said, now offering the wine and water to Aquila. 'You know that I have even rescued eagles,' the general added.

'I know,' Quintus nodded. 'You brought back the eagles stolen by Parthia at Carrhae. You restored a friend to Rome by placing Tigranes on the throne of Armenia. One of my own contubernales saw the eagles placed in the temple in Rome.'

'He must be noble to have been so close.'

'No, sir. But as a ward of the Vestals, he had a guide — and a privileged view.'

Tiberius nodded. 'This eagle of the Fifth Alaudae,' he said, pointing, 'was not so much lost as borrowed. You have some of Legio Five with you, do you not?'

The sudden change in the direction of the conversation took Quintus by surprise. 'We do, sir. Ones we rescued from the forest.'

'And from themselves, I hear.'

Quintus was astonished at the information Tiberius possessed. 'They fought bravely, sir. They are re-sworn to the Ninth.'

'On your authority?'

'Sir,' Quintus said quietly.

Tiberius made a quizzical face at this, but did not speak of it, instead going back to the eagle. 'It could go back to the Larks,' he said, 'but I think not. They are reconciled to its loss. Sadly, their commander has forgotten that it was ever taken. In time the Fates will find him, and the Furies, I have no doubt.'

'I planned to take it to Rome, to Caesar Augustus,' Quintus blurted out, 'along with information we gleaned in Britannia. Information about the Druids. Information that would help in the conquest of the island.'

Tiberius shook his head and sipped his own heavily watered wine. 'My father has no wish to cross Oceanus, no wish to conquer the Britons. For a while he dreamed of it, but no more.'

He did not apologise, although he must have seen that Quintus was crestfallen. Aquila put a supporting hand on his friend's shoulder.

'He is focused on Germania,' Tiberius continued. 'My brother Drusus and I have beaten the Raeti and the Vindelici, and have brought Noricum into the fold. I intend, along with my brother, to make Germania safe for passage from Rome to Tres Gallia. He has pacified the mountains now; the rest will be easier.' His confidence was absolute. 'It will go to Rome when I return. For now, it has been taken from its pole, and from its aquilifer and will be packaged for transport. It will not fly again.' He looked at Aquila. Aquila merely sat tight-lipped. He was lucky to have been allowed to bring the eagle to Tiberius himself — the two centurions sent to escort him would happily have taken it from him.

'Do you plan to return soon, sir?' Quintus dared to ask.

'Oh, no,' Tiberius laughed. 'We are not about to return to Rome. We have more tribes to beat first. You should know this from your own journey.' He patted Aquila's knee. 'Your aquilifer has told me of your battles and conquests — including the oppidum taken, and the death of the renegade leader. You have done well. He tells me that you can lead, that you have gained *auctoritas* with these men, that if you were of the right blood they might even hail you imperator.' He smiled dismissively and shook his head. Of course, this could never happen. Only the blood of Augustus could now be so acclaimed.

Tiberius stood, gesturing for the centurion and the aquilifer to stay seated as they began to rise.

He pointed away from the mountains. 'We are going east, then north, not south. My brother is already waiting for us, following another of the great rivers that flow from these mountains. We have a job to do. It seems to me that you should wish the same.' He looked at Quintus closely with his sharp eyes. 'We are following the waters of this land until we reach the sea. Your legion is not here, but we can add you to our numbers. Is that not wonderful news?'

Quintus could almost see the walls of Rome gleaming through the passes of the Alps. He could feel the sun of Italia on his back. He clutched the package containing Ursus' will and copper armband and turned his back on his home.

'Of course, sir,' he said. 'Wonderful.' Fist to heart, he saluted.

HISTORICAL NOTES

Romans were notably superstitious — the cry of an owl in daylight foretold a death, thresholds had to be crossed left foot first and the *lemures* (the malevolent spirits of the unquiet dead) were everywhere. The warding sign of the horns was used as we might cross our fingers or fling salt over our shoulder. Even the days of the year were each designated as *fasti* or *nefasti*. *Dies nefasti* were 'unlucky' days on which business should not be transacted.

So it is no surprise that there were certain days when Roman legionaries would not fight. *Mundus patet* is one such day, when the stone covering a vaulted pit — the legendary entrance to Hades — on the Palatine in Rome (the *lapis manalis*) was ceremonially moved aside to allow the spirits of the dead access to the world of the living. It is a little like our own All Hallows' Eve, traditionally the night when the veil between the world of the living and the spiritual world is at its thinnest.

Mundus patet occurred the day after Volcanalia on 24 Sextilis (Martius, named for the war god, was the original first month; Sextilis, the sixth month, would be renamed for Augustus in 8BCE) and no general would plan an action on this day, as men might refuse to fight, or fight only reluctantly. On such a day, the auspices would not even be taken.

Schoolboys were taught the consequences of ignoring auspices. When the sacred chickens refused to eat before the Battle of Drepanum in 249BCE, Consul Claudius Pulcher threw them into the sea, saying 'let them drink' (*mergi eos in aquam iussit, ut biberent*. Cicero, *De Natura Deorum*, 2.7). He was subsequently soundly defeated by the Carthaginians. This episode was used as an example to prove the gods were listening and served to strengthen superstition, particularly amongst the legionaries.

GLOSSARY

Agmen formate — the order to form square. This would be a hollow square, with shields facing outwards.

Aquilifer — the standard bearer who carried the legionary eagle (aquila). He was also often entrusted by men as a banker, and with their wills.

Aquilam defende — the order to defend the eagle (at all costs), a command of last resort.

Auctoritas — having the authority to issue commands and be obeyed, acquired rather than bestowed. Augustus accrued more *auctoritas* than any contemporary. Quintus has gained *auctoritas* with his men.

Aut vinceri aut mori — 'Either conquer or die', attributed to Scipio Africanus before the battle of Zama against Carthage in 202BCE.

Campus Martius — Mars' field, the sacred civic space outside Rome where voting took place, temples and monuments were raised and soldiers were recruited, billeted and trained.

Capsarius (pl. *capsarii*) — a field medic, essentially a first aider. In a full legion he would be under the command of a specialist centurion, the *medicus ordinarius*. A *capsarius* can be found bandaging wounds on Trajan's column.

Carthago delenda est — 'Carthage must be destroyed'. In 152 BCE Cato the Elder started to use this phrase to round off every speech he made. It came to mean a thing was inevitable.

Castra — a camp, *castra hiberna* is a winter camp; *castra incognita*, a hidden camp.

Cineres credis curare sepultos — Queen Dido's sister Anna asks, 'Do you believe the ashes of the dead are bothered?' Virgil's *Aeneid*, Book IV.

Congrega — the order to assemble or muster in a particular place.

Cornicen (pl. *cornicenes*) — a trumpeter. In a full legion there would be a number of brass players of different instruments. This one played the *cornu (q.v).*

*Cornu (*pl. *cornua)* — a brass instrument roughly in the shape of a capital G, with a vertical brace to take the weight on the player's shoulder. It had no holes or stops, so produced notes through the action of the player's lips. *Cornua* is also used to mean the warding sign of the horns made with the little and index fingers pointed downwards.

Cursus honorum — the 'greasy pole' of Roman politics, a set of steps from the lowliest magistrate to the Senate and ultimately the Consulship.

Cursus publicus — the road used by imperial couriers. It relied on citizens providing horses and post stations.

Delicia — young slave boys and girls treated as 'pets' by Roman nobility, often allowed licence at feasts or festivals to make risqué jokes and bold suggestions.

Deorum voluntatem — the will of the gods. In the Christian era it became 'deus vult' or 'as god wills it'.

Dignitas — there is no direct translation. It does not mean 'dignity' but social standing, influence and reputation. It would be built up throughout a citizen's life.

Divi filius — 'son of a god', apparently Augustus' favourite title. His adopted father Julius Caesar was deified.

Domum servavit. Lanam fecit — 'She kept house. She span wool'. This is a well-known tomb inscription for women, being the final line of the epitaph of Claudia (150BCE) found near Rome. It praises the matronly virtues of the deceased.

Evocatus (pl. *evocati*) — a legionary who has served his time and been honourably discharged, then voluntarily rejoined the army.

Fides — acting in good faith in all dealings of business or state

Gladium stringe — the order to draw swords. One of the most effective tactics of the legions was for a rank to draw swords (*gladii*) simultaneously and strike in concert.

Gravitas — being serious or earnest when required, a sense of the importance of acting appropriately in a situation.

Hastile — see *optio*.

Honestas — not honesty but respectability, the action of projecting an honest image of oneself.

Imaginifer — see *signifer*.

Ius iurandum — see *sacramentum*.

Lex exercitus — military law, literally 'the law of the army'. Commanders held absolute power, including the death penalty, over all their subordinates.

Lugubri sono — the mournful note, a call for the absolute destruction of an enemy fortress or position. It is the equivalent of 'give no quarter'.

Mare nostrum — 'our sea'. The Mediterranean Sea, considered by Rome to belong to them.

Optio (pl. *optiones*) — the second in command or 'chosen man' of the centurion. His helm was crested and he carried a *hastile* (pl. *hastilia*) a long staff whose original purpose was to push men who might be wavering in battle back into line.

Pietas — although often translated as piety, this has a wider meaning of respect for state and family and an acceptance of the way it is ordered.

Pontem aureum – the golden bridge as advocated by Scipio Africanus in the Punic wars. To weaken resistance and shorten battles. To allow the enemy one route to escape; the way you want them to go.

Ponto nox incubat atra — a darkness lies upon the sea, part of the description of the storm conjured by the gods against Aeneas and his fleet. Virgil's *Aeneid*, Book 1

Praefectus castrorum — an officer responsible for military logistics who commanded a legion if the senior commanders were absent. He was usually a seasoned soldier, promoted from centurion.

Quadratum defende — the order to defend a square formation.

Quam mox oblivioni sunt horrores — 'How soon the horrors are forgotten'. M Tullius Cicero quotes an unknown source in a letter to his friend Atticus.

Sacramentum — and *ius iurandum* are both cited as military oaths, the first made the soldier sacred to the gods (and bound to the state), the second was an oath to his comrades.

Scutum (pl. *scuta*) — the legionary's shield. It took various shapes through the ages but at this time was rectangular and tall, with a curve that helped protect the soldier's flanks.

Semper honoratum habebo — the full quote is *Quem semper acerbum, semper honoratum habebo* The day is at hand which I shall keep ever as a day of grief, ever in your honour. This is Aeneas on the death of Dido. Virgil's *Aeneid*, Book V.

Signifer (pl. *signiferi*) — a standard bearer. There were specialist bearers such as the *imaginifer*, who carried the image of Augustus.

*Tesserarius (*pl. *tesserarii)* — a junior officer whose key task was to set watchwords. These were usually not words as such but questions that required a specific answer. He derives his name from the early republic when watchwords were written on tesserae or tiles.

Testudo — a formation made by interlocking shields to imitate the shell of the tortoise, thus providing legionaries with protection from missiles.

Virtus — excellence of character and courageous leadership.

A NOTE TO THE READER

Dear Reader,

I cannot thank you enough for taking the time to read this, the fourth Quintus novel. I hope you enjoyed it. Although each novel in the series may be read as a stand-alone, the next in the series, whilst starting in the Alps, may finally return Quintus and his comrades to Rome and the welcoming arms of the Emperor.

Who was the Emperor of Rome? He is named in an early chapter by the messenger, and a few of his titles listed. To contemporaries, however, he was not known as 'Emperor'. It is we observers, over two thousand years later, who refer to him as such. 'Imperator' was just one of his many titles. It was an acclamation by victorious legionaries and signified that they believed in their general and in his '*imperium*', the power to issue orders that were obeyed. Many generals were so acclaimed: Scipio Africanus, the dictator Sulla Felix, Pompeius Magnus, Marcus Antonius and Julius Caesar all qualified at some point as, of course, did Augustus. It allowed the general to apply to the senate for a Triumph. Generals had to relinquish command before they could enter the city, as imperium could not be exercised within its walls. This caused problems at many junctures of the late Republic.

Quintus' 'Emperor' was, as the adopted son of Julius Caesar, known as Caesar and from 27BCE carried the honorific Augustus, along with the titles and honours bestowed by the Roman people. For example, by the time of our story he had been 'elected' consul eleven times. (His favourite title, apparently, was *divi filius*, 'son of a god', his adoptive father having been deified.) The coins minted at the time give a clue. Only after 27BCE, when Augustus decided that, as head of the army, only he could Triumph, did they include 'Imperator'. By 15BCE coins struck to commemorate Drusus' victories on the Rhine carried the legend 'IMP X', meaning 'proclaimed imperator ten times'. To modern historians he is titled the 'princeps' or 'prince', and the empire itself as the 'principate,' although it was still known as the res publica by its inhabitants.

For ease of recognition, I call him Emperor or Augustus or Caesar, or a combination of these. It didn't really matter what he called himself as he had an abundance of *auctoritas*, one of the defining Roman virtues. It implies status, reputation and prestige, and the ability to command. No-one outshone Augustus in this respect.

Quintus earns his own *auctoritas* through bravery in battle, his natural leadership qualities, and the tacit agreement of the men under his command. I had considered calling the book *Auctoritas*, but as the other titles in the series are all ranks or stations, settled on *Centurion* for consistency.

While I try my best to be accurate, if you find any errors I shall be delighted to hear from you and, if you're right, correct future editions. I can be found on **Twitter at @NeilDenbyAuthor** and **Facebook at NeilDenby-Writer**.

Reviews by knowledgeable readers are an essential part of a modern author's success, so if you enjoyed the novel I would be grateful if you could spare the short time required to post a review on **Amazon** and **Goodreads**.

Neil Denby

Sapere Books is an exciting new publisher of brilliant fiction and popular history.

To find out more about our latest releases and our monthly bargain books visit our website: **saperebooks.com**

Printed in Great Britain
by Amazon